GLAMOUR GIRLS

GLAMOUR GIRLS

A NOVEL

Marty Wingate

alcove
press

Copyright © 2021 by Marty Wingate

All rights reserved.

Published in the United States by Alcove Press, an imprint of The Quick Brown Fox & Company LLC.

Alcove Press and its logo are trademarks of The Quick Brown Fox & Company LLC.

Library of Congress Catalog-in-Publication data available upon request.

ISBN (hardcover): 978-1-64385-527-1
ISBN (ebook): 978-1-64385-528-8

Cover design by Lynn Andreozzi

Printed in the United States.

www.alcovepress.com

Alcove Press
34 West 27th St., 10th Floor
New York, NY 10001

First Edition: January 2021

10 9 8 7 6 5 4 3 2 1

To Leighton, with all my love

GLAMOUR
GIRLS

CHAPTER 1

August 1944
Royal Air Force West Malling, Kent

Rosalie stood on the flat roof of the control tower with the others, all of them staring into the piercing blue sky. No one spoke. Barely six o'clock and already it was so hot even the birds were quiet. The silence pressed against her like a great weight and she found it difficult to breathe, but she knew no one would utter a word until the first plane had been sighted. That would signal the return of the squadron from its overnight sortie.

They would be counted in. It was a ritual as much as a practical act. Did as many return as left? Not always—not even usually, if Rosalie faced the truth. The pilots flew across the Channel and all the way to somewhere in Germany, she supposed. Rosalie certainly wasn't privy to the secrets of war, although she could fly Britain's fighters and bombers as well as any of the RAF boys. Go ahead, put her in a Moth, Spitfire, or Mosquito—she could do it.

What she couldn't do well at all was wait. As the minutes ticked by, beads of sweat popped out on her forehead and upper lip. Bits of airborne chaff from the dry fields floated into her line of vision, and she waved them away.

"Alan's a good pilot," Declan said, breaking the silence without moving his gaze away from the sky or taking the cigarette from his lips. "He's made it through almost two tours; he won't let anything happen now."

Rosalie swallowed hard before she could answer. "Yes."

One of the Women's Auxiliary Air Force plotters in the group said nothing as she cut her eyes at the exchange. Rosalie saw the guarded admiration mixed with a tinge of envy that she had grown accustomed to from women since she and Alan had been together. Together, that is, when the war and their jobs allowed.

Their jobs had brought them together and torn them apart—RAF Squadron Leader Alan Chersey and Second Officer Rosalie Wright of the Air Transport Auxiliary. They were both pilots, but whereas her assignments sent her crisscrossing England and Scotland, ferrying planes to RAF aerodromes and maintenance units, Alan's took him into the thick of it. He was a fighter pilot, currently flying Mosquitoes out on night missions with his navigator, each journey taking its toll on the crew and the aeroplanes. Until now, Alan had remained unscathed. Would his luck hold?

"There—two o'clock!"

All eyes squinted at a point just off to the right. A black speck emerged from the blue, and as it took shape, the faint rumble of an engine confirmed the sighting. Soon, three other specks appeared, and then more—six, no, seven. But they needed twelve returning. Twelve was the magic number.

The ground crew emptied out of the nearby hangar like ants overrunning a picnic. The men chased after the aeroplanes as they touched down and slowed to a canter across the grassy field, bouncing slightly when they hit a rabbit hole. The doors, just below the cockpit, burst open one by one and pilots and navigators tumbled out to be greeted by the crew, who then pushed the men aside to tend to the planes. No one left the field. Instead, they, too, took up sentry watching the skies.

Rosalie, her nerves stretched to the snapping point, remained on the roof with the WAAFs and Declan, who had stubbed out his cigarette and now gripped the metal railing. She knew who was missing. Alan—and his navigator. The squadron leader would be the last in, chasing his crew home. But would he return? And, with the guilt of the survivor, however imaginary the loss, Rosalie began to blame herself. Was this her fault? Had she done this to him?

A controller from ops came out on the roof. Taking refuge behind field glasses, he muttered, "Radio's out."

She had no time to take this in before a shout came up from the ground. "There he is!" followed quickly by "No wheels down!"

Field glasses were no longer needed. Everyone could see it, the Mosquito limping in with its wings at a tilt and a stream of black smoke trailing behind. Alan's plane.

The WAAF who had given her the cutting look now grabbed Rosalie's hand and squeezed as they watched the scene play out. The plane, with no landing gear, evened out just in time and hit the ground on its belly with unbelievable grace. But then it skidded halfway across the field, made a sharp right turn—barely missing one of the other planes—and at last came to a stop on the far edge as black smoke engulfed the cockpit.

CHAPTER 2

September 1939
Lime Farm, Cambridgeshire

The sky rumbled, and Rosalie, lying back in the wooden cart at the edge of the field where the ewe lambs grazed, opened her eyes. The first of September and not a cloud in sight. The glorious day belied the mood of the country as it waited for the inevitable, but Rosalie dismissed war from her mind as she sat up and dragged a stem of straw from her mass of short brown curls, all the while searching the skies for the aeroplane she'd heard.

There. A Gipsy Moth just coming over the copse of oak to the south. She jumped up so quickly that the cart rocked and creaked and she had to put a hand out lest she went over the side. Steadied, she watched the plane come closer and closer until it was nearly overhead, and she saw Reg Mulden, her flight instructor from nearby Yelling airfield. She waved, Reg waved back, and then the plane banked to the right and climbed.

Lucky sod, she thought. But she didn't say it aloud, of course. Rosalie had promised her mother she would clean up her language, and she had done so. For the most part. It was one of many conditions her mum had laid out two summers ago before she grudgingly agreed to her daughter's flying lessons. When lessons started, Rosalie believed not even the sky was the limit for her.

She had wanted to be a pilot since the day in the summer of 1932 when veteran aviator Sir Alan Cobham set up his Flying Circus at

Reg's airfield. Rosalie had seen a poster in the village shop window offering public joyrides for four shillings, and her heart had thrummed at the idea of going up in an aeroplane. She had run home, sought out her father, and told him she knew exactly what she wanted for her upcoming eleventh birthday.

So, her dad had taken her to the airfield and paid the four shillings, and Rosalie, without a second look, climbed into a biplane, took the seat in front of the pilot, waved at her father, and took off. He felt his heart in his throat as he watched the aeroplane climb and circle the field with his beautiful girl in it, but when at last it landed and he saw Rosalie's smile amid her mop of brown curls, which were even more disheveled than usual, his furrowed brow melted.

As soon as her feet were on the ground, she streaked over to him and declared, "I want to fly, Pop!"

"You want to go up again?" he asked.

"No—yes, but I want to fly the aeroplane. I want to be the pilot!"

Rosalie settled for another joyride, but only just, after which she reluctantly followed her father to the car. Usually a reticent girl, she couldn't stop talking all the way home.

"It was glorious, Pop! I could see the world. We flew over the farm, and I could see the wash on the line and the geese hurrying off to the barn. I know how the aeroplane works. Take off into the wind—that's what he said. The pilot showed me all the controls, and I know I can do it."

Her father had a soft spot for his only daughter. She didn't have it easy with two older brothers who alternately chivied her into working harder and coddled her like a baby. Flying lessons for a girl? Well, for his girl, why not.

Her mother reacted as if she'd just been told her daughter intended to become prime minister. Flying lessons? They must cost a fortune. Not a fortune, Rosalie said. She had no idea how much it would take, but without a second thought, she promised to pay for the lessons herself, disregarding the reality that anything over a shilling would put shed to that idea pretty quickly. She followed her statement with an offer to take sole responsibility for the chickens and geese if she could keep part of the money from selling eggs and the birds.

Her mother countered by pointing out that Lime Farm was home and that Rosalie, although not yet eleven years old, had responsibilities in the house and on the land that went beyond poultry. She needed to learn skills that would teach her how to get on in life. Rosalie knew the phrase "get on in life," as far as her mother was concerned, meant "marry a farmer."

Rosalie had no objection to other women marrying farmers, and she believed her parents' marriage to be happy. She could see it in the way her father smiled and her mother blushed, their low conversations and easy laughter. Rosalie hoped for that herself, in an abstract sort of way. But she was an obstreperous learner in both the kitchen and on the land and couldn't help worrying that if she applied herself to those skills, when would there be time to fly?

A moot point, as Rosalie was forced to wait for lessons until she turned sixteen. It was a struggle, but she determined to stick it out for the five years and immediately began saving her pennies. Perhaps her mother thought her passion to fly was just a girl's fancy that would soon pass, remembering the brief time when seven-year-old Rosalie had been enamored of Doctor Dolittle and decided to be a veterinarian. But her love of flying—her need to fly—did not diminish, and during those five years she read all she could find about aeroplanes and pilots. That's how she came across Pauline Gower.

An aviatrix. An English woman pilot who ran an air taxi service. Rosalie put her case forward to her father. If she couldn't fly herself yet, couldn't she be flown again? And so one spring he drove to Hertfordshire so that his daughter, who was mute with excitement, could climb into an aeroplane with Gower. Rosalie's voice didn't return until the journey home, during which her father listened to every detail of the event twice.

Over the five-year wait, the pennies in Rosalie's post office savings account increased—augmented by the occasional half crown from her father—and by the time she turned sixteen in late summer of 1937, she could just afford the fifteen shillings a lesson. She spent her birthday at the local airfield with Reg, who took an inordinate amount of time orienting her to his setup, showing her diagrams of the controls on the Moth, and giving her a safety talk.

"We take off into the wind," she told Reg, who studied her for a moment and then replied, "That we do, girl." He continued his lecture before allowing her to climb up into the front seat. There, he labeled everything on the control panel, and Rosalie repeated the names after him—every dial and lever, as well as the control stick. She remained undaunted through the morning, and at the end of it all, they flew.

★   ★   ★

But it had all been for naught, Rosalie now thought. She dropped her gaze from the empty sky and down to her small flock of ewe lambs. Although a halfhearted farmer, she had been a dedicated student of aviation. She remembered the thrill at takeoff on her first solo flight—alone in the Gipsy Moth with Reg on the ground watching her. She felt again how her emotions had leveled out just as she'd leveled the wings of the biplane, making a calm and competent circuit before she landed with only a bounce or two.

Here, two summers later, she had chalked up an impressive number of solo flying hours. But not enough to get her license before Reg shut down lessons in the first week of August. War loomed, and he hoped the RAF would want his airfield. Cambridgeshire, he said, would be vital to the war effort. "I'm sorry," he told Rosalie, "because you're a good pilot—you could probably fly anything. But there'll be more important uses of my Moths than lessons for girls. You wait and see. You'll be needed for other duties. We've all got to do our part when this thing starts up."

A bitter disappointment had taken root in Rosalie's mind that even this quiet afternoon with her ewe lambs had not dispelled. She stood and stretched, brushed the rest of the straw from her coveralls, and crammed the stopper back into the tea thermos. Retrieving the greaseproof paper that had held her cheese sandwich, she folded it and stuck it in a pocket to be used again.

Empty pails waited for Rosalie by the kitchen door upon her return from the field.

"Damsons are ready for you," her mum said. "The boys have found a few lads to pick the apples, but you'll need to keep an eye out or we'll lose half the harvest to missiles as they play at war."

Rosalie murmured an assent, filled a glass from the tap, and drank the water down.

"We'll soon be glad of any food put away for ourselves," her mum continued, a dire warning she offered up daily after listening to the news on the wireless, and which she repeated now as she leaned over a steaming pot of beets. The sharp odor of pickling caught in Rosalie's throat. "You don't remember what it was like. The things we had to eat the last time."

The last time was the Great War, and Rosalie didn't remember because she hadn't been around. Her brothers, Will and Leslie, born in 1912 and 1913, said they had memories of men in uniform marching through the village. Rosalie had come along well after, in 1921. A surprise.

"Sort yourself out today for the market tomorrow so you won't be late. Carrots, onions, courgettes, beetroot, cabbages," her mother reminded her. "Eggs."

"Righto," Rosalie muttered, and immediately hoped the hiss of the hob covered her reply. Slovenly speaking, her mother called that word—at least when it came out of her daughter's mouth.

Rosalie swung two empty pails in each hand as she crossed the yard, heading toward the orchard to pick the damsons. She spotted her father coming out of the barn and called out.

"Pop!" That wasn't her fault, either—what she called him. It was all she'd ever heard. She tried not to take advantage of every opportunity to blame her brothers for her faults, but Will and Leslie were awfully convenient.

"There's my girl," her father replied with a grin. He drew out a handkerchief and wiped his flushed face. "Just in the office, working."

His office was actually a storeroom attached to the barn. A cozy place where he could read the paper and have a smoke in peace. He'd kitted it out with a worn easy chair covered in a rug and a desk where he worked on the farm accounts. A single lightbulb dangled from above, and he made his tea on a spirit lamp.

"Pop, Reg flew over. Did you see him?"

"Giving himself one last look before there's no more flying, was he? I'm sorry you're grounded too, love." Her father patted her arm, mopped his face, and headed for the house as he added, "But don't you worry—I'll find a way to get you back in the air. You're a good pilot."

"Rags!"

She heard her brother call over the rattle and cough of the new tractor as he drove it into the yard. The geese set off an alarm at the commotion, honking in protest and skittering out of the way like a white wave.

"Will, shut that thing off—you're frightening my birds," Rosalie shouted as she automatically pushed the hair off her forehead with the back of her hand. Her brothers had dubbed her Rags long before she was able to offer an opinion on the matter. It had come about when her mother dug out an old rag doll from a trunk in the attic and the boys compared its brown hair to their new baby sister's curls.

Will raised his voice over the noise of the engine. "This machine represents the way of the future." He switched off the tractor, jumped down, and patted its fender. "A Fordson tractor will make us a modern farm, not something from Queen Victoria's time."

"Don't you let the horses hear you say that. At least they give us something in return."

"Never fear—the beasts are safe. You need the fertilizer for your precious strawberries. As far as I can see, we'll never run out of horse sh—"

"Hello, Mum!" Rosalie waved to an empty space behind Will. He clapped his mouth shut before looking over his shoulder and then turning back to her with a grin.

"Nice one."

★　★　★

That was the last lighthearted moment she would remember for a long time. On Sunday morning, the third of September, her father returned early from church to call Will and Leslie out of the fields and Rosalie from the chickens and his wife from the roast so that they could gather round the wireless in the lounge and listen to Neville Chamberlain announce that Germany had invaded Poland, and Britain was at war.

Two days later, Rosalie found her father dead. She'd gone to look for him in his office and found him slumped over in the chair, the newspaper spilled at his feet. It took her a moment to recognize such a small figure as the giant of a man she knew.

"Pop?" Her voice shook as she tapped his shoulder, causing his body to shift and slip in the chair.

Only later, when the doctor had been called and her mother put to bed, did she and her brothers—who were never to be called boys again—learn that Pop had been warned about his heart. More than warned. The doctor had told him straight out that he could go anytime, and wouldn't it be best to prepare his family. But would that have helped?

Rosalie imagined the pain her father must've felt at the end, and that pain seemed to transfer to her own heart, which she was sure would break into pieces at any moment. But the family held together, each in his or her own way. Her mother mourned quietly in the kitchen, using the steam rising from cooking pots as an excuse to wipe her eyes. Will threw himself into tending the land, and Leslie spent evenings out with friends "before they signed up or got conscripted." The brothers would not fight in the war, because farmers were on the "reserved occupations" list. A country at war needed to be fed. The decision forced Will and Leslie to show their worth, and so they added to their workload, taking on sixty acres of wheat from an elderly neighbor.

Rosalie moved through the next months as if negotiating her way through a darkened house—slowly and with a great deal of bruising.

She kept to her chickens, geese, sheep, and crops, slogging about in the rain throughout the day to return to a mug of tea and the *Cambridge News* in the office Pop had set up for himself. He had promised she would be a pilot, that he would see to it, but he was gone, and this was her life now. Escape was futile.

The paper was filled with news that the war had started but hadn't quite got off the ground yet. The dire prediction that it would rain bombs on London had not come true, and many children who had been sent out of the city for safety had already returned. Even so, the country remained on alert and on edge while—at the same time—bored. There was talk of food rationing, perhaps after Christmas.

One day in December, just after the butcher had come to take away five of her geese, Rosalie huddled near the paraffin heater in Pop's office and clasped her mug of tea, perusing the paper from three days earlier. That's where she was when she saw the article about Pauline Gower, her heroine of so many years. Gower had been appointed to the Women's Division of the Air Transport Auxiliary, the organization that would move aeroplanes around the country to where the RAF needed them. A photo accompanied the article about the eight women who would fly for her. The first group of women ferry pilots.

Rosalie stared at the article and ran a finger across the photo. The *first* eight women, it said, not the *only* women. She read it again, and was well on to memorizing the article when Leslie pushed the door open.

"Rags."

A gust of cold air rushed in behind him. "Close that before I freeze," Rosalie said, then followed with, "My, don't you look nice."

"Dance at the tennis club this evening—don't you want to come along? Ellen would be glad of the company."

Bless him, he's a terrible liar, Rosalie thought. Ellen had about as much use for her as she had for Ellen.

"She says Theo will be there." Leslie raised his eyebrows and looked hopeful.

In the spring, Rosalie had attended one dance at the tennis club and had enjoyed the attention from Ellen's brother until, over glasses of lemonade, he explained to her that the idea of a woman flying an aeroplane was against all laws of nature.

"You go on, Les," Rosalie replied. "I'm all right here."

"Righto. 'Evening."

When he'd gone, she rummaged in the desk and found a pencil. From the back of the account book, she pulled out a yellowed receipt for the delivery of hay, turned it over, and sucked on the pencil tip thoughtfully before setting it to work.

Dear Senior Commander Gower . . .

CHAPTER 3

October 1941
No. 15 Ferry Pool Hamble, Hampshire

"Second Officer Rosalie Wright, ma'am."

Rosalie handed her papers over to Hamble's commanding officer, Margot Gore, and stood at attention—which was completely unnecessary, as the Air Transport Auxiliary was a civilian group, not a military one. Still, she thought it showed respect. She'd taken off her forage cap, and her mad mop of curls had sprung forth. She attempted to tamp it down while watching Gore scan her assignment.

"Welcome to Number Fifteen Ferry Pool Hamble," the CO said. "Be proud that you are part of this all-women ferry pool. You'll be billeted with Mrs. May. She's not far—just in the village. Number Six Satchell Lane. Anyone can tell you the way. She has another pilot there already, Caroline Andrews. Caro. You start flying tomorrow. Come in here first for your chits. I'll warn you now, we can't predict how busy a day will be until we get the assignments in early on. It may be that you pick up your first aeroplane here, or you may need to take an air taxi elsewhere to collect it. Or you may be the pilot of the taxi, leaving off and collecting other pilots from airfields. No matter your destination, be prepared for detours along the way. That means, in addition to your parachute, be sure to take a bag with whatever you need for an overnight." She set the clipboard down and smiled. "Well then, Second Officer Wright, you have come far in a short time, haven't you?"

It seemed to Rosalie that it had taken her forever to become an ATA ferry pilot. At least the better part of two years.

She had sent her first letter to Pauline Gower after Christmas, in January 1940, and received a polite response. Yes, women would be ferrying aeroplanes to RAF airfields, but regretfully, Rosalie was too young and had too few solo hours to qualify for such a job.

Four months later, when a few more women had been added to the ATA rolls and, according to the newspaper, more would be needed to "get our boys in the air and winning the war," Rosalie wrote again, and again was turned down. But at the bottom of this letter were the only words that mattered to her: "We will keep you on our list." She read the sentence over and over, and Commander Pauline Gower's promise lodged in her breast and fluttered like birds' wings.

News of the war became their daily bread on Lime Farm. In May came the stories of British soldiers being rescued from a place called Dunkirk—not only by any little English boat that could cross the Channel but also by air, Rosalie noted. She spent her days moving the sheep into the next field, collecting eggs, and tending her strawberries, but she kept her eyes on the sky, imagining she played a different role in the war.

She waited until she could wait no more, then wrote to Pauline Gower again in July, and was invited in two months' time to Hatfield in Hertfordshire to be tested. Only then did Rosalie tell her mother of her plans, and even so, she approached her brothers first for support. They didn't let her down, wearing away her mother's resistance by coming up with an answer to every imagined problem.

Will and Leslie had assured their mum that the farm was in good hands. More hands than they'd ever had: the Women's Land Army had sent them five Land Girls, and they could well handle the extra work. Rosalie wouldn't be in danger, because there would be no flying into battle, only ferrying planes around the country. And after all, it was what Pop would've wanted.

That last one did the trick. Rosalie's mother gave her reluctant permission to try for the Air Transport Auxiliary in September 1940 as German bombs wreaked havoc on London.

Rosalie's attention was brought back to the present when Gore checked the papers in front of her and looked up. "I see you passed your test at Hatfield without difficulty."

During Rosalie's "three circuits and down" test, she had managed to fly into a bank of fog, and when she came out of it, she had no idea of her whereabouts and had to put down in a field, ask a woman hanging out washing where she was, and then take off again. When she landed in the proper field, she confessed her mistake. The woman instructor didn't speak for a moment, her pencil hovering over a checklist. Rosalie didn't move, although her heart beat at a gallop. The woman gave a brief nod before saying, "Knowing how to get out of a pickle is more important than thinking you'll never get in one in the first place."

That had been her first step to this moment, at Hamble. "Yes," Rosalie told Gore. "I passed my test."

CO Gore leaned against her desk and said, "It took Commander Gower time to convince the ATA more women were needed. I'm glad you could wait."

Having passed the test in September 1940, Rosalie had been put on another list, leaving her in an uncomfortable limbo at Lime Farm until the following April, when word came for her to report to Hatfield for training. Will and Leslie took her into their village pub—a rare treat—to celebrate. Parting with her mum the next morning wasn't nearly such a joyous occasion.

"We're not good enough for you," her mum said as they stood with the table between them.

"Pop wanted me to be a pilot," Rosalie shot back.

Her mother flinched as if she'd been stung. "He always let you do whatever you wanted. Let you fill your head with such ideas."

"Can't you be happy for me?"

At that moment, Leslie beeped the horn of the farm lorry, and Rosalie went out and climbed in.

Now her commanding officer gave her a smile. "Did you enjoy your training?"

Rosalie had become one of the sprogs—the female pilots in training. During one run at Hatfield, she had taken off in a gaggle with three others, all in Moths, which were open-air. It was a bitterly cold morning, and the wind smacked her in the face until she could feel nothing. When they finally landed, it took thirty minutes before she could speak, and in the Mess, the tea she had longed to drink dribbled out the side of her mouth.

"Yes, ma'am, I did."

"Good. Well, you'll meet the others in the morning, although there may be a few still in the waiting room this evening. Take a look and introduce yourself if you like."

"Thank you, ma'am."

Dismissed, Rosalie dutifully headed for the waiting room, which she'd passed on arrival. It had gone eight o'clock now. Her air taxi had not taken off from Hatfield until four that afternoon, and they'd dropped other pilots off at Brize Norton and Cosford before getting to her new home, here on the south coast. Hamble would be almost as close as you could get to the action of war, but in her last letter home, Rosalie had made light of that.

She pushed the door of the waiting room open an inch and peered in. Four women sat at the end of a table on the far side of the room, cups of tea in front of them. One woman was knitting and one reading a newspaper, and all were chatting and laughing. Rosalie eased the door closed. Perhaps she would join them another time. That was what she had told herself at Hatfield too, where she'd stayed on friendly but distant terms with the other women trainees. Her natural reluctance had left her alone in her billet most evenings while the others would think nothing of dashing into London for a dance or the cinema or a club, even during the Blitz.

Rosalie had lived in a two-bedroom flat shared among four women and cherished any quiet time she could find, preferring to curl up with her *Ferry Pilots Notes* or write letters home. Those she addressed to Mum, Will, and Leslie, but she only ever heard back from her brothers, who wrote a few breezy lines and usually wrapped up by sending regards from the sheep. She could well have returned home occasionally—Hatfield to Lime Farm on the other side of Cambridge wasn't that far. But the memory of the stilted, painful parting with her mother, unspoken anger filling the room, remained fresh in Rosalie's mind and made the journey seem too far to travel. She missed them, of course—Will, Leslie, even her mum. And Pop. In her loneliest moments, she even had a sentimental thought for the geese.

★　★　★

Rosalie walked into Hamble village and down Satchell Lane and saw the brick terrace ahead, her path lighted under a moon that was almost full. There was no number on the white door, but she could see the rusty outline of a 6 and the holes from the nails that had held it. The War Office had directed the removal of road signs so that it would be difficult for invading Germans to find their way. Perhaps Mrs. May had taken this personally.

Here was Rosalie's home for the foreseeable future. She gave a knock, and looked round the road while she waited. No front garden, but perhaps her landlady had a bit of land at the back. Here it was, the beginning of October, and Rosalie felt the urge to plant. Now would be the time to put in cabbage and cauliflower. Hampshire was warmer than Lime Farm, and so it would do to start peas for an early harvest. Perhaps Will would send her a handful of onion sets.

The door opened so abruptly that Rosalie jumped.

"Well, don't just stand there—get in before the Jerries see us."

The woman before her, with a glowing pinny, pale skin, and a halo of silver hair, looked entirely white against the blackout curtain behind her. If the Germans needed a beacon, she'd do fine.

The woman did not move out of the way, and so Rosalie slipped past her with a "Yes, sorry."

Pushing the door closed, the woman gave it a shove. "Sticks," she said. "Always give it an extra go to be sure. Are you the new girl?"

They stood in a narrow entry, Rosalie against the wall at the bottom of the stairs. Mrs. May had what could be described as firm features, including the line of her mouth, which suggested neither grimace nor smile. A ceiling light threw a dim pool of yellow onto the floor between them.

"Yes, hello, good evening. I'm Rosalie Wright. You're Mrs. May? I've my billet here—"

"I'll take your ration book." The woman held her hand out. Rosalie grappled with her bag and came up with several maps that marked the RAF bases in England and Scotland—it was her hope to memorize them—a recent letter from Leslie mentioning his girl, Ellen, and, at last, her ration book.

"Here you are."

"Come up now."

Rosalie followed Mrs. May up the steep stairs. At the first-floor landing, the landlady paused and waved to one of two closed doors. "Your other one—don't think she's in this evening. You each have your own room for the time being, although I'd say I'll be getting another of your kind before long." She nodded to the other door. "The bath is in there along with the necessary. We're quite modern here, you'll find. Of course, we still have the one out back." She swung round and began the next climb, but stopped and added, "You won't be wanting a bath this evening, will you?"

"No, certainly not."

Mrs. May continued, ending on the second-floor landing, where she flung open the door. "This is you."

It was a small room filled with a bed, nightstand, chair, and wardrobe. The wallpaper—a heavy rope-and-woodbine design—seemed to take up a great deal of space. A window overlooked the back. Rosalie walked to it and parted the curtains to look down.

"Blackout!" Mrs. May shouted. "Have you not heard of it?"

Rosalie snapped the curtains shut. "Sorry, it's only that—I wondered if you had a garden."

After a moment's pause, the woman asked, "Why do you want to know?"

"If you needed any help tending it or planting, then I'd be happy to give a hand. My family has a farm. I rather miss it." She surprised herself by saying it, but immediately and silently swore she'd never mention geese.

Mrs. May glared at her—Rosalie wondered if she had any other expression—before replying, "Breakfast at eight." She walked out.

No garden, then. Rosalie unpacked her case and took off her uniform, giving it a shake before setting it out for the morning. She pulled on her dressing gown, took her bag of toiletries along with the thin towel draped on the back of the chair, and headed down to the first-floor landing. A bath would've been nice after all, she thought. It might've calmed her nerves about the next morning and helped her sleep.

In the bathroom, she found that her fellow pilot had made herself at home. Stockings hung over the rail; a toothbrush stood up in a glass at the sink. Was that her soap, or did it belong to the house? Rosalie would need to clarify the bath rules in the morning.

Returned to her room, she switched off the light and pulled back the curtains just enough to look down into the back garden, but the almost-full moon had gone to the other side of the terrace, and she saw only a large dark space below. She closed the curtains, switched the lamp back on, and stood in the middle of the room. The house was quiet, and Rosalie, annoyed with herself, found she missed the chatter of the women at her Hatfield billet. Too late for regret. She decided to write home and tell the family of her arrival, and she had just propped herself up in bed when a tapping came at the door.

"Yes?"

Mrs. May came in—rather, first came a cup and saucer, held out much like a peace offering, followed by the landlady.

"Cocoa?" Mrs. May asked. "It's only that, I figure it won't be long before milk is on the ration, so we might as well drink it while we can get it. I thought, as you'd probably had a long journey today, you might like something to settle you down."

Rosalie wondered if Mrs. May had an evil twin or a second personality like Dr. Jekyll, but she accepted the cocoa gratefully, after which the landlady left again, this time with a "Good night."

★　★　★

Rosalie awoke early and listened. From outside, she heard gulls crying and jackdaws complaining, and possibly, from below, the rattle of pans in the kitchen. But she heard no footfalls on the landing below, and so she crept out of bed and down to the loo. She washed up and ran damp hands through her hair in less than five minutes—a talent she'd had to learn growing up with two older brothers who seemingly waited for her to go into the bathroom only so they could beat on the door demanding their turns.

Dressed and ready for the day, she had hopes of tamping down the butterflies in her stomach with a strong cup of tea. Rosalie descended to the kitchen, glancing first into the empty lounge, where she saw two photos on the mantel of young men in uniform, one RAF and one army, before she continued to the kitchen, hesitating in the doorway. "Good morning, Mrs. May."

"Mmmm. 'Morning." The landlady stood hunched over the hob, struggling to stir the glutinous contents of a pot. Porridge. "Tea on the table."

Rosalie poured herself a cup and stirred in milk. She'd have to be careful of milk if it was to be rationed. She had been known to drink an entire glass at a meal, but she'd have to give that up now.

"There!" Mrs. May whacked the wooden spoon on the side of the pot, and bits of oatmeal flew through the air. She wiped her hands on her pinny and gestured toward the back door. "I've something to show you."

Rosalie took her tea and followed the landlady out, but stopped next to the outdoor water closet because the back garden consisted almost entirely of an enormous hole. Rosalie peered in—it looked at least ten feet deep. What space remained at ground level was covered in tall piles of dirt, like a cluster of miniature Egyptian pyramids. This was excavation on a grand scale for such a small terrace house.

"Bomb," Mrs. May said, as they both contemplated the pit.

"You were hit?" Rosalie gasped.

"No, not strictly speaking—it didn't explode. Went straight down and there it sat, looking back at me like Hitler himself with a grin." She gave the hole a hard look, and Rosalie thought that in a staring contest with Mrs. May, any bomb had better beware.

"How dreadful," Rosalie said. "But they took it away?"

"They did, but first they had to make certain it wouldn't go off, and so all these fellows arrived and the entire terrace had to wait behind a line"—she waved behind them—"over the other side of the road. All day, it took. They dug and dug to get down close to the thing and the expert of them disarmed it, and only after that could they take the thing away in pieces. And left me with this."

Tufts of weeds and grass had sprouted on the dirt pyramids. Rosalie thought the bomb must've fallen early in the year. She had heard that the last hurrah of the Blitz hit the south coast hard.

"April," Mrs. May said, answering her silent question. "If my boys were here, they would see to it, but one is somewhere in Africa, last I heard, and the other in Scotland, God knows why. Pity, too. I had my veg growing here, you see. And raspberries at the bottom of the garden."

Rosalie squinted. "Looks like they survived."

"And so you see," Mrs. May said amiably, "I couldn't quite say what space I had or didn't have. What I do have is this." The landlady gave her a sideways glance. "Of course, if you wanted to plant your cabbages and onions and whatnot, I wouldn't complain. All you would need to do is sort this out—between you flying the aeroplanes."

"'Morning!" a voice called from the kitchen. "Are we having church out at the bomb site?"

Mrs. May grumbled, and Rosalie turned to see a tall woman with fair skin and black hair cut in a shingle so short that it stopped above her ears.

"Good morning," she said, stepping back into the kitchen.

"You're Rosalie—I'm Caro Andrews. Did they tell you I'd be here? We women are taking over the house, Mrs. May, aren't we? What will your sons say to that?"

Caro poured herself a cup of tea, and Mrs. May returned to the hob and muttered, "Makes no difference to me as long as I have your ration books."

"Are we having an egg today, Mrs. May, to celebrate Rosalie's arrival?" Caro asked.

"One egg a week, and you want to squander it on a Monday?" the landlady replied. She took up her spoon, filled two bowls with molten porridge, and set them on the table. "Bit of sugar there."

She turned to the sink, and Caro gave Rosalie a grin. "We'll go halves, shall we? After all, Mrs. May, you'll be getting twice as much food now with Rosalie here." Caro leaned over the table and, in a low voice, added, "Good thing sugar isn't rationed at the airfields."

Rosalie took her spoonful of sugar and thought about how much room there would be once the pit had been filled. Enough space for a chicken or two. She rather liked an egg for breakfast or tea.

"I was at Hatfield, of course," Caro said, when they compared notes from their journeys, "but I must've left before you arrived. I went on to White Waltham before coming to Hamble a fortnight ago. I've been here long enough to watch most of the men leave. We've got the place almost to ourselves now."

Caro continued to natter. Rosalie found it comforting, and it even had an effect on Mrs. May, whose grumpy facade had faded by the time they left for the pool.

"Mind how you go," Mrs. May called after them.

"She's all right, really," Caro said as they walked up to the airfield. "It's just that she's worried about Fred and Terry, her sons. Her husband died right at the end of the last war, just when she thought he would make it home. Sad, really. Look, I have a car that I keep at the airfield, so if you're ever in need of it, you let me know."

"Oh, I don't know how to drive," Rosalie said. "I only know how to fly." And they both burst out laughing.

CHAPTER 4

Caro led them to the waiting room. She introduced the six other women to Rosalie, who attempted to keep hold of the names, but the more she tried, the more they seemed to slip through her fingers. Her mind was on the day, wondering which aeroplanes she would fly and where she would make deliveries. She did take note with relief that the other female pilots wore uniform trousers. Good thing, too, because Rosalie wasn't about to pilot a plane in a skirt. As far as she could tell, those were saved for more formal occasions and for photographs, which ended up in the newspapers with headlines such as *Ladies Aloft!* and *Heroines Give Hitler a Scare*. In cold weather, Rosalie wore the Sidcot suit to fly—a khaki coverall that zipped up to her neck—but she would forgo the leather helmet and even her uniform forage cap if possible. Her curls resisted confinement.

A woman put her head in the door. " 'Morning, all. Assignments are in."

A cheer went up. Newspapers, books, and knitting were abandoned as the group rose and streamed into the next room, where Rosalie had had her induction the evening before. Aircraft collection chits covered a large table, each with a pilot's name and details about the aeroplane to be delivered. The assignments were also written on a chalkboard that covered one wall. Rosalie scanned the table as the other women claimed their assignments by slapping their hands on the slips of paper.

"Carlisle," one said. "I'll be up north, Brenda. Any message for Snug if I see him?"

"Hurricane to Yeovil. Is that it?" another asked, and received a quick reply of, "They'll have something else for you there."

At last, Rosalie found two chitties with her name on them. She was to fly Airspeed Oxfords, one to Aston Down and then another to Kemble. Short journeys both. Was that it for her first day—was she not to be trusted?

"Spitfire to Brize Norton," Caro called to her, waving her chit across the table. "Plus three others. I may be in late tonight."

Rosalie stuck out her chin to hide her disappointment, gave Caro a wave, and followed the others out. She'd been trained on Spitfires and Hurricanes too, but if she needed to prove herself on an Ox-box, then she'd do her best and be proud of it.

They collected their two-penny bars of chocolate and their parachutes. Not for the first time, Rosalie wondered what good a parachute would do them. ATA pilots were required to fly below two thousand feet, but most, she had learned, stayed at a thousand feet or lower. Not really enough time for a parachute to save you, but rules were rules, and she always carried hers with her.

The pilots checked with Maps and Signals for hazard warnings and the Met Office for weather alerts, then headed to the field to find their planes. Rosalie let the other women go before her so that she wouldn't feel hurried. She studied her map again and laid a finger on the aerodrome at Aston Down, happy to see that a handy railway line would lead her almost the entire way. By the time she looked up, hers was the only aeroplane and the ground crew stood waiting. Lesson one: don't be a slowcoach.

She climbed into the Oxford's three-person cockpit, hurrying through the ritual she'd learned from Reg of touching the controls. No radio, of course, not for the ATA. Next, she spoke aloud her checks. "Hydraulics, trim, tension, mixture, pitch, petrol . . ."

The nervous excitement over her inaugural journey as Second Officer Wright dissolved into the thrill she felt at each takeoff. Once up, a calmness settled on her as it had on every flight she'd ever taken. Troubles, worries, fear were left behind. The world was hers.

She kept well below the high clouds, spotted her landmarks, and put down at Aston Down without incident. Good thing she didn't expect to be congratulated for carrying out her first assignment, because when she handed the plane over to the ATA duty officer—a fellow who looked as if he might've fought in the Great War—she was greeted with a question that sounded more like a challenge.

"Can you fly a Tiger Moth?" he barked at her, waving a chit in the air.

Rosalie narrowly avoided shooting back *I grew up on a Tiger Moth!* because it wasn't strictly true, and instead replied, "Yes, sir, I can."

"Right," he said, "we've got one to go to the maintenance unit at Little Rissington. You can take it."

"I'm to go back to Hamble and collect another Oxford for Kemble."

"Oh, one of the new ones, are you?" His voice softened as if he spoke to a child. "Are you saying you cannot get yourself from Little Rissington to Hamble?"

She snatched the chit from his hand, picked up her parachute, and headed back to the field.

She'd trained on the Tiger Moth at Hatfield, and it was much like the Gipsy Moth she'd first flown with Reg. She scanned the takeoff information in the pilots notes, carried out her tactile cockpit check, and took a quick look at her map. Takeoff should be no problem, and she could sort out landing on her way there. Once ready, she gave a nod to the fellow waiting to move the chocks.

★   ★   ★

At the Little Rissington maintenance unit, Rosalie had an hour to wait for an Anson air taxi back to Hamble, and so she went in search of a lavatory and a cup of tea, in that order. She feared the MU had only men, and that meant she would have to either dash into and out of the facility—praying no one would walk in on her—or make for the tall hedgerow beyond the hangar. She had started off in that direction when a coveralled figure approached.

"Hello," the woman said. "ATA?"

"Oh, yes, I am. Say—"

"I am Zofia Pasek. I have my break now—you would like a cup of tea?" she asked. "Only two women here, the rest men." She shrugged her shoulders.

"I'd love one, really I would, but first I most desperately need the loo."

"Loo." The woman laughed. "Yes. Follow me."

The lavatory block was thankfully nearby and empty. The woman pulled a red kerchief out of a pocket and tied it to the door handle and nodded Rosalie in.

"They know this means keep out," she said. "They are good lads."

After, as she buttoned up her trousers, Rosalie told herself that in the future, she'd need to be judicious about that second cup of tea before flying. But now, she could quite do with one.

She sat in a modest Mess—more a hut, actually—with Zofia, who was Polish and an experienced pilot with many more solo hours than Rosalie had.

"Why are you a mechanic? You should be flying with us."

"Five of us escape as the Germans come," Zofia said, pulling off her head scarf and running fingers through frizzy blond hair. "My mother is a chemist and much wanted for her work. She say, 'Go and we will follow,' but she and my sister, who is younger, are still in Poland. At least, I believe this. We five who escape . . . first, we are in France, and then come here. We are pilots. I want to fly. I write letters to say so. Many letters."

That sounds familiar, Rosalie thought.

"You are at Hamble?" Zofia asked. "Do you know Caro Andrews?"

A man stuck his head in the Mess. "Anson taxi!"

"That's me away." Rosalie stood and gathered her parachute. "I do know Caro. We're billeted together. How do you know her?"

"We met at Hatfield when I arrive. My first friend."

"Well, cheerio, Zofia," Rosalie said. "Keep writing those letters."

She climbed aboard the Anson, and they were off. Once airborne, Rosalie took her turn first at cranking up the undercarriage. It was one of the quirks of the aeroplane—144 turns to retract the landing gear. With its typical crew of four, there would be a man assigned to do the cranking, but for ATA taxi flights, there was only the pilot, and so passengers helped out.

"Are you for Hamble?" the pilot shouted above the engine.

"I am," Rosalie said.

"It's Chipping Norton first, then Aston Down, and then you."

Once she was at Chipping Norton, they were looking for someone to take a Fairey Battle to Exeter, and Rosalie put up her hand. "I will."

After that, it was another air taxi to Hamble in time to take the second Oxford to Kemble and a wait before she could get back to her pool. At the end of the day, Rosalie realized that two chitties in the morning did not mean she would lack for work. She might not have flown a Spitfire or a Hurricane, but she had made her scheduled two deliveries plus two others.

She tarried at Hamble, catching a cup of tea on her own in the Mess. She arrived back at her billet at seven o'clock to find Mrs. May in the kitchen, where she'd left her, but this time with the aroma of something savory emanating from the oven.

"Good evening, Mrs. May."

"You'll be relieved to know I take a broad view of the time for the evening meal," the landlady said as a greeting. "Better to cook something that will keep than to cook a meal that will go over as it sits there waiting to be eaten." She turned to Rosalie, who stood in the doorway. "Where's the other one?"

"Caro had a full day. She said she could be late," Rosalie said. "Should we wait for her?"

"And how long would that be?" Mrs. May replied. "I had a fellow here before you girls. He took an aeroplane to Scotland, and I didn't see him for three days."

"You had men billeted here before us?" Rosalie asked.

"You'll wash your hands, won't you?"

Rosalie, about to slide down onto a chair, popped back up without a word, having heard much the same question all her life. She took the stairs to the first floor, washed, and made it back just as Mrs. May was using a tea towel to pull a pie out of the oven. It landed on the table with a *thunk*, and she attacked it with a knife, scooped out a steaming mass onto a plate, and handed it over.

"Oh," Rosalie said, stabbing a large white cube with her fork, "swedes."

"I had only the one pilot, bear of a man. Thank God I had no one else—he took up that much room. But he had no interest in filling the hole in the garden for me."

Mrs. May nodded toward the back, and Rosalie realized she was now on the hook for sorting out a new veg patch for the landlady.

"I'll have thirteen days on, and then I'll have a couple off," she explained. "I'll get stuck in after that."

"Lord Woolton's pie," the landlady stated. "We're to use what we have, and Mrs. Potts over the road has more swedes than she knows what to do with."

Rosalie felt as if their conversation was out of sync. Was that what any prolonged discussion with Mrs. May was like—ask a question and get it answered two turns later?

"The carrots are sweet," Rosalie commented.

"He had only one eye," the landlady replied. "Didn't know they let you fly an aeroplane with only one eye."

"Ancient and Tattered Airmen," Rosalie said. "That's what they were called in the newspapers. The ATA has men who are too old for the RAF and others who have physical problems. I hear one of them is missing an arm."

"Ancient and Tattered . . ." the landlady repeated. "And so, what do they call you women?"

Rosalie's face reddened with both embarrassment and pride.

"They call us Attagirls."

★   ★   ★

Rosalie didn't see Caro until the next morning at breakfast, when she found her hunkered over a bowl of porridge and glowering out the back door at the heavy sky and mizzling rain.

Mrs. May set another bowl on the table, noticed Caro's look, and said, "A bit of rain is good for the garden."

Rosalie looked out the door to see rivulets running down the mounds of dirt, turning the landscape into a quagmire.

"It had better lift," Caro said. "Otherwise, we'll be cooped up in the waiting room all day. I don't knit. Do you?"

"Oh, yes," Rosalie said. "I had to set a good example for my sheep."

Caro's stormy face broke into a grin. "Did you knit them their own jumpers?"

Rosalie laughed. "No. We bring someone in for the shearing, and the wool goes to the cooperative mill after that. I get a bit back and knit a jumper or two to show how good the wool is."

"You're from a sheep farm?"

"I'm from an everything farm. Sheep, crops, chickens, geese, a few cows. Pop thought it best to diversify."

Mrs. May had stopped what she was doing at the sink and turned an ear to listen.

"Do you miss it?" Caro asked.

"No, I don't," Rosalie said with conviction and a nervous look at her landlady. Filling in the pit here at Mrs. May's and planting a few onions was one thing, but she didn't want to give the idea that she had any interest in becoming a farmer again—no matter how tiny the small holding.

The weather broke later in the morning, and so there was flying to be done. Rosalie took a Tiger Moth to White Waltham and then flew one back from the MU at Kidbrooke near London. The next day, she had another Tiger Moth.

The day after that, it was a Miles Magister—another basic trainer aeroplane. Here she was on her fourth day at the ferry pool, and all Rosalie had flown were trainers. She wouldn't dare complain. At least, not aloud. Instead, she kept her head down and studied her chit to hide her disappointment while all round her, women were waving assignments and talking of the fighters they'd flown just that week.

Caro bent her head to catch Rosalie's eye. "You've a Magister—that's a trainer for a Spitfire."

"But I've already flown a Spitfire," Rosalie said. "Don't they know I can do it?"

Once. She'd taken a few circuits round the airfield at White Waltham. She'd done the same with the other darling of the fighters, the Hurricane. Rosalie had trained on the Blenheim, too, and a few other light bombers, but there was something about being in a small fighter that gave her the feeling that she could conquer the world.

"You'll have time," Caro said. "The war won't be over anytime soon."

Guilt shut Rosalie up. She wanted the war to be over before there was nothing left of her country, and yet, what would she do afterward—go back to her sheep?

"Wright? You've missed one."

Rosemary Rees, deputy CO at Hamble, handed over one more chit to Rosalie, then turned to add it to the chalkboard.

R. Wright: Spitfire.

★   ★   ★

Her gum boot made a sucking sound when she pulled it out of the mud of Mrs. May's back garden, but Rosalie smiled despite it. She had ended her first thirteen-day stretch on a high note, by flying a Spitfire up to North Weald in Essex and taking the slightest of digressions to fly over Lime Farm on her way. She kept low enough to recognize people but spotted only a couple of Land Girls in one of the fields and another on the tractor. Rosalie had hoped Will or Leslie would walk out of the barn, look up, and wave. She wished with all her heart that Pop could see her.

It had made her free day all that more bearable, even under a dripping sky. She had donned gum boots and waterproof trousers that came up to her armpits and tied her curls down with a scarf, knotting it at her forehead. Mrs. May had provided the trousers and a canvas jacket. Both had obviously belonged to one of her sons—miles too big. In one jacket pocket, she'd found a half-smoked cigarette and in the other what her mother would have called a smutty book. The cover showed a woman, the strap of her shift slipped off her shoulder, holding a gun at an indistinguishable figure. Rosalie had seen similar books in the hands of her brothers or tucked away behind the horses' feedbox in the barn.

Caro was flying, and as it was Saturday, the landlady had armed herself with ration books and gone shopping, so Rosalie had been left alone with a shovel and her thoughts. She attacked the nearest dirt pyramid.

By midmorning, heated from exertion, she had shed the jacket, rain or no. She broke for lunch, cleaning her hands just enough to eat the dried end of a loaf and an equally dried hunk of cheese, washed down with a cup of tea containing—much to her dismay—evaporated milk. She wasn't fond of cows on a personal level. They were large, their cries sounded plaintive in her ears, and they had the unnerving habit of walking right up to you with their enormous heads and staring at you as if you had something they wanted. No, although Rosalie enjoyed the reasons for a cow's existence—milk, butter, cheese, beef—she had always left the tending of them to Pop, and now to Will and Leslie.

By late afternoon, one entire pyramid had been shifted. As the light failed, Rosalie regarded the remaining five, then took a step forward to gaze down into the pit. But her foot went out from under her on the slick mud. She waved her arms wildly, stumbled backward, and landed hard on her bum with a *splat*.

"Bloody hell," she said.

"We're not having this, Rosalie."

She gasped and looked round, half expecting to see her mother, but instead found Caro leaning against the kitchen doorpost grinning at her.

"What's this about?" Caro asked.

"I told Mrs. May I would help," Rosalie said, clambering out of the mud. "It was my first night and I'd just arrived and I was feeling . . . I could see pieces of the bomb that had been left at the bottom of the pit—at least, scraps of metal. I don't suppose it matters that I'm burying them?"

"If they had wanted them, they should've taken them along in the first place. Now, come indoors and get yourself cleaned up. We're off to the pub."

"Are we?" Rosalie said. "Now? Is Mrs. May returned from shopping?"

"No, and she won't be anytime soon. I've learned that Mrs. May's shopping days include a great deal of talking with the shopkeepers and popping into other people's houses for cups of tea. Of course, if you're still at work when she returns, she could be so pleased with your progress, she'll have you apply for an allotment."

"Let's go." Rosalie stowed the spade, pulled off the gum boots, and stepped out of the waterproof trousers. She would've walked out the front door that minute, except she noticed she had mud up to her elbows. "Perhaps I'll just have a quick wash."

Caro put the kettle on. "Don't be long."

Rosalie knew how to be quick, and twenty minutes later, she and Caro stood in the snug of the Bugle, Rosalie undecided about what to order. The small room, specially set off for the ladies, had only a short bar, the rest of it being on the other side of the wall in the public area, which was populated by men and the rare bold woman. The snug came with its own wood shutter above the barman's head so he could pull it down just in case. In case of what—the women became rowdy?

"A sherry?" Caro suggested.

Rosalie hadn't spent a great deal of time in pubs, but she considered sherry a drink for when the vicar came to call. "No, not sherry. I'll have a pint of the mild."

"Good on you," Caro replied, and ordered two. They took their beer over to a table, nodding to the only other occupants—two women who sat with their coats on, scarves tied under their chins, and handbags in their laps. In front of them on the low table, they each had a glass of a clear liquid. Gin, Rosalie guessed.

She and Caro chatted about flying—how and when they began. Rosalie asked about Caro's family and learned she was the daughter of a country doctor near Colchester and had started flying lessons at fifteen. Feeling hard done by, Rosalie complained that she had had to wait until she turned sixteen. Occasionally while they talked, Rosalie would glance at the dark surroundings, all oak and slightly shabby upholstery, and think, *Here I am in a pub. If they could see me now.* She wasn't quite sure if "they" were her brothers, her mum, or the girls from school. Rosalie had never had what she would call a close friend, but she was enjoying the evening with Caro, and found it much like bantering with Will or Leslie. How lucky she'd been to be assigned to Mrs. May's.

"Boyfriend?" Caro asked.

"No. You?"

Caro shook her head. "But now you can choose from all those handsome RAF pilots."

Rosalie wrinkled her nose. "I'm not good at meeting people. Although, I suppose it would be nice to find a man who didn't think flying was just a lark for me. Theo did that. He told me women didn't have the brains to fly. Shows he knows sod all."

Caro laughed and said, "There aren't any more like you at home, are there?"

Rosalie laughed too. "No. Oh, wait, you mean do I have a brother? Yes, two older ones. Will and Leslie. But I think Will is sweet on one of the Land Girls, and Leslie has Ellen, of course. So, they're taken."

Caro leaned back against the settle. "It's just as well."

Chapter 5

November 1941

A month passed in an instant. Rosalie no longer concerned herself with which aeroplanes she delivered. She had flown further afield each week, and had learned to work her way back to Hamble any way she could. Air taxi if at all possible, a train as a last resort—they were overcrowded and unreliable. But the afternoon of the day before, she had taken a Blenheim north to Halfpenny Green in Staffordshire, and because of the weather, her return air taxi had to put down almost immediately near Kidderminster for the night. She managed to fly into Hamble the next morning, the Anson landing in what Deputy CO Rees described as "deplorable conditions."

"We're grounded until it clears," Rees told her. "The others are in the waiting room. Go along and join them."

Rosalie considered going back to No. 6 for a quiet cup of tea instead, but as she passed the waiting room, Grace, one of the other pilots, came round the corner.

"Made it back, did you?" Grace asked sharply. "Stuck somewhere?"

"Yes," Rosalie replied. "I had to put up in a hotel last night."

"I hope it was suitable," Grace said. "There's been a terrible drop in standards lately. Even in London, you're just as likely to get a bad martini as you are to be bombed."

Grace acted as if the goal of the war was to inconvenience her, and Rosalie had learned the woman had a narrow band of what she considered suitable. Grace's good looks—tall and lithe—did little to soften the delivery of her cutting remarks, which could be aimed at one of the other women just as easily as it could a hotel. Rosalie had yet to be the recipient of one of these barbs, but remained wary.

When Grace opened the door, a burst of laughter and conversation came forth. She nodded at Rosalie.

"Oh," Rosalie said, "I need to go back to my digs for something."

Grace raised an eyebrow at her, but went in alone. Rosalie, however, was not to find escape, for when she turned to go, there was Bridget Hill.

"You aren't leaving, are you?" Bridget seemed a nice sort, quite cheerful and outgoing. Rosalie was sorry to disappoint her.

"It's only that I'm a bit weary." It sounded a weak excuse even in Rosalie's ears.

"Well, then, what you need is a cup of tea and good company." Bridget put her hand on the door. "We won't bite, Rosalie. I'm sure if you make an effort, you'll end up enjoying yourself. C'mon."

Rosalie followed her in and looked round for a quiet corner.

"There you are now," Caro said, looking up from the newspaper. "Come on, tell us all about it."

Rosalie dropped her parachute and bag and did as she was told. She got herself a cup of tea, took a chair, and told her story, aware that all eyes were on her. "We heard planes overnight. They said it was the Luftwaffe heading for Liverpool."

"I had to put up in a pub last week," Catherine said. "Didn't mention that in my letter home, though." She blushed. As the daughter of a Methodist preacher and fiancée to a fellow in the army, this was racy business.

"When you're stuck at a base, you should ask to bunk in the officers' wing. I did that once. My dad knew the CO." Anne was accustomed to the military, as most of her male relatives were officers of some sort. She claimed they could trace their ancestors through their military service back to Henry II.

Brenda, daughter of a policeman, shook a knitting needle at them and grinned. "Watch those officers, ladies, or one of them might entice you to share his bunk."

"I'm engaged," Bridget reminded them. "That would be off-limits for me."

"But what if we want to be enticed?" Anne said.

They laughed, and now that the spotlight was off her, Rosalie could join in.

But not Grace. Instead, after the laughter had died out, she muttered, "No need to worry about Caro being enticed by an RAF officer."

Caro shook out the newspaper and resumed reading. Brenda rolled her eyes, and the others went back to knitting.

The conversation picked up again in a few minutes. Once drawn—or dragged—in, Rosalie enjoyed the gregarious nature of her fellow pilots, if only as an observer. When Caro and the others went into Southampton for a film or down to the Bugle, they would do their best to include Rosalie, but still, most evenings, she could be found in the sitting room at Mrs. May's, reading a book. Unless the landlady started in about the garden.

Rosalie tried to put Mrs. May off the subject by saying, "We've really passed the time to plant anything," but even so, the remaining dirt pyramids haunted her. She'd had another go at them—again in the mud and rain—but had made little progress. Now, when the subject of spring sowing arose, Rosalie would excuse herself by saying she needed to write a letter home.

Which she would've done at that moment, except that Commanding Officer Margot Gore walked into the waiting room.

"Is it clearing?" Caro asked.

"Looks like it," Gore replied. "But before you go, I want you to meet our newest—but quite experienced—pilot. Second Officer Pasek."

"Zofia!" Rosalie exclaimed, and heard Caro like an echo, "Zofia!"

Second Officer Pasek, standing alongside the CO, gave them both a wide smile. She looked smart in her ATA uniform with her forage cap set at a jaunty angle. Quite a change from the mechanic's coveralls she'd been wearing when Rosalie met her.

"Zofia is from Poland," Gore explained. "She and a few others escaped to France and then made their way here. We're pleased she's joined us at Hamble, and I know you will all make her welcome."

Gore went round with names and then said, "Zofia was to be billeted in Bursledon, but that hasn't worked out. But not to worry. We'll find her a bed before the end of the day. Right, now to your assignments."

She gestured for Zofia to go ahead of her, and the rest of the women followed the CO out the door, but Caro hung back and tugged on Rosalie's sleeve.

"We've got a place, don't we?" Caro asked. "I mean, there's an empty bed in my room."

"So there is—should we ask Mrs. May first?"

"Oh, I don't know," Caro said, looking at the door. "Isn't she expecting it? Let's see what Margot thinks."

★ ★ ★

"In for a penny, in for a pound," Mrs. May muttered that evening, crowded into the narrow entry with Zofia, Caro, and Rosalie. She continued to study the billet form in her hand.

"For you, also," Zofia said, and handed over her ration book.

Mrs. May's countenance lightened considerably at the sight. She slipped the book into the pocket of her pinny, gave it a pat, and said, "Well, then, the meal is on the table, and there's plenty for all. Come through."

Four of them round the kitchen table made for close quarters, but no one seemed to mind. "You're lucky to land here at Mrs. May's," Caro said. "Isn't she, Rosalie?"

Rosalie agreed. It seemed they had stitched together some sort of home here—she, Caro, and their landlady.

"You have two sons, Mrs. May," Zofia said. "Caro tells me they are in the war."

Mrs. May had received a letter from the son in Scotland only that morning, and with a bit of encouragement, she retrieved it, and read aloud his tales of encountering the locals, whose speech, he said, was completely unintelligible. He ended the letter with *Miss your porridge, Mum.* Caro snorted, and Rosalie covered her laugh with a cough.

Good spirits excused a great deal, including the food. Fortunately. Rosalie looked down at the occasional fleck of fatty bacon mixed into the mound of large white cubes on their plates and wondered if they would ever finish with Mrs. Potts's swedes. But Mrs. May didn't want to look ungracious by refusing her neighbor's gift, because Mrs. Potts had a daughter who had a friend with hens and one rooster, and hopes were high that in the spring, the landlady might get hold of a few chicks.

"Don't let's go up just yet," Caro said, after they'd finished and she stood drying the plates that Rosalie had washed while Zofia wiped the table. "What about the wireless, Mrs. May? Couldn't we find a concert or a dance band?"

"I don't know where you get your energy," Mrs. May said, shaking her head. "But all right, go on, then."

They piled into the sitting room, negotiating overstuffed chairs and rickety tables. Caro switched on the wireless, and out came a riotous sound of horns. Rosalie made for a chair in the corner, but Caro caught her arm.

"I know that one!" she exclaimed. " 'In the Mood.' Come on now, dance with me!"

Rosalie laughed, took a few turns, and then excused herself by saying, "Zofia, what about you?"

Zofia took over as Caro's partner. Mrs. May sat down with a newspaper, and Rosalie picked up her knitting.

*   ★   ★

Rosalie looked at the three chitties with her name on them. Hawker Hinds—biplanes, much like the Moths. She sighed.

"Wright," her CO said, "every plane we fly is an important delivery."

"Yes, ma'am," she said automatically. "I realize that."

"No one can deliver a Spitfire every day. At least, not at the moment."

They all wanted to, because the Spit was the darling of the ATA. But Rosalie didn't mean to complain, and replied again, "Yes, ma'am."

Over the CO's shoulder, Caro waved a chit and mouthed the word *Spitfire*, then danced out the door. Rosalie tried not to look at her. "The Hinds are going to maintenance units?"

"Yes, the MUs will get them ready to be redeployed for training. We're all part of the effort."

"Yes, ma'am."

Her three deliveries crossed the country. It seemed easy enough, but it was November, and cold, and she would be in an open cockpit. But, as she asked herself each time something didn't go quite her way at Hamble, would she rather be back at Lime Farm spreading horse manure on the strawberry beds? She zipped her Sidcot suit up to her chin and went forth.

Her last delivery went to White Waltham, ATA headquarters near London, and when the duty officer asked if she would deliver yet another Hind on her way back, she said yes in an instant, not wanting to look as if she thought she could pick and choose her aeroplanes. Her destination, Stoney Cross in the New Forest, was near to Hamble, which suited her evening plans.

Caro had talked Rosalie into going out with a few of the women from the pool to the cinema in Southampton. "You'll enjoy yourself, you know you will," Caro had said. Rosalie knew she was right, but still it took an effort to be sociable after a lifetime of sitting at home with her parents and her brothers.

Occupied with those thoughts, she flew into a cloud before she knew it. Its heavy moisture smacked her in the face, and she pushed sodden hair out of her eyes, hoping she would come straight out of it again. But she didn't. Should she go above? That seemed a bad idea—without seeing the ground, she would have no idea of her location. Go below?

ATA pilots flew low all the time, because, with no radio or radar, they needed to see landmarks to find their way. But if she ducked down now without knowing her position, there could be a hill directly in front of her or she could become entangled in a cluster of barrage balloons floating like enormous fat silverfish in the sky, and she wouldn't know until it was too late. Danger above and below. She glanced down. The fuel gauge had dipped—given just enough to make her destination, she hadn't the luxury of continuing to waffle.

She dropped below the cloud, and the sun, low in the sky, cut across the nose of the plane. She let out her breath—not even aware she'd been holding it—as she spotted the airfield, circled, and put down. Taxiing to a stop, she completed her landing checklist and sat in the plane for a moment, grateful to be on the ground.

Wet, cold, and exhausted, Rosalie gave over her delivery to the duty officer and asked to use the telephone. She rang Hamble and talked with Caro, who told her to hold tight, she would be on her way, and that they would go directly to the cinema from there.

Desperate for warmth, Rosalie dragged herself into the Mess and saw a few RAF pilots huddled round a table. It felt no warmer indoors than out. She poured herself a cup of tea and noticed at the other end of the room a one-bar electric fire burning, looking as good to her as a blazing inglenook fireplace. A bear of a man wearing an ATA uniform was shouting instructions to an orderly, who scurried over with a straight-back chair and set it down next to the fire. The bear walked out the door after the orderly, and so Rosalie hurried over and slipped into the empty chair. But the man returned and made straight for the electric fire, acting as if he didn't even see Rosalie and looking as if he might just sit right on top of her. At the last second, he cocked his head and jumped at the sight.

"What are you doing there?" he bellowed. "Who the hell are you?"

"Second Officer Wright," she shouted in return. "Who the hell are you?"

He squinted his right eye at her.

"Second Officer Durrant," he barked. "That's my chair."

"Well, Second Officer Durrant, I've had a very long day. I'm tired and cold and wet, and I have to wait until I can make my way back to my pool." She decided not to mention that Caro would arrive in a car within the hour. "So, I am not going to move from this spot, and as you don't outrank me and we're civilians to boot, you have no right to turf me out of a chair in the Mess of an RAF airfield." She sniffed indignantly.

"Wright, is it?" Durrant said, as if filing her name away for future reference. "What makes you think your day has been any worse than mine? I've had three deliveries today."

"So have I."

"Blenheims to Luton, Henley, and Speke." He threw the names down like a challenge.

Hoping to avoid mentioning her trainer planes in the face of his bombers, she shot back, "No, wait—I've had four." He took a step closer, looming over her, but with two older brothers, she'd long ago become inured to intimidation. She gave a short laugh and took a sip of her tea. "You don't scare me."

He ran his hand through his short, untidy brown hair. His jaw worked as if he was sorting through his vocabulary to choose just the right response, but before he spoke, a musical female voice drifted across the room.

"Oh, Snug?"

He turned, and Rosalie leaned over to look round him. She saw a WAAF, still in uniform but with what looked to Rosalie—even from across the room—like a fresh and quite thick application of cherry-red lipstick.

"I'm ready now." The woman flashed him a big smile.

"Well, Second Officer Durrant," Rosalie said with a smile of her own. "Looks like you won't be needing this chair after all." Durrant grunted, and as he walked away, she called after him, "Have a lovely evening!"

★ ★ ★

Will and his Land Girl, Jean, were getting married. His letter had arrived in the post that morning, just as Rosalie was leaving. She took it along and read it as she walked to the airfield, stopping abruptly to let off a single *whoop!* Continuing on her way, she scanned the rest of the contents and then tucked the letter into her pocket to read again later.

The ceremony would take place in early January at Lime Farm. A small affair. Her brother had been careful to explain why they weren't waiting longer, as if she might get other ideas about the timing. He wrote that it was better to marry now in winter, when it was quieter on the farm. And, he added, Jean would have a chance to settle into the house, where she and their mum could get used to each other. Although it was short notice, he hoped Rosalie would be there. *How can I get married without our Rags?*

Later that afternoon, when Rosalie sat by herself with a cup of tea in the Officers' Mess at Honington in Suffolk, she took the letter out of her pocket and read it again. Will sounded happy, and she was happy for him.

But his request for her presence made Rosalie uneasy. This would be her first visit to Lime Farm since she'd left earlier that year, and she was unsure of her reception. Her brothers would welcome her, of course, but what about her mother, whose sole communication had been secondhand through letters from Will and Leslie, and then only a brief *Mum sends her love*. Had she?

If Rosalie could find a way to Lime Farm, she could be back at Hamble on Sunday. That would be two nights at home—perhaps the less time she spent with her mother, the better off they'd both be. And now her mum would have Jean, a proper daughter. By marriage.

What of Leslie? Rosalie wondered. She hadn't seen Ellen's name mentioned recently and felt a touch of apprehension at asking. If Will was in love, then Leslie deserved to be too. Meanwhile, she thought ruefully, she would continue to fly.

The door of the Mess opened, and Rosalie watched a pilot step in and glance round the room before he walked over to the tea station. He was tall and slender and had sandy-brown hair and, from what she could see of it, a pleasant face that seemed to border on a smile. He took a spoonful of sugar and stood stirring his tea, making a further examination of the people in the room. Rosalie cut her eyes round, wondering if he was looking for someone in particular. She was the only woman—the rest were men scattered about at the other tables.

A few of them acknowledged the new arrival, and he nodded back to them. Finally, his gaze landed on Rosalie, and she dropped her eyes, her face warm at being caught out. She opened Will's letter to read again, but in her peripheral vision she saw the pilot strolling toward her until he stood at her table and she had to look up.

Her eyes flitted first to the insignia on his sleeve—two stripes, which meant a flight lieutenant, if she remembered correctly—then to his face. He smiled as if he was terribly pleased to find her there.

"Hello, I'm Alan Chersey. Mind if I join you?"

Rosalie's face heated up further as she gestured to the empty seats and mumbled something incoherent.

"Sorry," he said, settling across from her and resting his elbows on the table, "I didn't catch that. What did you say your name was?"

She cleared her throat. "Rosalie Wright."

"Rosalie," he repeated, with no indication that he noticed her scarlet face. He nodded at her wing patch. "ATA, I see. I daresay you fly as many miles as we do."

She thought they probably did, but felt it impolite to agree. After all, the ATA carried no ammunition, and they neither dropped bombs nor engaged in midair battles.

"Where are you based?" Alan asked. He had a congenial manner, and Rosalie was grateful he took no notice that she wasn't holding up her end of the conversation.

She took a deliberate breath to slow her racing pulse. "Hamble."

Alan took a drink of his tea. Rosalie folded Will's letter, but she didn't trust herself to pick up her cup and so instead kept her hands and eyes on the table.

"Letter from home?"

"Yes. My brother is getting married." Her reply was a bit rushed, but at least she spoke like a normal person.

"Is he RAF?" Alan asked.

"No, he's in a reserved occupation."

"Ah."

Did Rosalie pick up a hint of scorn to Alan's reply? Her face, only just cooled, heated up again with righteousness.

"He's a farmer. He and my brother run our family's farm and have taken on an extra sixty acres to grow wheat. Farming is vital to the war effort. How can we fight if we can't feed our troops? Why, your breakfast could've—"

"Come from your farm?" Alan finished. "Don't I know it. We'd be finished before we started without people like your brothers. British farms will win the war." He smiled again. "So tell me, Rosalie—what do you grow on your farm?"

She wanted to say it wasn't her farm, but instead replied, "It's mixed. Sprouts, cabbages, savoys, cauliflower, turnips, runner beans. Beets and onions and peas. Hay and straw . . . geese and sheep . . . chickens." Her voice faded away, as she feared she sounded as if she were giving a report to the Ministry of Food.

Alan sighed. "You must miss it terribly."

No. Yes. No.

CHAPTER 6

December 1941

On the eighth of December, they awoke to a world at war. The wireless reported that the day before, the Japanese—a German ally—had attacked both British and American bases in the Pacific.

At the ferry pool, there was heated excitement in the air, along with an enormous amount of speculation. Would their work increase? Would they fly American planes? Would the war be over soon?

"We need to concentrate on our job," CO Gore told the women. "We have a vital role in the war." She swept her arm over the table that was covered in chitties. "You've got your assignments. We need to go about our business as usual—Maps and Signals, the Met. Looks like the clouds are staying rather low today, so you'll need to stay lower. Now, let's get to work and continue to do our part."

The atmosphere on the ground might have been charged, but once Rosalie had taken off on her first run of the day, she left the chatter behind, and her mind calmed. In the air, she took a circuit before spotting the railway line that would guide her most of the way to Lyneham in Wiltshire. There, she would deliver her Oxford to the maintenance unit.

The gray skies were like a frame for the scene below: patchwork fields, villages you could hold in your hand, and the leafless woods looking as if they'd been scribbled in with a rusty-colored pencil. England. The latest events had not changed the scene—it looked much the same that morning as it had the week before. After two years of war, even bomb-damaged houses and churches had become part of the landscape. The same, but different, for now there was hope.

At the end of the day, Mrs. May and her three lodgers sat at the kitchen table hovering over that morning's copy of the *Hampshire Telegraph*, which had been passed up and down the road. The news had been repeated at every airfield the young women had flown to, and they'd seen other newspaper accounts, but they read the stories again because the day held great significance.

"Pearl Harbor," Mrs. May said, tapping the name in the headline. "All the way on the other side of the world. Well, now we aren't alone—the Americans are in it."

"The Americans will make Hitler even more angrier," Zofia said, shaking her head. "Maybe it will be worse before better."

"Now, none of that doom and gloom," Caro said. "We've cause to celebrate. And to help us—see what I have." She plunged a hand into the pocket of her coat, brought out an oblong tin, and set it in the middle of the table on top of the newspaper. "There you have it—Spam. It's from America. Apparently, it's quite popular there and they've sent a boatload over. There's a Canadian unit where I landed today, and they'd got hold of a supply and were giving them out."

Rosalie, Caro, and Zofia watched as Mrs. May turned the tin over and over in her hands. She pulled a key off the bottom, caught a loose piece of metal in it, and wound the key round all four sides, peeling off a strip until the top of the tin came free. They all peered in at the pink chunks held together in a gelatinous block.

"What sort of meat is it?" Rosalie asked.

"The tin says ham," Caro said. "Looks like chopped boiled bacon, do you think?"

"I could mix a bit of it in with the swedes," the landlady suggested.

"Oh, please don't," Caro said. "Why don't you slice it up and fry it—doesn't look as if it needs any extra fat."

The aroma of the meat sizzling in the skillet set their mouths watering. It was much like boiled bacon, that is, quite tasty, and because it was from America, it made the evening meal seem nothing short of a feast.

"I wonder if there will be more of this Spam," Caro said.

"If there is, it'll be rationed like everything else," Mrs. May said. "We'll have to see how many points it costs."

"Perhaps next time we should not eat the entire tin at one meal," Zofia said, gazing at the empty container.

★ ★ ★

The excitement of America entering the war faded as the days went on and nothing seemed to change, apart from Rosalie being shot at by Germans.

She began her morning taking a Fairey Swordfish from Brize Norton in Oxfordshire to an airfield near Norwich. She'd checked with Maps and Signals and the Met and learned that neither barrage balloons nor clouds should be in her way, and so she had strapped on her leather helmet against the wind and set off, heading northeast across the country.

Taking note of passing airfields, she had not long cleared Lakenheath when something caught her eye off to the left. She looked, but saw nothing. The moment she took her eyes off the spot, there it was again. The hairs on her arms rose as she stared out into the gray until a trail of white smoke streaked past her port wing at a steep angle from overhead. Her heart stopped and then started again, thumping in her chest. Tracers— someone was firing on her from above. There went another.

"Bloody hell!" she shouted. What now? What were her instructions if under attack? There was no question of fighting back. The ATA flew nonoperational aeroplanes—no ammunition. She had no radio to call in the emergency. She daren't fly up into the cloud cover to escape, because that's where he was. He—or them?

She pushed the stick forward, and the plane's nose dropped. As she did so, she shoved the stick to the right until she was vertical, then pulled it back and shot left, almost sending herself into a roll. She leveled out, panting. Probably not much of an evasive action compared with real fighter pilots.

As Rosalie scanned the ground, looking for a place to put down, a Spitfire came out of nowhere, appearing from below to the right and cutting in front of her, shooting up into the clouds. Its wing looked so close to the nose of her plane that she gasped and threw herself against her seat, as if that would keep her out of the way. She looked back over her shoulder, straining to see, and caught a glimpse of his tracers shoot out as he fired. Was he after her attacker? "Thanks for that!" Rosalie called to the pilot. She opened her throttle and left them to their dogfight.

Thirty minutes later when she landed at Langham, her nerves had calmed, although her hands still shook. She told herself it was the cold, although she remained in the cockpit until the ground crew came up to take over the plane. When she told them what had happened, the first thing they did was inspect her aircraft. Not a bullet hole to be seen.

"Lucky you," one of them said. She picked up her bag and parachute and walked away.

Even her hands were steady by the time she handed her chit over to the duty officer, but her voice, high and strained, betrayed her.

"I was shot at!"

"You what?" he asked.

"From above. This side of Lakenheath. I saw the tracers."

"Was your aeroplane hit?" he asked.

Rosalie knew that it was aeroplane safety first, pilot safety second, but still, a small amount of annoyance seeped through her limbs, and this worked to calm her further. "The plane is untouched," she reported. "And I'm fine too."

"Well, I can see that, can't I?" The duty officer signed her chit and continued. "I heard they've been up and down the coast today. The Jerries in their 109s. Our boys have been on the hunt. Must've chased one of them this far inland trying to finish him off. Best for an ATA pilot to stay clear of that business."

It hadn't been her intention to get between a Messerschmitt and an RAF ace, but Rosalie thought it best not to point that out. She knew her assignment—to deliver aeroplanes and not be frightened out of her wits by the enemy.

"There's your taxi." The duty officer nodded to the Anson that had just arrived.

"Right."

Safe inside the Anson, the engines rumbling comfortably, Rosalie nearly fell asleep. When her head fell back, she felt it cushioned, and that was when she realized she still wore her leather helmet. She pulled it off and ran her fingers through her curls. Back at Brize Norton, she didn't even mention the incident.

★   ★   ★

Dear Rags, Leslie wrote, *I can say easily that you would be more welcome than Father Christmas here at Lime Farm. Can't you manage it? Borrow one of those aeroplanes and come for the day?*

Will wrote separately. *What a jolly time we'd have with you here at Christmas. All the Land Girls are staying. Uncle Trevor and Aunt Peg are leaving their bolt-hole in Cumbria to venture forth. Think of the groaning board!*

Rosalie missed her family and was well aware that Mrs. May's ration-defined Christmas Day dinner could not replace the feast at Lime Farm, but the fact was that the delivery of aeroplanes did not stop even if the battles on air, land, and sea might slow for a day or two. Also, wouldn't she be there in January for Will and Jean's wedding? And then there was her general ill-defined reluctance about going home and the uneasiness between her and her mother. Pop had always been their buffer. She wrote each brother and offered her regrets, but reminded them she'd see them soon enough.

Few of the women at Hamble made a request for Christmas leave, apart from Grace, whose parents were throwing a party to announce her engagement to Commodore Harold Utley of the Royal Navy. She had told her fellow pilots about it as they waited out the weather on a dark day when the clouds hung so low a person could dash from one building to another and get a soaking. Everyone offered congratulations and asked about the wedding date, the dress—all the usual enquiries. Later, Brenda told Rosalie that Utley was a friend of Grace's father and a widower with children older than his bride-to-be. But he was titled, and that would make Grace *Lady Elvington*. "That's all she really cares about."

All three lodgers remained at Mrs. May's. Caro said her father stayed too busy to enjoy Christmas—as the village doctor, he was always on call—but Rosalie thought Caro's concern was more for Zofia, whose family remained in Poland. Plus, how could they leave their landlady, whose two sons were away in the war? And so, they formed their own put-together family, and on Christmas Eve, they followed behind Mrs. May like ducklings to the late service at Saint Andrew's. Blackout curtains covered the stained-glass windows—two of which had been broken out by the bombs the previous spring—but candles had been lit, and when the familiar strains of "O Little Town of Bethlehem" started up on the organ, tears glistened in everyone's eyes in gratitude for the present and fear for the future.

The next morning, Rosalie met Caro coming out of the lavatory on the first-floor landing.

"Happy Christmas, love," Caro said, giving her a kiss on the cheek and then yawning. "I wouldn't mind looking in today to see if there isn't an aeroplane that needs to be somewhere. What do you think?"

"I don't know," Rosalie replied. "Mrs. May has something up her sleeve for dinner. You wouldn't want to miss it."

"I would if swedes are involved."

When Rosalie came out of the bathroom, Zofia was waiting.

"Happy Christmas," Rosalie said.

"Happy Christmas to you," Zofia replied with resignation.

Although Zofia had declared she'd given up on receiving news about her mother and sister in Poland, each morning, when the post dropped through the letter box onto the floor, Rosalie would see her dive for it, flip through the letters, and then leave them on the table with a sigh. Zofia also searched for news from the Eastern Front in the papers, but they offered nothing of substance about the war and instead touted uplifting stories—dogs lost and found or the unlikely friendship between a hedgehog and a house cat.

Now Rosalie heard the creak of the letter box opening, and Zofia flew down the stairs. Caro came out of their room, and she and Rosalie descended at a more leisurely pace to the entry, where Zofia distributed the post—Christmas greetings from Lime Farm, a card for Caro from her father, and one from each of Mrs. May's sons. Nothing from Poland.

Caro put an arm round her. "No glum faces on Christmas. Tomorrow could be the day that a letter arrives. Now, come along." She marched off toward the kitchen, singing "Once in Royal David's City" along with the choir voices that came drifting out from the wireless in the lounge.

In the kitchen, their landlady, busy at the hob, hummed along tunelessly, pausing to exchange greetings and say, "Scrambled eggs for your breakfast."

Powdered, of course, but the change from porridge was much appreciated. They spread margarine on their toast and turned attention to the gifts at each of their places.

For Caro, it was a fountain pen—perhaps not a new one—and for Zofia, a hair comb. Under Rosalie's plate was a booklet printed on tissue-thin wartime paper titled *Raising Chickens: Little Cost, Great Reward*.

"There you are, Rosalie," Caro said, "bet you didn't know anything about chickens before this."

Rosalie made a face at her and said, "Thanks so much, Mrs. May."

The landlady set the plate of eggs on the table and cut her eyes out the window. "Looks to me as if Father Christmas arrived in the back garden."

The three exchanged glances.

"Has he?" Rosalie asked, leaning over to look out and see the pile of well-aged boards stacked at the side of the pit.

It was their surprise for Mrs. May. Caro had overheard Bisby, the publican at the Bugle, say that an old unused shed at the back of the pub was on the verge of collapse and he intended to pull it down and sell the wood—that is, the pieces that weren't already crumbling with rot. Caro had got it into her head that she, Zofia, and Rosalie could build a henhouse with the best pieces. After all, she said, make do and mend. It would be a present from the three of them not only to Mrs. May, but also to one another.

To acquire the wood, Caro had come to a complicated arrangement with Bisby that involved the exchange of a bottle of whiskey her father in Essex had received in payment for medical treatment. The bottle had arrived a few days earlier—Dr. Andrews had wrapped it in cotton wool and packed it in a sturdy box with a layer of old magazines on top.

When Rosalie questioned the deal, Caro had told her that she'd been dreaming of eggs for breakfast. "And it isn't black market," she said, "it's bartering."

Bisby had delivered the wood while they'd been at church on Christmas Eve. The fact that Mrs. May didn't seem terribly surprised to see her gift made Rosalie think that a secret was a difficult thing to keep in Hamble.

"Caro and Zofia and I will get busy," Rosalie said. "All we need is a hammer and a few nails, and we'll be ready for spring."

"And finished with swedes," Zofia said.

"We might have to use up old ones."

Rosalie hoped Mrs. May wasn't talking about the vegetable. "Nails? Yes, of course—perhaps the old ones are still in the boards. We'll pull them out and straighten them. They'll do."

"Mrs. May, what's the word from Fred and Terry?" Caro asked.

"They need a roost," Mrs. May replied. "They like to be up a bit off the ground."

After a moment of silence, Zofia said, "And a box to lay?"

"They've no days off, same as you," Mrs. May said. "It's the war." And with that, the landlady walked out to inspect the wood, leaving them to wonder if she meant her sons or the chickens.

The three young women stayed indoors. The cold, dark, wet day precluded any outdoor activities. Mrs. May declined their offer of help with the meal, and so Rosalie, Caro, and Zofia spent the rest of the morning in the lounge amid the holiday decorations. Those consisted of a sprig of mistletoe hung over the doorway, a paper chain made from newspaper that looped its way unevenly round the room, and, on the mantel, a wooden crèche, which was spread out from shepherds on one end all the way to the Magi at the other.

Rosalie scanned the bookshelf and found the offerings heavily influenced by two boys growing up in the house—*Treasure Island*, *Kidnapped*, *New Arabian Nights*, and several others by Robert Louis Stevenson. But she did spot the first Biggles book, *The Camels Are Coming*, an adventure story set during the Great War. Zofia found *Martin Chuzzlewit*. "My old friend," she murmured, taking it off the shelf. Meanwhile, Caro studied the chicken booklet, jotting down notes on a scrap of paper and making an occasional venture outside to measure the wood. Eventually, they detected pleasant aromas from the kitchen.

"Is that sage?" Caro asked, eyebrows raised and looking hopeful. "Might we have a turkey for our Christmas dinner?"

Rosalie smelled the sage and apples too. What she could not detect was the smell of a roasting bird.

"Go sneak a look," Caro whispered at Zofia.

But there was no time. The landlady arrived in the doorway.

"He hasn't started yet, has he?" she asked, pointing to the wireless. "The King?"

Caro turned an ear and listened for a moment. "No, still 'To Absent Friends.'"

"Right," Mrs. May said, and sat in a chair, hands in her lap. Caro joined the other two on the sofa, snuggling into a tight spot next to Zofia and wiggling round to get settled.

"To Absent Friends" drew to a close, and the King began his Christmas message. "I am thinking of all those, women and girls as well as men, who at the call of duty have left their homes to join the services or to work in factory, hospital or field . . ." By the time he'd neared the end—"If the skies before us are still dark and threatening, there are stars to guide us on our way . . ."—the three young women along with Mrs. May had grown pensive and remained quiet after the BBC went to the next program, a holiday play.

Mrs. May reached over and switched off the wireless. "Now, then—our dinner."

They followed her to the kitchen. When they were seated, she took a casserole from the oven, set it before them, and straightened up.

"Mock goose," she announced, with hands on hips.

Caro raised an eyebrow. "Who is it mocking?"

Zofia narrowed her eyes at the dish. "Is it related to the Mock Turtle?"

The dish looked much like any other meal at Mrs. May's—a layer of mashed potatoes covering . . . something. Rosalie feared it would be Mrs. Potts's swedes, and just when she thought they'd finished them off.

"Lentils, apples, bread crumbs, sage. The Ministry of Food promises it's the next best thing to the bird."

They watched as the landlady scooped out generous, steaming portions onto their plates. True, there was a hint of sage, and the apple smelled good. But goose it was not. Rosalie gave a thought to the dinner table at Lime Farm, knowing they'd be slicing into the real thing.

The young women stared down at their plates until, at last, Zofia sighed and said, "There never was such a goose."

Mrs. May's mouth took on its familiar firm line. "What's that supposed to mean?"

"That is your Charles Dickens," Zofia said, and clicked her tongue at their surprised looks. "*A Christmas Carol*. My father studied at Oxford for one year, but then the war came—the first one—and he went back to Poland, carrying all books by Dickens. It's how he taught us English. Although," she added, "please tell me this wasn't the goose of which Dickens wrote."

They assured her it was not. Caro picked up her knife and fork, and Rosalie and Zofia followed suit and no one left the table wanting more. It was all they could ask.

After the kitchen had been cleaned, they retreated to the lounge, where Mrs. May produced a bottle of brandy from what seemed like thin air. After pouring out four small glasses, the bottle vanished again. They raised a toast—and with that, 1942 loomed on the horizon.

CHAPTER 7

January 1942

"Crikey, Rosalie, it's a wedding, not a funeral," Caro said. "Why so glum? You're happy for your brother, aren't you?"

"Of course I am," Rosalie said.

Friday morning, and Caro had come up to help her pack for the wedding weekend. There was little to do. Rosalie had added a skirt and jumper to the overnight bag she carried on every ferry delivery, plus her only pair of shoes other than the flight boots she wore.

"What shall we tell your pilot if he comes calling?" Caro asked, a bit of mischief in her voice.

"Caro!" Rosalie blushed and giggled. Caro had that way about her—she could winkle a good mood out of Rosalie's most sullen moments.

She had told both her housemates the story of meeting Alan Chersey at Honington and how he had asked her to stay and go to the pub with him for a drink. She had declined, of course, but not without a flutter of pleasure. Since that afternoon a few weeks ago, she'd been to Honington twice more, and each time, ever so casually, she had scanned the faces of the men in the Mess. But she had not seen Alan again.

Rosalie cinched the straps of her bag and then stuck her hands in the pockets of her trouser uniform.

"Done."

"You won't be wearing that for the ceremony?" Caro asked with raised eyebrows.

"Certainly not. I've a dress from my school leaving." Although Rosalie remembered the dress as an odd shade of blue—the color had made her look bilious. But it would do, because it was not her day. Will had written to say that their mum had got hold of a piece of rose-colored chiffon to sew onto a pink day dress Jean had from before the war, and so, the bride had been sorted, and that's what mattered.

"You'll be the talk of the village," Caro said, taking Rosalie's bag and heading for the door. "A pilot returning home."

Rosalie rolled her eyes. "I doubt that will impress anyone."

"You mean it won't impress your mum. But I'm sure she's proud of you."

Is she? Rosalie didn't feel she could complain. Caro's mum had died ten years earlier, although she still had her dad. Zofia's dad had died and now she could only hope her mum and sister were still alive back in Poland. Pop had died, but Rosalie still had not only her mum, but also Will and Leslie. And now Jean.

Zofia came out of the first-floor bedroom as Caro and Rosalie passed.

"You will not wear your uniform to the wedding?" she asked, and followed them down.

"No," Caro replied, "she has her school leaving dress."

On the ground floor, Mrs. May stood at the front door.

"I'll be back Sunday evening," Rosalie said.

"You take your time," the landlady said. "It's a bright spot in a dark time, and no one can begrudge you a bit of celebrating."

Mrs. May longed for her Terry or Fred to be married, but as they were both off doing their part, they had little opportunity at the moment.

"You aren't wearing your uniform for the ceremony?" the land-lady asked.

Rosalie pulled her forage cap down on her curls and picked up her parachute. "Does no one in this house trust my fashion sense?"

★ ★ ★

Rosalie zigzagged across England to reach her destination. First, she caught a lift with Caro, who flew the Anson taxi to West Malling in Kent, then hopped on another transport up to Doncaster, which overshot Cambridgeshire by a fair bit. Rosalie wondered how many journeys it would take to arrive near enough to Lime Farm.

As they flew, she gazed out the window at the winter fields below, some of them dusted with snow. She recognized aerodromes as they passed and named them off one by one under her breath. Having flown to a fair number of places in her first three months with the ATA, Rosalie had the idea that there were so many RAF bases, maintenance units, and aeroplane manufacturing plants across the country that a person could walk from one to the other from Southampton to . . . somewhere in Scotland without ever stepping off war-related land.

Not that the untrained eye could tell. Most places were disguised. The roofs of the buildings were painted or covered in fake foliage to look like woodland. Sometimes runways had been disguised by making them look as if a building, a hedgerow, or a lane crossed them, as if they didn't exist. Anything to confuse the Germans.

At Doncaster, she arrived to be told that an Anson taxi was about to leave for Bourn, an airfield only seven miles from Lime Farm. It was already afternoon. There might not be another flight anywhere until the following morning, and she feared being a late arrival to the wedding—showing up in her uniform after all—and so she trotted off in the direction the duty officer had waved. She saw a few ATA pilots emptying out of the aeroplane.

She dashed toward them and called, "Bourn?" to the first one she reached—a bear of a man. He stopped, cocked his head, and squinted an eye at her.

"Second Officer Wright, isn't it?" he asked.

"Oh, yes." Here was the pilot whose chair by the electric-bar fire she had taken. Second Officer Durrant.

Would he shout at her for asking a question? She glanced round for someone else, but the others had continued on their way.

"Is that the taxi to Bourn?" she asked Durrant again.

"Are you planning to steal another pilot's seat?"

Rosalie raised her voice as a Spitfire rumbled by them. "I will if I have to. Now, is that Anson going to Bourn or isn't it? I've got a wedding to get to!"

Durrant's eyes widened. "It is. And congratulations."

Rosalie dashed off, but over her shoulder called out, "Not me. My brother!"

On board the Anson, she pushed curls off her forehead with the back of her hand, heaved a great sigh, and tried to relax. She glanced at the two other ATA pilots across from her and nodded, but the engine noise precluded any conversation. For the next hour, Rosalie sat lost in her thoughts.

At Bourn, she rang Lime Farm. Will answered and told her Leslie would collect her. She went into the Mess, but she couldn't sit still and soon came out again to watch for him. When he arrived and climbed out of the old red Morris lorry, she threw her arms round him first thing. He caught her forage cap as it slipped off.

"Rags, I would hardly know you—look at this, uniform and all."

"I haven't changed," Rosalie argued, at once both pleased and annoyed that he'd noticed a difference in her. "I'm the same sister who cried when the cows surrounded me in the yard."

"You were only eight," he said.

"Not to say I wouldn't cry again if it happened tomorrow," she said. "Now, let me look at you."

He held out his arms. "You see before you a weary specimen of a farmer."

"No wonder. What possessed you to add village warden to your list of duties—don't you have enough to do at the farm?"

Leslie's face hardened briefly, and then he broke out into a grin. "There's nothing brave about being a farmer—who'd want to marry one?"

"Apparently Jean does," Rosalie said, but she realized Leslie wasn't talking about Will's girl. Before she could say more, he took her bag and parachute and strode off, pointing out to a runway as he did so.

"That's a Wellington, isn't it? Have you flown one of those?"

"Not yet," she said, following him. "But I could, and daresay I will before long. I'd only have to check my *Ferry Pilots Notes*."

Rosalie watched her brother as he tossed her bag onto the seat of the farm's lorry. Leslie was the same brother she had left the previous year, but at the same time, he too was different, as if he carried a heavy but invisible burden on his back. He caught her watching him and smiled, but the act only accentuated how tired he looked. She touched his cheek.

"You look as if you could use a kip," she said.

"On patrol last night, so I didn't get much sleep," he said. "Two days ago, we had bombs drop on Manor Farm at Madingley—missed the house but hit the barn, and they lost three cows. Bloody Germans probably just chucked the things out on their way home."

He held open the door for her but put a hand on her arm. "You never say for sure in your letters, but . . . you aren't in the thick of it, are you, Rags?"

Rosalie thought of the pit in Mrs. May's back garden and how the Spitfire factory in Woolston—not five miles up the coast from Hamble—had been nearly destroyed the previous year. And how many nights and days they heard the air raid sirens and aeroplanes passing high overhead and out of sight. The war still raged, and they would likely be in the Germans' sights again, but most people went about their business, because what else could you do?

"No, of course not. They don't even know we're there."

★   ★   ★

When Leslie pulled the lorry into the yard, Rosalie saw Lime Farm as a still life. Her mum in the kitchen door. Will perched on the seat of his Fordson. The geese, wings spread, caught in semiflight as they careered off round the corner of the barn. And a tall, thin young woman wearing coveralls and holding a hayfork in her hands.

Her face was a mass of freckles, and her ginger hair hung over one shoulder in a thick plait. The Land Girls had arrived before Rosalie left Lime Farm, and so she had met Jean, but all five of the women had become jumbled in Rosalie's mind. But surely this was she?

Rosalie slid out of the lorry as Will jumped off his tractor and greeted her.

"And here's Jean," he said. "You remember her."

"Of course I do," Rosalie said, arms halfway raised but unsure of how to greet her almost-sister-in-law.

Jean laughed as she put a hand up. "I'm a fearful mess. You don't want horse manure all over your uniform."

"You've been turning the compost?" Rosalie asked. "A fine job the day before your wedding."

"Ah well, we all muck in." Jean smiled, and her face glowed a pleasant pink. Will watched her and beamed.

Rosalie hadn't forgotten her mother, who had remained at the kitchen door. She turned now and went to her.

"Hello, Mum."

"Now then," her mum said, and clutched Rosalie in a brief hug that squeezed the breath out of her. "Haven't you eaten anything since you left us? Come in this minute and have a cup of tea. Jean, love," she called, "clean yourself up and join us."

Rosalie helped put the tea on the table, and when the bride-to-be returned, the three of them settled in the chairs and Jean asked, "Shall I pour?"

From out the door, Rosalie heard the rattle of the tractor as Will drove it off. The geese continued to complain, and Leslie whistled as he went off to the barn. The familiarity overwhelmed her—she could have believed she'd never left Lime Farm at all if Jean hadn't been at the table. But the sounds of the farm receded as, far off, she detected the rumble of aircraft, and she remembered herself.

The tea was a bit weak—with rationing, Rosalie had become accustomed to that—but the bread was her mum's best, with real butter and bramble jam. Rosalie had found the food at Mrs. May's and in the Mess at Hamble not too bad under the circumstances, but it couldn't hold a candle to the farm.

"Jean's put in all new strawberry plants with fresh runners," Rosalie's mum announced.

"That's grand," Rosalie said. "Better cropping this summer for sure."

"Couldn't improve on your straw mulch, though," Jean replied. "It keeps the fruit that much cleaner."

"She's asking two and eight for goose eggs," Mum said, "and no one minds."

"Well, they're so large." Jean shrugged her shoulders. "And not rationed."

"Biggest harvest of potatoes in years, because we switched over another field to main crop."

"That wasn't my idea," Jean said in a rush, her face splotchy red. "It was in a leaflet from the Ministry of Food."

Rosalie told herself she didn't mind that Jean was a better farmer than she had been—it meant that at last Mum would get the daughter she had always wanted. But Mum's boasting seemed to embarrass Jean, and so Rosalie changed the subject by asking about the wedding. That sent the bride-to-be to chattering gaily about what they'd made do with.

"And Mother Gladys"—she caught herself—"I mean, your mum, has worked wonders. Not just with my dress, which is so lovely, but also with the cake. Come and take a look."

Jean led her to the dining room, where, in pride of place on the sideboard, sat a highly decorated, round, tiered cake, its edges rimmed with thick sugar roping and a pile of sugar roses resting on top. "I can't believe you did all that on rations," Rosalie said.

Laughing, Jean picked up the cake by its sides, and Rosalie saw that it was only a cover and under it was a large, plain, one-layer cake studded with dried fruit.

"It's all the rage now," Jean said, and she tapped on the cover. "It's made of cardboard and a bit of plaster, see? We've borrowed it. We just scraped by with the sugar—Mother Gladys said the damsons were extra sweet this year and we didn't need as much for the jam, so we saved some there too."

"If Mum made the cake, then no matter how much sugar she had, it will be delicious." Rosalie looked round. The doors to the lounge stood open—the ceremony would be in there and the reception here in the dining room. Good thing they were a small family. "Are your parents coming?"

Jean twirled the cardboard cover in her hands. "No, they . . . travel is so difficult now, and Scarborough is quite far."

"Well, perhaps you can send them a photograph."

"Yes," Jean said, her good cheer returning. "Can you believe they've even restricted photography? Still, we're allowed two photos. So there will be one of us and one of the whole family. Will and I thought we'd include the vicar, Mr. Thrush. He's been ever so kind."

Rosalie had recognized the three bottles on the mantel—the vicar's homemade plum wine. Good thing they'd have something to pour in the glasses they'd raise.

"Your mum is such a dear," Jean said. She shot a glance at the door. "I know how lucky I am, Rosalie. I'll make the best wife for Will. I promise." Jean's voice caught in her throat.

"I've no doubt that the two of you will be very happy."

"Oh, listen to me going on," Jean said, and sniffed. "You've had such a long journey. I'm sure you'd like a rest. Look, I don't know if they've told you, but I've been sleeping in your room since Will and I set the date. I hope you don't mind—"

"Certainly I don't mind," Rosalie replied with feeling. "What good was it doing empty?" Although it felt as if the rug were being pulled out from under her.

"I'm back in the stables with the other Land Girls for tonight, though, and then Will and I go away to Cumbria to your aunt and uncle's cottage until Monday." Jean replaced the decorated cake cover and said, "So, now, let me take you up," as if Rosalie were only a visitor.

Well, aren't I?

She retrieved her bag and parachute from the kitchen and told her mother she'd be down shortly to help with dinner.

"No hurry. The other girls will be in later, and Jean has got us a good piece of beef. She's cooking it with some of her herbs she has growing in old chimney pots."

There you are, then.

In what had once been her bedroom, nothing seemed to have changed—the counterpane on the bed, and on the dressing table the porcelain figurines of little girls with baskets of flowers. Rosalie couldn't quite remember liking them, but they'd always been there.

Jean came in behind her, closed the door quietly, and then stood with one arm hanging and the other hand clasping her elbow. She was all arms and legs and yet had a casual grace. Although at the moment, she was a bit twitchy.

Rosalie dropped onto the edge of the bed and patted the space beside her.

"You must tell me all about yourself. So, you're from Scarborough. Do you miss the sea?"

Jean sank onto the bed. Beads of sweat had appeared on her forehead. She clasped her hands in her lap and twisted them.

"Rosalie, I want to tell you something. Will said it would be all right because you're a woman and you would understand. I haven't told your mum—I don't know that I can."

Is this why the wedding was so quick? Her brother had said it was the war, but it looked as if the war had taken second place to other circumstances.

She put a hand on Jean's and felt her tremble. What did Will think his sister knew about such things?

Jean looked up at her, green eyes bright and freckles popping out against ivory skin.

"I have a little boy."

Her voice was barely a whisper, and Rosalie thought she'd heard wrong.

"You . . . you're . . ."

"I have a little boy," Jean repeated, only a fraction louder. "He's five years old, and he lives with Bridie, a cousin of my mother's in Pontefract. The . . . father . . . was a boy in my school, you see. But I was fifteen, and so, when I found out I was . . . Well, his parents took him away and I left school early and my mum and dad sent me to a mothers' home near Leeds, and that's where I had the baby. Then I went to Bridie's, and after a month, she went and got him. She's taken in children before and now she has two evacuees too, and so it didn't seem so unusual for her to show up one day with a baby. I stayed with her for a month, as if I were visiting to help out, and then went home again. I've seen him only three times since. Best to break it off clean, you know. That's what Mum and Dad told me."

Rosalie's mind had emptied of all thought, and she groped for something to say, but Jean didn't seem to notice as her hand went to a pocket in her dress and she drew out a dog-eared photo. A boy no more than two years old stood in front of a goods shop. Rosalie thought she could see freckles and imagined his light-colored hair to be ginger.

"Oh, he looks so like you. What's his name?"

The tiniest hint of a smile appeared on Jean's face, and it broke Rosalie's heart.

"Robert."

Rosalie gazed at the little boy. "You were right to tell Will—you were right and very brave."

Jean looked down at her hands. "We haven't told your mum yet. But we will. Soon. She'll understand, don't you think?"

Will she? But Rosalie couldn't dash Jean's hopes yet, so instead she smiled and looked at the photo again. "Who wouldn't love this little fellow?"

CHAPTER 8

The next morning, Rosalie sat up when the rooster coughed—his first try at announcing the new day. She stretched and sighed, saw her breath, and dived back under the covers of the camp bed. The evening before, she had insisted that Jean stay in the house, and Rosalie had taken herself out to bunk with the Land Girls in the stable block converted into workers' accommodations. The other women had welcomed her, and she had spent the rest of the evening listening to their lively talk about the war—as it related to the men at RAF Bourn. They had grilled Rosalie about the pilots she'd met, and none of the women could understand why she wasn't out dancing every single night.

"I would, even if I had two fields to plow the next morning. Who can resist a man in uniform?" one of them said, and they had all laughed.

On the rooster's second attempt, Rosalie heard one of the Land Girls stir, and was pushed into action. She threw on her clothes and made a dash for the house, where she could warm up in front of the stove. Her mother stood at the counter slicing bread.

"Morning, Mum." Rosalie put her hands round the teapot and felt its heat. She poured herself a cup. "It's clear as a bell out there. What a fine day Will and Jean have."

"They deserve that and more," her mum replied. "I'll put your egg on now. Shall I do you two?"

"Yes, please," Rosalie replied, with a twinge of guilt when she thought of the one egg a week they got at Mrs. May's.

During the morning, the kitchen filled with the comings and goings of Land Girls, Will and Leslie, and the neighbors come to help out for the day. When the vicar appeared at ten, Rosalie slipped upstairs to get herself washed. She then joined Jean and the other girls in the largest bedroom—her parents' room, but only until the newlyweds returned from their weekend in Cumbria. After that, it would be Will and Jean's, and her mother would move to the ground floor.

Rosalie found her dress and discovered that her mother had added a length of wide, dark blue ribbon to the collar. She pulled on the frock and went downstairs to look at herself in the uncrowded entry mirror. The ribbon had banished the bilious hue from her face. Her mum came up behind, and Rosalie said, "Oh, it's lovely, Mum—thanks so much." She turned and gave her a peck on the cheek.

"You won't forget to comb your hair," her mother said in response. Rosalie had already combed it, but went upstairs for another attempt.

The wedding, albeit small, was lovely. Rosalie's eyes pricked with tears at the sight of Will and Jean gazing at each other as they said their vows. If only Pop could've been there. She saw her mother's chin quiver and reached out a hand. Her mum found it and gave a squeeze.

When the ceremony finished, everyone sat down to the post-wedding luncheon, followed by the cutting of the cake and toasts with glasses of the vicar's plum wine. Late in the afternoon, Jean and Will departed in the farm's Morris lorry for their weekend, signaling an end to the festivities. Friends went home, and the Land Girls went into Cambridge. That evening, Rosalie, Leslie, and their mum took their tea at the kitchen table, sighing contentedly over plates of cold meat and bread and butter.

"Will's thinking of getting rid of the sheep," Leslie said.

"Is he? Why?" Rosalie asked.

"He says the land could be put to better use—pigs or some such."

Rosalie knew that pigs provided more in wartime than did her sheep, which were meant only for wool. Still, she'd be sad to see them go—their field had always been a bit of a refuge for her.

"I believe I'll go up," their mum said at last. "It's been quite a day."

Her children wished her good-night and promised to wash up. After she'd gone, they left the kitchen table as it was and drifted out into the lounge, Leslie bringing along the last of the vicar's plum wine. He poured out what was left between two sherry glasses. It made for about a thimbleful each.

"The happy couple," he said, and they raised their glasses and drank the wine. "They will be happy, won't they? If they can't, I don't know who could."

Before the newlyweds departed, Will had pulled Rosalie into the lounge while the others gathered out in the yard. In a furtive whisper, he had thanked her for understanding about little Robert. "It means the world to Jean that you will support her. We want the boy to come and live with us. He has a proper mother, and he should be with her. I'm sure Mum will understand."

Rosalie didn't believe any support she could offer would sway her mother an inch, but she had given her brother a kiss on the cheek and said, "What a wonderful husband you are, Will. And Jean is lovely. I'm sure it'll all work out."

"And, so, we can count on you? In case Mum asks you about it."

Knowing that would never happen, Rosalie had readily agreed.

Now she held out her glass to Leslie. "Of course they'll be happy." He turned the bottle over, and they waited until the last drop fell. She stretched out her legs and leaned her head against the sofa. "I haven't had the chance to ask—what about Ellen? Was she not able to come today?"

Her brother looked into the bottom of his empty glass. "Ellen joined the WAAFs in the spring. She said she'd rather be called up than work in her dad's law office. She's up at Castle Camps near Essex and engaged to some fellow." He frowned.

"Oh, I am sorry, Les," Rosalie said. "That's rotten."

"He isn't even a pilot—he's a fitter, one of those fellows who starts up the aeroplanes for others."

"Well, I can't imagine what she sees in him. I know those fitters and they are a rum lot."

Leslie smiled and patted her knee. "We've missed you, Rags. And what about you—no dashing pilot capture your heart yet?"

She'd noticed a few dashing pilots, but they'd never taken any notice of her, apart from Alan Chersey. But she hadn't made a good impression there—she'd barely been able to put two words together.

"I think they go more for glamour girls, and we both know I'm not the type. Do you know, there's a woman in our ferry pool who will land her plane but won't get out of the cockpit without first putting on lipstick? I can't compete with that."

★ ★ ★

It was Sunday morning, and Rosalie stood in the kitchen with her uniform on and pack and parachute in hand.

"Rags," Leslie said, "did you tell Mum that you're flying Spitfires now?"

The subject of aeroplanes had come up once during dinner on Friday evening, but her mum had made no comment. She'd never spoken directly about Rosalie's vocation, because if her daughter wasn't a farmer, what use was she?

"You've packed your sandwiches," her mum said now, proving Rosalie's point.

"Yes." Along with sandwiches for her journey, Rosalie had packed an onion, and two jars—one of beets and one of piccalilli. Treasures from the farm.

"And here's this," her mum said, handing her another jar wrapped in paper and tied with twine. "From Jean. You take care, now."

"I will." She gave her a kiss on the cheek. "Jean is lovely, isn't she, Mum?"

"She's got a head on her shoulders," her mother replied. "She understands the farm and how to run it."

Rosalie silently agreed that Jean was the perfect farmer's wife. But that wasn't the point she'd intended to make, and so she tried again. "Jean and Will are so well suited. They'll make it through good times and bad, won't they? They remind me of you and Pop."

Rosalie noticed a slight warming to her mother's face. *There*, she thought, *that's about all I can do for you now, Jean. I wish you luck.*

Leslie took her bag and parachute, and they were off to Bourn. Rosalie left on an Anson from there going to No. 9 Ferry Pool Aston Down, Gloucestershire. Not terribly far from Hamble, so she should be back at Mrs. May's in good time. Rosalie took the first twenty turns at cranking up the undercarriage on the aeroplane before giving it over to one of the men. As they rose, she felt a weight lift from her shoulders, and her outlook, gloomy upon awaking in her old bedroom at Lime Farm, cleared. She was going home. To Hamble. She looked out at the receding landscape, surprised at the realization and yet, at the same time, not.

At Aston Down, the air taxi did two circuits before putting down, by which time her morning cups of tea had caught up with her. There was a lavatory block just off the runway here, but the only one for women was on the far side of the aerodrome near the WAAF quarters. Perhaps too far. Once her feet were on the ground, she made a sharp right turn and hurried off to a copse of beeches on the other side of the runway, kicking through the sea of fallen leaves until she could stop just behind a large trunk where she was well hidden.

She was just pulling up her trousers when she heard the crackle of snapping twigs, and a voice bellowed, "Wright?"

It was him—that bear of a man, SO Durrant. Had he followed her?

"What do you want?" she called out, her fingers fumbling with her trouser buttons.

"What are you doing in there?"

"None of your business!" she shouted, and he guffawed in response.

She picked up her parachute and her bag and walked out to meet him on the edge of the wood.

"You should've found someone and asked," he said. "You could've used the men's. One of us would've kept watch for you."

"I couldn't really spare the time to enquire." She brushed a bit of leaf mold off her sleeve.

"Waiting for another taxi?"

"Yes."

He looked round them and then at the buildings across the way. "Tea?"

Not even a bear could keep her from a cup of tea. "Go on, then," she said.

They walked to the Mess, and as they did so, a WAAF on a bicycle called, "Hiya, Snug!" She let one hand go to wave, which sent her front wheel wobbling.

Durrant responded with a wave of his own.

They reached the Mess just as another woman came out the door and greeted them with, "Snug! Are you for the pub later?"

"I could be if you're there," he said, and gave the woman a wink as he held the door open for Rosalie.

Durrant poured their tea, and they took seats at the end of an empty table. She pulled a couple of sandwiches from her pack and offered him one.

"You sure?" he asked.

"Pork," she said. "My brother Leslie joined the local Pig Club. Go on."

He took it with a "Thanks" and bit off half. Chewing, he asked, "How was the wedding? Your brother's?"

Rosalie was surprised and then remembered shouting at him as she ran for the air taxi.

"It was lovely. It was my brother Will's wedding, not Leslie's." Rosalie took a bite of sandwich and licked a bit of mustard off her finger. "They're both older than I am. He married Jean, one of the Land Girls. They'll do a fine job of running the farm along with Les. Mum can start to take it easy."

"What took you off the farm? Didn't you want to stay and tend the"—Durrant waved his arm vaguely—"the cows or whatever it is you have?"

"I don't tend the cows. And," Rosalie said, "I left because I wanted to fly. What was your job before the ATA?"

"This and that. I worked in the pub," Durrant replied. "My mum is the manager. It's her whole life. But pouring a pint or milking a cow can't hold a candle to this, can it?"

She didn't correct him again about the cows, because she knew what he meant, and besides, he had started to sing in a rough but melodious voice: "*How ya gonna keep 'em down on the farm, after they've seen Paree?*"

Rosalie sputtered. "What's that?"

"It's a song the Yanks brought over the last war," Snug said.

"You'd best forget all about *Paree*," Rosalie said. "They won't let ATA pilots fly to France."

"That isn't what I meant," Snug growled. Then he caught the smile she tried to hide and grinned.

"So, Snug, is it?" Rosalie popped the last of her sandwich into her mouth. "Do you have a proper Christian name?"

"I might," he replied. "But not one I use if I can help it. And you?"

"Rosalie."

"And do you have one that isn't proper?"

Rosalie's face heated up. "I don't know what you mean."

"Two older brothers, I daresay you do."

She frowned but didn't answer, and Durrant continued, "Are you based at Hamble?"

"I am," Rosalie said. It was an easy guess, as there were only three all-women ferry pools.

"I was there until September, when all of you moved in. That's when I came here to Aston Down."

Rosalie recalled her landlady's description of her previous tenant, and the penny dropped. "Were you billeted with Mrs. May? Are you the pilot she had before us—the one with only one . . ." She caught herself, but not in time.

"*Eye* is the word you're looking for," Snug said. "I've two of them, actually, but only the right one works properly. It's always been that way. That shows you how desperate the country is, doesn't it? Taking on a one-eyed pilot?"

"Not a bit of it," Rosalie shot back. "It means the country knows a good pilot when it sees one. If you can fly, it doesn't matter if you've got only one good eye or . . . or if you're a woman."

"Attagirl."

Rosalie took that as a compliment and nodded. "How is it she didn't get you to fill in the bomb crater in the back garden?"

"Busy," he replied. "I made sure I was always busy. Don't tell me she's got you on it?"

"I'm afraid I volunteered. It seems as if I spend the days I'm not flying covered in mud."

He laughed and she glared.

"Oh, Snug!" Another WAAF buzzed toward their table.

"I see how busy you stay," Rosalie said, glancing at the woman.

"Durrant!" the duty officer called from the door of the Mess, and Snug strode over to him.

The WAAF remained at the table. "Hiya," she said to Rosalie. "You're ATA, I see. I'm Marjorie. Plotter."

Plotters worked in operations, using long sticks to move pieces that represented aeroplanes around enormous maps. Like a giant board game.

"Rosalie Wright. Lovely to meet you."

"Yeah." Marjorie glanced over to Durrant. "Snug's good fun, isn't he?" Rosalie had no reply to that, but Marjorie didn't seem to need one. "A girl deserves a good time, even if it is the war. Or because of it. Might as well both the men and women take advantage of the situation. Look, I'd best push off. Maybe I'll see you later."

There was a call for the Anson taxi. Rosalie said good-bye to Marjorie, squeezed past Durrant, who stood blocking the doorway, and headed for the field.

"Wright," he called to her, "try to keep out of the mud!"

★   ★   ★

Sunday night, in inky darkness, Rosalie made her way on foot from the ferry pool to Mrs. May's. Her journey had taken hours and hours. The Anson taxi had taken off that afternoon from Aston Down but had to put down again almost immediately, as one of its engines had failed. It bounced onto the runway at touchdown, but no one was the worse for wear.

Rosalie, determined to make it back to Hamble, had taken an air taxi to Brize Norton—heading in entirely the wrong direction. But from there, she pieced together a journey: another air taxi, a train, and a lift from the cook at the airfield at Eastleigh to Bursledon, the village just up the road from Hamble. There, she borrowed a bicycle from Brenda, one of the other pilots, who was billeted in a cottage with an older couple.

She left the two-wheeled transport outside the Mess at the airfield, walked into her village, and headed down Satchell Lane. She had no moon to light her way but no longer needed the aid, having learned to negotiate her way to No. 6 even in the dark by the familiar patterns on the windows along the terrace. Some people had chosen to tape their glass as a precaution against bombings, crisscrossing the panes like lattice in hopes of keeping any blast from shattering the glass and blowing shards everywhere. Others had not bothered. But glass was expensive and practically unattainable, and so Mrs. May had taken great care and used a good deal of tape.

Entering No. 6, Rosalie kept the blackout curtain closed as she gave the door its extra shove and heard the *snick* of the lock.

When she parted the curtain, the world was a brighter place. A light spilled out from the lounge, and Rosalie looked round the door to see Caro and Zofia sitting close on the sofa, laughing, their fingers intertwined. Caro caught sight of her and jumped up, saying, "At last! We've been waiting for you. Come in, now, and tell us about the wedding."

Rosalie let her bag down on the floor, shed her coat, and turned to hang it on a peg as their landlady came in from her bedroom at the back.

"Thought you'd gone to Scotland," Mrs. May said.

"No," Rosalie said, and was reminded of Snug, her landlady's former tenant. "But it was a long journey back. I'm glad I'm home."

CHAPTER 9

March 1942

When the winter weather cleared, they were back at it, and in the last of February and into March, Rosalie counted fifteen days straight of flying. Most of their deliveries were made around the south of England, but even then it could be quite cold, as she learned the first day of March when she collected an open-air Hawker Hart and flew it to Castle Camps.

Her route took her over Cambridgeshire, and when she spotted the airfield at Bourn, Rosalie dropped down and flew low over Lime Farm. One of the Land Girls—it wasn't Jean—was working in the yard unloading hay. She didn't even look up. Neither Leslie nor Will was about. Rosalie considered putting down and having a cup of tea or a spot of lunch—she knew many an ATA pilot took such detours. Lime Farm looked serene from three hundred feet, but Rosalie knew that turbulence, although invisible, could still do damage. What was the atmosphere in the house? Will had made no mention of it in his letters. Had their mum been told, and if so, had there been a terrible row? Or did the subject, yet to be broached, instead hang heavy in the kitchen or lurk in a corner of the yard like one of those unexploded bombs?

Rosalie flew on, dragging an extra load of guilt with her.

She landed at Castle Camps in bright winter sunshine but with ice crystals in her hair, handed over her chit to the duty officer, and said, "I've a Blenheim to collect."

"Mmm, yeah, Blenheim, I see that. Not ready yet, so go get yourself a cup of tea, and we'll let you know."

On the way to finding the Mess, Rosalie pulled out a chocolate bar and stuffed half of it in her mouth. She reached the door just as it was pushed open toward her, and there was Alan Chersey.

She leapt back, and he might've thought she was about to topple over, because he put his hands on her arms and steadied her. Rosalie felt a warmth even through her thick Sidcot suit.

"Sorry about that," he said, and then, still holding her, he smiled. "Wait now—Rosalie, isn't it?"

Swallowing the last of the chocolate, she could only nod and whisper, "Yes." The man would think she was a shilling short of a pound if she couldn't do a better job of talking than she had the first time they met. She cleared her throat. "Yes, hello. You're Alan, I remember."

"It's lovely to see you again, Rosalie." He dropped his hands, and immediately Rosalie missed them. "Brought an aeroplane in?"

She mumbled something about a Hart.

"Well, I'm certainly the lucky one to run into you. Do you have time for lunch? I've just this minute come in for mine."

Alan had been leaving the Mess as she arrived, but she wouldn't point that out.

"Yes, I suppose I could do."

They sat across from each other in a room empty except for a handful of men sprawled in easy chairs in the other corner.

"It's cottage pie," Alan said. "Not bad, but not what you're used to on your farm."

Perhaps, but Rosalie had learned that the food in an RAF Officers' Mess was always better than what you could get on rations. When the orderly brought over the plates, she could see actual minced beef in the dish. It was a relief from Woolton pie, now such a common dish in the country that the *Lord* had been dropped.

But Rosalie wasn't sure she could enjoy her lunch, afraid she'd need to reply just as she filled her mouth. Where this worry had come from, she didn't know. Hadn't she spent her entire life doing those two things at the same time? Still, she quickly landed on a strategy—ask a question, and then chew and swallow while Alan answered.

"What do you fly?" she asked, and dug into the pie.

"We're training on a new aeroplane. A fighter-bomber for night ops."

"What is it?"

"Mosquito. It's a twin-engine."

"Twin-engine," she repeated. "That'll be class four. I'm qualified, but I'll most likely need extra training for it."

Alan shook his head. "It's amazing to think you women climb into those aeroplanes all on your own and fly."

"Not so amazing," Rosalie replied, modesty vying with pride for top billing. "We don't have guns or bombs. We don't engage the enemy."

"Still, you're quite brave."

Rosalie gave a brief thought to telling him about the time she had been fired at, but the shock had faded, and now it seemed incidental when she compared it with stories she'd heard from others.

"So, now, your farm—where is it?"

"Not far from Cambridge, a village called Dry Drayton."

"Well, just what are they doing there at this moment?"

"Oh, er, barely spring, you know."

"What comes along at this time of year, as far as crops are concerned?"

Rosalie rattled off a litany of plowing and planting, again feeling as if this were an enquiry from the government.

"It's a life's work, isn't it—the land?" Alan asked, pushing his plate aside and setting his forearms on the table. "I understand, you see, because we have a few farms. My grandfather runs them. I've only ever been there for summer holidays, and I was always too young to be of any use. But if I badgered them enough, they'd let me spend my days with the gardener planting beans and hoeing and the like."

A few farms? That's an estate, that is.

"Where is it?"

"Kent."

Rosalie waited, then asked, "The entire county?"

Alan laughed. "No, not quite. Right square in the middle of Kent. Easton Hall."

"But you don't live there?"

"No, mostly we stay in London," he said. "Even now, my parents refuse to leave. Well, my father is with the War Office, and so his work is there, and Mum runs several charities for the war effort."

"That's very good of her."

"Eventually, my brother will take over the running of the estate, of course," Alan said. "Firstborn and all that. But that suits me fine, because it leaves me to do the hands-on work. I wanted to stay with my grandfather for the war, but I had a couple of friends from school who were going for flying and I thought, why not? But after the war—well, I'm sure you understand. It'll be good to get back to the soil."

Alan continued to quiz her about farming, and Rosalie silently despaired that he would think the only thing she knew was harvesting barley and lambing and shearing, but she answered him regardless. They were interrupted when one of the ground crew put his head in the door, spotted her, and walked over. "A bit of a problem with your Blenheim."

"What sort of problem?"

"Won't start. But we'll get it sorted before the end of the day."

"I need to go back in daylight," she reminded him.

"You don't want to fly an unsafe plane," Alan cut in. "Look, you fellows take your time. Rosalie's well taken care of here."

"Will I need to find a place for the night?" she asked. "Is there a hotel or a—"

Alan put his hand over hers. "Let me sort this out." The ground crewman snorted, but Alan ignored him. "Some of the WAAFs are on night shift in Operations, so you can take one of their beds."

Rosalie registered this solution in only a vague way, as all she could think of was the warmth of Alan's hand on hers.

He dismissed the mechanic and turned back to Rosalie. "I've the rest of the day free. Would you like to see my Mossie?"

★ ★ ★

Rosalie looked back on that afternoon as if she had been in a magic bubble—no war, no worries about Lime Farm, only the kind and close attentions of Alan Chersey, RAF pilot. Once she'd stripped off her Sidcot coverall, she left it, her bag, and her parachute in the WAAF quarters, and he took her out to one of the blister barns where Mosquito fighters lined the walls. He greeted the crewmen at work with "All right, there? We're just taking a look-see."

"Yes, sir," they replied, and went about their business.

"Here we are," Alan said, taking her over to one of the aeroplanes. Its cockpit hood was open, and a short ladder sat near the wing. "I trained on a Blenheim, so this has been an easy transition so far."

Rosalie gazed up at the twin airscrews on the craft. "May I look inside?" she asked.

"Climb aboard, Officer Wright," Alan said.

Without another thought, Rosalie scrambled up the ladder. "It's a two-man cockpit," she called over her shoulder.

"We'll have a navigator for missions," Alan said.

Rosalie scanned the controls and automatically went into her cockpit check, saying the name of each dial and lever aloud the way Reg had taught her all those years ago.

"Say what?" Alan asked.

"Oh . . . er . . . how are takeoff and landing?"

"Good. Easy—although, on landing, there's a bit of drag with the wheels and flaps down, so be careful not to undershoot."

"Right, I'll watch for that," Rosalie replied, as if she were about to strap in at that moment. She turned to climb down, and Alan held out a hand to steady her. "Of course," she added, "the *Ferry Pilots Notes* will have all those details."

"Don't you train on every plane separately?" he asked.

Rosalie shook her head. "There wouldn't be time. But if an aeroplane is in the same class as another we know, we can sort it out."

Alan's blue eyes flashed. "Beauty and brains," he said, keeping hold of her hand. "I'd best watch myself."

Rosalie, caught up in the excitement of a new aeroplane and Alan's attentions, turned pink and replied, "Yes, I suppose you had."

He found two bicycles for them and took her out on the lanes around the airfield. She feared for her curls, knowing they would end up blown out of all proportion, but she tried to put her appearance out of her mind.

The afternoon was cold but clear, and Alan was a charming host, even though he stopped at every bare field and asked if she know what had grown there or what had just been planted. She answered as she could. When stubble remained, she would tell him wheat or oats or barley, but the fields that had been harvested and already plowed only occasionally gave up their secrets.

Once, they rested their bicycles against the trunk of a twisted hawthorn and discussed potato yields, Rosalie gladly passing along Lime Farm's decision to grow more main-crop spuds. But then they both paused and cocked an ear. Engines rumbled overhead. Aeroplanes—certainly more than one, probably a squadron, but too high up to see.

"What do you think?" Alan asked. "Ours or theirs?"

Rosalie closed her eyes and concentrated on the fading sound. "Spits, I'd say. So, ours."

When she opened her eyes, it was to find Alan quite close. He put a hand under her chin and his thumb stroked her cheek lightly, and then he leaned over and kissed her. A light but lingering kiss.

"It was my lucky day, meeting you," he said. "You're different from the other girls. You know that, don't you?"

Rosalie had only ever known she was different from other women by her inexperience when it came to men, and by her lack of friends in general. But now she did have good friends. She had Caro and Zofia, and she'd apparently caught the eye of a man, and so perhaps she wasn't such an oddball after all.

"Hang on, now," Alan said, looking over her shoulder. He walked across the lane and picked up a white object covered in dirt and held it out.

"Parsnip?" he asked.

"Sugar beet," Rosalie replied. "There's been a great increase in acreage, because we can no longer import sugar."

"You're brilliant," Alan said, tossing the vegetable back into the field. "Come on—pub."

They cycled off side by side back to the airfield first, where Rosalie had a chance to stop at the lavatory and run damp fingers through her hair. No need to pinch color into her cheeks, as they were cherry red from nervous excitement. She returned to the Mess to find Alan waiting for her at the bar.

"Here you are now," he said, and took her arm, steering her back toward the exit. Over his shoulder, he called, "Right, lads, be seeing you."

"No introductions, Chersey?" one of the men called.

But they were already out the door.

The pub was heaving with pilots, WAAFs, and locals, but the din was only a faint background noise to Rosalie. The entire evening, she sat perched on a stool at the bar with Alan close at her side. Winston Churchill himself could've been sitting behind her and Rosalie wouldn't've noticed.

Alan ordered her a sherry, and she made it last the entire evening. He asked about her family, and she told him about her brothers and the geese and the Fordson tractor—he was particularly interested in its time-saving qualities—and about Will and Jean's wedding.

"She's from Scarborough, and I don't think she's had an easy life. Her dad worked in the mines but had to quit a few years ago because of his lungs. Jean had never grown anything more than geraniums in a pot before this, but she's really taken to farming."

"He married a Land Girl who is the daughter of a miner?" Alan said with obvious delight. "Well, there you are, then."

Rosalie told him about taking flying lessons from Reg. "Did you start on a Moth?" she asked.

"Tiger Moth, oh yes. That was a year ago, when I turned twenty. Hadn't a clue what I was doing at the beginning. What about you?"

"My first was a Gipsy Moth. I started lessons five years ago when I was sixteen."

"Let's see," Alan said, "that gives you four more years of flying than I have. Well done."

Rosalie colored at the compliment. "Pop always wanted me to be a pilot. He knew how much it meant, even though Mum didn't approve. I'm not sure she thinks it's proper. I wish he could see me now."

Their talk wandered into farming again, and Rosalie found herself presenting a treatise on hilling up leeks. Then Alan told her a tale from one of his summers at Easton Hall where he'd fallen in the pigsty. "I ended up covered in muck from my chin to my toes," he said. "I was meant to be up in my room the entire day on the books, but Briggs let me sneak in the house and clean up before Mum caught me."

"Briggs is your . . . butler?" It was a stab, but she took it.

"Cook. Fortner is the butler. I had to steer clear of him, because he's been with the family for years and you can't trust him to keep his mouth shut."

This led to another story about stealing the first ripe grapes from the hothouse, during which heist Fortner did catch him. Rosalie smiled. She was warm from the sherry and the feel of Alan's arm against hers on the bar, and she thought he could've been reading her the shipping news and she'd have been listening.

At closing, a stream of pubgoers made their way back to the airfield, and Alan, staying at Rosalie's side, chatted with several of the men ahead of them. She was aware of a group lagging behind. She cut her eyes back and saw that they were WAAFs, but she didn't know how to strike up any sort of a conversation. At the base, the other women filed into their quarters, but Alan pulled Rosalie aside before she could follow.

"I'll be away early tomorrow, so I won't see you, but"—he paused, and his brow furrowed—"may I write you?"

She hoped her blush went unseen in the darkness. "Yes, of course," she replied, and he gave her another gentle kiss and was gone.

The next morning, she woke in a strange bed—one of many lined up in the room—and pieced together the previous evening, attempting to separate fact from a night of dreams, the details of which rapidly faded. In the Mess, the overnight crew had come off and a few sleepy-eyed WAAFs wandered in. Rosalie poured herself a cup of tea and sat down to spread margarine on her toast.

"Blenheim?"

It was one of the ground crew—a different man from the day before—standing in the door of the Mess, looking round.

"That's me." She took her toast with her and followed him out.

"Rosalie?"

At the sound of her name, she turned to see a woman approaching. It took a minute to realize who she was. "Ellen?"

Leslie's girl—former girl. Ellen's face had lost that soft complacency Rosalie remembered from school. Here stood a soldier at rigid attention. Perhaps that's what wearing a uniform did to anyone, causing Rosalie to wonder if she, too, looked harder than she had a year ago. She certainly felt different. Perhaps Ellen did as well. The war had changed her from the daughter of the village solicitor to a woman with responsibilities.

"I didn't realize you were here," Rosalie said, but now remembered that Leslie had told her.

"Yes, I joined up in the autumn. I'm a driver," Ellen said. "I saw you last evening at the pub."

Rosalie blushed. She hadn't seen anyone but Alan.

"You should've said something."

"Alan has a way of capturing your full attention, doesn't he?" Ellen looked down. "Everyone says so."

"I was stuck here overnight," Rosalie explained. "He was only being kind."

Was that all it had been? In the cold light of dawn and without Alan to disagree, Rosalie thought perhaps her words were true, that he'd taken pity on her and provided a few hours of entertainment.

"Mum told me Will married one of your Land Girls."

"Jean. They're very happy." She hoped. At least, as happy as you could be with a secret child by another man.

"And I'm told you're engaged," Rosalie said. "Congratulations."

"Yes." Ellen lifted her chin. "Ned is—"

"Blenheim!" the crewman shouted from somewhere up ahead.

"Yes, coming," Rosalie called, hitching her parachute on her shoulder. "Ellen, I'm sorry we didn't get more of a chance to talk." But how would that have gone? She and Ellen had always rubbed each other the wrong way, but the war seemed to turn everything on its head.

"Another time," Ellen replied. "And, Rosalie . . ."

She'd been almost away. "Yes?"

"How is Les?"

What do you care? That was the response of a defensive little sister, but aloud Rosalie said, "He's very well, working hard and really pulling his weight in the war effort. The farm couldn't do without him. Shall I say you asked after him?"

Ellen dropped her head. "Oh. Well . . . yes, of course."

CHAPTER 10

Another spate of bad weather, and the women were kept grounded and grumbling in the waiting room at Hamble, where sounds were limited to the turning of pages, the clicking of knitting needles, and the shuffling of cards. On the second day, they all jumped when Caro shot out of her chair.

"I'm fed up with this. Look, it's just gone ten o'clock. We've got the day. Let's go into town—shopping, cinema, lunch. It's Saturday, should be fairly lively, and we can go in my car. Who's in?"

Zofia's and two other hands went up. Caro went to ask for permission and came back with the news from the Met office that the weather would not lift for two more days, and so there would be no flying.

"Rosalie?" she asked.

"No, thanks. Think I'll head back to Mrs. May's. Write a few letters."

"Or wait for the post," Caro replied. "Why don't you write him first?"

Rosalie's face went hot. During the fortnight since her day with Alan, Caro had discovered Rosalie lurking in the entry at No. 6 waiting for the post. "I couldn't do that. What would I say?"

"I don't believe that would much matter," Caro replied. "Sounds as if you could instruct him about how and when to plant beetroot and he'd be fascinated."

"With the beetroot, probably. I'll see you later."

Rosalie returned to their digs to find Mrs. May at the front door with her coat on, scarf tied under her chin, and string bag in hand.

"I'm off to the shops," the landlady said. "I see you've brought in reinforcements to work in the garden. Good thing I located a second spade. I expect there'll be great progress." And with that, she set off down the road.

Reinforcements? Rosalie went to the kitchen and peered out the back door to see Snug attacking one of the pyramids and shoveling soil into the pit.

"What are you doing here?" she asked.

He paused, resting his arm on the top of the spade, and grinned. "We're not flying either, same as you—we've got snow and ice and it's a right mess. Then I thought of all those months I was here and didn't lend a hand and you working on it now. I felt guilty, I suppose. Although"—he squinted an eye and cocked his head at the bomb crater—"doesn't look as if you've got much done."

Rosalie laughed. "That's because I was waiting for you. I'll be right down and join you."

Upstairs, she changed into coveralls and came down again, wrapping a scarf round her curls and knotting it at the top of her forehead. She pulled on the old coat belonging to one of Mrs. May's sons, took up her spade, and they set to work. As they labored, they talked about their favorite aeroplanes. Rosalie leaned toward the Spitfire, which seemed built to suit a woman, while Snug preferred the Wellington. "Something with a bit of room for me," he said. But soon the physical exertion was enough and they fell silent, the only noises the squish and clank of the spades sinking into the rocky, wet soil.

After a couple of hours, Rosalie's arms felt like jelly, as if she'd cranked the Anson's undercarriage up by herself. Good thing they'd all but finished. The crater had become a mound, which would settle with the rain.

"Tea?" she asked Snug.

"I wouldn't say no."

They washed up in the kitchen sink and Rosalie put the kettle on, uncovered the loaf, and cut several thick slices of bread. Mrs. May couldn't begrudge a bear some food if he had given her room for a garden and chickens.

"I'm afraid it's margarine," she said, "but there's this." She went to the pantry and dug out the nearly-empty jar of damson jam from the far back corner—Mrs. May's vain attempt to make it last. "I brought it back from the farm."

They made a feast of it and, revived, began chatting again, exchanging close calls as if they were playing cards.

"Ack-ack almost brought me down over Manchester," Snug said, speaking of the antiaircraft guns from the ground. "Our own men, mind you. Could they not see the roundels on my wings?"

"I got in the way of a dogfight a few weeks ago," Rosalie said. "I never saw the German, only his tracers, but a Spit cut past me as if I wasn't even there and went after him."

Snug nodded. "Never a dull moment, is it?"

"How did your mum's pub do in the Blitz?" Rosalie asked. "It's in London, right?"

"Just down from Liverpool Street station. The Bishop's Finger. Building next door was hit right at the end of May, and the place is still just a pile of bricks. There was an old fellow killed." Snug shook his head. "The Blitz may be over, but they're still getting hit. I wanted them to leave, get out of the city, but Mum flat refuses. Says it's her life there."

"You must understand that," Rosalie said, licking jam off her thumb. "I mean, what if she said to you, 'Snug' . . ." Rosalie stopped for a moment. "Is that what she calls you?"

"What's that supposed to mean?"

"Well, it isn't your proper name, is it?" Rosalie asked with all innocence. "Doesn't she use your Christian name?"

"Never you mind what she uses," Snug said, and glowered.

"Mmm," Rosalie replied, but gave up on that front. "So, if she said to you, 'Snug, that ferrying aeroplanes all about the country is dangerous, and I don't want you to do it any longer,' what would you say to her?"

Snug watched her, his eyes small and dark.

"You'd tell her," Rosalie continued, wagging a finger at him, "that you're a good pilot and you can't think of anything else in the world you'd rather do, danger or no. Right?"

He grinned. "That's what Mouse says too."

"Mouse?"

"My auntie. She drives an ambulance in London and lives above the pub with her friend."

"She's called Mouse?" Rosalie asked. "Is she small?"

Snug seemed to consider the question for a moment. "No," he replied at last.

They were interrupted by a commotion at the front door—key in lock, voices raised in laughter. Rosalie called out, "In here."

Caro and Zofia came into the kitchen with Mrs. May behind. The landlady scooted past them and went straight to the door to look out. "Well, now, would you look at that. We've a back garden again." She stepped out for a closer examination.

"So," Caro said to Snug, "there you are. Brenda was wondering."

Rosalie's focus shifted abruptly and left her dizzy, as if she had moved her field glasses too quickly. "Oh," she said with a smile, "so that's why you're here today—a date with Brenda!"

Snug paused, but only for a second. "What's the time?" he asked. "A few of us were going into town. You're welcome to come along." He looked at Rosalie but also nodded to the other two.

"If you're going to the cinema, be forewarned," Caro said, "they're still showing *Inspector Hornleigh Goes to It*. And I'm not sure Rosalie wouldn't rather spend the evening in her room reading her post."

At that, Caro reached in her pocket, drew out a letter, and handed it over. Rosalie saw her name and in the return space *Chersey*, written in a brisk, dashed-off sort of script. As if from a great distance away, she heard Caro add, "He sent it to the ferry pool."

"Right, well, I'm off," Snug said, but he hadn't got as far as the front door before Mrs. May returned from the back garden to call out a reminder. "We'll see you again, won't we? There's the henhouse yet to build."

Once the door closed, Rosalie stripped off her muddy clothes, flung them at a peg on the wall, and dashed up two flights of stairs in her bra and knickers, calling out, "Must clean up. Be down later."

In her room, she dived under the covers instead of putting clothes on and held Alan's letter against her chest as she tried to steady her breathing.

She opened the letter carefully, because the thin, wartime paper ripped so easily.

Dear Rosalie—I've been remiss about writing and then worried that you wouldn't even remember that I'd asked you if I could. It's quite possible you're wondering who this cheeky fellow is who has the nerve to pretend that he knows you. Perhaps I should start at the beginning again.

Hello Rosalie—My name is Alan Chersey, and you may not remember this but we spent one of the best days of my life together when you were waiting for a Blenheim at Castle Camps. I look forward to our next meeting. I confess to scanning the Mess for your face each time I walk in and then must carry on, pushing my disappointment aside. I've thought about putting in a special request for you to deliver our next Mosquito. Do you think that would work?

Rosalie laughed. It had been only a fortnight since they'd met, but she was buoyed by the idea that Alan hadn't forgotten and wanted to see her again. After reading the letter twice more, she tucked it into the bureau. Something at the window caught her attention, and she looked over to see sunlight cutting through the curtains and throwing its sharp profile onto the floor. She blinked at the brightness. Spring had come at last.

★ ★ ★

But, two days later, the promise of spring ended in dull pain as three ATA pilots were killed in a crash near White Waltham. It was late afternoon on a Sunday, and Rosalie had returned to Hamble from delivering a Hurricane to Brize Norton. She was delighted to notice that the hours of daylight were increasing—she could land at six o'clock and still see.

When she reported to the duty office, it was to find CO Margot Gore staring at the assignment chalkboard, holding a rag loosely. Rosalie stopped just inside the door and watched as Gore slowly lifted her hand as if it were a heavy weight and erased a name: *Bridget Hill*. A lovely, happy young woman who would always put herself out to help a fellow pilot. No words were needed—the grief in the room was palpable, sucking up the joy of life.

"Bridget?"

She must've spoken aloud, because Gore turned to see her standing there.

"Yes, I'm afraid so," the CO said. "Along with two from other pools—Betty Sayers and Graham Lever."

"What happened?"

"It was a Fairchild taxi. The engine stalled coming into White Waltham, and he was too low to pull out. It crashed into a bungalow just off the airfield, and the petrol tank exploded. One pilot was thrown clear."

"But Bridget . . ."

There had been other ATA crashes that ended in death. The most famous was Amy Johnson, the world-renowned aviatrix who was killed when she got into trouble with her Oxford and bailed out over the Thames Estuary. But that had been in January of last year, before Rosalie was even accepted for training. Amy had been well known, but Bridget was a friend.

Gore noticed Rosalie's gaze go back to the board, and the CO regained some of her composure.

"It's an assignment board, Wright, not a memorial. We know this can happen. It's the nature of our . . ." She sounded calm and quiet, as if trying to close the book on the incident, but she twisted the rag in shaking hands, betraying her emotions. "Stop into the waiting room; there are others there. It's a good time to be together."

Rosalie would rather have gone back to No. 6 to be alone, but it had been Bridget as well as Caro who nudged her into becoming more sociable. In Bridget's memory, she made straight for the waiting room.

Inside, no one spoke, and the atmosphere felt compressed, as if the very air weighed down on them. Four women sat staring at their bridge hands. A few others had newspapers lying unread in their laps. Rosalie heard the click of knitting needles and longed to hold her own wool—the mindless handwork had a way of comforting.

Zofia sat on the sofa, staring at the floor, and Caro was at the tea table, pouring two cups. She looked up at Rosalie and reached for a third.

"Her name's gone from the board," Rosalie said, taking her tea and joining Zofia. "It's so final."

Anne shook her head. "There was a child in the bungalow. Unhurt, thank God."

"She's to be buried at Maidenhead."

"That's the nearest cemetery to White Waltham, so it feels like it's ours," Caro said, perching on the arm of the sofa. "It's where I'd want to be buried. Why not?"

"Why not?" Grace looked up from her bridge hand. "Easy for you to say, Caro, as you won't have a husband to be buried next to."

"Be a bit tight next to yours, won't it, Grace?" Brenda asked sharply. "Going to cozy up to the first wife, are you?"

"Leave it, Brenda," Caro said.

"You don't have to put up with this," Brenda replied. "She should mind her own business."

Rosalie, bewildered at this bickering when a friend had died, stood and rubbed her face to keep the tears from falling. "I'm going home."

"We will go too," Zofia said, and she and Caro followed Rosalie out.

They returned to No. 6 in silence. Darkness was falling, and it had started to rain.

Inside, they shook themselves off and hung up their coats. "Rosalie, come into the lounge with me," Caro said. "I want to talk with you."

"Is it about Grace?"

"There now," Mrs. May called from the kitchen, "no dallying. The plates are on the table."

"Or Bridget?" Rosalie asked.

"No, not Grace, not Bridget," Caro replied. "But it'll keep."

In the kitchen, Mrs. May announced, "We've sausage rolls for our meal."

She assured them that there was indeed sausage in the mixture along with vegetables and bread crumbs and seasoning and stood back as if waiting for the usual joke about the swedes, but the women picked up their cutlery without a word.

"What's this then?" the landlady asked.

Caro explained about Bridget, and Mrs. May sank into a chair, her face gray and her indomitable energy gone. "The poor thing," she said, and then sniffed. "You three," she warned, "you mind your-selves, do you hear?"

They nodded, promising they would, but knowing that Mrs. May's real fear was for her sons, Fred and Terry, whose letters arrived sporadically, whose locations were unclear, and whose writ-ings contained more memories of home than details about their present lives.

"I like this sausage roll," Zofia said, the first to dig into the meal. "We have sausage in Poland too—kielbasa. It is an excellent sausage. When the war is finished, I will have my mother send kielbasa and you will see."

And with that, they were reminded that Zofia's family was also far away. Even less was known about them than Fred and Terry, except that they had been in danger when Zofia fled. She'd had no replies to her letters. Pauline Gower herself, commanding officer of the ATA, was making enquiries for Zofia and the other Polish pilots. Rosalie told herself she was lucky to be alive and with a family intact. Apart from Pop. She would write to Will and Leslie before bed and tell them she was well.

Without comment, all of them helped with cleanup that Sunday evening, and no one lingered in the lounge to listen to the wireless.

In her room, Rosalie began a letter home with good cheer, telling them about the progress on the henhouse and how Mrs. Potts had promised chicks later in the spring and how she hoped Snug would come back and help.

She'd have liked to talk with Snug at that moment. He must've known Bridget and the others who had been killed. How did he manage?

As they all did, she supposed. For the next day, life went on—they picked up their chits and flew. Nothing would stop that, apart from the weather. The war continued, men and women died, and aeroplanes were needed. This is what they knew.

★　★　★

The women gathered in the assignment room on an April morning and found no chits on the table. At first, there was stunned silence, and then murmurs. Anne was first to voice their worry. "Aren't we flying today? What's happened?"

CO Gore walked into the room holding a stack of chitties. "You will indeed be flying. Conditions on Malta are desperate. The island has been under siege from the Germans and Italians for months. They have few operational aeroplanes left and limited supplies. We've received priority one orders from Central Ferry Control to deliver Spitfires immediately. You'll be flying from Chattis Hill, Brize Norton, or any another aerodrome to collect your Spit and ferry it to Glasgow. The aeroplanes will be fitted with radio and ammunition before sending them off to Malta. You will make your way back as soon as you can, because there will be more waiting for you. Good luck."

Gore held out the assignments and the women dived at them, locating their own, passing others along until each paper had reached its pilot. Every delivery of an aeroplane held significance, but this assignment seemed of even greater importance, because all the pilots were working together on a concerted effort and they knew the immediate goal. For five days, they waved good-bye to one another in the morning, and perhaps crossed paths again at RAF Renfrew when they landed in Glasgow. Rosalie had never been there, but there was no time for sightseeing, because after each delivery, she had to find an air taxi to take her at least part of the way back to Hamble.

One day, she got only as far as a small airfield at Doncaster, and as it was late in the day, they put her up in the group captain's private quarters and he stayed elsewhere. The next morning there was a knock at the door, and Rosalie sat up wondering for a second where she was. She remembered just as the orderly backed in with a tray.

"'Morning, sir," he said, not even glancing at the bed. "Looks a good day for—" He turned to see Rosalie and nearly dropped the tray. "Blimey! Good Lord, miss, you did give me a fright."

"I'm terribly sorry." Rosalie held the blanket up to her chin and tried to quash a giggle. "I'm ATA and came in late, and they said it was all right to sleep here. I can be away in two minutes, really I can."

"Not at all," the orderly replied, patting his chest and taking a breath. He was an older man, possibly as old as her pop had been when he died, and he gave her a fatherly smile. "As you're here and so is the breakfast tray, you should take it at your leisure."

Rosalie told her story in the Bugle that evening, prompting others to add their own tales.

"I got as far as London the other day," Brenda said, "and had to sleep in an Underground station with my parachute as a pillow. Have you been in one? There's a tea hut, and they had a little band playing on the platform."

Anne shuddered. "I'd feel like a mole spending the night down there. Didn't you?"

"The fellow on the trumpet chatted me up," Brenda said, "and said he'd take me out to all the clubs next time I was up. So there you are—I don't mind being a mole for one night if I get a date out of it."

CHAPTER 11

May 1942

Dear Rosalie, I think of you often, and have gone over the moments of our day together—now two months past—so many times I could give it to you word for word. I remember how I felt when I was with you, and I imagine I know how you felt. I hope I haven't pulled that last part out of a hat. Thoughts of you have become a sort of refuge for me as we have begun operational flying.

Will you come to see me? Next month, NAAFI puts on a dance for everyone here at Castle Camps. It's held in the village hall. Quite a do, I'm told, but it wouldn't be nearly as nice if you weren't here.

You won't have to worry about accommodations—there's a woman in the village, Mrs. Colby, who lets rooms and I will book a place for you there. This is all on the up and up, I promise—she doesn't allow a man to set foot in her house, so we'll be as proper as sunshine.

Please say you'll come. I've enclosed details and await your word.

All my best,
Alan

The letter had come in the afternoon post, and with Mrs. May out shopping, it lay on the floor of the entry when Rosalie, Caro, and Zofia returned to No. 6. Rosalie spotted Alan's scratchy handwriting at once, snatched the envelope, and ran upstairs, calling that she'd be down later to help with the meal.

She stretched out on her bed and read through the letter quickly, then studied it. Their correspondence had been light and breezy and a bit teasing, perhaps, but in this most recent letter, received only two days into the new month, Rosalie detected a need and a sadness. Alan had started flying night ops, and she thought this must be part of the change. She fell into a light sleep, clutching the letter to her breast, and when she awoke, read it again. Then she got out of bed and went downstairs, the letter burning a hole in the pocket of her trousers. Zofia waited for her at the bottom.

"Ah, I am ready to come and find you, thinking perhaps you were asleep. A kip, as you say."

Caro looked out from the kitchen and eyed Rosalie. "All right there?"

"Oh yes, fine. Quite hungry." She marched past, knowing Caro could probably read her face too well, as always.

Mrs. May had returned from her day out full of ideas about the back garden, which she passed on to the women over her shoulder as she stood at the hob.

"Mrs. Potts is advising me on what to plant."

"Not swedes, I hope," Caro said.

"But," said Mrs. May, "we'll have to take care they don't get eaten."

"No trouble there," Caro whispered to the other two.

"They'll peck at anything, it seems," the landlady said, ignoring Caro apart from a quick look out the corner of her eye.

"The hens?" Zofia asked.

"Will they eat the swedes?" Caro asked. "That would solve all our troubles."

"They might pull up seedlings," Rosalie said, "but as we don't have the hens yet, we might as well plant."

"A bit of hoeing every day . . ." Mrs. May continued.

"Every day?" Caro asked incredulously.

"It'll all be worth it in the end."

They continued to discuss vegetables through the meal, which resulted in more ideas than space, but Rosalie thought what seeds were available might put shed to some choices. Caro was on the rota to clean up, and when they finished eating, she shooed the others away.

"I'll help you," Rosalie volunteered.

Mrs. May was already out the door and on her way to switch on the wireless. Caro gave Zofia a nod, and she followed. Rosalie didn't speak during the washing and drying. When the table had been wiped and the tea towel draped over the hob, Caro took Rosalie's hand, pulled her down into a chair, and said, "So, then, how was the latest missive from Alan?"

Rosalie flushed. "It's a lovely letter."

"Yes, I could tell that. But there's something else, isn't there?"

In a moment, the letter was out of her pocket. She thrust it into Caro's hand. "Go on, read it."

When Caro had finished and looked up at her, Rosalie asked, "Should I go?"

"Do you want to?"

"Yes." The word sent a thrill through her. She tapped a finger on the letter. "Look there. You see that NAAFI's doing it, and don't they put on lovely events and run the canteens? They're quite respectable. And see, Alan says I'll have my own place to stay, so we'll be . . ."

"As proper as sunshine?" Caro asked. "But there's something that bothers you, Rosalie."

"Two things, actually." She frowned. "I've been to only one dance—it was at the tennis club. And I've never had a boyfriend proper, so I don't know how to act. I thought you could give me some advice, because you probably have more . . . experience . . . with men."

Caro laughed. "Well, you're wrong there. But listen." She put a hand on Rosalie's arm. "The important thing is that you feel comfortable with him and that he treats you with respect. Could you tell that on your one day together?"

Rosalie nodded. "Yes, he's kind. I can see that."

"And you wouldn't mind spending the evening with his arms round you on the dance floor?" Caro asked.

That thrill again. "I wouldn't mind."

"Well, then, what's the other problem?"

Rosalie's face seized up with worry. "I don't have a dress."

★　★　★

A return letter had gone out in the morning post the next day. Yes, she would go to the dance. That was the most important thing. After that, try as she might, Rosalie hadn't been able to put all her thoughts into words, and she relied on Alan's reading between the lines.

Rosalie thought she'd never be able to wait the entire month to see him again, but the war gave her plenty to do.

At the tail end of April, the Germans had begun bombing some of England's most beautiful cities—Bath, Exeter, Norwich, York, and Canterbury. The Baedeker raids, they were called, after the series of German guidebooks that spotlighted places of cultural importance. In this case, the guides told the enemy just where to strike to make it hurt. The bombing continued into May, adding more cities to the mix, forcing Rosalie and the other ATA pilots to plot their routes carefully with Maps and Signals before they flew, as they needed to account for not only weather and barrage balloons but also renewed attacks.

In June, the Germans started in on Southampton again. They'd been hard-hit during the Blitz, resulting in Mrs. May's crater in the back garden from an unexploded bomb. Southampton was close enough that Hamble Civil Defense needed help lest the whole coast go up in flames and requested that ATA pilots be put on fire watch each night in case of a German incendiary attack.

Rosalie did her bit, sitting out on the flat roof of the control tower. Long periods of nothing during which she kept awake by cups of tea alone were broken by bouts of aeroplanes rumbling overhead and, from the ground, antiaircraft guns firing into the sky. Apart from being shot at by a Messerschmitt that one time, she'd seen no war action, although at the ferry pool they'd certainly heard the air raid sirens go often enough. Most people paid no attention to them and went about their business.

Now, the silent night was broken by earsplitting *ack-ack*, and the dark was interrupted by flashes of fire from the guns. Rosalie had to steel herself, clenching the railing that lined the flat roof and staring out into the night, waiting for the world around her to burst into flames.

But fire watching did not dismiss her or the other women from ferrying aeroplanes the following day. At six o'clock the morning after her first night watch, she stretched out on a sofa in the waiting room, hoping to get an hour's kip. She didn't sleep, and started her day by downing a cup of tea and a slice of toast before picking up her chits. After dragging through her assignments, Rosalie returned to No. 6 in the late afternoon, fell asleep across her bed still wearing her uniform, and awoke three hours later to find it was time to go back for another night's observation.

She existed in a sort of limbo on tea, toast, and two-penny chocolate bars for three days and nights and then Zofia took over, but the arrangement with the fire wardens didn't last much longer. CO Gore complained that her pilots had too much work of their own to do and that if crashes occurred because they hadn't enough sleep, it would be the fault of the Civil Defense, not the ATA. The loss of aeroplanes was too great a risk, of course, and the women were relieved of the extra duty.

When life at the ferry pool returned to normal, Rosalie's thoughts were once again filled with the upcoming dance.

Caro helped immensely with plans. She'd offered to find a dress and took hold of her assignment with zeal, first making a list of all the women at the pool and then narrowing the possibilities down one by one until only a handful remained.

"Grace is about your size," she said one evening at No. 6.

"No!" Rosalie said. "I won't wear one of Grace's. I doubt she's the lending type, anyway."

"I wouldn't mind asking her," Caro replied, "just to see what she says."

Rosalie didn't understand this bristling squabble between Caro and Grace. The latter, of course, could get up anyone's nose, but she seemed to aim her sharpest barbs at Caro.

"There must be someone else."

"I've five possibilities left. Tomorrow I'll begin the interviews."

Rosalie laughed.

As it turned out, Catherine had a lovely frock that fit Rosalie perfectly after they'd taken up extra darts in the back. It was red. Not strictly red, but a shade that suggested a sunrise in summer, that layer above the horizon touched with pink. It suited Rosalie, and had a skirt that might almost be called full. At least enough to stand out a bit when she twirled. Brenda lent her shoes so that Rosalie wouldn't be forced to wear her flight boots—they'd had a laugh about that—and she practiced in the lounge at Mrs. May's, taking turns dancing with Caro and then Zofia. The next day, she completed her outfit by spending two precious clothing coupons on a pair of stockings.

Mrs. May made it clear that flying off across the country to go to a dance with a man Rosalie barely knew wasn't the proper way for a young woman to conduct herself. "What did your mother say to this?"

Rosalie hesitated. She hadn't mentioned Alan's invitation in a letter home, thinking it would be better to report on it after the fact. Fortunately, Caro saved her.

"It's the war, Mrs. May. It's changed everything. And some of it for good, don't you think?"

The landlady muttered her reply, and none of the young women were inclined to ask her to repeat it.

The time flew by in such a rush that it made Rosalie quite breathless, and suddenly it was the evening before she would leave for Castle Camps. Several of the women gathered in the waiting room at the end of the day to help Rosalie plan her route.

"Would that you could order an Anson to fly you direct," Brenda said. "As it is, you won't know how long it'll take."

"Get on the first taxi out tomorrow morning," Anne said, "no matter where it goes. You'll get a head start."

"No," Grace said, entering the discussion for the first time. "Take the first taxi that goes to a sizable airfield. You've a better choice there, and you'll be more likely to get closer on the next leg. Rosalie, did you say your fellow is a squadron leader?"

Grace had missed most of the women's talk about the impending dance, and Rosalie was loath to go over it all again, as if talking about Alan too much at this early stage might put a jinx on them.

"Flight lieutenant," she said.

"Mmm," Grace replied, and went back to her newspaper.

★   ★   ★

Hamble north to Brize Norton and then east to White Waltham, the headquarters of the Air Transport Auxiliary. Surely Rosalie could find an aeroplane going north from there.

"Stradishall," the duty officer said when she checked on the next available taxi. "That's as close as I can get you. And we've nothing else coming in today."

RAF Stradishall lay a good twenty miles from Castle Camps, but this could be her only chance. There might be a bus.

"Yes, that'll do. Thanks."

When she climbed aboard the Fairchild taxi, she recognized the ATA pilot but couldn't recall his name. "Any chance you could put down at Castle Camps?" she asked.

He gave her a nod, and after landing at three airfields, he at last put down at Rosalie's destination. She grabbed her bag and parachute, stuffed her forage cap into a pocket, and clambered out of the aeroplane.

She did not find Alan waiting near the field, in the duty officer's hut, or in the Mess. She stood outside the door weighing her options. Nearly five o'clock—he didn't fly during the day, so where was he? Two pilots sauntered past her and pushed open the swing door without giving her a second look. Had Alan told anyone she was coming, or would they think her mad for asking after him?

The idea of sitting in the Mess with a cup of tea waiting for who knew how long and having to explain herself didn't sound ideal. No, she would make her own way into the village and find Mrs. Colby's guesthouse. That seemed reasonable, because Alan would know to look for her there, and perhaps a walk would do her good. It might banish the nervous energy that made Rosalie vibrate as if she still sat in the Fairchild with its engines rumbling.

She struck out and had almost reached the gate when she heard her name called and turned to see him running, his jacket unbuttoned and flapping. He made such a ruckus that a few men stopped to watch and a woman in uniform stood at the corner of the Mess. Rosalie hoped it wasn't Ellen.

"I'm sorry," Alan said, panting as he took her bag and parachute and dropped them on the ground. "I'm so sorry. I've been watching for you, I have, but for one instant I got busy and I missed you. There now." He put his hands on her arms and squeezed. His breathing had calmed and he smiled. "I'm awfully glad you're here."

At his touch, Rosalie's nerves calmed, but they were replaced by a flutter in her midsection.

"It's all right. I thought I'd better make my way to Mrs. Colby's to . . . you know, get ready."

"I'll walk you there," he said, with a glance back.

The observers had remained, and whether they were actually watching or not, Rosalie would be glad to be out of their sight. After all, this was a private reunion.

Alan hoisted her gear onto his shoulder and put a hand at her waist. The sky was a dull gray and the still air muggy and close. She didn't care. They walked into the village and stopped at the pub first. Alan ordered her a sherry before she could say she'd rather have a glass of the mild, but no matter—she'd tell him next time.

They sat at a table in the corner near a window with wavy yellow glass—although half of it was missing and had been boarded up. Alan enquired about her journey, and Rosalie asked how the night ops in the Mosquito were going. He took a long drink of his pint before he answered.

"We've lost two pilots. Chalmers, and after that Peters. Good pilots, the both of them. And their navigators. Four men." Alan's eyes grew dull, and his face lost its animation. "Chalmers went down near the coast returning early one morning. They spotted his plane the next day against a cliff." Alan tapped the edge of his glass on the table. "Had he been hit, or was it something else? And then, three nights later, Peters. I didn't see it, but they say he stalled and that sent his Mosquito into a spin. Why couldn't he pull out of it?"

The question had no answer. At least, not from Rosalie. She reached across the table and took both of Alan's hands in hers.

"That's when I wrote you," he said. "That night, asking you to come. It calmed me, I can't tell you." He smiled and kissed one of her hands, and his good spirits returned. "This evening, we can forget all about the war."

They finished their drinks, and he walked her to Mrs. Colby's, whose house sat across from the village hall, where the dance would be held. The bell was answered instantly by a short, pillowy woman with ruddy cheeks that plumped up even further when she smiled.

"Good afternoon, Mr. Chersey. Ah, now, this must be Miss Wright we have here. I'm Mrs. Colby. You're very welcome."

Alan handed over Rosalie's gear and stood back at attention. "Well, Miss Wright, I'll leave you in Mrs. Colby's capable hands and return to collect you at eight." He gave her a wink and walked away whistling.

Mrs. Colby nattered on in a good-natured way as she led Rosalie up to her room. "I provide what your parents would if you were at home. That is a safe place for a young lady to stay whether for one night or longer. You're my only visitor tonight, but I do have a regular lodger, a widow whose husband was killed in Norway. That's nearly two years ago. She came to me in the autumn and is trouble free."

"It's very good of you to offer rooms," Rosalie said. "Last time I was here, I put up in the WAAF quarters."

Mrs. Colby huffed. "Those young ladies need a bit of supervision, if you ask me. Here, we have house rules." They had reached Rosalie's room, which was barely big enough for the bed. "I'm sure Mr. Chersey has explained. A gentleman may call on a young lady for tea, and I will be there to serve it and keep an eye on things. Otherwise, the only man that crosses my threshold is the odd workman. I won't have any girl's parents worried about what's going on here. Now, I'll put the kettle on and expect you down in ten minutes. All right?"

"Yes, thanks."

Rosalie got the idea that Mrs. Colby's soft outside hid a core of solid steel, but she wouldn't want to test it. She shook out her dress, draped it over a chair, and stopped in the lavatory. Ten minutes later, she sat in the lounge with a cup of tea and a thin slice of sultana cake.

"Dried fruit has gone on the ration," Mrs. Colby said, shaking her head. "Even sultanas are dear. So, Miss Wright, do you actually fly aeroplanes yourself?"

Rosalie explained the ATA, after which Mrs. Colby said, "I can't imagine why you'd want to do that. Couldn't you have been a driver or a Land Girl?"

She'd been a Land Girl of sorts her entire life and had no desire to return to it, but fortunately Rosalie didn't have time to reply, because the door opened and closed and there was a woman a few years older than her—perhaps twenty-five or twenty-six—who wore the brown uniform of the Navy, Army, and Air Force Institutes. NAAFI. Her brimmed hat was set at a jaunty angle and nestled against a sleek roll of auburn hair.

"Ah, there we are now," Mrs. Colby said. "This is Miss Wright who is staying the night with us. Miss Wright, Mrs. Barlow."

"Very good to meet you. I'm Deborah."

"Rosalie."

"You're ATA?"

"Yes, and you're NAAFI?"

"Yes, I run the local works round here. Mrs. Colby is very good to put me up on a semipermanent basis, aren't you?"

"You must've had a hand in the dance tonight," Rosalie said.

"It's all mine," Deborah explained. "Dances, sandwiches, entertainment, cups of tea—we run the canteen too. Where are you based?"

"Hamble, in Hampshire."

"You've come a long way for a dance."

"Mr. Chersey asked her up," Mrs. Colby explained. "And made arrangements for her accommodations here."

"Alan?" Deborah asked. "He's a fine dancer. Haven't we heard that, Mrs. Colby? Well, Rosalie, I do hope you'll share him this evening."

★   ★   ★

Rosalie came down to the entry fifteen minutes early. The lavatory had only a tiny round mirror and she wanted to get an overall effect—or as much of one as the half mirror in the hallstand would give her. She stood on her tiptoes and turned to the side and then the back and peered over her shoulder. Not too shabby. Catherine's lovely sunrise-pink dress did seem to suit her.

"Now, Miss Wright," Mrs. Colby said, hurrying in and standing between Rosalie and the door. "I hope you weren't thinking of answering the bell yourself, because that wouldn't do. A proper young lady waits for her young man in the sitting room. In you go. And may I say, don't you look lovely."

Rosalie struggled with a reply, wanting to point out that she was twenty years old, not twelve, and certainly she could answer the door when Alan called. Instead, she stepped into the sitting room and looked out the front window to watch him walk up. He caught sight of her and stopped. She waved and dashed off to the entry as he rang the bell.

Mrs. Colby answered. "Good evening, Mr. Chersey. Now, I don't need to remind you of the rules." But she did, although Alan didn't seem to pay much attention. He stood on the front step admiring Rosalie, who, under his scrutiny, turned a shade not far off that of her dress. Eventually, when Mrs. Colby had finished, she stepped aside and Alan offered Rosalie his arm.

They took off at a brisk pace. "Good evening!" Alan called over his shoulder.

"Eleven o'clock, Mr. Chersey," Mrs. Colby replied. "You remember. I'll be waiting."

"And if you're late," Alan murmured in Rosalie's ear, "she turns you into a pumpkin."

Rosalie slapped her hand over her mouth to muffle a shriek of laughter as Alan directed her to the far side of a large oak tree, in the shade of its dark canopy. Across the road, the door of the village hall opened, and a few bleats from the orchestra warming up drifted out before it closed again.

"I want a moment with you all to myself," Alan said, "before you catch the eye of every man in the room."

Would she? Wouldn't Mrs. Barlow in her NAAFI uniform cut a better figure than Rosalie? But that didn't matter, because she didn't want all those other fellows to look at her—only Alan, the way he looked at her now. He kissed her, his arms sliding round her waist as hers slipped up and round his neck. He pulled her closer, and she leaned into him and they kissed again. Rosalie liked it, the warmth and softness of his lips and the hard crush of him against her body.

They broke apart when a shout went up, but it was only a few men coming out of the pub up the road and heading to the dance.

"Just as well," Alan said, taking a deep breath as he took her hand. "I promised to behave."

At that moment, Rosalie wasn't entirely sure she wanted him to.

★　★　★

Looking back, the evening was a blur accented by clear snapshots and snippets of scenes. Later, Rosalie recalled sandwiches—bacon and something that aspired to be cheese—and lemonade and tea. She had a clear memory of the band. Although it had been patched together from village and base musicians and the church organist was on trombone, they did their part admirably and with great vigor. Rosalie thought Caro would probably have known each tune they played.

The room had been set with tables and chairs at the back, but Rosalie didn't remember sitting for long. Mostly, she remembered being in Alan's arms, the dance floor alive with couples, the band blaring, the laughter above it all. She especially enjoyed the slower dances when Alan rested his cheek against her forehead. Should she encourage him to ask other women to dance? Rosalie wondered if that was what they were waiting for—the women standing at the edges of the room. She could feel their eyes on her, and when she turned, she would see one or two of them quickly look away.

Then she spotted one she knew. At the end of a number when Alan had gone off to get lemonade, Rosalie made her way over to Ellen, and they exchanged greetings.

"I never realized you enjoyed dancing so much," Ellen said.

Of course, Ellen had seen her dance only at the tennis club that one evening. She'd never seen Rosalie at home, dancing with Pop or dragging Leslie or Will up out of a chair to show her the right steps.

"I'd love to meet your fiancé," Rosalie said. "Ned, is it? Is he here?"

Ellen glanced about, as if looking for him. "No, he's gone off to the pub with a couple of friends, but I'm sure he won't be long."

The band started up a fast number, and three of the horn players put down their instruments and began to sing.

"Wait, I know this one," Rosalie said, and sang along with the few words she remembered. "*How ya gonna keep 'em down on the farm.*" She laughed. "That's Snug's song."

Alan came up behind Rosalie with two glasses. "Hello, er . . . Ellen. Lemonade?" He held out the second glass.

"Thanks, I won't," Ellen replied. "I'm only waiting for my fiancé to return. Oh, there he is now. Good evening."

"Engaged?" Alan asked, watching her walk away.

"To Ned. He's a fitter."

Alan frowned. "Do you know her?"

"She's from my village. Her father is a solicitor. She was Leslie's girl before the war."

Downing his lemonade, Alan took Rosalie's hand. "Let's step outside, why don't we? It's like a furnace in here."

An evening breeze cooled Rosalie's skin, damp from dancing. Another couple stood under the oak, and others had taken all the available cozy spots where a man and a woman might have a bit of privacy. Alan and Rosalie stood at the corner of the building, and from nearby, she heard low laughter and caught the whiff of a cigarette.

"I'm sorry," Alan said, "I haven't even asked. Do you smoke?"

"No."

"Right, neither do I. At least, not often. Is it too cool for you out here?"

"No, it feels good at the moment."

Alan reached over, took one of her curls, and twirled it round a finger. Rosalie knew what her hair must look like. "I tried to put a comb in it to hold it down, but my hair rejects all intervention."

"Your hair is perfect, Rosalie," Alan said, leaning down to her just as a couple came barreling round the corner and knocked into them.

"Is that Chersey?" the man said.

"Yes, Massey," Alan snapped, "no need to run us down."

"Sorry, old man, had my eye on other things." Massey took hold of the woman next to him. "Come along, sweetheart."

The band had started up again, and others were returning to the dance. The magic moment having been broken, Rosalie said, "I was told to share you. Should we have a dance with someone else?"

"Share? I don't like the sound of that. But all right. As long as it's a fast number."

They went back in, and Alan scanned the room, eventually nodding over a gangly fellow with slicked-back red hair.

"Here now, this is Declan Mackenna. Mack, Rosalie Wright."

"Hello, Declan," Rosalie said.

"Howdoyado?"

"Have a dance, you two," Alan said, "but do be careful with her, Mack, won't you? No crushed toes. I'll be checking." He gave Rosalie's arm a little squeeze before he went off.

Declan was a good dancer, but he did scoot round the room rather quickly with his long strides. Rosalie had to take two steps to each one of his.

"You WAAF?" he asked over the band.

"No, ATA. I'm a pilot."

"You aren't," he said, but in awe, not skepticism. "I've mostly seen only the blokes. In fact, I had a run-in with one of them. Large fellow and a bit scary looking, I must say. Found him in my favorite chair in the bar one day and tried to turf him out. Thought he was going to punch me in the nose. Turned out all right, though—he took me down the pub for a drink."

Rosalie laughed at the familiar story. "Oh yes, he can seem a bit ferocious at first."

"You know him?" Declan asked.

But Rosalie didn't answer, because at that moment she caught sight of Alan and his partner. It was Deborah Barlow, and she was not dressed in her brown uniform. Instead, she wore a pale-blue dress with bare shoulders. Her hair hung down in one long, thick, silky curl. She had her hand round the back of Alan's neck, and he had placed his firmly on her waist. They were quite close and laughing about something.

The music ended, but Rosalie didn't notice and tried to drag Declan off for a few more steps.

"Oh, sorry," she said, and in the next moment, Alan was at her side.

"You still in one piece?" he asked her. "Good work, Mack, thanks. There now," he said to Rosalie, "our duty done for the war effort. Look, it's near to eleven, and I don't want to rush our good-bye. Why don't we go."

Gladly, Rosalie thought. They got at least ten steps outside the door before she said, quite casually, "You were dancing with Mrs. Barlow. She lives at Mrs. Colby's."

"Deborah? Yes. She's a good egg. Does an enormous job of keeping our spirits up round here. I don't know what we'd do without the NAAFI canteen out at the dispatch hut."

How petty you are, Rosalie told herself. These were fighter pilots flying sorties every night, putting themselves in danger, and all they got was a cup of tea and an occasional dance. She stopped abruptly and turned to Alan.

"I've had such a lovely time."

He led her to the oak tree, blocking the view from Mrs. Colby's front window. There he took her in his arms and they said a proper, long good-bye.

At last, Rosalie sighed and nestled her head into his chest.

"I wish you weren't so far away," Alan murmured in her ear. "I wish the war would be over and you could stop flying."

She lifted her face. "But I don't want to stop flying."

There it was, her looming conundrum. The war being over was a good thing, something to look forward to—but it always carried with it this specter of loss. The idea that women, once again, wouldn't be suitable as pilots.

"No, not stop. Not altogether," Alan said. "But when we're both finished with this, there could be other important things that might steal away your attention. Don't you think?"

With his lips on hers, she conceded the possibility.

CHAPTER 12

July 1942

Rosalie skirted the barrage balloons that ringed Southampton and turned west, flying low over the New Forest. It was a day to glory in. The sky was so blue it almost hurt her eyes. She had forgotten to pull on her leather helmet, and the wind whipped through her curls, but it didn't matter.

She brought the control stick toward her to climb a bit higher and aimed her Tiger Moth toward its destination, Aston Down. After nine months at Hamble, Rosalie no longer felt slighted when she received a chitty saying she was to deliver one of the open-air trainer biplanes. In fact, she rather looked at it as if she'd run into an old friend again. After all, soon enough she would have her class-four-plus certificate. She'd written Alan to tell him that when that happened, she'd be flying Mosquitoes, and he reminded her about not undershooting her landing. He didn't mention his own flying, only that he hoped to see her soon.

Why not? The next time she had two days off, she could make her way to Essex for another stay with Mrs. Colby. Perhaps they could escape her strict rules and take a picnic out. Go to the seaside, or was that too dangerous during wartime?

She spotted her runway at Aston Down and circled once to see her way clear. Then she squared up, eased back on the throttle, and pushed the stick away from her, dropping the nose of the aeroplane until she could level out, touch down, taxi to the end of the field, and turn round to make her way back to stop near the duty officer's hut.

When she was about a hundred feet off the ground, an aeroplane, large and lumbering, appeared from nowhere coming over a copse, directly at her. Rosalie had no time to think. In a split second, she had pulled back hard on the control stick, sending her nose up sharply and her plane just barely over the top of the other aircraft. Her Moth bounced as the updraft from the other plane hit her underside and sent her wobbling. A quick look back told her she'd almost collided with an Avro Anson. If she had, she knew who would've come out the worse for it.

Safe, she broke out in a sweat and then shivered. Clearing the copse of oaks the Anson had appeared from, she pulled left, thinking only to put down as soon as she could before the shock got the better of her. There she saw a clear field on the other side of the hedge from the airfield.

But the field was short, and by the time she stopped completely, the nose of the Moth was in the hedge and the starboard wing had scraped alongside a patch of brambles. She heard something snap, and the stern warning in the ATA pilots book—"The country does not pay you to break aeroplanes"—rang in her ears. Then, anger stirred.

"Who the bloody hell was that?" she shouted, her voice thick. "Could he not see me coming in?"

Her entire body shook, and she forced herself to breathe slowly in and out before she could regain composure and venture out of the plane. She knew landing mix-ups were not all that unusual, but the ATA flew in daylight, and pilots were supposed to be able to stay out of one another's way. At least, she told herself, she was more agile in her Moth than the pilot of that Anson.

There now, that's better, she thought as her heart rate steadied. She wiped the sweat off her face and huffed. Time to report to the duty officer—someone else would need to figure out how to get the Moth out of the brambles.

But leaving the plane would not be that easy, because when she climbed out onto the wing, it was to meet a crowd looking up at her in anticipation, as if she were about to give a speech. A crowd of cows, that is—ten or twelve of them. She could hear the puffs of breath coming from cavernous nostrils, and their wide heads were just about level with her feet. One of them came close enough for its huge tongue to snake out and lick the aeroplane's wing, as if conducting a taste test. Rosalie stumbled back, catching herself before she could fall into the cockpit.

So much for getting away from the aeroplane and into the Mess, where she might have a cup of tea and recover. Had anyone seen what had happened? Would they come looking for her, or would she be trapped with her Moth until the cows lost interest and wandered away? How long would that be? Should she make a run for it?

"Wright?"

Snug, across the field, was climbing over a stile.

"Are you hurt?"

"No," she shouted, her gaze dropping back to her captors.

"Well, are you planning to have lunch out here? Wouldn't you rather come indoors?"

He strolled across the field toward her, and the cows took no notice of him. Behind him, three other men, ground crew, came over the stile. Rosalie clutched her parachute to her chest and tried to lean forward without toppling off the wing.

"Get them out of here," she said to Snug in a furious whisper.

He stopped at the edge of the group.

"Sorry?"

"Get them out of here," she repeated, trying not to shout.

He turned to the ground crew. "It's all right, lads, she's fine. We'll let you know when the Moth is released."

They shrugged and returned over the stile and to the airfield.

"Not them," Rosalie said. "Them!" She pointed to the nearest cow, then drew her finger away quickly when it stretched its neck up toward her.

Snug coughed, wiped his nose, coughed again, and then roared with laughter.

"Are you afraid they're contemplating something nefarious?"

"I don't know what's on their minds, and I have no desire to find out. Now, shift them, please, because I'm in desperate need of a cup of tea. And I wouldn't mind a bun."

Snug waved his arms, but the cows only looked at him. He clapped and waved and gave a shout, and they trotted off in all directions. He held a hand up to Rosalie and she took it, jumping down off the wing.

"Bloody animals," she muttered, and Snug choked back another laugh. She shot him a look, then snickered as they headed back to the airfield.

"It's a bit daft, isn't it?" she agreed. "Pop said one of our cows chased me when I was two years old. I fell over in the field and screamed bloody murder, but Mum said all the cow did was lick the back of my head." Rosalie shuddered.

"Terrible memory," Snug said with a grin.

"I don't actually remember," Rosalie admitted, "but my brothers like to remind me of it. They don't mind cows. If you want to know about the beasts, you drop in at Lime Farm and Leslie will tell you everything and more."

"He gives farm tours to strangers?"

"You're not a stranger—they know who you are. I wrote them about how you helped out with Mrs. May's bomb crater."

Snug went with her to report to the duty officer, who was already getting an earful from a short fellow in an ATA uniform. The pilot of the Anson. He looked up at Snug and then shifted his beady gaze to Rosalie.

"Are you the pilot of that Moth?" he asked.

"Yes, I am," Rosalie said. "Did you do a circuit?"

"I might've known it was a woman," he replied.

"Yes," she said, "you might've known it was a woman who could maneuver quick enough to get out of your way. You were nowhere to be seen when I circled."

"I have priority. I'm bigger than you."

"You're not," Rosalie said, taking a step closer to show she had a good two inches on him.

"All right, all right," the duty officer said, "just hand over your chits, please."

"She pulled up just in time," Snug said. "She saved you an aeroplane, that's for certain."

The Anson pilot glared at Snug.

"I put down where I could," Rosalie explained. "It's in the field on the other side. I'm afraid there might be a bit of damage."

"Shed a few tears, why don't you," taunted the pilot. "See if that helps."

"Push off!" Snug shouted in his face, and the man jumped back before turning and stalking away.

"Napoleon complex, if you ask me," the duty officer said, and looked over Rosalie's chit. "Let's see, Wright. Well, I'll take all this down and hand it over to the accident committee. You'll need to write up your own account."

Rosalie sighed.

"Come on," Snug said. "That cup of tea."

On the way to the Mess, Snug cut his eyes at her and said, "You handled that well."

"Shouting at that pilot?"

"No. Well, yeah, that too. But you handled yourself in the air."

She had, it was true—but she didn't mind him mentioning it.

"You heard about that RAF pilot Gilbert," Snug said.

"Yes," she replied.

It had been the talk of Hamble. Glamorous ATA pilot Diana Barnato's fairy-tale story of becoming engaged after knowing Humphrey Gilbert for barely a month had ended in unexpected and unnecessary tragedy. In May, he had crashed his Spitfire on a joyride, killing himself and a friend he had taken up with him. It was foolish, but they'd been drinking and had apparently lost all common sense, cramming two people into a cockpit suited for one.

Rosalie stopped at the door of the Mess. "You wouldn't do that, would you?" she asked Snug.

He grunted. "First of all, I grew up in a pub, so I know when to stop drinking. Second of all, I can barely fit myself into a Spit, let alone another person. Pity, though, losing a good pilot."

And Diana losing her fiancé.

Inside, Snug brought over tea, sandwiches, and the bun Rosalie had been hoping for, and then he took her mind off the incident with a story of his mum discovering that the local air raid warden was scavenging from bomb sites and selling on the black market. The fellow had managed to weasel out of the charges, Snug told her, but not the name his mum had stuck him with: Light Fingers Carter.

"I told Leslie about your mum running the pub, and he said he wished a woman could take over our village pub."

"Well, you tell him if he wants to see how a woman manages, he's welcome to stop into the Bishop's Finger just round the corner from Liverpool Street Underground."

"Your dad—is he not around?"

"He's never been around," Snug said in a matter-of-fact way. He pushed his empty sandwich plate aside and brushed a few crumbs from the table. "Mum's never said where he is. Or who he is."

An unmarried woman with a child to bring up—that's what Jean had avoided by entrusting her Robert to a cousin. But now the boy could have a father in Will. Still no word from Lime Farm on that front.

"It must've been tough on your mum all on her own," Rosalie said. "But I'm sure you were quite a good little boy for her, weren't you?"

Snug's head shot up. He looked as if he might snap at her; then he grinned.

"That's where your name comes from, isn't it?" she asked. "The pub?"

"Yeah. Mum would leave me in the snug because she knew the other women would keep an eye on me. More often than not, I'd wake up with my head on the lap of some lady I didn't even know."

"Does your mum own the pub?"

"She's worked there since just after I was born, so they tell me. But it's Mouse, my auntie, that owns it. Bought it in '31. She'd been an ambulance driver during the Great War and this bloke said she'd saved his life, and he left her a bit of money when he died."

"And now she's driving an ambulance in London," Rosalie said. "There's something that takes fortitude."

"She's got fortitude in spades, Mouse does."

"Mouse." Rosalie liked her. She liked his mum too.

"So, Wright, what's the word on the henhouse?"

Rosalie shook her head. "The wood is in worse condition than we thought. We'll need to wrap it with wire to hold it together, but we aren't going to find any wire anywhere, that's for certain. Still, we've pulled out and straightened all the nails and have put the best pieces in as posts. Just as well the hens haven't arrived."

Snug squinted his good eye at her. "Are they late?"

"Mrs. Potts's daughter's friend overpromised, apparently. We've been shifted to further down the list, and the birds are now expected to arrive within the month. So, if you've a spare afternoon and would like to lend a hand with the building, I know you'd be well compensated in eggs. Could you use them?"

"I could give them to George," Snug said. "I'm billeted with him. He runs a garage in the village, and my room's above it. All I've got is a spirit lamp to make tea."

A WAAF buzzed over to their table.

"Hiya, Snug. Hiya, Rosalie?"

"Hello, Marjorie," Rosalie said.

"We're talking chickens," Snug said.

Marjorie laughed and gave him a little slap on the arm. "Go on with you." She looked at Rosalie. "No, really, chickens?"

She didn't get an answer, because the duty officer put his head in the door of the Mess, spotted Rosalie, and came over. "We've a Lysander to go to Tangmere. You interested?"

"Might as well. I should be able to get back to Hamble from there."

Snug walked her out to the dispatch hut.

"Have you seen a Lancaster yet?" he asked. "Four-engine bomber. I'm going to the conversion course for it."

"Four-engine bomber?" Rosalie asked in awe. "That's class five. That means you'll be . . ."

Snug smiled. "First Officer Durrant."

"You'll be insufferable, won't you?"

"I'll try my best."

She laughed. "Well, I suppose you'll have earned it."

Chapter 13

August 1942

The days went by, and it seemed that ferrying took Rosalie everywhere except to Castle Camps in Essex—the one place she wanted to go.

She and Alan had exchanged several letters since the dance. He made only casual mentions of flying as a defensive night fighter. *It's as if when we're up there, we exist in a separate world.* And he made life at Castle Camps sound generally dull, apart from the NAAFI organizing a football match. *I don't know what we'd do without that bit of entertainment.*

Football and flying aside, each letter became more personal as they examined their evening together in detail, including the long good-bye at the oak tree. Rosalie spent quiet moments replaying the scene over and over. She felt his kisses on her lips, her neck. She remembered where he had put his hands, and where she wished he had put them. The dance had been weeks ago, but this was a fever that would not abate.

She slept fitfully, thrashing about in bed as images of Alan segued into thoughts of the crash that had killed ATA pilots. Of Bridget's engagement and how little time she'd had to live. Of Humphrey Gilbert being lost to Diana Barnato after only a month. Then, one late afternoon, Rosalie stopped in the waiting room before going back to Mrs. May's and found Catherine in tears on the sofa and Anne beside her.

"Missing isn't dead, you remember that," Anne said. She looked up at Rosalie, her eyes pleading for help. "Catherine's Bill has been reported missing."

Rosalie sat on the low table across from the women and put on the best face she could. She took Catherine's hand and looked straight into her red, swollen eyes. "Missing means that soon he'll be on the captured list. And, well, then, they will have taken him to a camp, probably, isn't that right? They'll have to treat him properly there—Geneva Convention and all that. Why, he might even be writing you a letter this very moment. And the Red Cross are taking care of the fellows, aren't they? He won't be lost to you."

Catherine nodded and attempted a smile, but her face was a study in misery. After a cup of tea, Anne took her off to her billet, and Rosalie returned to No. 6.

Catherine's news made the need to be with Alan too real. He flew night ops and had already lost men from his squadron—probably more than he mentioned. Rosalie flew aeroplanes in daylight, when she could see where she was going most of the time, and so she knew Alan's task was not an easy one, and certainly not safe.

A letter from him came in the post the next morning. She heard the flap on the letter box creak open and ran down the stairs, snatched the letter, and went back to her room to read it in private.

My darling, he wrote, *if only we could meet, I would have another memory to take along when we fly into the darkness. If I could see you, I would have the chance to speak my mind and my heart. I am able to get a break from ops, for a day—that is, night—or perhaps two. Shall I book you a room at Mrs. Colby's?*

That day, Rosalie ferried a Spitfire to Speke near Liverpool, where she had time for a cup of tea and her chocolate bar before returning to Hamble. Without another assignment, the rest of the day was hers.

Here it was, then, an opportunity. And like that, her decision was made. She went back to Mrs. May's and up to her room and wrote Alan.

I will come to you. Tell me the days and we will meet in a place no one knows us. Not Mrs. Colby's—somewhere we can be together.

That was clear enough, wasn't it? She read it over twice, sealed the letter up, and hurried down to the post office window in the local shop. Once the letter was on its way, her taut nerves eased.

It seemed her letter barely had time to arrive before it was answered. Alan had made discreet enquiries and learned of a small hotel nearby. He would have two days before the end of the month. *I will take care of everything,* he wrote.

From where Rosalie had stood at the beginning of August, the end of the month appeared as a distant dot in a murky future. How would she endure until then?

Rosalie kept Alan's reply in her pocket and spent the evening in the lounge with Mrs. May listening to the wireless. She wrote a letter home, remembering that Leslie was particularly interested in the Spitfire. *Do you know that if the field for takeoff is short, one or two of the ground crew must sit on the tail as we taxi! It's because the Spit is nose-heavy and needs a bit of extra help getting pointed into the air. Otherwise, it's a dream to fly.* Enough about aeroplanes. Perhaps her mum would say it was too much. She searched her mind for another snippet of news. *Snug's aunt is called Mouse and she's an ambulance driver in London. Wouldn't want to try that!*

A letter soon came from Alan to say arrangements had been made and he would see her next week. And that he loved her. Those words floated in her vision, obscuring details until she blinked and reread the letter.

In a slight panic, Rosalie went to Rees, Hamble's deputy CO, and asked for the days off.

"You're well due for two days. Home to the family?" she asked.

"It's been ages since I've seen them," Rosalie replied, with a stab of guilt at so adroitly lying and yet telling the truth at the same time.

That evening, she knew what she must do. She must talk with Caro.

All through their meal, Rosalie fiddled with her food until Mrs. May threatened to serve it to her again the next evening. She cleaned her plate in three bites.

Zofia was on kitchen duty, and Mrs. May went to switch on the wireless. Caro and Rosalie followed her in and listened to a radio play about . . . Rosalie had no idea what it was about. She attempted to knit, then looked at a magazine, all the while wondering how she could get Caro on her own without looking obvious. Zofia joined them eventually, and at the end of the evening, the landlady switched off the wireless and said, "I believe we can stretch the milk to include cups of cocoa tonight."

This was a rare event, although they knew the cocoa would be mostly dry milk and the fresh saved for accent.

"What a treat, Mrs. May," Caro said. "Zofia, could you help, and we'll be with you in just a minute. There's something I want to ask Rosalie. About the henhouse."

Mrs. May looked pleased at that. Zofia gave Caro a quizzical look but followed the landlady out. Caro pushed the door almost closed as Rosalie asked, "What about the henhouse?"

Caro sat across from her. "Forget the henhouse. I got the idea you have something on your mind. What is it?"

"Oh. Yes. I . . ." Rosalie, ever so grateful for Caro's intuition, found that the opportunity she sought had opened up, but she didn't know how to begin. She took a deep breath and dived in.

"Alan will have two days off ops soon. He wants me to go for a visit. He said he'd book me a room at Mrs. Colby's. I wrote back and said could he find a hotel where we could stay. Together." Her voice shook when she spoke, but perhaps Caro hadn't noticed. "And so he did, and it's Friday and that's three days from now, and I'm—"

"Are you having second thoughts?"

"No," Rosalie said emphatically, and Caro laughed. "No, but I wanted to tell you, because you're a sensible person and can give me advice on men."

Caro gave her a puzzled look. "Rosalie, love, I need to explain something." She shook her head. "No, never mind now. Look, first, as long as you're certain it's what you want, you need to be practical. He must wear protection."

Rosalie felt her face go hot. "He said he would take care of everything."

"You must make sure. It's best to say it outright."

"Caro, I can't ask him that!"

"You must be certain he has something, or else you may find yourself"—she dropped her voice to a whisper—"in the pudding club. And you don't want that, not now."

Jean's predicament had already come to Rosalie's mind. She swallowed hard. "All right. I'll do it." But how? Maybe instead she could go to a chemist herself and buy them. Did women do that?

Zofia called out from the kitchen, and they rose to go.

"What did you want to explain to me?" Rosalie asked.

Caro put an arm through hers. "Another time."

★　★　★

Two evenings later, Rosalie retired to her room directly after the meal, and soon after, Caro knocked.

"Oh, that's a lovely frock," she said, nodding at the navy-and-white dotted shirtdress laid out on Rosalie's bed.

"It's Anne's. I'm trying to sort out how to pack without crushing it. And Brenda gave me the loan of her shoes. I thought I might have to wear my uniform skirt, but now I believe I'll look quite presentable."

"Even better than how you'll look," Caro said, reaching in her pocket, "is being prepared. I've sorted something out for you, just in case Alan hasn't."

She handed over two small, sealed, square paper packets with a picture of a woman in a flouncy dress and wearing an enormous sun hat with a bunch of roses on it. She held a fan in front of her and stood in a garden, as if she had no idea what might be inside the packet.

Rosalie knew what it was. A French letter. Just thinking the words made her feel racy.

"She looks happy enough, doesn't she?" Rosalie said, and they both burst out in a fit of giggles. "Did you go to the chemist for them?"

"Never you mind," Caro said. "You just . . . have a lovely time."

"Yes, thanks." Rosalie had feared that Caro might want to go over the basics of lovemaking with her before she left and was both relieved and disappointed when she didn't try. It wasn't the basics Rosalie needed to know—she'd grown up on a farm, after all—but she was unsure of the nuances.

★   ★   ★

Rosalie had wanted to change out of her uniform before arriving at the hotel so that she would look like a civilian when they checked in. So she would look like a wife, because that's how they were booked, of course. Mr. and Mrs. . . . something. Alan hadn't said, and she hadn't asked. But changing clothes at the airfield meant that others would see and wonder and comment. No, better to stay in uniform.

He waited for her at the edge of the duty officer's building, leaning against the wall and smoking. He dropped the cigarette the moment he saw her and stamped on it, coming out to meet her and taking her bag and parachute. They stood for a moment and smiled at each other.

Then a car motored up behind him. "Here now," Alan said, "one of the drivers will give us a lift."

In a cold rush of fear, Rosalie imagined Ellen as the driver leaving them off at a hotel and then telling her mother back at home and then her mother telling Rosalie's mum what was going on with her daughter.

"He's got a delivery, so we're on his way."

He—that was all right, then.

Rosalie had yet to mention Alan to her family. The only people who knew about him were at Hamble, and apart from Caro, they knew him only as some fellow she was seeing. She had examined this reluctance to tell her mum and brothers of Alan's existence and decided that although her feelings for Alan were anything but casual, they were private, and that for the moment, she'd prefer them to stay that way.

The driver let them off at a small hotel with a hanging sign in need of repainting that displayed three white feathers. The place had probably seen better days before the war, but it looked like the Ritz to Rosalie. There was a man at the desk who looked up at their entry and offered a welcoming smile. He introduced himself as Wilkes.

Rosalie stood to Alan's side and a little behind as he signed the book. The man spun it back toward him and said, "Mr. and Mrs. Jones, lovely to have you here at the Feathers. Here now, let me take your bags. Perhaps you'd like a drink in the bar before dinner? My wife is a dab hand at making do, and we have fish on the menu this evening—actual fish from our own waters, which are not the safest place these days, you can imagine, but then there you are, anything for our guests."

It was only when he came out from behind the desk that Rosalie saw he had one leg shorter than the other and walked as if he were aboard a rocking ship. He took her bag and parachute and made for the stairs, and Alan said, "Oh now, sir, allow me to—"

"Not a bit of it. If I'm not to fight, then I will do my part to make you RAF boys as comfortable as you can be." He puffed as he went up the stairs but kept talking. "We intended to put in a lift, but then the war came and what have you. Still, you're on the first floor, so not too far." At the landing he nodded to a closed door marked LAVATORY. "Necessary and bath on your right. And here we are."

He unlocked the door of the room and stood back for Rosalie to enter, then carried in her bag and parachute and Alan's bag, setting them inside.

"Good evening," Mr. Wilkes said.

Rosalie remained just inside the room and Alan just outside as they watched the man plod down the stairs. When the thumping had ceased, Alan turned to her.

"Why don't I head down to the bar, and you can—" He waved his hand into the room.

"Get ready for dinner," Rosalie offered. "Yes, I'll see you down there directly."

"Good." They stood looking at each other for a moment, and then he leaned across the threshold and kissed her.

"Are you all right with this?" Alan asked.

"It was my idea, remember."

"I don't want you to think . . ." he began, then faltered. "I want you to know I have something . . . protection. I would never—"

Rosalie kissed him again, relieved that the packets with the flouncy lady could remain at the bottom of her bag.

"On your way now," she said. When the door closed, it took her only five minutes before she showed up at his side in the bar with her hair patted down. She even wore a bit of lipstick borrowed from Brenda. Rosalie had applied it so sparingly that when she looked at herself in the mirror, she couldn't tell any difference.

Alan was jolly during their meal, and Rosalie wasn't sure if he was trying to put her or himself at ease. The food was all they had expected. That is, not terribly good. They broke into silent laughter as they attempted to identify what "fish" this was that they were eating. They talked of the weather to avoid talking about the war. Rosalie explained why in spring some crops shouldn't be planted until the ground had dried out. The meal was interminable and, at the same time, went by in a flash.

They were served cups of dreadful coffee after the meal and drank them even as they speculated on the contents, coming to the conclusion that it might be little more than warm water colored with gravy browning. Their conversation petered out, and Rosalie worried what to do next.

"Would you like to go on up?" Alan asked. "Why don't I stop in the bar first?"

"Yes. All right."

Upstairs, she quickly changed into Brenda's silk nightgown— even Rosalie knew her usual striped pajamas would not do—and stood there waiting and shivering until there was a quiet knock. She let Alan in, and there they stood.

"Hello," he said.

"Hello."

"Rosalie, are you sure?" he asked, and she erupted in a huff of indignation.

"Yes, I'm sure," she said. "Why do people keep asking me if I'm sure?"

Alan looked alarmed. "Who keeps asking?"

She waved the question away. "No one. That is, Caro, my friend."

Alan reached out and stroked Rosalie's arm, and a flood of longing shot through her body, banishing her worries. If she could figure out midflight how to land an aeroplane she'd never flown before, surely she could manage this.

★   ★   ★

It was an odd journey back to Hamble after two nights with Alan—odd in that Rosalie couldn't quite remember how she'd got there. She vaguely recalled Alan putting her on a bus that took her to the gates of RAF Debden. There, he said, she would be in a better position to catch an air taxi south. He had been right. And so here it was, the afternoon of the same day she'd left him watching her bus pull away.

The usual group occupied the waiting room toward the end of the day, and Rosalie found herself drawn to them while still unsure of how she came to have so many friends. Caro gave her a quick look, and Anne said, "You look rested." Rosalie blushed.

Grace looked up from her cards. "Oh good, we need a fourth. You play bridge, don't you?"

"Sorry, no I don't. I played Happy Families at home."

"We played Happy Families too," Caro said. "I was always keen to get the first four for a set, no matter if it was Bung the brewer or Grist the miller. Lovely to have a complete family."

"But to what end, Caro?" Grace said, going back to her cards. "Where has that got you—it isn't as if you'll have your own happy family, is it?"

Catherine, across the table from Grace, said, "I doubt if a card game is meant to prepare you for life."

"Are you defending her?" Grace asked with wide-eyed inno-cence. "What would your Methodist father say?"

Catherine laid down her bridge hand. "I'm done in, girls. See you tomorrow."

That broke up the group. Rosalie, Caro, and Zofia walked home silently, each with her own thoughts. Rosalie wanted to bring up Grace and her attacks against Caro, but inside No. 6, Mrs. May called them into the kitchen.

"See here," she said with a flourish toward a clear glass crock on the table. It held an egg in water.

"Shouldn't the water be boiling if you're cooking it?" Caro asked.

"It isn't cooking, it's preserving," Mrs. May explained, "and it isn't water, it's water glass. This is an *experiment*."

"You are Marie Sklodowska Curie," Zofia said, and nodded. "She was Polish, you know. A woman and a scientist."

"It's like isinglass, isn't it?" Rosalie asked. "Mum used that occa-sionally. It'll keep the eggs for six months, and you can still use them."

"Isinglass is hard to come by now," Mrs. May said. "Or so I'm told."

"When we do finally have hens," Caro said, "won't we want to eat the eggs fresh?"

"But the hens won't lay much in winter, if at all," Mrs. May said. "This way we'll be able to keep some for the slow time."

"How do we know it works?" Caro asked, squinting at the experiment.

"If you crack the egg open and it smells bad," Rosalie said, "then it didn't work."

Caro frowned. "Whose rationed egg are we sacrificing to this trial?"

"You'll thank me in the end," Mrs. May said. "Off with you now, and let me cook the meal. I've added a bit of minced Spam to the Woolton pie. Bless the Americans."

The three trooped up the stairs, and at the first-floor landing, Zofia disappeared into their room, but Caro hesitated.

"You look happy," she said to Rosalie. "Everything went well?"

Rosalie nodded and smiled and might have gone a bit pink. What words were there to describe how she felt after this most important event—her first time with a man? With Alan. "Yes, it was . . . Alan was . . ." Startling. Overwhelming. Calming.

Caro patted her on the arm. "That's all I needed to know."

In her room, Rosalie began a letter to Will, hoping she could ask in a roundabout way—in case her mum read it—about little Robert. For a while now, she'd been meaning to offer them more of this "support" her brother had asked for in January, nearly nine months ago. But her support could come only after their mum knew about Jean's son, so really the question to Will was: Have you told her? She couldn't figure out how to word that. Perhaps she should learn a secret code the way spies did. Rosalie left the letter unfinished and went downstairs to the lavatory. Caro and Zofia's door was partly open, and she paused when she heard Grace's name mentioned.

"I don't mind what she says," Zofia said, "but that it hurts you."

"She can't hurt me," Caro replied. "I feel sorry for her."

"She looks for the opportunity to . . ." Zofia paused. "It's like her words are a knife."

"She's afraid," Caro said. "She is afraid she will never have love. And so, she tries to push her anger off on others."

"I don't know how you can be so kind to her," Zofia said.

Rosalie agreed, and pushed open their door to say so. She stopped when she saw Caro and Zofia in each other's arms and kissing— not the way Caro kissed Rosalie, on the cheek, but the way Rosalie kissed Alan and he kissed her back.

For a moment, she didn't move, and then Caro and Zofia broke apart. Rosalie fled into the lavatory, closing the door quietly and holding stock-still. She heard the two women in quiet conversation, and then there was a knock.

"Rosalie?" Caro asked.

"Yes?" Rosalie leapt back from the door and called, far too loudly, "Sorry—what?"

"Are you all right?"

"Fine. Am I taking too long? Is the meal ready? I'll see you down there." She sank down on the edge of the tub.

"No hurry. I only—"

Rosalie turned the tap on full, but only for a few seconds or Mrs. May would be up to find out why she was wasting water.

She stayed where she was and went over what she'd seen. Then gradually she began to make sense of it, piecing together images from their life at No. 6. Caro and Zofia under the mistletoe, sitting on the sofa holding hands, dancing quite close to music from the wireless. She recalled Grace's cutting remarks aimed at Caro. Light began to dawn.

Was Rosalie the only one who hadn't known? Mortified at having eavesdropped—as well as being a dullard—and unwilling to chance running into Caro on the landing, she waited ten minutes before cracking the door open an inch and peeking out. Their bedroom door was closed, and so she crept upstairs and soundlessly closed her own. A moment later, there was a knock.

"Rosalie, may I come in, please?" Caro asked.

"Yes, of course." Rosalie opened the door, and Caro slipped through and closed it behind her.

"Come on, let's sit down. You saw us, I know, and I want to explain."

"You don't have to explain anything," Rosalie said, hoping she would. "I know about these things."

"Do you?"

Not really. At school, she'd heard talk about one of the girls who preferred to be around other girls and would never be "the marrying sort," but few details were provided and Rosalie had no close friends with whom she could dissect what little she understood. Only since leaving Lime Farm had she realized how much she'd missed out on learning the ways of the world.

"Look," Caro said, "it's like this. The way you and Alan feel about each other, that's how Zofia and I feel. We're different like that and have been our whole lives—it's just the way it is. This upsets

Grace, and that's why she's always saying things to me like she did earlier."

Rosalie thought about Alan and her love for him and tried to imagine how it might be like that with Caro and Zofia. Could she understand that? Maybe or maybe not, but what she did know for certain was that this was Caro, Rosalie's first true friend. No, more than that—Caro was a sister to her. They could share anything. And yet Caro had been reluctant to tell her this.

"Is this what you've been wanting to explain to me?" Rosalie asked.

"Yes, and I'm sorry it's taken me so long."

"It isn't your fault—I should've known. Perhaps I did know. At least I could've cottoned on to those terrible things Grace says to you."

Caro shook her head, and her short, straight hair fell down onto her forehead. "Don't pay her any mind—it doesn't bother me, not really."

But Rosalie knew Caro well enough to see that it did, and hot indignation rose up in her. "Well, it bothers me," she said, with such force that it startled the both of them.

They laughed, but Caro's eyes filled with tears—an almost unheard-of betrayal of emotions. "Are you all right about it, then?" she asked. "You're dear to me, and I wouldn't want to think this changes our friendship in any way."

Rosalie hugged her. "Of course I'm all right with it." Although she thought it might take some getting used to. Caro probably knew that too. "But I'll tell you this—that Grace had better watch what she says."

★ ★ ★

Her brother Will must've understood Rosalie's unwritten question in her last letter, because he wrote in late August to tell her he'd met little Robert for the first time and what a fine boy he was and how they sincerely hoped he would be coming to live at Lime Farm, but that would have to wait. *You know how it is, Rags—it isn't easy to change*

Mum's mind about anything. Recently, she's just been on about the daughter of someone in the WI and how she's unmarried and off living with a distant aunt and now waiting for a baby to come. It's too close to how it was for Jean and it was a difficult conversation, as we had to listen and say nothing. We don't want to tell her quite yet. So, we knock on together, and hope for the right moment.

Leslie wrote and asked about Ellen after Rosalie had mentioned meeting her at Castle Camps. Also, he wanted to know if Rosalie had gone to the dance with Snug. What an odd thing to ask. At least, that was her first reaction, but then she reminded herself she'd yet to mention Alan.

She had been relieved to find that Alan felt the same sort of protectiveness of their relationship. In bed the second morning of their time together, he had said, "I don't see why we should tell just anyone right now. What we have is ours alone, and private. Does that make sense?"

It had made great sense to her, but it was more difficult to explain to Caro, who had good reason for keeping her relationship with Zofia on the quiet side but couldn't see why Rosalie and Alan felt the need.

"You don't wonder if he's hiding something?" Caro asked.

"This wasn't his idea," Rosalie explained. "I'm the one who wants to keep quiet, and he thinks the same. It won't be a secret forever."

"And when you say *secret*," Caro said, "what you mean is a secret from your family?"

"Have you told your father about Zofia?" Rosalie asked, hoping to deflect attention and, at the same time, make a point.

A slow smile spread over Caro's face. "Yes," she said, "I have."

"What did he say?"

"It can't be easy for him," Caro said, "but he's a good dad. The way you talk about your pop reminds me of my dad. He wants me to be happy, and he knows what makes me happy isn't the same for other people. He wants to meet Zofia."

"Wouldn't that be lovely?" Rosalie said.

"And now, returning to my original point—your family may not know about Alan, but you do realize that everyone here knows?"

Perhaps she and Alan had more in common with Caro and Zofia than it might seem. But the atmosphere at the ferry pool was rather like that of a large, close, yet disjointed family. And, apart from Grace, no one seemed to be terribly bothered.

Previously unaware of the difference between Caro and Zofia's relationship and hers with Caro, Rosalie now wondered how she hadn't seen it all along. The way they could communicate with a look or smile or the squeeze of a hand. And they were happy with each other. They were both dear to her—Caro more so, of course—and Rosalie hoped the best for them.

★   ★   ★

On the last day of August and without any warning, Snug appeared at No. 6. He arrived just as Rosalie was leaving for the pool a few minutes behind Caro and Zofia and said he'd come to help with the henhouse. He was out of uniform—wearing a flat cap, canvas trousers, a brown jumper, and a jacket that had pockets stuffed with wire, which he said he'd got off a fellow who had it spare in his shed from long before the war. It looked rusty enough, and so she believed him.

The landlady had gone with Mrs. Potts to a Women's Institute meeting in Southampton to talk of the WI setting up a market stall, and so Rosalie handed over the henhouse plans and left Snug to it.

"Make yourself a cuppa when you want. I'll see you later," she called as she left, with only a twinge of guilt that Snug would be on the ground while she flew.

Rosalie had only one aeroplane to ferry that day. She took an Oxford to Little Rissington and returned to No. 6 in the early afternoon to find Snug putting the finishing touches on as complete a structure in the back garden as she could hope, held together with old nails and bound with rusty wire.

"Would you look at that? Where did you come up with a hinge?" she asked, lifting up the door on the nest box and peering in. Snug stood by, arms crossed like a genie admiring his work. "Looks fine.

With a few handfuls of straw and a branch for a roost, we're in business." She glanced behind them at the garden bed. "And see here, you didn't even trample the cabbages. I'd say you've earned your lunch."

"And just in time," he replied. A fine mist had begun to fall, and Snug took off his flat cap and gave it a shake before following her into the kitchen, where she put the kettle on and made them sandwiches from the last tin of fish paste. They sat across from each other at the table.

Snug swallowed a mouthful of sandwich, chased it down with a swig of tea, and said, "Have you heard back from the accident committee about that thing with the—"

"The incident with that Anson pilot full of himself?" Rosalie filled in.

"I was going to say the incident with the cows," Snug said, and she laughed.

"I've received the letter," she said officiously. " 'The pilot of the Tiger Moth, SO Rosalie Wright, is held not responsible.' " It had been a relief to see those words.

"Good on you."

When Snug reached for the teapot, Rosalie spotted a hole the size of a half crown in the side of his jumper.

"Here now, take that off and give it to me," she said.

He paused midpour. "Sorry?"

"You don't want that to get any bigger. Come on, now, off with it. I can do a bit of repair, and it'll last longer."

Snug's cheeks colored. "I've only my vest on underneath."

"Well then, put your jacket back on. Now, off with it."

She turned to the sink to give him a bit of privacy, and when he thrust the jumper at her, she took it upstairs to her room, found a reasonable match to the yarn, and took her darning tools back down with her. She drank her tea and ate her sandwich while she worked and they talked.

"Do you remember that feeling the first time you went up solo?" Snug asked, looking out the window to the gray weather. "How light you felt, how—"

"Free," Rosalie said, thinking of being alone in Reg's Gipsy Moth, nose to the sky. "Like it was yesterday. I still feel that, don't you?"

"Yeah."

"When did you first take lessons?" Rosalie asked.

"Five years ago, starting when I was about eighteen. One of the regulars at the pub knew a fellow who owned his own aeroplane, and Mum was looking for something to occupy my time to keep me out of trouble. You?"

"Five years ago for me too. I had to wait until I was sixteen."

"Funny that."

They looked at each other, silent for a moment, and Rosalie's fingers paused over their darning.

Then the front door flew open and they both jumped.

"Rosalie!" Caro shouted.

"In here!" Rosalie's heart leapt to her throat.

Caro and Zofia came tumbling into the kitchen, holding hands, with flushed faces and smiles. In her free hand, Zofia waved a letter.

"They are in France! My mother and my sister are in Vichy!"

Rosalie leapt up and embraced first Zofia and then Caro. Snug joined the celebration too, standing and taking the letter that was thrust at him.

"It is a letter from my mother trying to find me, and it was passed from hand to hand until it arrived at Central Ferry Control," Zofia said.

"Pauline Gower kept asking questions on behalf of all the Polish pilots," Caro explained. "And it paid off."

"That's the best news," Rosalie said.

"They escape Poland, but could take nothing with them," Zofia said. "Nothing from our home—but they are safe. Perhaps now my mother will be chemist to help win the war."

Caro looked round the kitchen, and at the heap of jumper on the kitchen table. "Well, what's all this?"

Snug had buttoned his jacket, but now he pulled the lapels together, too late to hide the fact he had little on underneath.

Rosalie retrieved her darning. "A small repair job on his jumper. It was the least I could do." She waved out to the back garden. "Look what we have ready and waiting."

Caro flung open the door and observed from the threshold. "Well done. I'd say this calls for a double celebration. We're going down the Bugle. Who's for it?"

"Oh yes," Rosalie said, and lifted her eyebrows at Snug. "Perhaps Brenda will come along."

"Everyone will be there," Caro said. "We've already spread the word. We'll dash up and change out of our uniforms. You'll change too, won't you, Rosalie?"

"Yes, let me just finish this off." She plopped down into her chair, and a few stitches later, the hole in Snug's jumper had vanished. She thrust it at him and said, "You get yourself dressed. And could you write a note to Mrs. May and tell her where we've gone?"

Rosalie skipped up the stairs, catching a bit of the chatter from Zofia and Caro's room on her way up. By the time she returned to the kitchen, wearing nonuniform trousers and her red sweater, Snug had both his jumper and jacket on.

"Here now," Rosalie said. She stood on tiptoe to reach up and pull the collar of his jacket out straight and then let her hands slide down his lapels.

"Thanks," he said.

"Well, thanks for the henhouse."

Caro cleared her throat. Rosalie turned to see her watching them and dropped her hands.

"Ready?" Caro asked.

★   ★   ★

They made a jolly group at the pub. There were the women pilots, the men who worked maintenance at the ferry pool, and a couple of RAF pilots Brenda had invited back from Eastleigh. A few stood at the bar, but Rosalie sat next to Snug on the long settle against the wall, with Caro on the other side of him and Zofia next to her. Anne took a seat beside Rosalie, and Brenda took the end of the table with an RAF pilot on either side. They raised their glasses to Pauline Gower and to the hope that the ATA might one day soon return to France, something they hadn't done since May 1940.

On the walk back, Rosalie found herself next to Brenda. "So, you and Snug . . ." she started.

"Me and Snug?" Brenda asked, and laughed. "You might as well put any name in place of mine."

"Are you not . . . ?"

"Snug's good fun, if you know what I mean," Brenda said, wiggling her eyebrows. "But that's all it is. Nothing serious on either side. So you don't have to worry."

"Me? No, I'm seeing someone. You know that. He's an RAF pilot at Castle Camps."

"Oh yes, that's right," Brenda said. "Mosquitoes, isn't it?"

"Yes. Alan Chersey. Do you know him?"

"I believe I've seen him on a delivery," Brenda said. "He's quite a catch."

Rosalie agreed. And it could still surprise her that she was the one who'd caught him.

CHAPTER 14

September 1942

A month elapsed before Rosalie heard from Alan, although she'd written him twice. Each morning, she haunted the front entry at No. 6, hoping to catch the post when it arrived, longing to see Alan's scratchy writing on an envelope. She had relived the two days they'd spent together over and over, but what of him? Did he have regrets?

At last, one warm morning in the middle of the month, a letter shot through the slot and straight into Rosalie's hands. She held it against her racing heart for a moment, then took it into the kitchen and poured herself a cup of tea.

The back door stood open and the sun spilled onto the kitchen floor. Rosalie heard the blackbirds *tuk-tuk* and saw Mrs. May bent over a garden bed. The landlady went out most mornings these days to admire the henhouse, which still awaited its lodgers, and then do a bit of hoeing and digging. The blackbirds had learned her ways and kept a close eye on the proceedings, rushing in the moment she turned over a worm.

Caro and Zofia hadn't come down yet, and the place was quiet apart from the molten *plop* of the porridge on the hob. Rosalie sat at the kitchen table and read Alan's single-page letter five times over. He made barely a mention of Mosquitoes, the squadron, or the war—

not even the most recent football match—and instead focused on his longing for their next meeting. *I cannot say when it will be*, he wrote, *but know that until you are in my arms again, you are always in my thoughts.*

She tucked the letter away just as Caro and Zofia came down the stairs and into the kitchen discussing ATA policies.

"What do you think?" Caro asked Rosalie. "If they said to you, 'Do you want a working radio in your aeroplane?' would you say, 'Yes, please?'"

"You know, I don't think I would," Rosalie replied. "It's rather nice being all on our own up there, no one telling us what to do."

After breakfast, they headed to the ferry pool. Along the way, Rosalie gave her pocket a pat and felt Alan's letter there, waiting for her to read it again. Perhaps after takeoff, when she was alone in the sky.

The sight of the chitties lined out on the table in the assignment room each morning brought hope to Rosalie. When she had located hers, the first thing she did was scan her destinations, and only after that did she look to see what aeroplanes she would fly. She had hoped to be assigned a delivery to Castle Camps so that she and Alan could at least lay eyes on each other, perhaps have tea and toast in the Mess and a quiet moment somewhere. But it was not to be that day.

Or any other. The weeks marched on, and it seemed as if Rosalie went to every other RAF base in England and Scotland except Alan's. In her most emotional and least rational moments, it was not an exaggeration to say that she began to feel as if the war, the RAF, and probably the King himself were all to blame for her flying schedule.

Rosalie had thought it might be possible to orchestrate a journey by patching air taxis together and ending at Alan's airfield, but when she tried it, she ended up at RAF Cark in Cumbria, about as far away from her destination as she could get. She didn't arrive back at Hamble until the next morning. That took some explaining.

But at last, one clear, golden day in late September, her assignment was to fly the Anson taxi herself, and one of her stops was Castle Camps.

She wouldn't arrive there until the afternoon, which would be for the best, because Alan didn't fly until it was dark, and so his days started late. *Our workday begins at sunset*, he had written. *Many nights we sit out in the dispatch hut waiting for orders that never come, and other evenings we're off on the spot and don't return until dawn.*

Rosalie spent the day in high spirits, delivering and collecting pilots at three other airfields. At last, she carried one pilot to Castle Camps—a woman from the ATA ferry pool at Cosford who had the job of cranking up the undercarriage all to herself. At the airfield, Rosalie's instructions were to wait for two pilots who would be delivering Mosquitoes and then to fly them to Aston Down. When she put down, they hadn't arrived, and with perhaps only thirty minutes free, she went in search of Alan.

She made directly for the Mess, where she found a scattering of men but no Alan. Back out through the swing door she went, and paused. Should she enquire at RAF command? Would they really care to look up her boyfriend for her? She imagined his commanding officer as a gray-whiskered, blustering leftover from the last war, yelling, "Chersey, some woman came demanding I wake you up. You just remember what your duty is here, young man, or you'll never make squadron leader." No, that wouldn't do. Rosalie hesitated at the edge of a small grassy area, uncertain of her strategy. Time was running out.

"Rosalie?"

Ellen stood near the door to the WAAF canteen.

"Hello," Rosalie said, crossing to her, relieved for the distraction, even if it was Ellen.

"Are you here for—"

"Delivering and collecting pilots," Rosalie said, before Ellen could ask if she was there to see Alan. Of course she was there to see him, much good it was doing her.

There was an awkward moment, and then Ellen said, "It must be terribly exciting flying aeroplanes. I remember when you took your lessons all those years ago. I was impressed. Did you think this is what you'd be doing?"

Impressed? Rosalie remembered a cool incredulity from the other girls at school when they learned of her passion. "Well, I didn't know about the war or the ATA, but I knew I wanted to fly. And how is it for you, being a driver?"

Ellen shrugged. "A bit less exciting than I expected. Have you seen Alan?"

"He isn't around, apparently. He's probably still asleep, you know, because of the schedule he flies."

Ellen glanced over her shoulder back to the WAAF canteen, or perhaps beyond, and Rosalie looked too but saw nothing. "Do you have time for a cup of tea?" Ellen asked.

The war did odd things to people—apparently, even making Ellen into a friend.

"I'm sorry, I don't today. I need to see about my aeroplane."

"Yeah, sure," Ellen said. "Well, if you've got an extra minute, you could walk back the long way, just in case Alan is about." She waved her hand in a wide circle. "You know, off and around the back of the canteen."

"I will, thanks," Rosalie said. "Next time we'll have that cuppa."

They parted, and Rosalie took the route Ellen had advised, in case she was watching.

When she turned the corner of a building, she saw him next to a Nissen hut with one of the blister barns beyond. He was standing with Deborah Barlow, who wore her brown NAAFI uniform, her auburn hair wound round and pinned neatly just under her brimmed hat.

They were talking, that's all. Deborah was leaning back against the building, and Alan, cigarette in one hand, had his other hand resting flat against the wall. But seeing them caught Rosalie by such surprise that she froze, wanting to continue and, at the same time, to flee—and feeling the fool for her indecision.

She took a step back, and the movement must've caught Alan's attention, for he looked over at her. At first, his face was a blank; then it broke into a look of sheer joy. He tossed away his cigarette and loped over.

"I can't believe this," he said, holding her at arm's length for a look. "You aren't a dream, are you?—because I'll be terribly disappointed. That's all I've had of you are dreams, and they aren't nearly enough."

She laughed at his enthusiasm, and when he kissed her, she returned it. Was such a public display allowed? Her eyes flitted over to where Deborah Barlow had stood, but she was gone. Rosalie and Alan seemed to be in a quiet spot, with the airfield's activity just beyond reach.

"I looked for you in the Mess," Rosalie said, "but you weren't there. I'm walking back to my aeroplane and just happened to come this way." But then she remembered it hadn't been an accident. Ellen had suggested the route.

"Well, I'm the lucky one, then," Alan said, and pulled her close. "Can you stay? At least for a while? Or even overnight? Then I might be able see you in the morning. We couldn't . . . it would have to be . . . it's only that I've missed you so."

That made the weeks of waiting worth it. Or almost.

"I can't stay. I'm the taxi pilot today, and I've got to get going." She stroked his cheek. "You could walk me to the duty officer's hut."

"With pleasure." Giving her his arm, he winked. "No, not exactly *pleasure*—not when I'm sending you on your way."

She reported for her assignment with Alan by her side, and the duty officer nodded to the Anson. "Your two pilots are out there."

"Right, thanks. If there's no one else, I'll be off."

But outside the hut, Alan took her elbow and led her to just inside the nearest blister barn and out of view. Rosalie backed up against the wall and slipped her arms round Alan's neck, hoping those fellows working on the Mosquito across the way would mind their own business.

Alan kissed her until she was breathless and then held her tightly.

"It isn't good to be so far apart," he said.

Rosalie agreed, but said, "I must go now."

They parted on the edge of the runway, and she made her way to the Anson. She called to the ground crew that she was ready and climbed up to find one of her pilot-passengers at the door of the aeroplane. It was Snug.

"Nothing like a bit of recreation in the middle of the day, Wright."

Her face flamed as she pushed past him. "I'm not late. It's your choice if you want to sit on the aeroplane waiting." Rosalie nodded to her other passenger—a woman with a book in her hand—and made her way forward.

Rosalie strapped in and began muttering her takeoff drill. "Hydraulics, trimmers, throttle, mixture, pitch . . ."

Snug took the navigator's seat. "So, that was Chersey?"

She whipped her head round. "Who told you?"

He looked out the window. "Andrews mentioned him."

Caro? Why did she . . .

"Now," Rosalie said in an officious manner, "let me just make sure I have my proper passengers. You would be First Officer Durrant. Wait, what did you say your Christian name was?" Rosalie lifted her eyebrows.

He glowered at her.

"Well, never mind," she said. "So, will you be bringing up the undercarriage all on your own?" She looked past Snug to the other pilot, who glanced up from her book and gave Rosalie a smile. Snug grunted.

When she landed at Aston Down, the ground crew scrambled around the Anson as the female passenger left and Snug remained.

"Tea?" Snug asked.

"I should get back," Rosalie replied, busying herself with wiping off the screen of the altimeter, desperate for that cup of tea as soon as he'd mentioned it.

"Are you in a hurry?"

"It's half past four," she said, not looking at him. "They'll be expecting me at Hamble."

"It's daylight for another four hours, Wright. Worried you won't be able to find your way back?"

She spun round in her seat. "I'm well able to—" He tried to swallow his grin, but she had seen it, and she let go of her anger. "All right, then. Tea."

It had become rather a habit with them. Rosalie often went through Aston Down, because it was not only a ferry pool but also an RAF base and a maintenance unit. That made it a frequent destination for her, delivering or collecting aeroplanes that needed to be or had been repaired, ferrying aircraft needed by the RAF to other bases, and even flying those that were fit only for scrap. Most of the time through the late summer and into autumn, if Rosalie didn't see Snug in the Mess, she'd track him down to find out if he was up for a cup of tea.

One midday in early October, she learned that he had returned that morning after a fifteen-day stretch of ferrying planes and had gone to his billet above the garage for a kip. She walked into the village, found the garage, and tossed pebbles up to his window to rouse him. She could hear him shouting even before he opened the window. At last he put his head out, saw her, and said, "Bloody hell, Wright."

"It's a lovely day," she called up, "and you shouldn't spend it sleeping. I've sandwiches and a flask of tea. Come out for a walk."

They took their lunch out to a gentle slope above a field of barley. Rosalie lay back in the brown grass and stared up into the sky.

"The chickens arrived," she told him.

"How's the egg supply?"

"Nonexistent—they're too young. Even so, Mrs. May goes out every morning to encourage them. She'll be terribly disappointed if they don't start laying before winter."

"Have you been back to Lime Farm for a visit?" he asked.

"Not since the wedding. I mean to, but it hasn't worked out. You know how busy we get." It wasn't much of an answer. "I doubt they miss me, anyway. It's quite a lively place these days, with the Land Girls in the stables and Will and Jean in the house along with Mum and Leslie. And one day, Jean's little boy will be there too."

She'd said it in such a matter-of-fact way, it didn't occur to her that Snug was the first person she'd told about little Robert. And yet, it didn't feel as if she was betraying a confidence. If anyone could understand the situation of a child with no father, he could. She filled in the rest of the details.

"Will wants him to live at Lime Farm just as much as Jean does. He would be such a good father—just like Pop."

"Your mum," Snug said, "she knows?"

"Not yet. At least, I don't think. I'm sure they'll work it out, though. After all, a boy needs his mum." She sat up. "Do you ever go back to the pub for a visit?"

"I was there a few weeks ago, just looking in."

"Do you write them? You know, to keep them up on things." Rosalie thought of the steady flow of letters between No. 6 and Lime Farm.

"I'm not much for writing letters," Snug said. "Hang on now." He reached up to pull a stem of dried grass from Rosalie's curls.

She combed her fingers through, came up with several other bits, and laughed. "I'm like a dust mop. So, the pub—the Bishop's Finger? Were they in the thick of it during the Blitz? Did they go to a shelter?"

"They're not far from Liverpool Street Underground station. Loads of people use it as a shelter, but not my mum. They have a Morrison shelter right in the back of the kitchen behind the pub. Looks like a bloody great wire cage. Air raid sounds, the three of them—Mum, Mouse, and her friend—pop under it."

"I've seen photos of a Morrison," Rosalie said. "I always thought it would make a fine henhouse. Good protection against foxes, you know. Must be sturdy."

"It had better be. I'm the one put it together for them."

They were quiet. Rosalie lay back in the grass again and had closed her eyes, about to drift off, when Snug stretched out and propped himself up on his elbows.

"So, how is Chersey? You see much of him?"

Rosalie opened one eye. "No. But it's the war, isn't it?" How easily Snug annoyed her, and to hit back, she said, "You should've asked Marjorie to come along with us this afternoon."

"What would Marjorie want with going for a walk?" Snug said, sounding fairly annoyed himself.

Rosalie made a little noise. "Or one of your others."

He laughed. "Here now, open up those sandwiches."

★ ★ ★

The next afternoon, she collected a Miles Magister and took off for Biggin Hill near London, where the RAF used the light aircraft as a trainer. Open cockpit. The wind whipped her hair into a frenzy, but she was heading east, and so the sun wasn't in her eyes. All in all, it was a pleasant flight until, near her destination, her engine cut out.

The world went silent in an instant. The aeroplane floated on as every nerve in Rosalie's body came alive. She tried restarting the engine. Nothing.

Out the window, she could see Biggin Hill growing closer. It was a large aerodrome, but she knew her destination and made for it. She was at five hundred feet and pushed the stick forward to drop gradually, attempting to slow her breathing, although her heart was racing. She cleared her head except for one goal—to put down in one piece. She'd never wanted to be the pilot of a glider, but here she was and she'd make the best of it.

No time for circling the field for a proper look at her surroundings, but a quick glance round told her there were no other aeroplanes about. Then she remembered how that Anson had come out of nowhere. If another plane appeared, it would be the other pilot's job to keep out of her way, because she could do nothing. Perhaps someone on the ground had seen her already and realized there was a problem and would . . . what? Well, at least they would have the fire tanker waiting. With that thought, cold fear shot through her veins. *Don't think that. It will be all right.* If she could touch down at a reasonable speed, she would be able to brake and everything would be fine. But with no engine, she had no way to throttle back while she was still in the air.

Perhaps I should make that circuit after all. Yes, that's what I'll do. I don't think even Biggin Hill has a runway long enough for me to touch down at this speed. Once on the ground, I can brake. And that will work fine, won't it? Perhaps their field is plenty long enough. Keep that in mind, Rosalie—there are always options.

There are always options—that's what Reg used to say to her during lessons, and when she remembered that the Magister was much like her old Gipsy Moth, a sob caught in her throat.

She took in a ragged breath. *Flaps down. Now, then, get hold of yourself, Wright. What would Snug say if he knew you were falling to pieces? This'll be a good one to tell him, won't it? Better than the cows, that's for certain.*

Rosalie hadn't realized it before, but the purr or rumble or roar of an engine always seemed to underscore her safety, and now she felt so alone. She took the circuit as the plane continued to descend.

No one about, that's good, isn't it? Clear the decks now, here we go.

She lowered her landing gear, and the ground rose up in a rush to meet her. She landed, bounced high and landed again, hard. As soon as the wheels were on the ground, she hit the brakes, but with too much force. The aeroplane juddered at the strain, and so she eased off. She passed the control tower in a *whoosh* and continued to press steadily on the brakes, watching the end of the runway hurtle toward her. She slowed and slowed until the Magister came to a stop, its nose all of six inches away from the trunk of an enormous beech tree.

She sat, numb and staring at the trunk and its smooth gray bark. She kept still for so long that a squirrel crept down from a high branch headfirst until it grew level with her. It stopped and looked at her, its cheeks stuffed with nuts. She laughed—high-pitched and sounding slightly unhinged in her own ears. She swallowed the laughter and wiped her face, which was wet from tears or sweat, she didn't know. Taking a deep breath, she let it out slowly. She looked behind to see the ground crew coming out to her, and by the time they arrived, she was tossing her bag and parachute onto the ground and climbing out of the plane.

"Sorry I couldn't turn and taxi back," she said, putting a hand out and taking hold of the wing, hoping to cover for her wobbly legs, "but I had no engine power. You'll want to take a look at that. I'll leave you to it."

It seemed an interminable walk to the duty officer's hut, but she made it at last and reported in.

"We saw you circling and heard nothing," he said, and she detected admiration in his tone.

"Yes, well, the engine cut out." Rosalie said. "But ATA pilots are trained to expect the unexpected."

"Any damage to the Magister?"

"Not a scratch."

★   ★   ★

On her return to Hamble, the noise of the Anson taxi and the vibration beneath her comforted Rosalie, but by the time the plane put down, she had a headache from the heat and events of the day. When she walked into the waiting room, it didn't get any better.

"I believe we have a responsibility to our country," Grace was saying. "My marriage will allow us to be an example to others."

She could've been talking to herself—no one responded as they attended to knitting or writing or reading. Caro and Zofia sat across a low table from each other playing Snap. Rosalie edged over to the tea table as Brenda yawned.

Finally, Catherine asked, "Will you stop flying when you're married, Grace?"

The wedding drew close—in four weeks' time, when her fiancé's battleship was to be back from its latest mission. Grace liked to keep everyone abreast of the plans.

"Until the war is over, Harold will spend most of his time at sea, and there's no point in me abandoning my work in order to . . . We may close the house, as the . . . Harold's children have moved on."

Harold's children had been Grace's childhood companions, but now that she was to marry their father, she took every opportunity to position herself in a new way. Rosalie wondered what they thought about the whole thing.

"I don't shirk from responsibility," Grace continued, as if answering the question *Why are you marrying a man old enough to be your father?* "I would never choose my own happiness over . . ."

That apparently didn't go in the direction she meant, and she stopped and started again. "We have to consider what our contributions to the nation will be. Don't you think, Caro?"

Caro lifted an eyebrow, but Rosalie jumped in.

"We supply the RAF with the aeroplanes they need to defeat the Germans. Wouldn't you consider that a contribution, Grace?"

"I think Caro knows that isn't what I meant, Rosalie, and there's no need for you to take up the banner and get yourself tarnished in the process."

"What business is it of yours what another person does with her life?" Rosalie demanded, in a voice louder than she had intended.

The clicking of knitting needles stopped, newspapers ceased to rattle, and pens stopped scratching as the other women cut their eyes at Rosalie. She knew they thought of her as the quiet one, but her emotions were still too near the surface after her afternoon incident. She felt an inch away from losing control, and Grace was an easier target than the Magister.

"Rosalie," Caro began.

"Look now," Anne cut in, "which of us is going to a conversion course next? I'm all for flying a Lancaster."

The rest of them seized on the topic, beginning a wish list of aeroplanes and what pages they might be adding to their *Ferry Pilots Notes*.

"What about you, Rosalie?" Anne asked.

"I'm up for a new aeroplane," she said, "but I want that plus rating for a Mosquito first."

"Room for two in that cockpit," Brenda said.

CHAPTER 15

November 1942

*D*ear *Rags,* Leslie wrote, *it's been absolutely ages since we've seen
you—can't you shake loose from your flying for a visit? It's a bit mad
here now with harvesting and sowing, but at least Mum won't put you to
work at the jam. I have to say, it might be good for all of us to have you in
the house. There's a bit of oddness hanging in the air. Mum has gone quiet,
and Jean is working more with the Land Girls than she is in the kitchen.
Will won't talk at all, and gets angry when I push. Do you know something
I don't? At least he was clear in this—he, too, wants you to come for a visit.
In other news, I saw Ellen recently. Her mum had an operation and she came
home for a fortnight to help out. It was awfully good to see her, although I
tell myself what's the point if she's marrying this fitter fellow. What's his
name again?*

It was like an SOS call from a ship at sea, and both guilt and
a longing to see her brothers and mum sent Rosalie back to Lime
Farm. That, and because Alan still had no days to spare. As soon as
the letter arrived, she made arrangements and wrote home.

At the end of her thirteen-day stretch of ferrying planes and the
night before she would leave for Cambridgeshire, she knocked on
Caro and Zofia's door.

"All packed, are you?" Caro asked, shifting her feet to give Rosalie room to settle at the foot of her bed.

"Not much to pack, is there?" Rosalie asked. "Except I'm hoping to take a bit of advice along with me. Here's the thing . . ." She drew her knees up, wrapped her arms round them, and told them the story of Will, Jean, and little Robert.

Zofia, brushing out her hair at the dresser mirror, turned. "You think they have told your mother and now they need you there to be peacemaker?"

"I don't know what good I would be at that," Rosalie said. "Mum thinks I'm mad for wanting to fly, and if she believes my judgment is flawed there, how would I ever be able to talk her over to any other side she doesn't want to go?"

"They should just go and get the boy," Caro said. "Your mum would love him on sight, and then it would all be sorted."

Caro, right about so many things, had never met Rosalie's mother, and so in this one instance, she could be wrong.

The next morning, Rosalie walked into the ferry pool with Caro and Zofia and left for Lime Farm, arriving at Bourn, where she didn't even need to ring for Leslie—he was already there. She saw him as they landed, waiting for her at the gate of the airfield, leaning up against the old Morris lorry with his coat buttoned up against the chill. He looked well and even had a bit of color in his cheeks, without that air of sadness she'd detected at Will and Jean's wedding in January, which seemed ages ago.

Apart from her reluctance to face a family drama, Rosalie had looked forward to her visit. She could be a layabout for a couple of mornings—didn't they have enough hands to work the farm? She would let Will take the lead on that other business.

On the way from Bourn, Leslie asked what new aeroplanes she had flown and did she have any good stories. No need to tell him about the Magister incident, because that had ended well, hadn't it? Instead, she drew on an older event. "Did I tell you Snug had to rescue me from some cows?"

Leslie laughed. "Is that when that Anson got in your way and you had to land in another field? You see, Rags, how Snug took charge of those cows. Even a bloke from London doesn't mind them. It's all in your attitude."

"And so you saw Ellen again, did you?" she asked, and out of the corner of her eye, she saw her brother's smile surface briefly.

"Well, couldn't help it, could I? She was home, and Mum sent me over with a crock of soup and a steak-and-kidney pie."

"Steak-and-kidney pie?" Rosalie asked in shock. "I haven't had a steak-and-kidney pie since . . . since . . ." She got hold of herself. "That's nice. Has Ellen gone back now?"

"Mm-hmm. Do you see her often?"

"I do seem to run into her regularly when I stop at Castle Camps. I'll tell you this, Les, she isn't all that thrilled with being a WAAF. She's a driver, and of course any war work is important, but it isn't as thrilling as she had expected, I think. And I'm not too certain this thing with Ned will stick. She misses home."

It didn't cheer her brother up as much as she'd hoped. "Don't we still have to get through the rest of the war, though?" he asked.

Will greeted them in the yard at Lime Farm, and her mum came to the kitchen door. Rosalie caught sight of the geese looking cautiously at her round the corner of the barn. One of the Land Girls came out from the stables and gave her a wave. It wasn't Jean, but then Rosalie reminded herself that Jean was no longer considered a Land Girl. She was a member of the family.

Rosalie embraced her brother and mother and looked round. "Where's Jean?"

"She's out planting the last field of wheat," Will said in a rush. "We've got an attachment for the Fordson, and she oversees the whole process. I've just come in from the cabbages, and we've carrots coming out next."

"She's really taken on a great deal, hasn't she? Good on her."

"You know what it's like at this time of year, Rags," Will said. "All hands on deck."

Rosalie gave up her hope of a lie-in the next morning. "Yes, true. But you must miss her in the kitchen, Mum."

"Enough of standing out in the yard," her mum said, "come in for a cup of tea." She waved at her sons. "You two, back to your work."

It was not in Rosalie's little-sister makeup to let such a thing pass. She turned to her brothers as she went into the kitchen and whispered, "You two, back to work."

The kettle was just coming to a boil, and on the table sat a cake.

"Oh, Mum, are those sultanas? Do you know, even though we can get them on points, Mrs. May says they're terribly scarce."

"Well, so they are, but isn't my daughter worth it?"

Rosalie was stunned into silence by this declaration.

Her mum put the milk jug on the table. "I could give your hair a cut this afternoon. Looks as if you could use it."

Rosalie's hand went up to her curls. "Yes, I suppose I could. I'm afraid I made a dog's breakfast of it the last time I tried."

The words hung heavy in the air. Improper language. Rosalie had been away too long.

"How is Ellen's mum?" she asked quickly, in hopes of distracting her mother. "Les said Ellen was here and he saw her. Did you see her? Do you think she's sorry she became a WAAF?"

Her mum cut a thick slice of sultana cake. "Perhaps Ellen needed to get this wearing-a-uniform business out of her system. The things girls get into their heads."

Rosalie knew where her mum was headed with this, and it wasn't about Ellen. Would she ever be able to put shed to the idea that being a pilot was only a passing fancy?

"We've had a few things growing in back at Mrs. May's—cabbage and leeks and beetroot. We had some lovely peas, although not enough to put up. The hens are settling in. And we've raspberries at the bottom of the garden. We ate most of them fresh, but we were able to come up with two jars of jam."

She reached for the cake but saw her mum open her mouth to speak. Rosalie popped up.

"I'll just go wash my hands."

★   ★   ★

When Jean arrived at the end of the day, Rosalie's mother's good spirits dried up and the temperature in the kitchen dropped several degrees. Rosalie hadn't had a word alone with Will, but it was clear as day that her mum now knew about Jean's son and she wasn't best pleased. As the evening wore on, the strain of staying jolly amid unspoken tensions became too much. Leslie did his part, and Rosalie pitched in, but the two of them sounded like a music hall act—telling stories and jokes and laughing at each other. In no way could the evening meal be called a success.

At last, Rosalie excused herself. "I'm just a bit weary from the journey, you know." Her journey had been one of the easiest ever. She'd had only one stop at Aston Down, with time for tea and toast with Snug before he went off to Leeming and she had boarded the air taxi to Bourn.

Before she went up, she offered to wash the dishes, but her mum turned down the help. "The boys will lend a hand." Jean stayed downstairs too—the invisible woman in the room. Rosalie gave everyone a "Good night" but suspected it wasn't really the end of her day.

She stood in the middle of her old room for a moment, trying to reconnect with all the objects that used to define her. How odd, she thought. This room where she'd grown up was larger than her room at Mrs. May's, but somehow it felt smaller. She wasn't taller or fatter and so couldn't quite tell how that worked and didn't try to sort it out. Instead, she pulled out her night things, dashed into the lav, and was back in ten minutes, sitting up in bed with the light on and waiting for the tap at the door when it came.

"Come in," she said.

It was Will. He took only one step inside and stayed near the door, shifting his weight from one foot to the other.

"We're awfully glad you've come, Rags."

"Oh, do come in and sit down. You've told Mum, haven't you? Is it as bad as all this?"

Will sat. "We'd been waiting for the right moment, and it seemed to have come. Leslie went over to—oh, Ellen was home, did you know?"

"Yes, he told me."

"Do you think there's any hope for those two?"

"Will."

"Yes, right. Leslie had taken some food over to Ellen's mother, and we sat Mum down and explained it all." Will's face drew up in pain. "Robert is six now, Rags. He needs his mum. He's a right proper little fellow, and even though I've only met him the once, I believe we'd get along fine. I want to be his dad."

"What did Mum say?"

"Nothing. Not for the longest time. It was as if she had turned to stone right there at the kitchen table."

"And then?"

"She said it was no wonder Jean's parents didn't come to the wedding, knowing as they did that Jean kept such a secret from people who were supposed to become her new family. She said it wasn't the boy's fault and she had no complaint against him, but wouldn't it be better for him to continue living where he was. 'Isn't that his true home now?' she said."

"His true home is with his mother, because she wants him. You both do."

"Mum doesn't agree. I know it's because she's afraid of what people will say. But it's none of their concern."

"That won't stop them from talking, though, will it? And asking questions."

Will made a noncommittal noise. "What do you think we should do?"

"First off," Rosalie said, "tell Leslie. He deserves to know, and he can tell something's wrong."

"Yes, I know, and I'm sorry I haven't done it yet. I feel as if I'm not a terribly good example to my younger brother. Or my little sister. Can't even sort out my own life. And I've let Pop down."

"And how have you done that, I'd like to know?" Rosalie demanded. "You and Jean have been truthful with each other—let the others rot if they don't like it. Not Mum, of course," she added quickly, and Will grinned. "Pop would be proud of you. You'll just have to talk to her again."

"I've tried and she refuses. She'll walk out of the room on me. It's hard on Jean, the strain—well, you saw her. And it isn't fair. Mum doesn't mind the work Jean does, of course, but I know she's sorry she ever moved out of her and Pop's bedroom for us."

When Rosalie came for the wedding, Leslie had been the one to look weary and Will the one on top of the world, and now they had reversed positions. Perhaps not entirely, but at least Les looked hopeful—Rosalie reckoned it had to do with Ellen—whereas Will looked older than his years.

"I'll speak to Mum," Rosalie said. "Tomorrow. But you know, Will, that it may come to nothing?"

The next morning, Rosalie managed to delay going downstairs until the Land Girls, Jean, Will, and Leslie had left and her mum was alone in the kitchen. The door to the yard stood open, and the diffused light from the gray skies gave the farm the look of a painting framed by the doorpost. Outside, a goose honked, and the Fordson tractor chugged off into the distance. Rosalie yawned and reached for the teapot.

"A lazy morning—all right for some," her mum said, but with a smile, and so Rosalie smiled back. "Two eggs?"

"Yes, please, but not just yet. Sit down with me for a moment, won't you?" Rosalie asked.

Her mother's good humor drained away, to be replaced by a wary look.

"All right, then. But you'll have the toast?"

Rosalie dutifully reached for a slice from the toast rack and began to butter it.

"Mum, you know about Jean and her son."

Her mother dropped her hands into her lap. "I know she misled us all. Will included."

"No, Will knew about the boy before they married."

"Still, she'd used her wiles until he had no other choice."

"Her wiles?" The knife clattered to the table. "Oh, Mum, really, what century do you think we're in? Jean is honest and loving, and if she made a mistake, then she's paid for it over and over."

"She thought she could be a daughter here, that she could slip in unawares and become a member of this family. But she isn't and she can't. I wish you'd come home, Rosalie, and give up all that other business." She flung a hand out. "Don't you see we need you?"

How had Jean having a son and Will wanting him to live at Lime Farm become about Rosalie flying?

"Are you saying my replacement hasn't worked out?"

Rosalie regretted it, but her mum ignored the biting comment.

"This farm is important work for the war too."

"Of course it is," Rosalie said. "But you have plenty of hands. And don't you know that my flying is both for the war and for me—it's my passion. Would you take that away from me?"

A black-and-white barn cat put its nose in the kitchen doorway and hesitated over the threshold. Her mother rose from the table.

"Puss-puss-puss," she said, getting a saucer and pouring milk into it. "She has kittens in the barn and comes here a-begging. Will you take the eggs up to the market this morning?"

★   ★   ★

"Thank you for trying," Jean told Rosalie on Sunday morning.

"We'll wear her down yet, you'll see." Although, when it came right down to it, Rosalie wasn't sure she would have the courage of her convictions, and she didn't know how she could wield an influence from faraway Hampshire.

Rosalie had arrived at Lime Farm with only the bare essentials so that she could repack with as much of the farm's bounty as possible. When she returned to No. 6 later that day, she made a show of struggling to carry her bag into the kitchen and then easing it onto a chair. Mrs. May, Caro, and Zofia hovered round the table as she drew out the gifts one by one like a magician pulling rabbits out of a hat—a marrow, a block of cheese, a jar of pole beans, and bacon.

She'd wrapped this last in two layers of greaseproof paper. Each item was received with acclamation.

It was too bad they couldn't end the year on a high note, but that wasn't to be. On the tenth of November, the Germans took Vichy, giving them all of France and cutting off communication between Zofia and her mother and sister, such as it had been. Despite the assurances of Hamble's CO, Margot Gore, that the ATA was doing all it could to get information on the situation, Zofia lost her spirit, and a pall settled over No. 6 that no Christmas celebration could dispel.

CHAPTER 16

March 1943

*M*y love, I am much due a rest and hope you can arrange a visit—our same place as before? Could you arrive Debden instead of coming to Castle Camps? Wouldn't it be easier for you to make your way there? Then, we could meet at the hotel. I'm sorry to say I'll have only the one night. Very sorry indeed.

True, Debden was easier, but still, Rosalie would've preferred to walk into the Feathers at Alan's side. Still, a return visit meant that perhaps Mr. Wilkes, who had been so friendly the first time, would remember her. Rosalie made her own arrangements, and when she stepped off the green bus, she held her head high as she crossed the road and walked into the hotel.

But kindly Mr. Wilkes with the bad leg was not behind the desk. Instead, it was a woman who looked up from her paperwork with a slight frown.

"Yes?"

Rosalie had half a mind to turn tail and run—take a walk down the lane and return in an hour when Alan was there and she wouldn't have to explain herself. Instead, she took a deep breath and a step forward.

"Hello, I'm looking for—"

Oh no, what name had Alan used before?

But before she could continue, he appeared from the bar. "Here you are now."

"Yes," Rosalie said, flushed and barely able to make a sound. "Here I am. I'm a bit late, aren't I?"

Alan put a firm hand on her back and ushered her up to the desk. "You see, Mrs. Wilkes," he said with a smile, "I knew she'd arrive soon. Thank you so much for your kindness."

What kindness had the woman behind the desk shown him? Rosalie wondered, because all she got was a hard look and pursed lips. Alan picked up her bag and parachute, and the two of them took the stairs to the first floor without speaking. They had the same room they'd had before, and once inside and with the door firmly latched, they broke out in a fit of giggles.

"Is that the way she greets all the guests?" Rosalie said, then sobered up. No, perhaps only the ones she knew weren't married.

"Never you mind about her," Alan said. "All that matters is that you're here." He stroked her cheek and ran a finger down her neck to the hollow place at the base of her throat. "I've missed you so."

Rosalie moved in closer and held still, letting his hands go where they might until she could stand it no longer, and she pulled him over to the bed.

"I said we wouldn't be down to dinner until eight," Alan murmured in her ear as he unbuttoned her uniform shirt. "Is that all right?"

At that moment, nothing else mattered. Even the prospect of coming down the stairs at eight o'clock to be met with a disapproving look from Mrs. Wilkes.

★　★　★

They'd had to hurry down at the last minute, dashing past the desk—empty, Rosalie was relieved to see—and arriving at the dining room at quarter past eight. The woman serving wanted to seat them in the middle of a surprisingly crowded room, but Alan smiled and asked if they could have the table on the far side, against the wall and near a window, if it was no trouble. No trouble, she said, and smiled in return.

It was only when they were seated that Rosalie noticed a hollow look about Alan's eyes that she hadn't seen in the dim light of their room. He seemed unsettled, fiddling with the cutlery and his gaze darting about the room. She reached across the table and touched his hand, and as if she'd pushed the *on* button, he started talking.

"I got a possible two nights ago," he said. "That's when you know you've hit an enemy plane but no one's actually seen him go down. It's often difficult to know for certain. Flying at night by instruments only—it's another world. You can't see where you're going, and you must put your trust in the dials in front of you and your navigator and the fellow on the radio. God, it's dark. But is a bright moon any better? They can see us just as well as we see them. We were in the thick of it last week. Junkers everywhere. You just pick one and start firing, if you can get close enough. And hope you don't get hit yourself. Instinct and training take over when I'm up there. There's no time for anything else."

His eyes became glassy. He held on to her hand but looked off across the room. "I saw one of ours get hit. Owens and James, his navigator. At night, the only light you get is when the guns fire. Theirs or ours. And, too, when an aeroplane blows up." Alan's hand tightened on hers. "That's what happened. It exploded—and it was as if, for one moment, it was Guy Fawkes night. The sky illuminated, pieces of aeroplane sent out in all directions like a dandelion clock. And they were gone, just like that."

Their meals, barely touched, sat going cold, but Rosalie didn't move until Alan's grip on her hand loosened and his gaze settled on her.

"They count us in, you know," he said. "When we return at dawn. I can see them on the roof of the control tower counting the aeroplanes as we land. To see if we've all come back."

"You need more of a rest than this," she said. "They can't send you up night after night without time to recover."

He smiled, and the color came back to his face. He kissed her hand.

"It's what we do—take our Wooden Wonders up and hunt for Jerries." He picked up his knife and fork, setting to work on his pork cutlet.

Rosalie glanced down at her own plate. She tried a bite and found the meat required more chewing than she had the energy for.

"And it's every night?"

Alan shook his head. "Some nights we sit in the dispatch hut drinking tea until five in the morning, waiting for them to spot enemy planes on the radar. If they don't see any, we're dismissed. Other nights we're off at two or three and may not be back until first light. Or we may go up at sunset. I'd rather be flying than waiting."

Rosalie understood that.

"It's odd that a night's flying can be divided into such discrete parts," Alan said, working his way through a heap of boiled potatoes. "Often when we take off and climb, there's still light in the west. It's quite beautiful, and I've plenty of time to think and my mind begins to wander. I remember summers in the country and begging my grandmother to let me spend every day in the kitchen garden. Planting beans and watching them grow, pretending the tendrils of the melons in the glasshouses were monsters coming after me, training the peaches against the brick walls."

"What do your parents think about you wanting to be a farmer?" Rosalie asked.

Without a moment's thought, Alan replied, "Growing peaches and melons is not a topic I'd bring up to either my mother or my father. But it's what gets me settled when I'm climbing, and when I reach twenty-five thousand feet, I can see the future. My mind skips ahead, past the entire war, and I see what I want. That kitchen garden but on the grand scale of a farm. And you there with me."

He'd recovered not only his color but also his good humor, and Rosalie was reluctant to say anything to spoil it. The waitress had come for their plates, returned with dishes of semolina pudding and blackberries, and left again before Rosalie said, "But I'll fly after the war. I'll continue to fly."

Alan scooped up a heaping spoonful of pudding and berries and paused with it in midair, watching her. "Well, then," he said, "I'll buy you an airfield."

He took the entire mouthful and chewed for a moment; then his face screwed up and his eyes twitched. Rosalie burst out laughing.

"And I promise you," he said, his voice strained, "after the war, we will never be short of sugar."

They declined the offer of coffee and went upstairs. When Rosalie came back from the lavatory, Alan was already asleep. She climbed in bed. He stretched, put his hand on her stomach, and murmured something.

Rosalie lay awake for another hour, staring at the ceiling. She tried to imagine what it would be like to fly at night by instrument seeing only blackness outside the cockpit. No, that wasn't her sort of flying. Then her mind moved on to Alan's flippant remark about buying her an airfield. It was a jest, and if she hadn't known that, she would've taken offense at the light way he dismissed her. But at that moment, it seemed to her more important for them to enjoy each other's company. They had loads of time to sort out the details of their lives.

At breakfast the next morning, a bowl of blackberries appeared on the table, again without any sugar. Rosalie nibbled hers and washed their astringency down with a swig of tea, but Alan left his alone and went for the toast and butter. Margarine, that is.

"You shouldn't have to take a bus back to Debden. We'll have them ring for a taxi."

"The coach leaves in half an hour and it's perfect for me, really."

Irritation at her means of transportation was only the latest in the morning's irksome events. Alan had already lost patience with the door to their room, which stuck, and with the strap on his bag for being willful. He had a few words for the table, too, when it wobbled and spilled tea into his saucer.

He poured the tea back into his cup. "I don't like us to be parted. It would be different if you were here. Closer."

"But there's no ferry pool nearby," Rosalie said, having already thought that through.

"You could join the WAAF. Think of all the things you could do."

"I couldn't fly."

He tapped the spoon on the edge of his cup. "No, you couldn't."

"And I don't want to be a plotter or a driver or . . . put on your football matches like NAAFI does."

His eyes flickered to her and away.

"No, you are not a NAAFI girl. You're different—you're better than that."

"I don't mean they aren't doing their part—"

"It's all right," Alan said. "I understand."

An awkward silence fell between them, and it reminded Rosalie of the first time they met, when she had been so tongue-tied. Not even a year had gone by, and yet that seemed like a lifetime ago.

"I'd better get my bag," she said. "You stay and finish."

She returned to find Alan chatting with Mr. Wilkes at the desk.

"Mr. Wilkes lost his son in Norway," Alan said.

"The younger son," Mr. Wilkes explained to Rosalie with a sad smile.

So many had been lost in the Norway campaign. Rosalie remembered that someone else had mentioned it.

"That's why we are happy to see the likes of you," Mr. Wilkes said, "a pilot and his wife, who also does so much for the war effort. You're always welcome at the Feathers."

They walked out just as the green bus pulled up. Rosalie held back while a few others boarded, and Alan put his arms round her waist.

"I've been terrible company, haven't I?"

It had not been the best of times, but what point was it to hash over the details? "Nonsense. We were together. That's what matters," she said, and kissed him lightly before getting on the bus.

★　★　★

Rosalie added the plus rating to her class four certificate, but that did not immediately add a Mosquito to her assignments. She had envisioned taking a Mossie into Castle Camps at the first opportunity to show Alan that she could fly the same aeroplane he took up every night. It wasn't to be. Not yet. But they made up for the awkward way they'd ended their last meeting by a series of wistful letters of longing that kept her spirits up as she continued to fly all manner of other aircraft or flew the taxi, ferrying pilots who would then ferry the aeroplanes. The weeks went on, during which the most exciting thing to happen was that the hens began to lay.

They had got the young hens late in the year, and there had been no eggs through the winter. But at last, with spring upon them, it happened. Rosalie had come down to the kitchen first and found the teapot cold, and so she was filling the kettle and putting it on the hob when Mrs. May marched in from the back garden, cupping a small prize in her two hands. "See here what we have," she said.

It was odd looking—small and a bit misshapen.

"I'm not sure which one it belongs to," the landlady said.

"An egg? I believe it's mine," Caro said, coming into the kitchen.

"It's the first, and so early in the spring. It may not look like a normal egg inside," Rosalie warned them. "Plus, the shell is soft."

"It might be the red one," said Mrs. May.

"The red one's mine, isn't it?" Caro asked.

"And if it came from one of the other hens?" Rosalie asked.

"Then it's still mine," Caro said, and they laughed.

Zofia came in the kitchen and went straight to the teapot, putting her hands round it. "Is there no tea?"

"I've my hands full, as you can well see," Mrs. May said, still cradling the egg. "Someone else will have to serve the breakfast."

★   ★   ★

Soon the hens were well at it. Mrs. May kept a logbook to record how many eggs were laid, when, the quality, and by which hen—she had taken to watching them to learn their habits. She also made note of how each egg was used. Much to Caro's chagrin, not every egg laid found its way to her plate.

One afternoon, Caro and Rosalie found themselves at Aston Down with time on their hands, and so they looked Snug up and went down to the pub.

"I'll get this," Rosalie said, stopping at the bar to order and pay.

"And I'll get the next round," Caro said. "After all, don't we get the same wages as all you men now?"

"I'll let you, then," Snug said. "Wouldn't want to hurt your feelings."

They settled at a table, and Caro reported the latest news about the hens. Rosalie thought she was as consumed with the topic of eggs as Mrs. May.

"What's she doing with them all?" Caro asked.

"We had that cake last week," Rosalie reminded her, "and though it had no fruit or anything else in it, it was the better for containing fresh eggs, don't you think?"

"It wasn't a Madeira, though, was it?" Caro asked. "When will we see a lemon again?"

"The last lemon I saw," Snug said, "was 1940. One of Mum's regulars brought it in to pay his bill."

"What was his Christian name?" Rosalie asked.

"James," Snug said.

"What's your mum's Christian name?" Rosalie said.

"Betty."

"What's your Christian name?"

Snug put his forearms on the table and leaned across to her. "You're going to have to do better than that, Wright. Now, I'm off to deliver a Lancaster to Scampton in Lincolnshire. Be seeing you."

"Braggart," Rosalie called after him, and he gave her a backward look and grinned.

"What's this about his name?" Caro asked.

"Well, it isn't Snug, is it?" Rosalie replied. "That isn't his actual first name. I'm trying to get it out of him."

"Why don't you ask his CO?"

"What would be the fun of that?"

CHAPTER 17

October 1943

"You'll be fine as long as you aren't flying west," said the fellow in the Met to Rosalie and Caro first thing in the morning. "There's a system coming in."

That was all right, because Rosalie was headed the opposite direction, to the aerodrome at Eastchurch in Kent, and Caro north to Castle Bromwich at Birmingham, each of them with Spits.

They walked out to dispatch together. "Let's talk Mrs. May into eggs for our evening meal," Caro said. "Because they won't lay as much come winter, will they? We should take advantage of our bounty."

The hens had carried out their duties all through the summer. Mrs. May had eased her restriction on eating eggs as eggs and had even occasionally bartered with neighbors for the odd ounce of tea or extra half pint of milk. Rosalie, unsure of the legality of these deals, looked the other way.

"She may want to try her hand at preserving eggs again."

Caro shuddered. "I won't be the one to crack open an egg that's been sitting in water glass for six months. Not next time."

Rosalie laughed. "You were too eager. At least remember not to hover over the dish when you crack it."

"She should've pickled them."

"Yes," Rosalie agreed, "and we could have a crock of them in the kitchen. Snug says his mum always had a jar of them sitting on the bar in the pub. Before the war."

Caro looked at her sideways. "Have you ever wondered about you and Snug?"

"What would I wonder?" Rosalie asked.

"If you two might be . . . something more than you are now."

"No, Caro, because Alan and I are together," Rosalie said. "You do remember that, don't you?"

If pushed, Rosalie would admit that when a month or two or more went by without the two of them seeing each other, it put a bit of a strain on things. It seemed they were either longing for each other's touch, to be alone upstairs in the room at the Feathers, or they were awkward in letters and in conversation. On the rare occasions when Rosalie delivered or collected an aeroplane at Castle Camps, she was seldom successful in locating Alan, and even when she did, he appeared distracted. On that account, it had been a difficult summer.

"Rosalie?"

She turned back to Caro and said, "And anyway, don't you think Snug has as many women as he can handle?"

"But is he serious about any one, or are any of them serious about him? I don't think so. What would it take for Snug to chuck them all away, I wonder?" Caro smiled at her, but didn't wait for an answer. "Look, if you see Margot when you get back, would you find out if there's any news about Zofia's mum and sister? I'm sure she's tired of me asking, and Zofia is afraid to hear any news because it might be bad."

Without Zofia present, Rosalie could express her fears. "Do you think they're still alive?"

"Yes, I'm sure they are. They're in the hills with the Resistance—they must be there." Caro shook her head. "Her only family. Without them, Zofia has no one."

"She has you," Rosalie said, and gave Caro a kiss on the cheek.

★　★　★

Rosalie returned to Hamble just before midday. It seemed a quiet place, as if everyone was still away or else holed up in the waiting room whiling away the time with a round of bridge. If that was the case, Grace would be involved, and Rosalie thought she might take a pass and go back to No. 6. She signed her flight log with the duty officer, and as she turned away, he picked up the telephone at his desk.

Approaching the waiting room, Rosalie noticed Commanding Officer Margot Gore standing outside her office. When she saw Rosalie, she said, "Wright, come in here, please."

Rosalie stopped. The world drained of color and became unfocused, and the air filled with a gray mist-like gauze that obscured the light of day. Without knowing why, Rosalie knew with certainty that she should not step into the CO's office at any cost.

"Wright."

"Yes, ma'am."

Rosalie followed Gore in but didn't move far. "Sit down," her CO said.

She obeyed, taking a chair against the wall nearest the door. Gore brought another chair over and sat in front of her.

"I'm afraid I have bad news."

Rosalie leapt up, but Gore took her hand, pulled her down again, and continued.

"There's no easy way to say this. There's been a crash, and Caro Andrews is dead."

Rosalie snatched her hand back, but she didn't speak, because Gore's words had made no sense to her.

"I know you and she were good friends," Gore said, and then cleared her throat. "She was a fine pilot, and we all greatly admired her."

"Caro." Rosalie's mouth formed the name, but no sound emerged.

"They believe her engine cut out as she approached Castle Bromwich. She could not make it over Brown Clee Hill near the aerodrome and instead crashed into it."

Rosalie's Magister engine had cut out and she had landed safely. Caro's engine had stopped and she'd died.

"Wright," Gore said, and then, softer, "Rosalie? I know what a shock this is. You are relieved of flying for a couple of days, and—"

"What?" In a panic, Rosalie jumped out of the chair, knocking it against the wall. "No, you can't do that. Please don't. I have to fly. I'm all right; please let me fly."

The CO rose. "Shock can affect you in ways you can't anticipate." Rosalie opened her mouth to protest, but Gore hurried on. "But we'll take this one day at a time. You aren't scheduled for another aeroplane today, and we'll discuss tomorrow in the morning."

Rosalie saw the minutes and hours and days ahead of her as a vast chasm, void of life and light. What was she supposed to do now?

"I want you to go into the waiting room," Gore said, "and be with the others."

The others. A thought broke through Rosalie's haze.

"Zofia? Does she—"

"Pasek won't return until later this afternoon, and so I doubt if she's heard." Gore frowned. "At least, I hope she hasn't. It would be better for one of us to tell her, but I have no way of cautioning every ferry pool and RAF base. We're all so terribly sorry." Again, the CO paused and coughed. "I've already spoken to Caro's father."

Dr. Andrews. If Rosalie's shock and grief were this enormous, what of Caro's father? His only child gone in an instant.

"There are arrangements to make," the CO continued, "and I'll let you know the details as soon as possible."

She meant the funeral. The burial. Caro in the ground. Rosalie could see her own father's casket being lowered into the earth.

"You shouldn't be alone now. The others know, and you can be a comfort for each other."

"Yes," Rosalie said automatically, but once out the door, she knew she couldn't go into the waiting room, because Caro wasn't there and would never be again. She turned away, thinking that if she couldn't fly, she would go back to No. Six, but that idea lasted only a moment. She couldn't go there either, and for the same reason. Rosalie remained at the corner of the building with no destination as inertia overcame her, slowing her blood to treacle and turning her feet to stone. But then she saw movement across the yard, and fearing it was one of the women and she would have to talk with her, Rosalie fled into the Mess.

A few of the ground crew sat at a far table, but otherwise the place was empty. She edged round the room, keeping her back to the wall, and finally sank into a chair in the opposite corner with no objective other than to keep from thinking. But it didn't work. Rosalie had ferried an aeroplane to Castle Bromwich in the past, and she knew Brown Clee Hill and how it loomed up out of an otherwise flat landscape. There had been other crashes there, and it took no imagination to conjure up the vision of Caro's Spitfire heading straight into it.

Intertwined in those images of the crash were glimpses of Caro, alive and happy. At No. 6 collecting eggs, in the waiting room playing Snap with Zofia, at the Bugle raising a pint. Laughing, cajoling, listening, understanding things before Rosalie had to explain. Round and round the film went in her head, until she was dizzy.

Once, Rosalie heard a woman—it might have been Brenda—say, "Oh, I'm so sorry. Are you all right here? Don't you want a cup of tea?"

"I'm fine," she replied, and shook her head at the offer. She was left alone again, truly alone, her hands in her lap and her eyes on the table and aware of nothing except that she was cold. Time passed—or didn't, she couldn't tell—until someone large enough to block out the light stood in front of her.

"Wright?"

She looked up, blinked, and squinted at Snug. It took a moment for his face to come into focus, and when it did, she could tell he knew. Even so, she said it.

"Caro is dead."

Rosalie slapped a hand across her mouth, as if letting the words escape had made it real. Her body shook and wouldn't stop, and so she stood, thinking to escape before someone noticed, but when she took a step, her legs wouldn't hold her up, and she collapsed. Snug put a hand out and caught her, and a moment later she was in his arms, her body racked with spasms.

She cried for the longest time without awareness of anything, but eventually she felt a vibration and realized that Snug was speaking in a low, calm voice. Regardless of the words, they began to have an effect. Her spasms became sobs and then petered out to ragged breathing. She became aware of his arms round her, and found herself disinclined to pull away. At last she realized the front of his uniform was soaked with her tears. She looked up at him, and he dropped his arms but held on to her hands and guided her back into the chair and then sat across the table from her.

She wiped her nose on the back of her hand, and Snug dug in a pocket and pulled out a handkerchief—not white, not ironed, and possibly not clean. She took it regardless and blew her nose long and hard.

They remained silent for a few more moments, and that was perfectly all right with her. He didn't seem bothered either. But at last she felt strong enough to speak.

"How is it that you're here?" she asked.

"I heard this morning and found a transport down. I didn't want you to . . . I thought you might want a bit of company or . . . well . . ."

Rosalie had never seen Snug uncomfortable before, and she noticed there was a slight pink color to his cheeks. Her spirits lifted, if only a minuscule amount.

"Look," he said, regaining a bit of his usual swagger, "cup of tea?"

"No," she said, stuffing his handkerchief into her pocket. "I want a drink."

Snug raised his eyebrows.

"A drink," she repeated. "Let's go to the Bugle."

He pushed the cuff of his shirt back and checked the time. "Yeah, all right. Come on."

They walked out, and Rosalie was blinded by the sun and couldn't, for a moment, understand why it was shining. Anger flared in her heart.

As they approached No. 6, Rosalie said, "Oh dear. Mrs. May will need to be told."

"Would you like me to go in with you?" Snug asked.

"No, she isn't home—there's a district WI meeting in Southampton," Rosalie said, surprised that the world could continue in such mundane ways. "Zofia will be back later. She's the first one I need to tell."

"I'd say she'll hear before the afternoon is over."

"But *I* need to see her," Rosalie said, stopping in the road. "*I* need to tell her. Help her take it in. You don't understand. They were close, Caro and Zofia." She cut her eyes at Snug, unsure of what else to say.

"Close?" he echoed.

"Yes, close," she said. Her hands closed into fists, ready to do battle. "Quite . . . close."

He nodded. "Oh, I see."

"What's that supposed to mean?" she shouted. "Do you find something wrong with it?"

Snug put his hands up in defense. "Oh no, you're not putting that on me. Haven't I lived with Mouse and her friend my whole life?"

"Mouse's friend? You mean . . ."

"Delfina," he replied. "She's Spanish."

"Delfina and Mouse," Rosalie said, and after a moment walked on. "What's Mouse's Christian name?"

"Agatha."

"What's yours?" Rosalie asked. Snug cocked his head and squinted his good eye at her, and her spirits rose a bit more. "Can't blame me for trying," she said, as he opened the door of the Bugle.

Inside, two old men, hunkered over their beer, ignored them. Rosalie took a table in the public area, and Snug went up to the bar.

Bisby eyed them both but said to Rosalie, "A glass of the mild?"

"No," she said. "I want whiskey."

"You what?" he asked, and the old men looked up.

"Whiskey," she repeated with force.

Snug leaned over the bar and spoke quietly to Bisby, after which the publican said, "Oh God, that's terrible." He glanced at Rosalie and then drew out a bottle from below. It was, she noted, the same bottle Dr. Andrews had sent Caro—the one used in bartering for the henhouse wood. When Snug tried to pay, Bisby waved his coins away.

"Water?" Snug asked her, holding a pitcher up over her glass.

When she shook her head, he brought the drinks to the table, handed hers over, and sat down. "I didn't realize you were a whiskey drinker," he said.

She'd never had a drop, but she wasn't going to tell him that.

"Caro," Snug said, and raised his glass.

"Caro," Rosalie repeated with no sound, and swallowed half her drink at once.

She thought her throat was on fire. Her eyes watered and her face went hot. The old men were keeping watch over their shoulders. Determined not to choke, she breathed in and out heavily, wheezing the entire time.

Snug took a sip of his, looking at her over the rim of his glass.

Rosalie set her glass down. "We left at the same time this morning. We both had Spits. I could've had hers, couldn't I? Then it would've been me, and Caro would still be alive."

Snug took hold of her hand and squeezed it tightly.

"Ouch."

He lessened his grip but said, "Don't you do that. Don't think you could've or should've taken her place. It's happened. There's no going back now, only remembering her for being a good pilot and good friend."

Rosalie took her glass and swirled the whiskey round. "Pop died before I joined the ATA. He so wanted me to be a pilot, and here I am and he doesn't even know." Rosalie frowned at herself. Why did one death bring up memories of others?

"You're doing him proud, though, aren't you?" Snug asked.

"Do you wonder about your father?"

"Oh, sure. I wonder what sort of work he did. Or if he worked at all."

"How could that be?"

Snug shrugged a shoulder. "Mum was in service before Mouse got the pub—before I came along. I reckon my dad was someone who didn't want to own up to having a baby with one of the servants. I reckon he was a toff."

"Or a criminal," Rosalie ventured.

Snug laughed. "Or both."

"Caro's dad seems a fine man," she said. "I've never met him, but from all she said, I know he loved her."

"She had a way about her, didn't she?" Snug asked. "She was confident."

"Did she ever tell you about the time she flew a Hawker Hind into Brize Norton and one of the ground crew said . . ."

And so they went, exchanging stories about Caro. Rosalie found herself comforted. The trouble was, at the end of it all, she would go back to No. 6 and Caro would not be sitting in the kitchen with a cup of tea.

"You two want to move to the back?" Bisby asked. "I don't mind."

Rosalie looked round and found that the old men had gone and the publican was locking up. Three o'clock, afternoon closing time.

"Zofia," she said.

"We'll go," Snug said to Bisby, "but thanks." He nodded to Rosalie's glass. "Are you going to finish that?"

She took the rest of her whiskey in a single swallow, and it went down much easier than the first. Snug rose and took their glasses back to the bar.

CHAPTER 18

Mrs. May had not returned, and so Rosalie and Snug continued to the ferry pool, where CO Gore told them that Zofia had boarded an air taxi at Woodbridge in Suffolk and was due in another hour. "Durrant, there's an Anson leaving for Aston Down, if you're interested."

Snug looked at Rosalie. She nodded. "You go on."

They walked out to his aeroplane together.

"You'll be all right?" he asked.

She shrugged.

"You won't stay out here, will you?" he asked. "Go back in and wait for her."

Were the other pilots still in the waiting room? "No, I don't think I can. Not yet." She put a hand on Snug's arm and then pretended to fix his collar. "Thank you. If you hadn't been here, I don't think—" The tears that had abated threatened once more.

He closed his hand over hers. "You're welcome."

Snug climbed aboard the Anson, and Rosalie watched it take off. She remained in place for another hour, realizing that if Zofia did not already know about Caro, she would certainly sense the tragedy when she saw Rosalie, just as Rosalie had known something was terribly wrong when she saw Margot Gore waiting for her. It was as if they emitted waves of sorrow.

When the air taxi landed, five pilots climbed out and crossed the field toward Rosalie. Even from a distance, she knew that Zofia had already heard. It was something in the way the others surrounded her, as if they could insulate her from hurt. No one spoke until they reached Rosalie, and then Anne said, "Will you bring her into the waiting room? Or will you be at the pub?"

"I don't know," Rosalie said. "I'm not sure. It may be better to give her some time to be quiet."

Catherine and each of the others said a few words until they had all passed and only Zofia remained, standing apart and waiting, her arms hanging at her sides, weighed down by her bag in one hand and her parachute in the other, her forage cap pulled down on her frizzy blond hair.

Rosalie went closer and could see the emptiness in Zofia's eyes. They embraced but didn't speak for a moment, until the sun dipped behind the beech wood to the west.

"Come on." Rosalie put her arm through Zofia's. "Let's go home."

They were quiet walking down Satchell Lane, and they both paused at the door of No. 6. Rosalie, key in hand, gave Zofia an enquiring look. Zofia nodded, and in they went.

Mrs. May had arrived and was busy at the hob, but when she turned and saw their faces, she dropped the spoon she held and clutched at her pinny.

"What's happened?"

Zofia didn't speak, and so Rosalie began. "I'm afraid it's Caro."

The landlady aged instantly before their eyes, her face as gray as her hair.

"Here, let's sit down," Rosalie said. She guided Zofia to a chair and put the kettle on. The story was told, and retold and questioned and told again, and eventually they fell quiet. Zofia, her eyes already red-rimmed, wept, and Mrs. May clutched her hand while wiping away the tears that trickled down her own cheeks.

The only sounds in the kitchen were the hiss and clatter and clink as Rosalie made tea. She sliced and buttered the dry end of the loaf and rejoined them at the table.

"I watched you three walk out the door this morning," Mrs. May said, "and I don't mind saying I thought how lucky I was to have you here."

"She knew your home as her home," Zofia said, and patted the landlady's hand.

"Wasn't she always trying to get round me about the eggs or some such thing, but I never minded, because she was such a happy soul."

They sat over their untouched meals until the food was cold, and then they dutifully ate as much as they could force down and gave the rest to the hens. After the kitchen had been cleaned, they trooped into the lounge as they did almost every evening. Mrs. May switched on the wireless and then went to her writing desk and picked out the most recent letters she'd had from Fred and Terry and reread them. Of course she would worry about her sons—Rosalie would not begrudge her that. They were both at war, and their mother was frightened for them all the time. Usually she could hide that, but not when death had come so close.

Rosalie took *Treasure Island* off a shelf, but weariness overtook her and she excused herself, thinking she would go to her room to write Alan and tell him what had happened. But once upstairs, the very thought of the activity exhausted her even further. Tomorrow.

She slept through the night, even though she'd thought she would not be able to close her eyes. It was as if her body said *enough* and put her in some sort of coma. She awoke not exactly rested, but no longer tired, and with a hint of steely resolution in her. She would carry on for Caro, ferry aeroplanes wherever she was assigned, even to Castle Bromwich. She would fly over Brown Clee Hill and cock a snook at it.

When she went down to the lavatory, Caro and Zofia's door was closed. Rosalie returned to her room, dressed, and went down for breakfast, noticing that the lounge door stood partway open. She looked inside and saw Zofia asleep on the sofa, still in her uniform and with a thin blanket thrown over her.

"I left her," Mrs. May whispered behind Rosalie. "Poor love. I didn't want to disturb the only sleep she might get. It's a terrible thing."

Rosalie wondered how much Mrs. May knew about Caro and Zofia. Whatever she knew, at least she understood the impact of losing Caro on those closest to her.

Zofia stirred, opened her eyes, and looked round, as if unsure of where she was. And then she remembered—Rosalie could see the change in her face, the emptiness returning.

"I'll bring you a cup of tea, shall I?" Mrs. May asked.

Zofia sat up and ran her hands through her hair. "No, thank you," she said, "I will go into breakfast, but first I must wash."

When she arrived in the kitchen, she had washed her face, combed her hair, and tucked in her blouse. She stood tall with her shoulders back.

"Thank you, Mrs. May," she said, taking a cup. "I will be better today. I must not let Caro down. I will help where I am needed—Rosalie and I both will. With death, there is always much to do."

★   ★   ★

At the ferry pool, Rosalie and Zofia went directly to the waiting room to be with the others until they were called for their assignments. The women moved round them as softly as possible, offering cups of tea, patting hands. It began to get on Rosalie's nerves. Was this what Caro would've wanted, or would she want them to get out there and fly the bloody aeroplanes?

The deputy CO, Rosemary Rees, came in and said the chits were ready. She remained at the door as the women filed out. Zofia hung back, and Rosalie waited with her until only they were left.

"You're all right to fly?" Rees asked Rosalie, who nodded. "Zofia, would you stay? Dr. Andrews asked if you would phone him, and Commander Gore has said you could go into her office. I'll take you."

Rosalie continued to the assignment room. Only four chits remained on the table. She would've taken hers and been off but for looking up at the chalkboard that tracked who was flying what that day. Caro's name had been erased. Just as Bridget's had. She had been obliterated from the ferry pool. Rosalie trembled but quickly got herself in hand, because she didn't want to be told she shouldn't fly. Also because she had noticed that one pilot lingered in the room. Grace.

Grace's September wedding had been postponed because the battle-ship her fiancé commanded had been diverted to help with an operation off the coast of Africa. Since then she had been rather quiet. But now, what sorts of terrible things would Caro's death prompt her to say? Had she held back on purpose to corner Rosalie or—even worse—Zofia? To tell them Caro had finally got what she deserved for not being the sort of person Grace expected every proper woman to be? Rosalie wondered what punishment an ATA pilot received for getting into a punch-up, because if Grace dared to open her mouth, Rosalie knew her nerves would snap. Well then, better not to give her the opportunity.

She marched over to the table, slapped her hand on her two chitties, and dragged them toward her.

"Rosalie," Grace said.

Rosalie walked out the door.

Commander Gore caught up with her and walked alongside. "Wright, how are you?"

"I'm fine. I can fly."

Gore nodded. "Zofia will stay back today. I see you've your assignments there, but tomorrow is Caro's funeral." She watched Rosalie carefully. "Her father has decided to have her buried at Maidenhead, the cemetery nearest White Waltham."

Rosalie willed her chin to stop trembling. This had been what Caro wanted—to be buried at the cemetery near the ATA headquarters. She had said that very thing the afternoon they'd heard Bridget had been killed in a crash. Was that foresight or foreshadowing? And where would Rosalie want to be buried? The thought came at her suddenly. Would she want to be in the parish church next to her father or in a cemetery slowly being filled with ferry pilots and other war dead? Should she decide now, this minute, in case something happened and no one knew that—

Stop it, Rosalie told herself. *How will it look if you fall to pieces now? As if you aren't fit to fly, that's how.*

"Not everyone can be there tomorrow," Gore continued. "But Zofia will go. And you, Brenda, and I will be there too. We will wear our uniforms and be Caro's pallbearers."

Rosalie's steps slowed as she felt a pain in her heart. Could she do this for her best friend—her sister?

"It's for Caro as well as for her father. He requested it."

"Yes, ma'am."

★   ★   ★

The day had started with low clouds. Too low for an ATA pilot to fly, and Rosalie worried that the air taxi to Maidenhead would not be able to take off. She asked the CO if they should look into the train from Southampton or ask for drivers from nearby Chattis Hill. "We should plan in case we can't take off, because we must be there. We must."

Gore suggested that Rosalie go have a cup of tea, and so she went off to the waiting room, where Zofia and Brenda sat on the sofa and offered weak smiles. She joined them and, for lack of anything better to do, began to fret. Zofia had been ever so quiet about her phone conversation with Dr. Andrews. Thoughtful or worried? Caro had said her father knew about Zofia, but face-to-face, what would his reaction be? It was enough that Zofia had already lost her mother and sister—or as good as, because there had been no word since the Germans took Vichy France. Would Dr. Andrews allow her to mourn Caro properly?

The clouds lifted, then broke up, and the Fairchild taxi flew them all to White Waltham in good time. Rosalie had been in and out of the ATA ferry headquarters a dozen times. She enjoyed being at the hub of things, always reminding herself that the ATA's commanding officer, Pauline Gower—still Rosalie's hero—was nearby. But today there was no time to linger, because cars waited, and they were driven straight off to All Saints in Maidenhead.

Dr. Andrews waited for them outside the church. Rosalie thought she would've known him anywhere. He had the same black hair as Caro, although his was brushed with gray at the temples, and he had a lift to one corner of his mouth just as she had. He must be a fine-looking man, she thought, when he wasn't weighed down by sorrow.

He spoke to each of them in turn, beginning with Margot Gore, saying how much Caro had appreciated serving under her. Next, he had kind words for Brenda and the spark of laughter Caro had said she brought to the ferry pool.

That morning Rosalie had given herself strict instructions to carry out her duties without falling to pieces, but when Dr. Andrews took her hand and told her how much she had meant to Caro, as a fellow pilot and almost a younger sister, tears rushed to Rosalie's eyes and all she could say, in a thick voice, was, "She was my dearest friend." Dr. Andrews moved to Zofia last, but Rosalie struggled to regain her composure and missed their exchange.

Inside the church, the light was dim and gray. The casket lay at the front with an untidy bundle of Michaelmas daisies on top—their blooms such a pale blue as to be merely a suggestion of color. There were no other floral displays. Flowers were hard to come by unless they were from the garden or roadside. If food couldn't get past the German lines, flowers certainly wouldn't.

The service passed, quiet and lovely. Only two things stood out in Rosalie's mind—trying and failing to find her voice in order to sing "Abide with Me" and, during the Scripture reading, hearing the echoing creak of the massive wooden door at the back of the church. When she turned, she saw Snug creeping into the last pew.

The churchwarden had given the pallbearers brief instructions, and Rosalie performed her duties without any trouble, although when the casket sat on her shoulder and they processed to the grave, she had to fight the urge to lean in and listen for Caro's voice.

★ ★ ★

After the church service and the burial, they followed the crowd to a pub for sherry, glasses of beer, and sandwiches. Rosalie stood in a corner and could see no one she knew until she was joined by Snug. "Drink?" he asked.

"Yes, please," she said, and as he moved off, she added, "I don't want—"

"Sherry," he finished. "You don't want sherry. Got it." He brought back two glasses of beer, and they stood watching the crowd. Soon Brenda made her way over with a clear liquid in her glass.

"Is that gin?" Rosalie asked.

"I know the fellow behind the bar" was Brenda's reply.

There was no sign of Zofia. The room seemed to be filled with mostly older people but also a good number of others in uniform.

"Do you know who they are?" Snug asked, as they observed the room.

"I met a few," Rosalie said. "Some of Dr. Andrews's patients drove over. He said they'd known Caro all her life. Plus a few aunts and uncles, and six or seven cousins."

"Seven?" Snug replied. "I don't have a single one."

"I have two older ones on Pop's side," Rosalie said. "And one on Mum's."

"I've about three dozen cousins," Brenda said. "Let me know if you want to borrow any."

Margot Gore looked in and scanned the room, and her gaze lighted on the three of them. She nodded toward the door. They finished their drinks, each taking a sandwich from the serving table, and followed her out. Back at White Waltham, they left Snug, who said he had a Hurricane to deliver, and returned to Hamble. Rosalie hadn't seen Zofia again until they were climbing aboard the Fairchild.

She'd looked exhausted but peaceful, leaning her head back and hugging her parachute. "My mother still doesn't understand about me," she told Rosalie. "She thinks it is something I will grow out of. But Caro's father understands, and he says he was glad to meet me, because Caro had told him. He's a kind man, but with few words. Perhaps he let Caro do the talking at home. Do you think?" She smiled and wiped the tears off her face. "My father was a kind man too, but he was big"—she gestured tall and wide with her arms and then laughed—"like a bear, with voice the same. Much like your Snug."

Rosalie laughed too, and it felt good.

★   ★   ★

That night, back in her room at No. 6, Rosalie was finally able to write a letter. She sat in bed, knees up and with a two-year-old copy of *Women's Weekly* under her writing paper, and began.

> *Dear Leslie, My friend Caro has died. You remember I've mentioned her—we were billeted together here at Mrs. May's along with Zofia, the Polish pilot. Caro was such a happy person and kind to everyone. Her aeroplane stalled and she crashed. Please don't tell Mum. I'm afraid she'll only worry about me, and there's no need. But I had to tell someone. It happened only two days ago, and today she was buried at Maidenhead, in a cemetery with other ATA pilots.*
>
> *Look, Les, if anything—*

But she scratched out the last line.

CHAPTER 19

November 1943

Rosalie told herself the reason she hadn't written Alan about Caro's death was because it would be better to tell him in-person. That way she'd be able to get the measure of him first. If he seemed exhausted from flying missions every single night and as stressed as he had the last time they'd met, it might be bad news at a bad time. He had enough to occupy his mind. Yes, in-person was best. They needed to see each other again.

Not that she hadn't started several letters to him that told him the news. *Caro is dead.* She gave up that version immediately—too abrupt. *Remember Caro, one of the pilots billeted here at Number Six? She crashed her Spitfire.* No, that put it too close to home, and he would worry. *My friend Caro died last month* might make him wonder why there had been three other letters between the event and the telling. She abandoned those pages, putting them in the drawer of the wardrobe. She couldn't throw them out, because that would be a waste. Perhaps she should rip them up and put the pieces in the henhouse as bedding.

At last a day came when she had delivered an Oxford to the maintenance unit at RAF Henlow in Bedfordshire and just happened to overhear the duty officer say to another ATA pilot something about a Mosquito.

"Do you need someone to deliver a Mosquito? I can do that. Where is it going?"

She held her breath while the duty officer looked at his paperwork. "Not far—Castle Camps. You on for it?"

"Yes, sure, I'll do it," she said, covering her relief with a casual shrug.

The paperwork filled out, Rosalie departed for the short journey, putting down at Castle Camps just before two o'clock and asking about an air taxi.

"Don't know that we have another coming in today," the duty officer said, "but if you stay, you could fly this Hurricane out tomorrow morning to Henlow."

Rosalie thought about Mrs. Colby and said, "Yes, put me down for that. I should telephone Hamble and let them know."

Once that was sorted, she stepped out of the hut and smiled. This had worked out better than she could've expected. Now she and Alan would have the rest of the day together. Perhaps, with a bit of luck, he wouldn't be flying tonight and so they would have more than the afternoon. Now, where was he? She went straight to the Mess.

No Alan in sight, but Rosalie spotted someone she knew—Declan Mackenna sitting alone and making short work of a plate of stew. She'd had one dance with him and hadn't seen him since, but she marched over to his table, hoping he would remember her.

"Hello, Declan," she said.

He stood up, knife and fork in hand. "Hello. It's Rosalie, isn't it?"

"Yes. I'm looking for Alan. Do you know where he is?"

Declan looked round the Mess. "He was here, wasn't he? Although that might've been a bit ago. Not in the officers' bar?"

"Oh, well, I'll take a look. I've missed the last transport out for ATA and thought I might put up at Mrs. Colby's."

"Mrs. Colby's," Declan repeated, and stared at the door as it swung open.

Rosalie whipped round, but it was not Alan coming in.

"Would you like a cup of tea?" Declan asked. "You could wait here and I'll go find him."

"Thanks," she said, "but I'll take a look in the bar first."

But Alan wasn't in the officers' bar, either. Without telling herself she was doing it, Rosalie walked about the compound, following the route suggested by Ellen last time she'd been there. Alan was nowhere to be seen, so she ginned up her nerve and asked after him at the squadron headquarters. "Like me to get on the Tannoy?" the clerk asked with a grin.

Rosalie blushed at the thought of her request being broadcast all over the base. *Second Officer Rosalie Wright requests Flight Lieutenant Alan Chersey to meet her at . . .*

"No need. I'll have a nose round."

Perhaps she should take care of her accommodations first. She started into the village, heading for Mrs. Colby's. She pulled her jacket close and cinched the belt—the sun had ducked behind the hills to the west, and the air had taken on a chill. She could see the guesthouse up the street and across from the village hall, but she came to the pub first and thought it wouldn't hurt to look in. She approached the door and gave it a pull, found it locked, and remembered it wasn't evening opening time yet. Well, off to Mrs. Colby's, and then she'd go back to the base.

But she heard voices from round the side of the building, and she recognized one as Alan's. A thrill went through her before she realized the other voice was a woman's.

Picking her way to the corner through the drifts of beech leaves at her feet, Rosalie stopped when she reached a climbing rosebush, practically leafless, twiggy, and dense but easy enough to look through. When she did, she saw, twenty feet beyond, Alan and Deborah sitting across from each other at a table in the garden.

Rosalie thought she should say something, call out so he would know she was there. But she didn't and wasn't sure why. She felt mesmerized by the scene, as if she were at the cinema and none of this was real. She watched as they spoke, their conversation too low for her to understand. Then Alan leaned across the table and kissed Deborah.

It sent Rosalie reeling. She turned and ran, plowing through the leaves without a care and not stopping until she'd made it back to the airfield and stood panting outside the WAAF quarters. She waited until she'd caught her breath before she walked in, looking for Ellen.

★　★　★

"It's only that I find myself unable to fly out until the morning," Rosalie explained to Ellen as they each sat on a camp bed in the long barracks lined with them. "So it's very good of you to sort this out for me."

"You haven't seen Alan?" Ellen asked, and Rosalie could not tell if the question was genuine or prying.

"I imagine he's on call or something. I didn't really have a chance to find out." Rosalie didn't meet her eyes.

Ellen had not been in the WAAF quarters when Rosalie arrived, and so she had asked the first woman she'd seen, who had suggested she check in the canteen.

The WAAF canteen was run by NAAFI—by Deborah Barlow— and although Rosalie felt sure she knew where Deborah was at that moment, she would not chance it, not until she had time to sort out what she had seen.

"Are you going that way?" Rosalie had asked the WAAF. "Would you mind terribly putting your head in and checking for Ellen, and if she is there, would you tell her I'm here and I'd like to talk with her?"

Rosalie received raised eyebrows as an answer, but then the woman nodded and left.

When Ellen arrived, she didn't ask why it was that Rosalie couldn't've walked the hundred yards to the canteen herself, and when Rosalie enquired if there might be a bed for her that night here in the WAAF barracks, Ellen had made no comment but gone off, made arrangements, and returned.

"Thanks so much," Rosalie said, wishing Ellen would now leave her alone.

"Would you like a cup of tea?" Ellen asked.

"Oh, I don't . . ."

"I'll bring one back for you, why don't I?"

"Yes," Rosalie said, and found herself so near tears at Ellen's kindness that she had to turn away. "I'll just get myself settled here."

She'd composed herself by the time Ellen returned. "Thanks for this," Rosalie said, accepting the tea.

"I saw Alan," Ellen said. "He was across the way talking with Declan Mackenna."

"Good, that's good. Well then, I'd better drink this up, hadn't I? I'm sorry to be such a bother. You can leave me to it now."

Ellen hesitated, but then offered a perky "See you later" and left. Her footsteps were the only sound in the long hall. Only when they had faded and Rosalie was truly alone could she open the door in her mind to what she'd seen and examine it for what it was. Alan kissing Deborah Barlow. Deborah, that "good egg" who organized football matches and dances and took care of the RAF pilots who needed looking after. Was this part of the service?

No, that wasn't fair. It was Alan's action, not Deborah's, that Rosalie must address. Was it that she and Alan were finished and he just hadn't thought to mention it to Rosalie yet?

True, she had also kept things from him. She hadn't told him about Caro, but that was because she needed to see him in-person to do so. Was that what had happened for him? He wanted to break it off with her but thought it would be better to do so face-to-face? Well, if that was the case, she would take it on the chin. She wouldn't be one of those weepy girls who begged him to come back to her.

Rosalie blew her nose. She would find him—find him and release him from their promises, although now she had trouble putting into words just what those had been. Had they talked of marriage? Not exactly. They both had said they would get through the war first and be together after. "After the war" seemed a faraway and blurry prospect, without definition.

A WAAF came in the door at the far end and said, "Rosalie Wright?"

"Yes?"

"There's someone out here wants to see you."

Alan stood just outside the door, so close that Rosalie almost ran into him when she stepped out. His face was flushed and his eyes shining bright and hot. He took her hands and held them to his chest.

"You're here," he said. "I couldn't believe it when Mack told me. I didn't know. Have you been here long?" He squeezed her hands and kissed them. "I'm so glad to see you."

His emotion overwhelmed her and sent her off course until he added, "Why are you in the WAAF quarters? Wouldn't you rather be at Mrs. Colby's?"

She took a breath and began. "I arrived earlier and I went looking for you, and when you weren't about, I thought I would get a room at Mrs. Colby's. I was about to pass the pub and thought I'd look in there first, but it had closed for the afternoon, and then I heard your voice and followed it and saw you with Deborah." A flicker of something that she imagined might be guilt crossed his face and disappeared. She went in pursuit. "I saw you kiss her."

"No."

She pulled her hands away. "I know what I saw."

"No, that isn't . . . that's . . ."

Two WAAFs pushed past them to get in, one of them sending Rosalie an envious look, the sort she'd seen at the dance when she was in Alan's arms.

"Let's go somewhere and talk," he said, taking hold of her arm. "Please, please let's talk, Rosalie. Where we won't be disturbed. Let me explain, won't you?"

She didn't know what sort of explanation might accompany the fact that he had kissed Deborah Barlow, but she nodded and said, "Yes."

He led her round the back of the Mess to a small Nissen hut. He opened the door and clicked on a single lightbulb. The place held shelves of stores and a table and two chairs. Alan closed the door and pulled her into his arms. When she didn't respond, he held her out at arm's length. He could've shifted her like a sack of potatoes—all her fight had vanished and she felt like her namesake, the rag doll at Lime Farm.

"I'm sorry," he said, and she could see tears in his eyes. "I can't tell you how sorry I am." Gently, he pulled her down into a chair and kept hold of both her hands. "It was a mistake, and I have absolutely no excuse for my behavior. What you saw meant nothing to me. This is what I want you to understand. It's you I love. It's only because of this bloody war and you being so far away and me missing you so dreadfully . . . I feel so alone that . . . well, I lost my head. It won't happen again. I won't even speak to her again if that's what you want. I swear. Please, please forgive me."

Alan waited and watched her, his faced washed of color but his eyes still on fire.

"Is that the first time you've kissed her?"

He didn't answer, and his silence caused Rosalie to leap from her chair and back away.

"No, wait, listen." He stood and caught her. "We knew each other before. At Honington. It was ages before you and I met. We saw each other now and then, that's all. But you see, you changed all that. When we met, I knew you were different. I knew we were meant for each other."

Rosalie remained standing. "If she was at Honington, how is it that she came here to Castle Camps where you are?"

Alan shrugged. "She's NAAFI. I don't know how they're managed. But it doesn't matter, because I won't speak to her from now on. I would never do anything to hurt you. I can't lose you, Rosalie—you're my only hope."

"You kissed her."

"It was nothing. It was only a kiss."

Rosalie looked at the floor and considered this. Did a kiss mean more to her than it did to Alan? Was that the way with all men?

When she said nothing, Alan continued. "It was wrong of me—I know that. Please, Rosalie, don't let what I've done ruin everything for us. What we have now and what we will have in the future. Can you forgive me?"

Rosalie strained to hear beyond his words. That he was upset was obvious—disheveled, worried, and he had that hollow look she'd seen when they'd last met. He looked sad. There was no doubt he was under enormous stress. So the question was, could she forgive him this one transgression?

If only Caro were alive and she could ask her what to do. But no, Rosalie must fly alone on this one. And after all, whatever had been between Alan and Deborah before was long over. As he'd said, this was only a kiss.

"I won't hold you to any promises, you know," Rosalie said. "If you find someone else—"

"You must hold me to every single promise I make to you. I expect it."

Rosalie paused for the longest time. Alan kept his eyes on her, and at last she said, "Even promising we'll always have enough sugar after the war?"

The smile that spread across his face banished the sadness, stress, and worry, and he was Alan again. She smiled in return.

As they walked back to the WAAF quarters, Alan said, "Wouldn't you be more comfortable at Mrs. Colby's? I'm sure she has a room."

"No, I don't want to stay at Mrs. Colby's."

Alan's glance darted to her and then away. "No, of course not." Just before they reached the barracks, he turned off the path, rounded the corner, and they were alone. "I love you, Rosalie. You know that, don't you?"

"Yes, I do know."

"And when the war is over, I'll take care of you."

He kissed her gently, then with longing. She pushed the image away that rose in her mind and concentrated on the moment. Then an announcement came over the Tannoy.

"That's for me," Alan said, "best be off. I'll write and let you know the first chance I have of a day."

"Caro died." She didn't mean to be so abrupt, but it was the one thing she had wanted to tell him, and she'd been sidetracked.

"Your friend?"

"Yes," she said, quickly giving him the story.

"I'm so sorry. Are you all right?"

She nodded. She would have to be.

Before he left her, he asked, "Can we find time for another night at the Feathers, do you think? Soon."

CHAPTER 20

Christmas 1943

Rosalie and Alan met at the Feathers in early December, and it was the one good thing about the days leading up to Christmas. Rosalie flew into Debden and had been bold enough to change clothes at the airfield before boarding the bus—no one had made a comment to her about being out of uniform. No one had even given her a second look. Once again, she had borrowed Anne's navy-and-white dotted shirtdress. Rosalie knew she really should buy her own frock, but that would use up eleven clothing coupons, and she'd already spent five on proper shoes and given Mrs. May five to help buy linens and towels. Three more had gone for a pair of knickers, and she had used two for a new handkerchief that she kept tucked away in the bag she took on every flight.

Alan waited for her where the bus stopped across from the hotel. He kissed her right there, and they took a moment to look into each other's eyes before they crossed the road arm in arm. They'd got past that business about Deborah and had written each other six times in just the four weeks that had gone by. Rosalie felt as if she understood a bit more about the relationship between a man and a woman and how they had to forgive and go on. She was glad to have Alan's arm round her. Just let people wonder if they really were married; she didn't care.

Although she wasn't so bold that she wasn't grateful to see Mr. Wilkes and not his wife at the desk when they walked into the hotel. He was kind and greeted them as he might old friends, and again he took hold of their bags, preparing to take them upstairs. But someone called to him from the dining room, and so he allowed Alan to take the bags and plodded off with his sailor's gait.

Since they'd last seen each other, Rosalie had built up such a longing for Alan's touch that she had returned to those restless nights at No. 6, unable to sleep for thinking of him. She knew he felt the same. She could see it in his eyes and feel the heat of it when he put his hand on her back as they walked up the stairs. They could barely get in their room and close the door before he'd pulled her skirt up and they'd tumbled onto the bed.

★ ★ ★

The December weather did nothing to cooperate with the ATA's need to ferry aeroplanes around the country—low clouds, heavy rain, fog. No matter that they fired up the electric heater to all three bars, the waiting room retained a damp and sullen atmosphere, and the women easily got on one another's nerves. Rosalie had resorted to carrying *Treasure Island* with her to ward off Grace's attempts to teach her bridge. It didn't help that Christmas was upon them.

Rosalie dreaded the holiday without Caro and could dwell on little else during the dark days. It would be the three of them—she, Zofia, and Mrs. May—each consumed with thoughts of their losses. Stoically, they would listen to the King's message in the lounge while surrounded by drooping paper chains and a sprig of mistletoe with no one to take advantage of it. They would sit like lumps at the kitchen table, dutifully eating their mock goose. Mrs. May longing to hear from Fred or Terry. Rosalie with greetings from Lime Farm. Zofia with nothing.

Guilt sat like a rock in Rosalie's stomach, because she knew that enduring a sad Christmas at No. 6 was preferable to entering the battlefield that was Lime Farm. Even if little Robert's name was not mentioned, the subject would hang in the air, overpowering any sense of Christmas cheer.

Will, Jean, and Leslie had all written *We need your cheerful self here at Lime Farm.* In response, Rosalie had explained that they were so far behind in delivering aeroplanes that if there were even a few hours' break in the weather, they must all be ready to fly—and that meant Christmas Eve through Boxing Day. They would see through that excuse in an instant, but she promised herself she would make it up to them with a visit in the new year. And, with Caro's voice in her head, she told them they should just jolly well go and get Robert and take him to his new home at Lime Farm.

On Christmas Eve, Mrs. May and her two ducklings following behind set off for church, the landlady looking back over her shoulder once or twice on the way.

"We are not going to escape," Zofia said. "Do not worry."

"She might be looking for Father Christmas," Rosalie said, to which Mrs. May replied, "I just might be at that."

★   ★   ★

Christmas morning, Rosalie pulled out her red jumper, noticed a small hole, and set to mending it. She thought she'd heard someone downstairs earlier, and yet when she passed Zofia's door, it was closed, and on the ground floor everything was quiet. Rosalie went into the lounge and switched on the wireless. She listened for a moment to "O Come, All Ye Faithful," humming as she pulled the blackout curtains away from the front door. The post hadn't arrived yet, and so she went through to the kitchen, where she found Dr. Andrews sitting with a cup of tea.

Rosalie jumped back and knocked into the door. "Oh, my!"

He leapt out of his chair, and she noticed his red-rimmed eyes and ashen face. "Hello," he said, looking sheepish. "Happy Christmas."

"Oh, yes . . . Happy . . ."

"I've startled you," he said. "I'm sorry."

"No, certainly not. Well, yes, you have, but—"

Mrs. May appeared at the door to the garden, backing in and talking as she did. "Winter or no, you'd think they would realize the importance of the day and offer us a gift of their eggs. Ah well, at least we have porridge."

As if in response, Rosalie heard a *plop* from the pot on the hob. "Yes," she said, "at least we have porridge."

The landlady turned, holding an empty egg basket. "Ah, you've noticed your Christmas surprise," she said, nodding to Caro's father.

"Mrs. May and I have been corresponding, you see," Dr. Andrews explained. "I needed to come down and collect Caro's things and make arrangements for her car, and Mrs. May was kind enough to invite me for Christmas."

"You don't need to be knocking round that house all alone," Mrs. May said to him. "I expected him last evening." She directed that at Rosalie. "A Christmas surprise for you two."

Definitely a surprise, and a bit of a shock at first, but Rosalie quickly warmed to the idea.

"I had an emergency," Dr. Andrews said. "The midwife needed a bit of help with a Christmas Eve baby. But I left as soon as I could, and anyone who needs a doctor today knows to call the next village over."

"You drove through the night?" Rosalie asked. That, at least, explained how exhausted he looked. "Well, this is splendid, it truly is. Does Zofia know?"

"No," Mrs. May said, dropping her voice to a loud whisper. "Has she come down yet?"

Rosalie shook her head. "Shall I go fetch her?"

"We'll wait."

The letter box squeaked open, and the post was put through. Rosalie went out to the entry and collected the few pieces as Zofia came down the stairs, pausing halfway at the sound of a man's voice.

"Who is here?"

Rosalie nodded toward the kitchen. "Go on." She followed after a moment to find Zofia clasping Dr. Andrew's hands while tears streamed down her face. Mrs. May stood at the hob, soaking up her own tears with a tea towel.

And so, Christmas did make an appearance at No. 6. It was the best porridge Rosalie could remember, because Mrs. May produced a jar of raspberry jam she had sequestered since it was cooked up in the summer—Rosalie sometimes wondered if the landlady didn't have a secret pantry of delicious but scarce foods hidden behind the one sparsely furnished with tins of fish paste and tomato soup—and they each stirred in a spoonful. For once, there appeared to be plenty of good, strong tea and fresh milk. When she enquired after the bounty, she learned that Dr. Andrews had brought down his own rations plus a gift or two from patients.

"The least I could do," he said.

Over breakfast and with prompting, he told them stories about Caro as a girl—headstrong, compassionate, funny. In response, they told him she was an excellent pilot, an almost-perfect lodger—"She was a bit too free with the bathwater at times," Mrs. May said, "but who can blame her?"—and the best friend.

"I don't know what I would've worn to that dance if she hadn't polled the women at the pool and found something suitable for me to borrow," Rosalie said.

Mrs. May chased them out of the kitchen so that she could get the dinner under way, and the three retired to the lounge. There, Dr. Andrews asked Zofia and Rosalie more pointed questions about being pilots—the training, the war, the day-to-day flying. "She never wanted to say too much about the dangers you face when you fly, I think," he said. "Didn't want to worry me. But I would like to think of how she went about each day. How each of you manages."

Rosalie and Zofia—who was more animated than she'd been in weeks—gave a glowing picture of their lives as ferry pilots and dredged up the funniest stories they could think of about the ferry pool and No. 6.

"The hens," he said, nodding to Rosalie. "Caro told me about Snug helping you out."

"I believe he felt guilty for skiving off work when he was a lodger here early in '41," Rosalie said, "and so he came back as recompense."

"Perhaps not only guilt," Zofia said. "Perhaps now he sees more reason to come to Number Six."

Dr. Andrews stood. "I need to fetch my bag—I left it in the car. Won't be a minute." He hesitated and then said, "I'd had several invitations for Christmas, actually, but I couldn't bring myself to accept any. When Mrs. May offered, it seemed right. It meant I would see where Caro lived, where she was happy. You all have made such a difference."

He soon returned and asked Mrs. May to join them in the lounge. He opened his case and said, "I hope you don't mind that I've brought a few gifts along for you—from Caro, really. She never was one to want a lot of things, but what she had, she loved. So . . ." He bent over his bag and at the same time took his handkerchief out and wiped his face. "Mrs. May, I brought this scarf back for her from Italy in '34."

The landlady shook out the silk. It was a riot of color and floated as light as a cloud.

"Rosalie, I remember Caro saying you didn't care for bridge, but that this was a favorite." He handed her a much-worn box of the card game Happy Families.

"Oh, yes—it's perfect."

"Zofia," Dr. Andrews said, and handed her a book, an old one by the look of it, leather bound. "She told me how you lost everything when your mother and sister escaped, including your father's library. I'm very sorry. But she said how much you loved Dickens."

Zofia stroked the book, a copy of *Bleak House*, and whispered, "Thank you."

Rosalie popped up, saying, "Shall I put the kettle on? I could certainly use a fresh cup of tea." She ran out without waiting for an answer, making it to the kitchen before she let out a sob, clutching the pack of playing cards to her chest.

Where were these happy families? Dr. Andrews had lost his only child; Jean wasn't allowed to keep hers. What hope was there for Zofia's mother and sister? Zofia and Caro had been like a family unto themselves, and look how that had ended. What of Rosalie's family—at Lime Farm and any to come? Nothing seemed certain.

Not a minute later, Mrs. May walked in the kitchen saying, "How is that tea coming along?" and found Rosalie backed into a corner, weeping.

"Now, love, what's this?"

Rosalie shook her head, unable to speak.

"There, now." The landlady cupped Rosalie's face. "We all miss her and will do for a long while, I'm sure. Do you want to go have a rest?"

"No, I'm better now. Let me just splash some water on my face, and then I'll come out."

Mrs. May left her to it. Rosalie blew her nose, washed her face, and put the kettle on. Then she saw the post that she'd set on the counter and forgotten about.

Only three pieces. There was a letter from Lime Farm and one for Mrs. May from a cousin in Australia. Last was a postcard addressed only to *Number Six, Satchell Lane, Hamble*. The illustration showed a black kitten with a red bow round its neck peeking out of a large boot that had a spray of holly tucked into its laces. The message on the back, written in a heavy and deliberate hand, as if the pen were too small or the hand too large, read, *Happy Christmas, Snug.*

Rosalie laughed. She put her own letter in her pocket and took the postcard and greetings from Australia out to the lounge. As she passed the front door, there was a knock, and she stopped to answer.

A man in RAF uniform stood there with a rucksack slung over his shoulder. He had the same chin and keen look in his eye as Mrs. May, and without being told, Rosalie knew for certain that this was Fred. Or Terry. She'd never got the photos on the mantel straight.

"Are you a surprise?" Rosalie mouthed.

He nodded. "Where is she?" he whispered.

Rosalie nodded toward the lounge and then put her hand up to tell Fred—or Terry—to stay put. As she closed the door, she pointed at him and made a knocking motion.

"Who was that?" Mrs. May asked when Rosalie sauntered into the lounge.

"Sorry, what?" she said. A sharp rap came from the front door.

"Did you not hear that?" the landlady said, getting up, waving Rosalie out of the way, and heading to the door while she muttered, "Aeroplane noise making you go deaf, no doubt."

They heard a shriek from the entry.

★　★　★

Over a cup of tea, Terry told them about being a senior controller in operations at RAF East Fortune near Edinburgh.

"Do you know it?" he asked the pilots.

"Yes, I have flown there," Zofia said. "Blenheim once and Mosquito another time."

"Two Blenheims for me," Rosalie said. "Just think, we might've crossed paths and not known it."

Mrs. May gave her son a tour of the henhouse, and upon returning, he marveled at the change in the garden. "And the bear built it? I didn't know he'd returned."

"He filled in the crater," his mum said, "and built the henhouse. Although it was this one that was in charge." She nodded at Rosalie.

"We did what we could with what we had," Rosalie said, "just as they ask us. Snug came up with the wire. Otherwise, I'm not sure our nails would've held the contraption together. Did you meet him while he was here?"

Terry shook his head. "But I heard Mum's stories. He sounds quite a character."

Too bad Snug wasn't here, Rosalie thought. Wouldn't that be a jolly group? Was he having Christmas with his mum, Mouse, and Delfina at the Bishop's Finger? Rosalie drew a picture in her mind of a smoky, dark pub decorated for Christmas with stems of red-berried holly tucked about the place and a sprig of mistletoe hanging in the middle of the room. The regulars would be there, pints sitting in front of them, and someone would break out into the wassail song. Funny how she could picture the pub and his mum behind the bar and she'd never laid eyes on them. What a comfortable, cozy place.

"Here we are now," Mrs. May said, turning up the volume on the wireless, "the King's message."

The King did his best to uplift their spirits with good news about the country growing its own food and winning battles, but he also acknowledged that they would always remember those who have been lost and those left behind: "Our hearts go out to you with sorrow, with comfort, but also with pride."

The next program picked up with a lively dance band, but at No. 6, no one moved.

"No word from Fred," Mrs. May said.

"He's all right, Mum," Terry replied.

"Do you know where he is?"

Terry shook his head.

Another silence.

"Is that mock goose I smell, Mrs. May?" Zofia asked.

"Oh, the meal." The landlady was off like a shot.

They revived over food and after, too, when Dr. Andrews presented Mrs. May with a bottle of brandy. He had taken Rosalie aside earlier to ask if that would be appropriate. "Oh yes," Rosalie replied. "She's another bottle somewhere—we saw it last Christmas—but it was running low then. Surely it's time to replenish."

They drank their brandy in silence, until the women heard a low snore come from Dr. Andrews, who held his empty glass upright and had rested his head against the back of the sofa. That brought up the subject of sleeping arrangements.

Dr. Andrews roused himself. "I'll go into Southampton," he said, stretching his shoulders back. "I'll find a hotel."

"I won't have it," Mrs. May said.

"Rosalie can come in with me," Zofia said. "I have the extra bed."

"I'll sleep on the sofa here in the lounge," Terry offered. "It's where you found me many a morning after one pint too many the night before."

His mother threw him a look, but it changed quickly to an indulgent smile. "Now, wait, all of you, and let me sort this out." The seconds ticked by, and Rosalie noticed Dr. Andrews's eyes grow heavy. Mrs. May tapped a finger on her chin as if puzzling out how to piece together a jigsaw. "Right, here's what we'll do. The girls together upstairs, Dr. Andrews in the top room, and Terry . . ."

Terry laughed. "You see, I was right. The sofa."

"Oh you," his mother said.

*　★　*

On Boxing Day, Rosalie hurried through breakfast and left for the ferry pool alone so that Dr. Andrews and Zofia could have a word in private and Terry and his mother could say good-bye. In her pocket, she carried with her the Christmas letter from Lime Farm. She'd read it twice but wanted another look later. She'd almost put Snug's postcard in her pocket too, because it made her smile every time she looked at it, but she'd decided that was selfish because it hadn't really been addressed to her. Instead she propped it up against the milk jug on the kitchen table.

CHAPTER 21

Winter 1944

*D*ear Leslie, I hope this finds you all well. Rosalie hesitated, wishing she could ask specifically about Will and Jean and little Robert but knowing that was a bad idea. She'd been too bold before Christmas. Usually her letters were passed round, and the post was no way to carry on a conversation about delicate issues. *The weather has kept us from flying most days and so I find myself working on a sweater with yarn so coarse and of such an unpleasant color, I don't really want anyone to wear it. Will tells me he's yet to get rid of the sheep. Whenever he goes through with it, give them a kiss goodbye for me.*

During the slow times in the waiting room, after letters had been written and wool had been knitted, Rosalie looked through her logbook and made lists of how many different aeroplanes she had flown—fifty-seven to date. She'd made deliveries to 193 aerodromes and MUs, and as for total flights made, well, she kept losing count and had to start over. She noted the busiest days, and put a star beside her favorite aeroplanes—Spitfire, naturally, with Hurricanes not far behind, but also the larger Wellington. Mosquito. Fairey Battle and Firefly and the Hawker Tempest and Typhoon. She became rather sentimental and admitted to a fondness for an old Moth. The exercise meant nothing to anyone else, but it kept her busy.

She'd had a quick letter from Alan, and she'd sent him a rather brief reply. It seemed as if there just wasn't much to say. Rosalie looked back on their one night together in early December and could not remember anything about it apart from being in bed with him. Hadn't they talked? Had they both been too preoccupied with other things? She was missing something, and it worried her.

Soon after Christmas, Zofia had begun again to watch out for the post. Rosalie waited for her to explain, but after almost three weeks, one dark evening as they returned to their digs, she could stand it no longer.

"Is it your mum?" she asked. "Do you expect to hear from them?"

"There is nothing yet," Zofia said.

They strolled along in the darkness. The blackout had started an hour ago—winter days were so short that they were often finished flying by three o'clock. Usually the women gathered in the waiting room to see if anything was on, perhaps deciding to go to the cinema or a dance in Southampton or for a drink at the pub. But without Caro, Rosalie and Zofia were rather sticks-in-the-mud and contented themselves with the wireless or books at No. 6.

Rosalie longed for spring just so they could fly more. And, too, so Mrs. May would stop fretting over the hens that were currently offering up only the occasional egg.

Zofia's steps slowed, and she glanced sideways at Rosalie. "But," she said quietly, "at Christmas, Dr. Andrews tells me he has a cousin who works for the War Office. Or some department—he isn't quite sure. But he says it is someone who might be able to . . . the word, it is like *ask*."

"Ascertain?"

"Yes, that is it. Ascertain the . . . situation of my mother and sister." Even in the dark, Rosalie could see Zofia's face was a mix of hope and fear, one overtaking the other, back and forth. "I try not to expect too much."

★   ★   ★

One day in late January, Rosalie found herself at Aston Down for the night. Snug wasn't about, and she didn't see Marjorie anywhere—perhaps they were off together. Did Brenda mind?

At the Watch Office, Rosalie enquired about a bed in the WAAF quarters, but when the duty officer asked if he looked like a hotelier, she gave up and instead told him she would need the first air taxi back to Hamble the next morning, and did he think he could manage that? She didn't wait for a reply but walked off, eating her two-penny chocolate bar.

The WAAF canteen was nearly empty, and the Officers' Mess was busy with officers but no ATA pilots, so Rosalie continued into the village, her bag in one hand and her parachute in the other. Once or twice she and Snug had had a drink in the Wheatsheaf, and it seemed as if Rosalie remembered they had rooms.

The pub, having just opened for evening hours, was already heaving. As she squeezed her way up to the bar, she heard Snug shout, "Wright!"

He sat at the head of a long table filled with a variety of men and women in uniform—ATA, WAAF, ground crew, Observer Corps, Home Guard. Rosalie made her way over and spotted Marjorie at the other end of the table, sitting on the lap of an airman.

"It's my birthday!" called Marjorie.

"Oh, that's lovely," Rosalie called over the din.

"Sit down," Snug said, nodding next to him.

The chairs on both sides were occupied, but the fellow on his left patted his lap and winked at Rosalie. "Here you are, love."

"Shift yourself!" Snug barked at him, and the man took his pint and got up, muttering.

"Drink?" Snug asked Rosalie.

"Yes, please. I also need a room—do you think they have one going?"

He came back with two pints, but instead of sitting, he pointed with his chin to the corner, where a tiny table and two short stools were hemmed in by the standing crowd. Rosalie got behind Snug and followed as he pushed his way through the mob.

"That's better," Snug said when they'd settled. "Here, give me that." He took her parachute and crammed it under the table, and she put her bag behind her against the wall. "You've got a room upstairs, second on the right. Cheers."

"Thanks, that's grand." Rosalie took a drink first, then added, "I have something for you." She pulled her bag back out, set it on her lap, and began searching by touch through the jumble—a fresh pair of knickers, her forage cap, a chocolate bar she'd forgotten about. At the very bottom, her hand came across a small, paper-wrapped square. Rosalie's face heated as she realized that what she held was one of the "French letters" Caro had obtained for her as a precaution. In her mind, Rosalie could see the painting of the flouncy lady. She hadn't needed them, because Alan was always prepared, and so they had lain forgotten in her bag.

"What is it you have for me?"

"I have . . . er, yes, let's see." She released the flouncy lady and located the correct item. "This!" She held out a clean, white, ironed handkerchief.

Snug cocked his head and squinted his good eye at the offering.

"Don't you remember," Rosalie said, "you lent me yours, the day you found me after Caro's crash."

"Is this one mine?"

"Good heavens, no. We use that out in the henhouse. This one is new."

"But that would cost—"

"Two coupons and a few pennies."

"A shilling, more likely." Snug took not only the handkerchief but also her hand, and he gave it a squeeze.

She squeezed back, and their clasped hands dropped to the table. Snug brushed the back of hers with his thumb.

"Thanks," he said.

"You're welcome."

The man standing next to Rosalie knocked into their table, and Snug released her hand in order to save his pint from toppling over.

Rosalie took a drink, looked round the pub, and said, "Do they do sandwiches here? I'm famished."

"Do you want me to go back over?"

"No, I'll ask later. Remember you were telling me about delivering that American bomber, the Fortress, to Kinloss up in Scotland? How is it to fly?"

They never seemed to have enough time to get through their news, and now Snug picked up on the story he had been telling her the last time their paths crossed, which had been at Lyneham the week before. At some point, he stood up and motioned to the publican, who understood whatever signs Snug threw at him, for in a few minutes he made his way over with a plate of sandwiches.

The bread was a bit dry at the corners, and the filling was, inevitably, fish paste. No matter; she was hungry enough to eat the whole fish. Rosalie had read the label on a tin of the stuff in Mrs. May's pantry. She couldn't really say what sort of fish a bloater was, but they must be plentiful. She shared with Snug, and two hours later, they noticed the pub had mostly emptied out.

"Oh, but you missed the rest of the evening with Marjorie," Rosalie said.

"It was just a load of us out together," Snug said. He stretched his legs out and leaned against the wall. "So, how is Chersey?"

"Fine." Her answer was clipped, and she played with the pile of bread crumbs in the plate. "It's a difficult assignment, don't you think?—night defensive fighter? Very stressful. I mean, it would put you on edge, so that you may do something without thinking . . . something that you don't really intend and then you realize it, and you're quite . . ."

She didn't know how those words had slipped out. Rosalie had thought she was truly past the emotional upheaval that had threatened to undo her the day she saw Alan kissing Deborah. But she and Alan had been apart too long, and uncomfortable thoughts had begun to resurface in her mind since Christmas. To combat them, she had taken to telling herself over and over what she'd just said to Snug.

Snug's eyebrows lowered. "What did he do?"

"Nothing," she said in a rush. "Nothing, I didn't mean . . . well, so First Officer Durrant, how's the Lancaster?"

He kept his eye on her and didn't answer.

"Lancaster," she repeated, "the aeroplane."

"Yeah, it's all right." He looked as if he might go back to the previous subject but instead added, "Had ice pellets bouncing off me the other day when I landed up in Lincolnshire."

"What're you doing flying in that sort of weather?" she demanded.

"It was fine when I took off—Met said it would be all right. Only when I got there, this thing came sweeping in, caught between the hills. But I landed. And there wasn't a cow in sight."

She laughed.

The publican rang the bell and called time.

"I don't know how it got to be closing time," Rosalie said as she stood and picked up her bag.

"Good night, then." Snug stood too and ran his fingers through his short brown hair, causing it to stand on end.

Wouldn't her mum love to take a pair of shears to that, she thought, and smiled.

"Yeah, good night." She took the stairs behind the bar, and before Snug was out of sight, she gave him a wave.

She'd been in the room not a minute when there came a knock, and she opened the door to Snug with her parachute.

"Oh, sorry," she said, taking it.

He shifted uncomfortably. "Look," he said, "I only want to say, that you shouldn't have to put up with . . . whatever it is that Chersey did. You deserve better."

She bristled. "He didn't do anything."

"He did—you think I can't tell that?"

"It's none of your business what happened," Rosalie said hotly. "It's private, and you have no right to tell me what I should do."

Snug's jaw worked as he glared at her, but at last he said, "No, I don't have any right, do I?"

He turned and stomped down the corridor, while Rosalie remained frozen in the open doorway. But she sprang to life when she heard him start down the stairs.

She dashed out to the landing.

"Snug?"

He stopped on the bottom step and turned, his face like thunder.

"See you in the morning?" she asked. "In the Mess? Cup of tea?"

The storm cleared. "Yeah," he said. "Of course."

CHAPTER 22

April 1944

"I'm here to pick up a Blenheim and take it to Little Rissington," Rosalie told the duty officer. She had flown to Castle Camps with no expectation of seeing Alan, because his squadron had moved on to Predannack in Cornwall. He'd written about it only a day before they left—all the notice they got, he said. Now she must hope for an assignment there.

He had written her again when they'd settled, a lovely letter that had arrived only a day ago. Barely in passing he mentioned he'd been made squadron leader. Most of the letter he told her how much he missed her, how he was looking for someplace they could meet whenever it could be arranged, how he'd had a dream of the war being over and the two of them spending a glorious summer in the country with no one else about, Rosalie whiling away her days in the cutting garden tending sweet peas. He remembered sweet peas, he wrote, from his holidays to Easton Hall, the family's home. *Sweet peas smell like heaven—like you.*

"Blenheim isn't ready," the duty officer replied, "but it shouldn't be long—give you time for a cup of tea."

Because there would be no Alan to look for in the Officers' Mess, Rosalie, head held high, marched off to the WAAF canteen, run by NAAFI. She hoped to see Deborah Barlow there, have a friendly chat, and lay that business at Castle Camps to rest. Alan's letter had put shed to any recurrent worries she'd had about him and Deborah. Rosalie regretted her unkind thoughts about the woman, and she wanted to put things right.

The WAAF canteen was a cheerful place, clusters of women here and there chatting and laughing. It hadn't seemed like that to Rosalie on her previous visits. A woman behind the counter was setting out a tray of cakes, and Rosalie could smell the sweetness from across the room. The services were never short of sugar. She took a slice and a cup of tea and was about to ask the worker where she might find Deborah when Ellen came up beside her.

"Mind if I join you?"

"Oh, please do; I was hoping I'd see you." It wasn't a lie—hadn't Rosalie promised they'd do this?

They sat at a table and chatted about nothing in particular, until Rosalie found the conversation turning toward Lime Farm.

"How are Will and his bride?" Ellen asked. "Wasn't it lovely that he married one of the Land Girls? How many did you say the farm has?"

"Five. Well, four with Jean married, although she still does her work and more."

"Five women working every day right next to them—to Will and to Leslie, I mean. So how could they not notice?" When Rosalie didn't answer immediately, Ellen prodded, "Don't you think?"

"Will and Jean fell in love," Rosalie said. "Not because she was a Land Girl, but just because they did. That they both love what they do makes it that much better, but it wasn't a requirement. And it doesn't mean Leslie will automatically fall in love with one of the others."

Because, of course, that was what Ellen was fishing for—news of Les.

"How is your mother?" Rosalie asked. "I hear that you were home to take care of her."

"She's doing well, quite well."

"And your fiancé? Ned?"

Ellen colored slightly, and her voice cooled. "We aren't engaged any longer."

"Oh, I'm sorry." But relieved, too, that she had been right to tell Les that this thing with Ned wouldn't last.

"It's for the best," Ellen said. "He's a bit of a . . . dullard. Says he has ideas for improving a car's gearbox, and he talks of little else. He doesn't read books and he isn't interested in anything but motors. I mean, look at Les, for example. He's a fine farmer, but he's fascinated with the world, and he can talk about other things. Remember the time he became so interested in St. Kilda?"

Rosalie remembered, and she had an image of Ellen rolling her eyes when Leslie would start in on the remote and deserted Scottish island.

"Why don't you write him, Ellen?"

"What? Me write Les? Oh, I don't think I . . . he doesn't want to hear from me." She cut her eyes at Rosalie. "Does he?"

"You won't know unless you try."

"It's too bad you're here today and Alan's squadron has left."

"Yes, he's in Cornwall now, but I'll see him soon, I'm sure." They finished their tea, and Rosalie scanned the room one last time. "I thought I'd say hello to Deborah Barlow while I was here. Have you seen her?"

Ellen glanced over her shoulder as if checking on eavesdroppers, then leaned over the table. "Rosalie, last time you were here and you put up with us, you seemed a bit . . . upset."

Had she hoped no one would notice she'd barricaded herself in the WAAF quarters and sent out emissaries with messages and on errands for tea?

"Did I?" she asked cautiously.

"Was it because of Deborah?"

Rosalie had told no one, but that was only because Caro was dead. She would've told her. No, Caro would've known before a word was spoken. Did Rosalie now have to drag this painful memory out of its drawer and examine it with Ellen?

"At the dance," Rosalie said, thinking in for a penny, in for a pound, "I remember Alan knew who you were. Had the two of you . . . ?"

"No," Ellen said. "Certainly not. We may have gone for a drink once or twice. But that was before—"

"Before Deborah arrived?"

Ellen picked up her empty teacup and then set it down again and offered Rosalie a smile. "He changed altogether when he met you."

"Not altogether."

The mere suggestion of a nod was all the confirmation Rosalie needed, but Ellen added, "I didn't know what to say before, but, you know, I might've seen them together. Once or twice. Just talking, that's all. I never saw anything else."

Yes, but Rosalie had. *It was a kiss. Only a kiss.*

Ellen brightened. "But it doesn't matter now, because Alan's squadron has moved off and Deborah has gone too."

"Where has she gone?"

Ellen shrugged. "I don't know. Another NAAFI post, I suppose. You could ask Mrs. Colby at the guesthouse—she might know."

Rosalie left to check on her Blenheim and was told it would be another hour. Plenty of time. She set off to walk into the village to say hello to Mrs. Colby and ask after Deborah. Had she moved to another NAAFI station to organize dances and football matches and run the canteen? Perhaps to Inverness or Ballykelly in Northern Ireland? But Rosalie had made it only halfway to the guesthouse when she saw the pub coming up on her right, and her steps slowed until she came to a stop. If Deborah Barlow had moved to another NAAFI post, then good for her. That should put an end to the incessant discussion in Rosalie's head.

She returned to find her Blenheim ready, but the duty officer told her why it was heading for the maintenance unit: it had been peppered by ack-ack guns. Friendly fire from the ground. "Said they couldn't see the roundels," he told her. "If that's the case, they'd better get their eyes checked. At any rate, the engine's in fine shape, and so off you go."

Rosalie walked round the aeroplane and saw holes scattered across the metal skin and the cockpit. She should've asked after the pilot, but then thought that if he'd been able to land, he couldn't have been too bad off.

Takeoff was no trouble and the flight went smoothly, although she could feel the cold air being sucked in through the bullet holes and swirling round her. It made her feel as if she were back in an open-air Tiger Moth. No matter, as the cold air blew away the last of the dark thoughts in her mind. She pulled the Blenheim up to a thousand feet and banked west toward Gloucestershire.

★　★　★

Five days straight of a thick, wet, gray mist kept the ferry pilots on the ground. The women chafed at their confinement and got on one another's nerves. Rosalie continued to be full of resentment at how Grace had treated Caro and so had made it her mission to avoid being in a room with the woman. If she spotted Grace at the bridge table in the waiting room, then Rosalie would find somewhere else to be. And so it was that during the prolonged dreary days, she would often return to No. 6 and work in the back garden.

First she carried out a thorough cleanup of the beds, then tied back the new growth on the raspberries before the thicket threatened to take over. After that, it was the henhouse—raking out the straw and turning it into the old beds to be planted with beans and marrows later in the spring when the soil had warmed. Next, she put in potatoes and rigged up something for the peas to climb on from a collection of sticks and thin branches hoarded over the winter. All the while, her companions, the hens, kept close in case she turned up a treat.

On the fifth day, there was the suggestion of blue in the sky. Rosalie waited with the rest of the women for word that they could fly, then gave up midday and went back and spent the afternoon in the garden.

Past teatime, Rosalie stuck her fork in the ground and used it as a support as she straightened and stretched. Although she'd done a good job of not stepping into the beds, she'd done a terrible job of keeping herself tidy. She'd got one of her gum boots stuck in the mud down at the bottom of the garden, and her coveralls were splattered. She put her head in the back door. The house was silent, and so Rosalie struggled out of her gum boots, stripped off the coveralls, and dashed up the stairs.

In the bathroom, she turned the tap and stood naked, chilled, and eager as she watched the water run and the steam rise. She was well due for a bath but knew to keep an eye out. She leaned over and closed the tap just as the water level reached five inches. Mrs. May liked to keep to the recommendation by the Ministry of Information, and Rosalie had learned what the proper level was by sight. After the war, when hot water would be plentiful again, she might just take a bath in six inches of water. Seven, even! Rosalie climbed into the tub, dipped the enamel jug in the water, and poured it over her hair before soaping up.

She was out of the bath in ten minutes and rubbing her hair dry with such vigor that she didn't realize anyone had arrived until she heard the voices downstairs. Rosalie finished drying herself, dressed, and went down to the kitchen. The last ray of sun streamed in the open back door. Mrs. May waited at the hob for the kettle to boil, Zofia was setting out the bread and butter, and a young woman with ivory skin and auburn hair—and wearing an ATA uniform—sat at the table. She leapt up when she saw Rosalie.

"Hello," she said, holding out her hand. "Third Officer Pamela Warnes, pleased to meet you. I've just arrived. I've been billeted here with you at Mrs. May's."

Rosalie looked from the extended hand up to the face—wide-eyed and eager—then to the landlady, whose hands were in the pockets of her pinny, and at last to Zofia, who gave a weak smile.

"Hello, Pamela, I'm Rosalie. Welcome."

It wasn't as if they hadn't known it would happen—that Caro's bed would be taken at No. 6—but that didn't mean they were prepared. Still, Pamela had no way of knowing she was replacing someone who couldn't be replaced.

They sat down to tea with bread and butter. Mrs. May gave the house rules, and Rosalie and Zofia asked Pamela about her training, where she was from, what her favorite aeroplane was. They got that and more.

Third Officer Warnes was a chirpy, cheerful, chatty woman who recounted to them moment by moment and without pause her entire life story—all of its almost twenty years. She had four sisters, but Pamela was the only pilot.

". . . and when Mummy saw me in uniform the first time, she squealed—really she did, just like this." Pamela's reenactment of her mother's delight brought them all to attention.

Rosalie wasn't sure she'd ever heard so much talk at No. 6. Through the evening meal, Pamela showed herself to be interested in not only herself but also everyone else. She quizzed Mrs. May about Fred and Terry, Zofia about life in Poland, and Rosalie about her two older brothers, nodding in a resigned fashion when she learned that one was already married. Rosalie found Pamela charming but exhausting and made it an early night.

Walking into the ferry pool the next morning, Pamela went into greater detail about her home near Worcester and her widowed mother, her sisters, the housekeeper who had been with them "forever," and her friends—the most exciting of whom worked in an unidentified "and terribly secret" government post and the least exciting of whom was a Land Girl. "I mean, really, she'll never be able to wash that smell off her. Ooh, sorry, Rosalie—I forgot about your farm."

Rosalie smiled indulgently, feeling older and wiser at twenty-one—twenty-two in August. It was experience that made the difference. And Rosalie didn't mind the farm reference, because she knew she smelled like sweet peas. Hadn't Alan said so?

They reached the pool just as the door to the assignment room opened. The pilots swarmed in and, eager to fly again, dived for their chits. Rosalie climbed aboard an Anson and was taken to Chattis Hill, where she collected her first Spitfire for the day.

At the end of a fortnight of nonstop ferrying of aeroplanes, Rosalie breathed a sigh of relief, for the next day, she would see Alan. It was a miracle that they'd been able to arrange this one night at the

Feathers in Essex, because now his squadron had moved to Wales. But he'd said he would sort it out; the hotel had become their special place. Rosalie's journey would be easier and familiar—air taxi to Debden and then the green bus. She already imagined Mr. Wilkes greeting them warmly.

★   ★   ★

Rosalie stepped off the bus that late afternoon into a sudden shower of rain. Alan was waiting, and he took her bag and kissed her. As the bus pulled away, she saw an older woman looking out the window at them, smiling. Rosalie smiled back.

They dashed across the road to the hotel as Alan asked, "Good journey?" Rosalie nodded. "Right, well then, steel yourself for our reception."

Mrs. Wilkes looked up from behind the desk, and Rosalie felt disapproval radiating from her.

"Hello, Mrs. Wilkes," she said bravely. "Lovely to see you again. And nice to be back at the Feathers."

"Yes, you're very welcome." Mrs. Wilkes offered a tight smile, as if to say that wasn't actually true and she would prefer that Rosalie and Alan stay away from her hotel. Regardless, she held out the pen for him to register.

Mrs. Wilkes did not hand over the key. Drawing herself up, she said, "I'm so sorry your room isn't ready yet. The girl we had has gone off and joined the Observer Corps—although if she couldn't see the dust on a table in front of her, I don't know how she would ever spot an enemy aeroplane—and it's left us quite short. You're welcome to wait in the lounge. I'm sure it won't be long."

A sharp ray of sunshine cut through the window to save them.

"Perhaps we could go for a walk," Rosalie suggested.

Mrs. Wilkes gave a sniff. "Well, certainly not the best of conditions for it—do mind the mud. You may leave your bags with me, and my husband will take them up for you."

They were barely out the door of the hotel before Alan drew Rosalie close.

"It's all a ruse," he whispered in her ear, and she shivered. "She didn't want us in the room because she didn't want to think about what we'd be doing up there," he said.

"She's fighting a losing battle on that front," Rosalie whispered back. She was perfectly willing to be annoyed with Mrs. Wilkes and her snooty ways, until she remembered the circumstances. "She's probably still quite sad about her son, don't you think? The one who was killed in Norway."

"Then why begrudge those left a chance for happiness?"

They chose a lane that went out of the hamlet and began walking. The air was damp and chilly, but the sun persisted. They paused on the grassy side of a muddy track, resting their arms on posts, and looked out into the field, neither of them speaking until Rosalie said, "You must've had quite a job to make it here."

"Caught a lift with a fellow taking his Mosquito back to Castle Camps, so it worked out."

"I was at Castle Camps again recently," Rosalie said. "I had a chat with Ellen."

She was a second away from mentioning the news that Deborah Barlow had moved on but bit back her words. Why mention her name?

"Shall we go back?" Alan asked.

The track ahead looked like nothing more than a series of muddy pools. Rosalie glanced down at her new shoes. "Yes, I suppose we should. Mrs. Wilkes was right, at least on this account." They returned to the hotel to find that fortune was with them, for Mr. Wilkes had taken the desk over from his wife.

"Terribly sorry I wasn't here to greet you," he said. "Your room is ready. I hope you didn't feel as if we turned you out."

"No," Rosalie said, "it gave us time for a bit of a walk."

"Well, then," Mr. Wilkes said, "your bags are in your room. Would you like a cup of tea?"

"I think not at the moment," Alan said.

"Then we'll see you at dinner."

Alan took Rosalie's hand, and they ascended the stairs in a stately manner. In their room, conversation again was kept to a minimum.

Later Alan went down to dinner ahead of her to wait in the bar. When Rosalie arrived, they were taken to the dining room, but not to their favorite table at the back. Instead they were shown to a crowded section, where they had to slip in between a party of five, doggedly making their way through plates of "fish," and an older man and woman. These latter two were apparently regulars, because Mrs. Wilkes soon appeared at their table and stood chatting for several minutes while she kept an eye on the room. She stood so close that Rosalie worried she would be overheard if she made a comment, and she thought to catch Alan's eye to share a silent joke about it. That's when she saw the hollow look had returned to his eyes, as if he had been able to keep it at bay for only so long before it rushed back in to overpower him. They had ordered, and the soup arrived before either of them spoke.

Rosalie plunged in first, filling in the silence at the table by telling him about Pamela's being billeted at No. 6 and rabbiting on for so long that she worried she might sound like the younger woman herself.

"And how is Wales?" she asked at last, hoping Alan would speak. "Do you have anyone to organize a football match for you?"

He stared at her for a moment, then reached out for her hand. "I love you, Rosalie."

How could those words bring a stab of fear to her heart?

"And I love you," she said.

The woman at the next table glanced over with one raised eyebrow, and it was all Rosalie could do to keep from telling her to mind her own business.

The soup was taken away and replaced by the main course. Rosalie hadn't felt like guessing at the fish and had ordered a plate of mushrooms and vegetables. Alan had a meat pie.

"Do you know by the end of August, I will have finished two tours?" he asked with wonder in his voice. "That is, if I make it that long."

"Of course you'll make it."

"Yes. I don't mean to sound as if I'm filled with doom and gloom. In fact, far from it when I'm up there and in the thick of things. I have complete concentration, I keep a cool head, and I know what I'm doing. It's as if I can predict the other pilot's next move. But did Wilson think the same? He's gone. Two nights ago. I saw him tear off after a couple of Junkers from the swarm we encountered. I radioed, but he didn't answer. Lost somewhere over the North Sea."

"You can't dwell on the losses." It was an easy thing to say, but harder to follow. She thought about Caro every single day.

Alan's mood lightened instantly. "No, and I don't. I think of you instead." He nodded to his plate. "Now, any guesses as to what the meat is?"

★ ★ ★

"I've never flown to Wales," Rosalie said the next morning at breakfast, "but surely you need aeroplanes to be ferried in or out of there. I wonder how I could sort out an assignment."

"We may be moving again before long. There's talk we may end up in Kent."

"Would you be near home—that is, Easton Hall?"

Alan played with his spoon. "The Yanks have taken the house. They've built airstrips in the fields and . . . It doesn't seem right to have the war that close to home, but there you are."

Didn't they all have to make accommodations? But would Rosalie be as pragmatic about it if the Yanks wanted Lime Farm?

★ ★ ★

Mrs. May walked into the kitchen at the end of April with the morning post. Rosalie, Zofia, and Pamela watched as, with exaggerated care, the landlady put the letters on the table, except for one, which she held to her chest for a moment before showing it to them. "Fred."

At last, a letter from her elder son. They watched as she opened and read through the short missive. She read it a second time before at last reading it aloud to them. Fred was out of North Africa, he reported, and unhurt, and he looked forward to seeing his mum when the whole thing was finished. That was all—except that he'd met a girl. Her name was Antonella.

"Italy," Mrs. May whispered. "That's where he must be. There's fierce fighting in Italy."

"Antonella," Rosalie said, hoping to distract her. "Such a beautiful name."

"What would you think, Mrs. May," Pamela chimed in, "if your Fred married her? Wouldn't she cook lovely meals?"

"She would bring with her olive oil," Zofia offered. "You could make new kind of Woolton pie with it."

Mrs. May frowned at the three for a moment and then sniffed. "I don't see what this olive oil could do that a knob of butter can't." She stuffed Fred's letter in the pocket of her pinny, gave it a pat, and went out to the hens.

Rosalie took her own letters along with her and read them over a cup of tea later in the day at Colerne, where she'd delivered a Mosquito.

Please come for a visit, Leslie had written. He now knew all about little Robert and fully supported his brother and Jean, but that had not helped one whit when it came to convincing their mother. *I'm caught in the middle and I'd like a bit of company. Also, did you know Ellen had left the WAAFs? She's going for nurses training.*

Will had written too. *We have a difficult decision to make, Rags, and we would all benefit from your common sense and strength.* Those were not attributes Rosalie ascribed to herself, and as much as she thought her mother in the wrong, she wouldn't gang up on her. Still, she would try to sort out a visit to Lime Farm.

CHAPTER 23

May 1944

In the middle of a swarm of women all comparing chitties, Rosalie felt as if she'd won the sweepstakes—here she held in her hand her second assignment of the day, which was to fly a Mosquito to RAF West Malling. Alan had only just moved there, and now she was to take an air taxi to Hatfield, where she would pick up the Mossie. She stifled a giggle as she imagined handing her chit over directly to him instead of the duty officer.

She optimistically had told Alan to be on the lookout for her any day—after all, West Malling was only Kent and not that far away. Alan had come up with a plan. *When you do get it arranged, why don't you telephone from your last stop. You can ask them to give me a message. I'd hate to miss you because you're looking in one place and I'm in another.*

For her first assignment of the day, she flew a Spitfire from Chattis Hill to Cosford, drank a quick cup of tea, and then climbed aboard the Anson for Hatfield. Her thoughts were her own, and she let her mind drift away in pleasant memories of her times with Alan. It was easier than looking ahead. The future remained amorphous.

This would be the first time in two months that they'd seen each other, and even if it was only over a cup of tea, it would be something.

She took off from Hatfield, avoiding the barrage balloons near Croydon, and gazed out onto the spring landscape. The hedgerows were white with cow parsley, hawthorn, and elder. The world seemed a hopeful place, and so it was with a light heart that she landed at West Malling and handed over her chit to be signed. Now, to find Alan.

"Your taxi will be here in twenty minutes," the duty officer said when she'd asked where to find the Mess. "Last one of the day—I wouldn't miss it."

"I'll be here," Rosalie assured him.

Or not. Because if she did miss her return to Hamble, she'd have to put up here at the aerodrome or nearby. That would mean many more hours with Alan before night fell and he was off on a sortie.

No longer worried what anyone would think, Rosalie stopped first at the squadron office, because she knew the duty officer would recognize her.

"He's about" was the reply she received. "Saw him not long ago. You could try the bar at the Manor."

Rosalie walked over to Douces Manor, acquired by the RAF and used for not only offices but also the Mess. As she approached, a pilot came out of the porticoed door, and when she asked about the bar, he directed her inside and downstairs. There she found a door with a sign that read TWITCH INN. She paused in the dark corridor. This was unfamiliar territory.

But when the door opened and a roar of laughter billowed out, she saw Alan at the bar at the same moment he saw her. His eyes lit up, and he slammed his empty pint glass down, pushed his way out, and took her in his arms.

"You are like an angel, do you know that?" he asked. "Appearing in my time of need."

"I'm an angel in desperate need of a cup of tea."

He watched her for a moment, his hands kneading her waist.

"I wish for more than that."

"Sadly, I'm not Aladdin," she said. "And actually, I don't even have time for the tea—there'll be an air taxi waiting for me." So much for missing her way back on purpose. Try as she might, Rosalie found it impossible to shirk her duty.

"Well, damn the war." He kissed her, and then a fellow bumped them on his way out of the bar. "Come on, then, I'll walk you back."

They went the long way—in a wide arc round the cluster of buildings and toward the blister barns and runways. They stopped on the far side of the duty officer's hut and out of view.

"Will you be here long, do you think?" Rosalie asked.

"They don't tell us much."

"You've moved so often in the last year, it must take a while for the rest of your life to catch up with you."

Alan's eyes scanned their surroundings and then came back to her. "You are all that matters. You know that, don't you? Everything else is just . . ."

An Anson rumbled past out on the runway.

"Oh, I suppose I'd better be ready," she said. "I wish we had more time."

"I've got my eye on a hotel nearby," he said, and pulled her closer than he should in public. "I'll let you know."

He left, and Rosalie went into the duty officer's hut to make sure he knew she hadn't missed her taxi. When she walked out to see the Anson reach the end of the runway and turn to come back, she suddenly didn't want to leave. She wanted Alan.

Rosalie turned and ran back, dashing through the maze of buildings, searching for him, hoping he hadn't got far. He was nowhere to be seen, but on the other side of crisscrossing paths in a wide-open space, she did spot someone she knew. She sucked in her breath as if someone had poured a pail of cold water over her.

Deborah Barlow. She wore her NAAFI uniform with her auburn hair neatly rolled and pinned under her brimmed hat. She spoke to another NAAFI woman next to her, their heads bent over a clipboard. Hard at work planning another dance? Rosalie didn't wait to find out.

★   ★   ★

She made it to the Anson in the nick of time. Inside, Rosalie sat engulfed in a black cloud that she had neither the energy nor the will to dispel. The two other passengers, both men, ignored her, and good thing, because she spent the flight dwelling on this latest discovery of Deborah at Alan's new assignment. Had she also been at Predannack in Cornwall, unnoticed by Rosalie? And the brief time he'd gone to Wales, had she followed him there? Was she traipsing after him all over Britain? And, more to the point, was this at his request?

Rosalie had the beginnings of a headache by the time the Anson put down. She had wanted Hamble, but here they were, landed at Aston Down. She had half a mind to stay put under protest until she was taken to her proper destination, but the pilot chivied her out. "I'm not the one you need," he said. "I'm headed north."

Toting her parachute on one arm and holding her bag in the other hand, Rosalie dragged herself over to the duty officer's hut to be told that a Fairchild air taxi would be along "in a bit" and it would take her on to Hamble. In the meantime, why didn't she go have a cup of tea?

She didn't want a cup of tea. Well, she did, but she was annoyed enough that she wouldn't admit to wanting anything anyone suggested. Instead of going to the Mess, she sat down under a beech tree not far off the runway to wait.

"Rosalie?" Zofia called to her from beside the duty officer's hut. Rosalie gave her a wave but didn't get up, and so Zofia walked over. "I am taking Spit to Brize Norton. You?"

"Just waiting for my taxi home."

"Funny place for you to wait. Why aren't you drinking tea or a glass of your mild with Snug?"

"No reason." Rosalie knew she should respond with something bright and cheery, but it was all she could do to speak.

"Mmm."

To Rosalie's great relief, a ground crewman called out to Zofia.

"I'll see you this evening," she told Zofia. "You'd best be off."

Returned to her own miserable company, Rosalie rested against the tree trunk and closed her eyes.

"What are you doing out here?"

Snug stood over her. Rosalie hadn't heard him coming because her thoughts were miles away at West Malling, imagining a scene that made her stomach turn.

She scrambled up off the ground and busied herself with brushing duff from her trousers. "I've . . . er . . . I'm waiting for the taxi." She fussed with the straps on her parachute so that she wouldn't have to look at him.

He didn't move. "You all right?"

"Yes. Fine."

"You're not."

"I am," she snapped, glancing up to see him frown—not an angry frown, but one that touched her and made her want to tell him her fears. She looked away and saw the Fairchild landing.

"Well," she said, in what she hoped sounded like a bright voice but keeping her eyes averted, "that's me away. See you."

She trotted out to the aeroplane and was out of breath by the time she boarded, sinking into her seat and putting her head back. Had she looked like an absolute idiot running to the Fairchild as if she were being chased? But she couldn't face Snug right now—she didn't want to face anyone. She would go straight home to No. 6 and up to her room to read *Treasure Island* and forget about the war and love and the entire messy world.

She was the only passenger and wished the pilot would take off, but he was looking over his shoulder toward the open door as if in anticipation. And then a large form appeared and cut off all light. Snug climbed in and sat across from her.

"Where are you going?" she asked.

"Isn't this taxi for Hamble?" he asked with as innocent an expression as she'd ever seen him muster.

She narrowed her eyes at him but gave up talking when the door was closed and the engine roared as the aeroplane made its way down the runway.

At Hamble, Rosalie clambered out of the Fairchild first and hurried across to the duty office, where she checked in. When she turned to leave, there was Snug.

"Are you following me?" she demanded.

"Yes, I am," he said.

She laughed despite herself, then said, "Stop it." She would not let him keep her from being miserable.

"The thing is, I fancied a pint at the Bugle," Snug said. "Is there anything wrong with that?"

"Certainly not. Have a lovely time—perhaps you'll see Brenda there."

The trouble with Snug going to the Bugle was that he would walk the same way as Rosalie did to No. 6. But she wouldn't talk to him. He couldn't make her talk.

He didn't even try. All the way down Satchell Lane they were silent, but even so, with each step, Rosalie felt the vise grip round her heart ease ever so slightly.

"Hang on a minute," she said when they'd reached No. 6. She let them in, dropped her parachute and bag at the bottom of the stairs, and called, "Mrs. May?"

The landlady came as far as the kitchen doorway and saw the two of them. "Oh well, all right then. You'll stay for the meal?"

"He will," Rosalie answered. She turned to Snug. "Won't you?"

"I wouldn't say no," he replied.

"We've Spam," Mrs. May said. "The little one won't be here this evening, but still I'll use the entire tin."

"Yes, that would be best," Rosalie said. "We're going down the pub. Would you tell Zofia when she returns?"

"Shoo, now," Mrs. May said as she turned away. "You aren't to be indoors, you know."

Snug threw Rosalie a questioning look as they left.

"It's all right," she said. "She's talking to one of the hens. They think an open door is an invitation. I caught one of them on the kitchen table the other day, looking as if she were waiting for her tea."

It was early in the evening, and the pub reflected that. The two old fellows had their usual places and were hunkered over their pints in silence. Rosalie could see through to the snug where three women sat, also not speaking. She heaved a sigh, releasing what she could of her fear and anger and confusion. Snug brought over her glass of mild and his pint, and they talked of other things—he said nothing about Rosalie inviting herself along to the pub, and she said nothing about seeing Deborah Barlow. Although the subject would not leave her mind. It lurked on the edge, waiting to get in. Biding its time.

Snug finished his pint, set his glass on the table, and said, "So."

Here it was—he was going to ask her what was wrong. What would she say? The words rose in her throat and she was just able to swallow them, although her eyes filled with tears.

"We'd better go," she said, leaping up from the table. "Mrs. May will have the meal ready."

On the way back to No. 6, Snug said, "You haven't said—where did you fly today?"

"Spitfire from Chattis Hill to Hatfield. Then I collected a Mosquito and took it to West Malling." Had she told Snug Alan's squadron had moved there? She generally didn't bring up his name, because it always caused a cooling in Snug's manner, as if he didn't think Alan was completely trustworthy. Rosalie couldn't hear that right now, because she was beginning to believe it herself.

They paused before the door of No. 6—that is, Snug paused, and so Rosalie held up too. He cupped her elbow in the palm of his hand, and he seemed to be about to say something. Rosalie didn't know what it was but found herself wanting to hear it. They looked at each other, and Snug leaned down ever so close and she tilted her chin up and—

Pamela opened the door.

"Well, there you are, then," she said. "I know I was supposed to be away, but here I am after all. Zofia's helping with the meal, and so Mrs. May was about to send me out on a recce."

Pamela turned back to the kitchen, and Rosalie followed. She didn't look at Snug but felt his hand drop from the back of her neck. She wished he had left it there.

Over the meal, Pamela kept up her usual nonstop narrative of her day, and for once it was a relief, because Rosalie had her mind on other matters.

Is that how it had been with Alan and Deborah—an accidental kiss? Because that was what had almost happened on the doorstep. Snug knew she was feeling low and he only wanted to cheer her up. He was good at that—it was a real talent. She knew he went further than a kiss when he cheered up Brenda and Marjorie and all his other girls.

There, that brought her to her senses, and she was able to enjoy the Spam-and-potato pie with greens from their own garden for a salad. As they progressed through the meal, Pamela's chatter waned, ending with an anecdote from her mother's most recent letter and then giving space for others to talk. Zofia told of a large, happy home when her father was alive. Snug talked of how his mum once poured a pint over a man's head when he'd slapped her bum. Mrs. May gave an example of what terrors her sons had been as boys.

Rosalie told them about the time she'd followed the shearers who took her sheep's wool to the cooperative, where she had taken part in the carding and spinning and even had a hand in the dyeing. "Both, actually," she said, "up to my elbows in the blue from woad. Wouldn't come off for ages."

When they moved into the lounge, the party continued, as Mrs. May surprised them by bringing out the bottle of brandy from its hiding place. "We'll have a drop, why don't we?"

After Snug left, Zofia took the glasses in to wash, Pamela went for a bath, and Mrs. May retired to bed. But Rosalie had lost the good spirits she'd found and now wasn't sure she had enough energy to get up off the sofa. She set her elbows on her knees and rested her chin in her hands and stared at the floor, her predicament coming back to her tenfold.

Zofia came in and took the chair across from her.

"Rosalie, you are happy and then sad, but nothing between. This evening is not first time."

She didn't reply, and Zofia continued. "Caro would not let this happen without a talk. It is always better to talk. So, talk to me."

Rosalie smiled. She caught Zofia's hand and gave it a squeeze.

"Is it Alan?" Zofia asked. "It is not Snug, I think, because the happy part of you is when he is here. So?"

"Alan may be . . . there's this woman he knew from before we met. She seems to be around again."

"But the two of you have . . . you understand that you will be only together? You are engaged?"

"Yes . . . Well, not in so many words. It isn't official or anything. We prefer it that way for now. Still, he says I'm the girl for him. He loves me. I'm different from anyone else." Rosalie wiped her nose on the back of her hand. "I saw them together once. But he promised me it was a kiss—only a kiss."

Zofia's eyes darkened. "That does not sound good."

★   ★   ★

British forces were on the move during May—keeping Rosalie and the other ATA pilots busy. One day she was the taxi pilot in a Fairchild, followed the next day by ferrying an Oxford and two Spitfires. She had not been to West Malling since discovering that Deborah Barlow was also there. She'd not mentioned the sighting in her latest letter to Alan. Rosalie managed to keep what she knew locked away in a separate part of her brain, as if it had nothing to do with the real world. It was there and it would have to be addressed, but she didn't know how.

Toward the end of the month, Rosalie began her day just down the road at Lee-on-Solent, where she collected a Hurricane to ferry up to Hawarden near Chester. This was as far afield as she'd flown in ages. The ATA had grown large enough that pilots mostly kept to their own part of the country, which, in Rosalie's case, meant the south.

As she took off out over the Solent—the strait that made its way up past Southampton and separated the mainland from the Isle of Wight—she saw a change. There were boats, many more boats than she'd seen in her two and a half years at Hamble. No, not boats. These were ships—large, military vessels, crowding the waterway. Amassing. A thrill of hope shot through her as she turned north.

Chapter 24

On the fifth of June, the ships were gone, and it was as if the country held its breath until the next morning, when the headlines shouted:

FRANCE INVADED
OUR ARMIES IN N. FRANCE
GREAT ARMADA ATTACKS

The very air was charged that day. Still, regardless of—or because of—events in France, aeroplanes were needed, and so the ferry pilots went about their business, gathering scraps of news between flights. That morning, Rosalie had taken a Spitfire in desperate need of repair to the MU at Cowley, near Oxford. She felt as though she were limping along in the sky. The landing gear had refused to retract on takeoff, and so she flew the whole way with it down. After an air taxi back to Hamble, she took another Spit to Aston Down. There the BBC midday broadcast came out over the Tannoy so that the entire place could listen to the report of D-Day.

She searched for Snug, but learned he was flying a Lancaster to Newmarket Heath in Suffolk. Too bad he wasn't about, as he might've returned to Hamble with her and gone to the Bugle for the evening, because surely there would be a crowd. As there was—almost every one of the ferry pilots, maintenance workers, and ground crew. So momentous an occasion was it that Rosalie, Zofia, and Pamela nearly persuaded Mrs. May to go along.

But the next day began like any other for the women, with chitties lining the table in the assignment room and the chalkboard filled with the names of pilots, aeroplanes, and destinations. A week later, an unpredictable element was added to their flying.

Doodlebugs. V-1s, unmanned rockets launched by the Germans from France and pointed in the direction of Britain. Hitler's revenge. The rockets buzzed along on their programmed route until all would go quiet and the bomb dropped to the ground and exploded. The noise of the rocket was bad enough, but it was the silence that people feared.

Rosalie heard her first V-1 after she'd delivered a Hurricane to Manston, near the Kent coast. She was standing outside the duty officer's hut searching for the chocolate bar in her bag and deciding whether to go for a cup of tea in the Mess. First, she noticed the ground crew out on the runway—they stopped their work and looked up. Then she heard a rough sound, like an engine missing. It came from a distance and grew louder and louder. Two maintenance workers came out of the blister barn to listen, and when a car pulled up and the driver—a WAAF—got out, she stopped too. The sound had just started to fade when a barrage of gunfire made them all jump. There was an explosion in the sky to the east, and a round of cheers went up from those on the ground at the aerodrome.

"Our boys shot it down." The duty officer had come out of his hut and stood behind Rosalie. "The ack-ack guns are all along the coast here. They got that one, but how many more are there to go?"

★　★　★

She would sometimes fly three Spitfires in a day, but at last, at the end of June, Rosalie's chits included a Mosquito that needed to go to West Malling.

On the air taxi to Henlow in Bedfordshire to collect the aeroplane, she considered what to do. She could telephone West Malling and ask to leave a message for Alan. Wasn't that what he'd suggested to her? That she let him know she was on her way, so that they wouldn't waste time and miss each other? Now she saw that alerting him to her appearance would give him another advantage—he could make certain he wasn't off at a pub, kissing Deborah Barlow.

Rosalie didn't telephone but instead landed at the aerodrome late that afternoon and went directly to the squadron office, where the clerk knew her.

He nodded at her request. "I'd say he's awake now and you might find him in the bar. They'll be moved out to the dispatch hut at seventeen hundred hours."

Rosalie made her way to the grand house and, just to be certain, looked into the Mess before heading downstairs to the bar. No Alan at either place. She stood in the dark corridor for a moment, rocking on her heels as if teetering on the edge of a precipice. Could she let this go—ignore the circumstances that seemed to paint their own picture of what was going on? No, she couldn't—it was eating away at her heart. Right, then. If the Allies had enough nerve to invade France, then surely she too could be brave. She made her way to the WAAF canteen.

A woman in the kitchen was just pulling a large tray of cakes out of the oven when Rosalie walked in.

"Tea's fresh," she said, nodding at the urn on the counter.

"Thanks," Rosalie replied. "Is Deborah Barlow here?"

The WAAF looked to the back of the kitchen, where a door stood half-open. "Yes, back there in her office. Go through."

Rosalie would much rather have taken one of the fresh cakes and a cup of tea and sat in the corner, pretending everything was right with her world, but instead she walked through the kitchen and found Deborah Barlow seated at a small desk with tidy stacks of papers at the corners and four clipboards hooked to the wall in front of her. Deborah looked up and wasn't quick enough to hide the look of surprise—her eyes widening and mouth dropping open—before Rosalie noticed.

"Hello, Rosalie. Lovely to see you again."

"Hello, Deborah." Rosalie gripped the edge of the door for support, noticed her white knuckles, and tried to relax. "I've just brought a Mosquito in and don't have to leave quite yet. I'm looking for Alan—do you know where I could find him?"

"I . . ."

Deborah hesitated so long that Rosalie thought some terrible confession would come spilling out of the woman. *Please don't*, she thought. *This isn't about you.*

"You might try the library in the house—it's on the ground floor in the far back corner. Not as busy as the rest of the place, and some of the pilots like the quiet." Her cheeks colored slightly.

"Thanks." Rosalie left as quickly as she could, passing by those fresh cakes that didn't look nearly as appealing now that her stomach had twisted into a massive knot.

Back inside the house, she hesitated in the entry and then heard footsteps coming up from the basement bar. It turned out to be Declan Mackenna.

"Hello, Declan, how are you?"

"Rosalie. Fine. I hope you're well."

"Yes. I'm looking for Alan. I was told he might be in the library."

Declan patted his chest in an absentminded fashion and looked round the entry hall. "Yes, the library. They've rather hidden it away. You go straight toward the back, and about halfway down, turn right, and walk to the end. Door on the left."

"Thanks."

Before she'd gone ten steps, he called after her. "Rosalie."

She turned.

"He talks a great deal about you," Declan said. "Always makes him happy too. The rest, you know—it doesn't matter."

Should that have made her feel better? Rosalie carried on, and at the end of the last corridor she pushed open the enormous carved oak door and surveyed the scene. At the far end, the late-afternoon sun poured through a tall window, but drapes covered the others, keeping the rest of the room dim and musty. Leather chairs and two sofas occupied the shady end. Every available wall space was covered with books that looked as if they hadn't been opened in a century.

No one was there apart from Alan, who lay sprawled in a chair, head back, legs straight out, asleep. He looked so peaceful. Then his eyelids fluttered opened, and he saw her.

He sat up abruptly, blinking, and then got up and came to her.

"I thought you were a dream," he said, and laughed. He kissed her and she kissed him back.

"Come on," he said. "Are you here for long? Do you want to go for a drink?"

"I don't have much time. Let's stay here and talk, why don't we?"

His eyes darted about the room as if looking for an empty seat. "Yes, all right." He led her to an upholstered settee in the corner, and they sat. He took hold of her hands and kissed one.

"How are you?" she asked.

"This business of invading France has made us busier than ever. It's as if we stirred the hornets' nest. But now all the activity is off the coast or we're sent further afield. Germans don't need to fly this far any longer, do they? Not with those V-1s. Must be making it hell for you."

"I was surprised to see Deborah Barlow here," Rosalie said, feeling her time was short and her need great.

Rosalie heard or imagined a hesitation in his voice. "Yes," Alan said, "yes, she is. She just appeared one day. NAAFI, you know. They must always be moving about the country."

"Was she at Predannack in Cornwall? Did she go to Wales when you were there?"

Alan straightened and frowned. "No, of course not. At least, I didn't see her there."

"But you've seen her here."

"Rosalie, I've explained that. What you saw was an . . ."

She waited for him to say *accident*, unsure she could keep herself in check if he did.

". . . aberration. And entirely my fault. But she means nothing to me. I love *you*. I want to be with *you*."

"What do you think we'll do after the war?"

It caught him off guard, she thought, because he didn't answer for a moment, and then he said, "We'll farm, of course. And"—he hurried on—"you'll fly, if you want to. Anytime."

"Will we farm on the land your family owns?"

A longer pause. Too long.

"Alan, I have to leave—the Anson will be here."

He took hold of her hands. "I'll see you again. Soon."

CHAPTER 25

July 1944

Rosalie had flown sixteen Spitfires in June. By the end of the month, she had become so accustomed to aeroplanes with holes in them or with dodgy flaps or with landing gear that remained down no matter what she tried that she paid little heed to the aeroplane's condition. She made her flight plans and flew.

Her Spitfire this day was, unusually, intact, and she was taking it back to Hamble. Along the way, she had a discussion with Caro. An imaginary conversation—Rosalie had not gone round the bend. But she needed to talk with someone, and she thought she could well imagine what Caro might say. So she spoke aloud her thoughts and fears, hoping to define her relationship with Alan.

"Why does it need to be a secret?" Caro would've asked.

"It isn't a secret," Rosalie replied, "it's only that it isn't the right time for him to tell his family and for me to say anything to my mum."

"Or to Will or Leslie," Caro would've pointed out. "Do you want to be with Alan after the war? Do you see the two of you together, getting married, having a family, living . . . where?"

After the war, as far as Rosalie's life was concerned, remained an impenetrable gray fog.

"I don't know. I can't . . ."

"Who do you truly want to live the rest of your life with?" Caro would've demanded. "Come on, just say a name—on my count. Three, two, one, go!"

Without a thought, Rosalie blurted out a name, but the next second, the engine of her Spitfire cut out, and her conversation with Caro broke off. All Rosalie could hear was silence.

She swore, using a word her mother would have been too shocked to even scold her for. She'd just cleared the New Forest and passed Southampton, and she could see the airfield at Hamble—she was that close to home. *Well, then, glide your way in—do a circuit and put down.* She'd done it before in a Magister, and so she could do it in a Spit. Caro hadn't been able to do it, though, had she? Brown Clee Hill had got in her way.

Rosalie started her circuit, pushing the control stick away from her and to the left as she circled the field. But only halfway round, the plane lurched, pushed heavily from behind by a blast of wind. It threw the tail up and the nose of her aeroplane down—down too much and too fast. She pulled back on the stick, but here was another strong gust. Dropping her landing gear as the wind buffeted the aeroplane, watching the ground come closer and closer and at such a speed, Rosalie wondered how she could feel so calm.

The wind eased, and she managed to regain some control and level the aeroplane. Her speed even slowed—but not nearly enough. At this rate, she would overshoot the runway, no doubt about that, but she couldn't pull up, not without any power. *Hang on then, here it comes.* The ground rushed up to her, and she landed roughly, her straps biting into her shoulders as she was thrown round in the seat. She felt the tail wheel touch and pressed both feet on the brakes—not too much pressure, or the plane would end up on its nose. But she knew there was a barn past the end of the runway. It had always been one of her landmarks when coming in, knowing she had to stop well short of it before turning and taxiing back. This time, though, she saw it hurtling toward her. Its doors were wide open but not wide enough for her Spit to go through. Rosalie slammed hard on the brakes, and she felt the aeroplane tip forward.

★　★　★

"Have you been here all night?"

Rosalie didn't recognize the woman's voice, but she didn't think the question was directed to her. And besides, she didn't feel like opening her eyes.

"No, Sister. They made me leave last night but let me in first thing."

Snug? Yes, she was sure it was he, although he didn't sound himself. So quiet, so compliant.

"You can't stay."

"I won't let her wake up without her seeing someone she knows."

There, that was more like him. Belligerent.

"Nurse!" Another voice came from further away, and Rosalie heard footsteps departing.

"Stubborn," she murmured thickly, her tongue stuck to the roof of her mouth.

"Rosalie?"

She opened her eyes then, and found herself looking at an unfamiliar ceiling—high and full of bright lights. The sun poured in from tall windows behind her. She saw a metal bedstead at her feet and a row of beds down each side of the room. A hospital ward. And then, in her mind, she was back in the Spitfire, the engine silent as she dropped out of the sky. Straight ahead of her was a barn. She jumped, her body almost lifting off the bed.

Snug was beside her in an instant, his hands on her shoulders, holding her gently.

"Rosalie," he said. "Look at me."

She did, gasping for air. His small, brown eyes locked on hers, and soon her breathing calmed. She wasn't in the aeroplane; she was on the ground and in hospital.

"What happened?" she asked.

He let go of her, pulled the chair over, and sat down close to the bed. "What do you remember?"

She kept her eyes on him and forced her mind back. "The engine cut out. I glided, and I thought I could land. I did it that other time in the Magister, remember? But . . . the wind caught me from behind and I couldn't slow down. I landed." She closed her eyes and felt the aeroplane's landing gear bump along the ground. "There was the barn, and so I used too much brake."

"You slowed almost enough. You tipped forward and sheared off one of the wings when you hit the barn. At least it stopped you."

She could see it all now, the ground coming up to meet her. The barn growing larger and larger. She opened her eyes, glad of the hospital view. Her head hurt.

"When?"

"Only yesterday. You've no broken bones, but a bump on the back of your head and a long gash on your left arm."

As if to call attention to itself, her left forearm began to throb.

"The doctor and the sisters said you were only sleeping and would wake up when you were ready." He chewed the side of his cheek. "Took you long enough."

The pain in her head subsided a bit. She was alive and nothing was broken. She was safe and Snug was sitting beside her.

"There will be hell to pay about the Spit, won't there?" she asked.

"Wasn't your fault the engine cut out." He looked her over as if to judge how much she could take, then added, "Good thing the cows were out to pasture."

He watched her. She managed a weak laugh and then said, "Ow," and put a hand gingerly to her head.

"Careful now," Snug said, and he leaned over, took her hand, and guided it to the lump.

It was the size of a hen's egg and felt hot.

"Well, I should go," he said, standing. "You need to rest."

"No, I don't want you to go," she said, reaching for him with her right hand. "Sit down."

He obeyed, keeping hold of her hand. They didn't speak, but she found his presence such a comfort. She closed her eyes and thought of nothing. At last, he cleared his throat.

"Ivor."

Rosalie opened her eyes and frowned. "What's that?"

"My proper name. Mum was a cleaner at Oxford when she was young and said there was a boy there, Ivor, and he was a great singer. Mum thought it sounded grand."

"Ivor," Rosalie said, trying it out. "Has a certain charm to it." Rosalie studied his face, feeling as if she could never get enough of looking at him. At last, she took a deep breath.

"Rags," she said.

Snug lifted his eyebrows.

"What my brothers call me," she explained. "It's my hair, you see. When I was a baby, my mum dug out an old rag doll, and Will and Leslie said it looked just like me. So there you are."

"Rags," Snug said, and shook his head. "No, I don't see it."

Rosalie knew better but was grateful nonetheless.

A sister walked through the door at the end of the ward, saw Rosalie, and walked over to the foot of the bed. "Came back to us, did you? We knew it was only a matter of time. Doctor?" she called over her shoulder.

The nurse edged Snug away from the bed, and at once there appeared another nurse and the doctor. They crowded round her, checking her pulse and looking into her eyes and asking her questions.

"Lie still now," Rosalie was told when she craned her neck to see where Snug had gone. She caught a glimpse of him, heading for the door. He turned at the last minute, and she saw him lift his chin in farewell.

★　★　★

There ensued during the following two days what the ward matron called a "parade of visitors" to Rosalie's hospital bed. They all came— Hamble's commanding officer, Margot Gore, and deputy, Rosemary Rees, as well as Brenda, Anne, Catherine, and more ATA pilots than she could count. The sisters tried in vain to regulate the flow, but as soon as they had ushered one or two out, three more would slip in behind her back. Zofia and Pamela smuggled in a large wedge of cake from the Mess, and Rosalie dutifully picked at it as they entertained her with silly stories about the hens. Zofia returned with Mrs. May, who looked as if she had been crying. The landlady clasped Rosalie's hands and gave her a kiss on the cheek.

Eventually, the ward matron limited visitors to one at a time and for only ten minutes. Rosalie protested, although the attention exhausted her and she would drift off as soon as someone had gone— sometimes while they were still there. Once, her eyes popped open when she thought Snug had returned, but he was nowhere to be seen. A dream.

CO Gore came back and explained that Rosalie's family had been notified and that the ATA had given her a fortnight's leave. "You have a concussion, and these things take time to heal. You may take more than a fortnight if you need it. Let us know when you're ready to return, and we'll welcome you back. We can't let go of a good pilot."

That they continued to think of her as a good pilot boosted Rosalie's mood ever so slightly. She thanked Gore but said nothing else.

Rosalie was content to let others make decisions for her, spending her time sleeping or awake and thinking. She drank the cups of tea and ate whatever food was on the tray brought to her. Once, there was a semolina pudding with slices of tinned peaches. Why were they feeding her this luxury? The orderly said the food at the hospital wasn't half-bad, as they were allowed special shipments from America.

The hospital released Rosalie on the third day. Zofia arrived with a packed bag of clothes—Rosalie's old trousers, a blouse, a jumper, and her sturdy shoes. "I put in also your uniform," Zofia explained, "for you to be ready, when you return. Do you want help with dressing?"

Rosalie declined the offer, thinking if she couldn't get herself dressed, the matron might decide she had to stay in hospital. She dressed carefully, every movement awkward and all parts of her sore. She sat down to pull on her trousers, eased her left arm through its sleeve first, and leaned against the bed to slip into her shoes. When she pushed the curtain aside, there, standing next to Zofia, was Leslie.

"Hello, Rags," he said. Rosalie's eyes filled with tears, and Les looked as if he might cry himself.

He gave her a gentle hug, picked up her bag, and shook Zofia's hand, then stood back for a moment to allow the two women a farewell.

Zofia took Rosalie's face in her hands and said, "You are strong woman."

Rosalie took a ragged breath and nodded.

Outside the front door of the hospital, the farm's red lorry awaited its return journey.

"How did you have enough petrol to get all the way to Hampshire?" she asked.

As he helped her in, Leslie explained that he'd used all the farm's petrol coupons plus coupons from Ellen's father, who, Les told her, had said that a war hero such as Rosalie deserved a comfortable journey home.

War hero? Not Rosalie. She had crashed a Spitfire that an RAF pilot could've used against the enemy. She must've done something wrong, made a mistake, although she could not sort out what. True, the engine had cut out, but wasn't she the responsible party? How would her accident report read?

Leslie told Rosalie it had taken him nearly four hours to drive from Lime Farm that morning. "I've never seen so much of the country," he said. "Half the time I didn't know where I was, as there are still so many signs down, so I just kept heading south. But you'll know where you are as we drive back, won't you? Haven't you flown over all of England and Scotland these last three years?"

She had, but looking down on villages and woods and railway lines was one thing; seeing them straight on was something completely different. Fortunately, Leslie didn't really expect her to act as navigator, and they spoke little as they went on their way. That suited Rosalie. It was sunny and warm. She carefully rested her left arm on the open window and stuck her head out to let the wind blow through her curls. It reminded her of being in a Tiger Moth.

When they stopped at the side of the road to eat sandwiches Leslie had brought, he finally asked about the crash.

"Do you remember it? You don't have to talk about it if you'd rather not."

"I do remember," Rosalie said, and gave him an evenhanded account—not difficult to do, because the further she got from the crash, the more it seemed to have happened to someone else. "And anyway, better that I tell you the details than Mum."

"God, yes," Leslie replied. "She's been in a right state since your CO rang. She wanted to come along today, thinking you'd need someone to look after you while I drove."

They returned to their sandwiches, and in the silence there came the rumble of an aeroplane off to the west of them, flying low. Rosalie pointed it out. "Anson. An air taxi, probably." She wondered who the pilot was and if she noticed a red lorry stopped along the road.

The rest of their journey, Rosalie dozed off and on, and she awoke when they pulled into the yard. The sight of Lime Farm, the late afternoon turning the barn and the stables golden, gave her a lump in her throat. She sniffed briskly—her emotions were far too near the surface since the crash, and she needed to get hold of herself. Leslie jumped down and slammed the lorry's door. The geese looked cautiously round the corner of the barn at her but skittered off when one of the Land Girls rode in on the Fordson tractor. Then her mum shot out of the kitchen.

When Rosalie climbed out of the lorry and was engulfed in her mother's embrace, tears got the better of her at last. "Now, love," her mum murmured, "there now."

"I'm fine, Mum, really I am," she said, and in only a moment or two, she was, and felt all the better for a brief cry.

Still, her mother led her into the kitchen as if she were an invalid, placing her in a chair at the table and in front of a fresh sultana cake that smelled sweet and fruity and made Rosalie's mouth water. Leslie came in as Rosalie peeled off her jumper so they could see the bandage on her left arm.

Her mother clicked her tongue and then cut her daughter quite a large slice of cake, prompting Rosalie to say to her brother, "I'm sorry there's none left for you." Her mum poured out the tea and sat across from her. Rosalie took a mouthful of cake and sighed. Then she realized what was missing.

"Where is Will?" she asked. "Where is Jean?"

Her mother rose to refill the milk jug. Rosalie turned to Leslie and waited.

"Will knows you're coming," he said. "He'll be in soon."

"Where is Jean?" Rosalie persisted. "Is she upstairs?"

Les looked at his mum's back. He exhaled loudly and said, "They aren't here, Rags."

"Aren't here?" Rosalie asked. "What does that mean? They live here."

"They've moved out to the cottage at the bottom of the far field—you know the one?"

Rosalie could hardly believe her ears. "They're living in the cottage? Isn't that where you keep your pig?"

Her mum spun round and snapped, "Leslie, don't. Rosalie, you don't need this now. We'll leave it until later."

"You didn't think I'd notice my brother and his wife were missing from their home?" Rosalie asked. "I may have crashed my aeroplane, but I haven't lost my mind!"

Her mother sucked in a breath. "How can you be so . . . you have no idea what I thought when I answered that telephone and was told you were . . . ." She put her hand over her mouth.

Rosalie would not be deterred. "Are you saying neither of them is allowed in the house?" She heard her own voice rising and tried to catch it but couldn't. "Why? Tell me why."

"Rags . . ." Leslie started.

"I want to see Will," Rosalie said, standing up too quickly and grabbing the table.

"You need to rest," her mum said. "Go upstairs, lie down. This will wait."

At the mention of resting, Rosalie could've fallen asleep on the spot, and so she relented. "Yes, all right. I'll go up, but I want to see Will as soon as he gets here." She turned to Les. "You send him up to my room the very minute."

In her old room, Rosalie had a thought to defy her mother and stay awake. She refused to even sit down. Instead, she wandered about, looking out the window and then examining one of the porcelain figurines on the dressing table. But her resolve weakened, and eventually she stretched out on the bed without turning back the counterpane and immediately fell asleep, waking later and listening. Had she heard something? There it came again, a quiet knock.

"Come in."

Will entered cautiously. He looked anxious and tired. She sat up and, unsure of how stable she would be on her feet, patted the bed next to her. Will sat and gave her a kiss and asked how she felt.

"Oh, I'm all right, I suppose. All things considered." They grinned at each other. "What about you? Tell me what is all this about you living in that dreadful cottage?"

Will puffed out his chest. "It isn't dreadful any longer—you just wait and see. We've made it into a home. We had to, Rags, because . . . well, you see, I followed your advice."

"I didn't tell you to move out!"

"No, you said, 'Just go and get him.' Do you remember?"

"Oh, that."

"You were right," Will said, "it was the best thing. But when we told Mum what we planned, she said wouldn't the house be too crowded and perhaps she should move out and go live with Uncle Trevor and Auntie Peg."

"She threatened you?"

"As good as. But we said no, that we would be the ones leaving. I don't think she believed us, but we spent two months getting the cottage ready and then we moved out of here and into there and went to collect Robert. Oh, Rags, he's a grand boy, and settling in so well. He'll start in our village school in September. Can you believe that? Mum would love him, I know she would, but I won't push her."

"She hasn't even met him? How long has it been?"

"Nearly a month now."

"You never mentioned it in your letters," Rosalie said.

"I didn't want to worry you. Look, Rags, you rest now."

Will left, and Rosalie stretched out on the bed and stared at the ceiling. Did she have the courage, let alone the strength, to help mend her broken family when her own life lay shattered in pieces?

CHAPTER 26

Rosalie managed to stay awake during the evening meal, and the three of them—Leslie, Rosalie, and their mum—talked about the farm, what was coming on, what needed to be done. Her mum told her in no uncertain terms that none of the work would be done by Rosalie. "You will rest."

The next morning after breakfast, Rosalie announced that she would go for a walk about the place. Her mum looked as if she were about to argue, but Rosalie added, "The matron said fresh air was the best thing for me." Those might not have been the matron's exact words, but if pressed, Rosalie could blame her concussion.

Her mother relented, but retained a bit of power by strongly suggesting that Rosalie should wear her jumper, even if it was a warm morning already. Rosalie thought it better not to argue and pulled her jumper on over her short-sleeved blouse—still keeping care of her left arm—and set off well covered, strolling down the lane until the break in the hedge, then crossing two fields and climbing up a rise. By the time the cottage was in sight, she had stripped off the sweater and dragged it along beside her.

The appearance of the cottage cheered her. It did look much improved, with the brambles cut back, a window box of geraniums, and a fresh coat of red paint on the door. Jean came out, looking happier even than she had on her wedding day and yet at the same time weary.

They greeted each other warmly, each asking in turn, "How are you doing?" and each in turn giving much the same reply: "Managing."

"I'm so glad you came," Jean said. "I was hoping you would. Oh, that's awful." She gingerly touched the bandage on Rosalie's left arm.

"No broken bones," Rosalie said. "I'd say I'm one of the lucky ones. But really, Jean, I can't believe it's come to this—you living out here."

"We're all right," she said, leading the way in. "I'm sorry for your mum not to know how lovely it is to have Robert here. You'll meet him soon. He and Will are just coming back from the village."

Rosalie surveyed the interior of the cottage. It had cleaned up well, and Jean put on a brave front, but even so, three rooms for the family, a kitchen with a pump handle instead of a tap, and electricity only because a single line had been brought in from the road? They deserved better.

"Warm today," Jean said, "isn't it? Wasn't the walk too much for you?"

At the mention of her trek, Rosalie felt herself flagging. "No, I'm fine. Just need to have a sit."

"No, lie down there on the sofa. I've wash to put out, and we'll have tea when the fellas return."

Rosalie complied. With the slight breeze from the open window at her head, it wasn't a minute before she drifted off to sleep, and she awoke some time later to find a ginger-haired boy standing over her, staring intently with blue, blue eyes. He was no longer the tot from the photo. What was he now, seven? Eight?

"Hello," she said.

"I'm seven years old," he said. "How old are you?"

Rosalie thought for a moment, hoping this was a test of her memory after the concussion. "I'll be twenty-three next month."

"You're my Auntie Rags."

She saw Will at the door watching them. "Yes," Rosalie said, "I am. And you are my nephew, Robert. I'm very pleased to meet you."

"Would you like to see my toads?"

"I would indeed. Might we have a cup of tea first?"

The four of them sat down to bread and butter and strawberry jam, and Rosalie walked back to Lime Farm with renewed energy.

* * *

"She's stuck and she doesn't know how to go forward," Rosalie whispered to Leslie at the breakfast table when their mum had gone out to the pantry for a jar of beets. "She only needs a nudge. I've a plan."

It was a week later, and Rosalie had been the acquiescent daughter as long as she could stand it. Each day she had gone off to spend time with Jean and Robert, and each night she had gone to sleep thinking about what to do. She had awakened that morning with resolve and renewed strength. The time had passed for discussing the issue, and she would no longer tiptoe round her mother. She was ready to take action.

When her mum came back into the kitchen, Rosalie reached for a slice of toast and began buttering it with great care.

"Mum, I'm making scones this afternoon, because I'm asking Jean and little Robert to tea." Leslie's eyes cut between his sister and his mother, who clenched the jar of beets with both hands. "Leslie will be here, won't you?" She didn't wait for an answer. "And I hope you'll join us. But if you don't feel that you can welcome the two of them, I'm giving you plenty of notice to make other arrangements."

Her mother made no reply, and nothing else was said about it the rest of the morning. Would she stay or would she go?

Rosalie had no answer until she opened the kitchen door that afternoon to find Jean and Robert, both well scrubbed and well dressed. Her sister-in-law looked a bit paler than usual, but her nephew's cheeks were aflame with curiosity, his eyes darting about the kitchen until they alighted on the plate of scones.

"Thank you for coming," Rosalie said. "Hello, Robert, how are you?"

Perhaps her voice was a bit too loud, but she wanted it to carry out into the front room, where she believed her mother lurked.

"'Afternoon, you two," Leslie said, coming up behind them from the yard and sounding like a jolly Father Christmas. He looked past Rosalie. "Hello, Mum."

She had appeared silently and stopped just inside the kitchen. Jean and Robert remained on the other side of the threshold. Rosalie made the introductions from the middle, like a referee at a boxing match. Then Robert stepped inside the kitchen, held out his hand, and said, "Hello, Grandmother. I'm very pleased to meet you."

Robert's grandmother crossed the room and looked down at his hand. Rosalie held her breath.

Her mother took the boy's hand and said, "Well, now, aren't you a fine young . . ." For a moment, she could go no further, but she got hold of herself and said, "I suppose we've all washed our hands?"

"I was just about to," Rosalie said. "Who will join me?"

They lined up at the kitchen sink, Rosalie's mother providing a stool for Robert to stand on.

"You have taps," Robert said as a matter of fact. "We had taps at my first house, but now we pump our water. It's work, but Daddy says it makes the water taste better."

Rosalie glanced at her mother, whose face had gone blotchy red as she reached out to touch Robert's hair.

Tea was a lively affair, and they finished with the table covered in crumbs and Robert's mouth purple with damson jam. When he asked his grandmother about the possibility of toads nearby, she didn't hesitate for a moment, and the two of them went off to the farm pond for a look-see, leaving three stunned adults behind.

Jean grabbed Rosalie's hand. "I don't know how you did it, but thanks."

"I knew they would be fast friends," Rosalie said with great nonchalance, brushing crumbs on the table into a heap and then into her hand.

"Will you go back to flying when you're well?" Jean asked, gathering cups and saucers.

"Of course she will," Leslie said.

Rosalie turned to the sink as Will came in and said, "Where's my boy?"

Jean's smile was as wide as her face. "He's with his gram."

★ ★ ★

As the days went by, going back to being an ATA ferry pilot seemed less and less likely to Rosalie. Physically, she healed—her headaches diminished, the long gash on her left forearm scabbed over and began to itch, she didn't need as much sleep—but as her body recovered, her mind and spirit slipped into a melancholy stoked by her own thoughts. She couldn't see herself getting into an aeroplane again. She had crashed, just as Caro had crashed, but Rosalie had survived. Shouldn't she count herself lucky and quit while she was ahead? She would live the rest of her life on the farm, the unmarried sister, growing old and alone, always the fifth wheel wherever she went.

Before she left hospital, Zofia had offered to write Alan. "Easy for me to tell him what has happened and you don't worry." Rosalie had blamed her quick acceptance of this offer on the concussion, which at first had made it difficult to act or make decisions. A week after she arrived at Lime Farm, a letter had come, and Rosalie had been able to slip it into her pocket before anyone noticed and asked her questions about the sender.

I could hardly believe the news from your friend, Alan had written. *Are you all right? Will you stop flying now? No one could blame you for that, not after what you've been through. I do love you.*

His words had left Rosalie strangely unmoved. Was this the concussion or some fault on her part? Perhaps failure was contagious, and now that she'd crashed an aeroplane, she was ready to destroy something else valuable—their relationship. She put the letter away in her bureau, and there it had stayed. She thought about it now and then, knowing she should get it out and send an answer. What would she write?

Her mother continued to forbid her to work, and Rosalie didn't put up a fight. Instead, she spent most afternoons doing nothing out at the field where her year-old ewe lambs had grazed. The sheep had been gone for months, but Will hadn't brought in pigs or plowed it up to plant. Growing up, the field had always been a refuge for Rosalie—her private corner of the world. And so it became again.

One afternoon, three weeks after her crash and more than a fortnight since she'd arrived at Lime Farm, Rosalie took sandwiches, a thermos of tea, and an old blanket out to the field with her. She clambered into the cart and lay back—half on the blanket and with her head resting in the corner on a clump of straw—and stared up into the blue sky. She closed her eyes. Time to address the problem of Alan.

But a rumble in the sky brought her back to the moment. She opened her eyes. Had she fallen asleep? The rumble receded and then grew louder again. A Spitfire. She jumped up so quickly that the cart rocked and creaked, and she had to put a hand out lest she went over the side. There it was, just coming over the copse of oak to the south. She watched the plane come closer and lower. He circled the field and then came in to land, turning at the far end and trundling back toward her. The engine switched off, and she waited until Snug climbed out of the cockpit.

Leaping down from the cart, she ran to him and pulled up a second before she threw herself in his arms. What would he think, that she'd gone mad? Instead, she laughed and said, "I hope you didn't think you were landing at Brize Norton. It would be a terrible thing for an ATA pilot to lose his sense of direction."

He beamed at her. "Oh, I know Lime Farm when I see it."

"Do you?" She paused. "Why didn't you come back to visit when I was in hospital?"

"You had plenty of company."

"Who told you that? Was it Brenda?"

"No," he said, frowning. "It was not Brenda."

Now she had annoyed him, and so with mock politeness she said, "Thank you for stopping to visit today."

He cocked his head and squinted his good eye at her. "You're welcome."

"As it happens, you're just in time for lunch. Come along." Afraid that he would turn round and fly off, she took hold of his hand and led him to the edge of the field, waving her arm at the cart. "Today, we'll be serving *en plein air.*"

He smiled at her and reached over to touch her hair—a light caress—and came away with a stem of straw. She put her own hand up and pulled out another bit. "I must look an awful mess."

"Not to me, you don't."

"I'm terribly glad you're here," she said, thinking how far she'd come in the healing process, because two weeks earlier she would've been crying, but now she only felt as if she might. She climbed up into the cart and he followed, and they settled across from each other, backs against the sides and legs extended. Rosalie opened her pack and handed over half a ham sandwich on thick bread with both butter and mustard. She poured out tea from her flask and they shared the cup. They ate in companionable silence for a few minutes, and when Snug finished his sandwich, he put his hand on her ankle beside him. It was really the easiest place to rest it.

"The sheep are gone?"

"Mmm," she replied. "Will has plans, but other things have got in the way. Little Robert has come to live with his mother and stepdad."

"Has he? What did your mum say?"

"She tried to put up a fight, but it took only one look at the boy and her resistance crumbled. Now they're fast friends, Robert and his gram. Will had his family living in a cottage a couple of fields over, but they'll be moving into the house soon." Rosalie folded up the greaseproof paper the sandwich had been wrapped in and asked, "Where are you taking it, the Spit?"

"Biggin Hill. But before it gets there, I thought you might like to take it up for a circuit."

"Me?" She'd never heard of anything so ridiculous in her life. "No. I . . . no, I don't think I . . ."

"Yes, you can."

"I didn't say I *couldn't*," she said hotly, "I said I didn't think I . . ."

Snug waited, but she refused to continue.

"Heard from Chersey?" he asked.

First aeroplanes and now Alan. Had Snug come to visit with the sole purpose of vexing her?

"Of course I have. He's written. He said he loved me and that he was terribly sorry about what happened." But resentment swarmed round her like a hornet in late summer, and she was tired of swatting it away. "Although for all his talk, you'd think he could've visited, don't you? You'd think he would've wanted to see me in my time of need. A fellow would hold vigil at the bedside of the woman he loved after she'd been injured in an aeroplane crash. He would do that for her."

A thick silence followed as it dawned on Rosalie who it was she had described. She cut her eyes at Snug, and he held her gaze for a moment, then looked away.

"The RAF never rests. He's busy, you know that."

Rosalie longed to say something, to ask if what she suspected were true, but the moment had passed and she couldn't see a way back.

"Yes," she muttered with a touch of bitterness. "I daresay he is."

She looked out at the Spit sitting in the field where once there had been lambs. Such a fine aeroplane, and there it was, waiting for her.

"It's a short field," she said.

"I'll hold down the tail," Snug replied.

Rosalie went out to the aeroplane, climbed into the cockpit, strapped herself in, and carried out her preflight check just as Reg Mulden had taught her in his Gipsy Moth all those years ago, and as she had learned in training at White Waltham. It was like greeting an old friend. She taxied the Spit to the edge of the field, turned, and waited for Snug to climb onto the stile and hop up on the tail. As she picked up speed, she pulled the control stick back and felt him slide off, and the plane rose, nose in the air, and Rosalie's spirits with it.

Her left arm complained a bit when she worked the throttle, but otherwise, the world was hers. She flew out as far as Reg's field and turned back to Lime Farm, coming over Will and Jean's cottage. They weren't home, more's the pity. Wouldn't Robert have loved to see her? Rosalie continued, flying low over the house. She slid back the hood and saw Leslie come out of the barn and look up, one hand shielding his eyes. She waved, and he waved back. Her mum came out of the kitchen, and Rosalie waved to her too and then continued back to the field. When she had landed, taxied up, and gone through a brisk landing check, Snug helped her climb out.

"How was it?" he asked.

"Glorious," she said, keeping hold of his hand and weaving her fingers through his. Now was the time.

"Snug, I've been such a fool."

"Snug Durrant?"

The call came from the end of the hedge that separated the lambs' field from the next one. It was Leslie, and he came trotting over to them.

"It is you, isn't it?"

Rosalie dropped Snug's hand, and he stuck it out. "And you're Leslie. Good to meet you."

"Welcome to Lime Farm. I saw the Spitfire go over a bit ago, low like, and I wondered why. And then I heard it again and came out and saw you, Rags."

"I've just dropped in on my way to Biggin Hill," Snug said. "Thought I'd see how Rosalie was doing."

Leslie glanced at his sister. "Much better now, I can see that. Will you stay? Mum will lay on a good tea, I'd say."

"Yes," Rosalie said. "Please do. Meet the family."

"I wish I could, but they're expecting this Spit, so I'd best be on my way." He looked back at the aeroplane. "Although, I'll need help taking off."

"It's a short field," Rosalie explained to her brother.

Leslie looked from the plane to the pilots, and the light dawned. "You mean I can . . . I say."

They walked Snug out to the aeroplane. He climbed into the cockpit, and just before he slid the hood closed, he said, "Good to meet you, Leslie. Wright—I'll be seeing you."

"You will," she replied.

He taxied to the end of the field and waited for Leslie to climb from the stile onto the tail. He held on to the rudder as the pilot picked up speed, dropping off just as the aeroplane put its nose in the air.

Snug flew a circuit and waved to them before continuing on his journey.

"He's just as I imagined from your letters," Leslie said as they walked back to the house. "Really seems a grand fellow."

"Yeah, he is," Rosalie said, missing Snug already—missing his cockeyed looks and the feel of his hand. Wishing she'd had time to say things properly. Because she remembered now whose name it was she'd spoken just before she crashed.

On the way back to the house, Leslie cleared his throat. "Look, Rags, I've had a letter from Ellen . . ."

"Have you?" his sister said with a sly grin. "You two are writing?"

Leslie's cheeks turned ruddy. "Well, yes, but only as friends."

"I don't believe that."

He laughed.

Evening meal preparation was under way by the time they walked into the kitchen. Their mum kept her back to them when Leslie said, "I'd always hoped Rags would fly over Lime Farm and wave to us. Aren't you glad she did, Mum?"

When there was no answer, Leslie shrugged at Rosalie. "Good luck," he mouthed, and escaped, probably out to his office that had been Pop's.

Her mother turned, her hands clasped in front of her. "You're going back, aren't you?"

"Yes, Mum, I am." It was a question she wouldn't have been able to answer that morning, but now she knew for certain. "I know you don't think it's much, me flying, and that I should do some proper work round the farm, but—"

"Proper work?" her mother echoed. "Don't I know you do your part and more every single day? And there's nothing wrong with loving your work. I know that because I love the farm. I never meant to make you believe the farm is all you should ever do. It's only that a woman being a pilot didn't seem possible. Although, I remember the day you and your pop came back from that aeroplane circus. You were such a little girl."

"I was eleven."

"But I saw that spark in your eye. I thought it was a phase and you would grow out of it, but it never left you. Until now. Until this accident and you came back hurting. I worried before, of course. I worry about all three of you when I can't see you. But since you've been back, I've worried more, because you had lost that spark, and without that . . . well, I'd rather have you happy and me worried than the other way round."

"I don't want you to worry, Mum. It's quite safe. Do you want me to tell you how I fly the aeroplane, and then it won't seem so difficult?"

"I do not." The kettle came to a boil, and her mum poured up the tea. "Now, this fellow who came by with his aeroplane. Is he the one you've written about so often?"

"Yes," Rosalie said, "he is. I did . . . there was another fellow I went to a dance with, and we saw each other a few times." Rosalie wanted her mother to know something of Alan, but she felt no compulsion to go into details.

"You've *two* fellows now?" her mother asked, and Rosalie didn't begrudge her the astonishment. After all, when had she ever had even one?

"Not really. That is, Snug—this fellow today—we've not actually . . . we've mostly been friends until now."

Her mother smiled. "Your father and I knew each other for ages before he called on me properly. I was ever so surprised. But it turned out all right, didn't it?"

Rosalie gave her mother a quick kiss and dashed up the stairs, calling back that she'd be down to help with the meal. Inside her room, she took out pen and paper.

Dear Commanding Officer Gore, I am ready to return.

★   ★   ★

At the end of July, Rosalie flew in an air taxi from Bourn all the way to Hamble, sorry that they didn't have a stop at Aston Down so she might look up Snug. When she arrived at her ferry pool, the lads in maintenance gave her a friendly wave and shouted, "Welcome back!" and when she looked into her CO's office, Margot Gore rose from her desk with a smile.

"It's good to see you, Rosalie. You are much needed here, both for your skill as a pilot and your good spirits. I hope you're ready, because you'll fly tomorrow. Why don't you stop in the waiting room now and say hello."

It was the very thing Gore had said to her upon her arrival nearly three years earlier. Rosalie had been too shy to do it then, but now she marched directly over and pulled the door open to find only one pilot, Grace, reading a newspaper with a cup of tea beside her. *Bad luck*, Rosalie thought. She'd made a successful job of avoiding Grace since Caro died almost a year ago. But there was nothing else for it, and so she bravely entered.

"How are you?" Grace asked, as if actually concerned. "We've missed you, you know."

"I'm fine," Rosalie said, and added, "Thanks." She moved over to the tea trolley and poured herself a cup, thinking that perhaps being polite would get her through this and out the door. "And you? Have you set another wedding date?" For Grace's nuptials to Lord Elving-ton continued to be delayed. Zofia said Brenda had speculated that the problem might not be the war but the bride, who could be—and with good cause—getting cold feet.

"No, we haven't," Grace said, still holding up the paper but not looking at it. "Rosalie, for a long time now, I've wanted to explain—no, apologize—to you for how I . . ." Her voice petered out. Rosalie stirred milk into her tea and waited.

"About Caro," Grace said at last. "I'm sorry for how I treated her. I can't quite explain why I was that way, except . . . she was happy, you see, happy in herself—and I couldn't bear it. The thought that she blithely went along and . . . we can't all be happy, can we?"

Rosalie had held this grudge against Grace for so long that it seemed sewn into the fiber of her being, and she wasn't sure she could be shed of it. "It isn't me you should be apologizing to," she said.

"I apologized to Zofia ages ago," Grace said. "To lose someone you love and not be able to stand in public as that person's survivor—I don't know how she bears it."

"Yes. The war. It must make you worry," Rosalie said, "knowing your fiancé is out there in danger every day."

Grace shook out the newspaper with a *crack*, and it folded itself into place. "Do all of you think I *want* to marry him?" she snapped. "My God, he was Uncle Harold to me growing up. But for some of us, marriage isn't about love—sometimes it's about duty. You should remember that."

Rosalie gulped down her tea, mumbled a good-bye, and left.

It wasn't quite the homecoming she'd expected, but it improved when she walked down Satchell Lane and arrived at No. 6. She let herself in, and Mrs. May called out from the kitchen, "Who's that now?"

"It's me—Rosalie. I'm back."

"Are you? Well, you'd best come through and let me look at you."

There was scuffling and snickering, and when she walked in the kitchen, she was met with cheers from Zofia, Pamela, and Mrs. May beating on a pan with a wooden spoon. On the table, in pride of place, sat a cake with three rows of raspberries marching down the middle.

"We've been waiting for you for ages," Pamela said, "and I'd just said to Mrs. May that this cake is in danger of being eaten if you don't arrive within the hour."

Zofia hugged her. "You are most welcome sight."

"We've beef hot pot and curried carrots for the evening," Mrs. May said, "and tomorrow morning—would you like an egg for your breakfast?"

"I tell you what I'd really like for breakfast tomorrow, Mrs. May," Rosalie said, attempting to control the tremor in her voice, "is a bowl of your porridge."

CHAPTER 27

August 1944

Rosalie eased back into ferrying aeroplanes and soon felt as if she'd never been gone. Memories of her crash remained, but they stayed in the past, where they could neither hurt nor frighten her. What would happen the next time there was a problem mid-flight? She would know the answer to that only when she came to it.

For two weeks, she collected her chitties, looking first at her destinations and second at the types of aeroplanes. She needed to find a way to West Malling. She needed to see Alan. He'd written a brief letter—only the second since her crash—to say that they'd soon be moving to RAF Swannington, near Norwich. She'd never have an aeroplane to deliver that far away, not these days. What Rosalie wanted to say to Alan was best done in person and, equally important, as a regular part of her day, not a specially arranged visit with all that would imply. She must get past this so that the rest of the year, the war—her life—would make sense.

It happened one afternoon that she took a Spitfire to Brize Norton. She was to return to Hamble, but they were looking for someone to fly a Blenheim to RAF Detling. Detling was only a few miles from West Malling, so here was her chance. She flew the Blenheim, but upon arrival at Detling, she could find neither bus nor aeroplane to take her those few miles. So, she borrowed a bicycle, because they seemed to have plenty on hand, and no one was bothered that she should return it. She set off for Alan's base, wearing her parachute and with her overnight bag perched on the handlebars.

It was early evening before she arrived at West Malling, and she knew that Alan would be flying that night, but she asked in the squadron office to be sure.

"They're out at the dispatch hut waiting," the clerk told her. "Too bad you've missed him."

"No, it's all right," Rosalie replied. "I'll stay the night. Mind if I telephone Hamble? Then I'll see if they'll put me up in the WAAF quarters, and that way I can see him after he lands tomorrow morning."

After she had sorted her accommodations, she made for the canteen, but stood outside a moment, her courage wavering. She pushed open the swing door far enough to sweep her gaze round the room, just in case Deborah Barlow was about. She wasn't, and so Rosalie had a sandwich and tea and spent the rest of the evening reading on her camp bed and chatting with a few other women before falling asleep. She woke when the WAAFs came in from night duty in operations, talking quietly among themselves. She caught the words "Hard going, apparently, and they aren't back yet. I would've stayed, but I'm knackered."

Rosalie, at first groggy from sleep, was now fully awake. She washed and dressed in five minutes and made for the control tower. She saw Declan heading the same way.

"God, Rosalie, I didn't realize you were here. I was going up to the roof."

"Is there something wrong?"

"No," he said quickly. "They had a rough time of it and just thought I'd, you know . . ."

"I want to go up too."

He looked past her.

"I don't care if Deborah is there," Rosalie said.

Declan flinched at this declaration, but then he shrugged. "C'mon."

They climbed to the roof, and despite her brave words, Rosalie was relieved not to meet Deborah.

★   ★   ★

From the roof of the control tower, Rosalie had watched Alan land with her stomach in a hard knot. Watched as the fire tanker came clanging up and as the ground crew managed to wrench open the cockpit and drag out two bodies. One of them appeared lifeless, but the other broke away from his rescuers, shook them off, and waved at his companion instead.

Which figure was Alan? Both men were covered in black soot, and Rosalie couldn't tell until the man standing had pulled off his leather flying helmet and she saw his light brown hair. Alan.

Now the group on the roof of the control tower began to disperse, and Rosalie considered what she should do. Alan was being escorted across the runway—walking there under his own steam, she noticed. He passed by the control tower but didn't look up. How could this be the right time to tell him what she had to say? He would need comfort, not confrontation.

"He'll have to go to medical quarters first," Declan said. "Want me to tell him you're here?"

"Would you? Thanks. I'll be . . ."

"You could wait in the library," Declan suggested.

They parted at the bottom of the steps, and Rosalie set off for Douces Manor and its vast, musty library. But at the last minute, she veered off and instead walked into the NAAFI-run canteen.

At the counter, a woman was using a short pole to lift an enormous muslin bag of hot, wet tea leaves out of an urn. She rested it across the top so that the tea could drain down into the pot, wiped her forehead, and looked over at Rosalie.

"Good morning," she said. "Tea's fresh, as you can see."

"Perhaps after I . . . Is Deborah Barlow in her office, by any chance?"

"Yes, just went in. Go through."

The knock prompted a "Come in," and Rosalie complied.

"Hello, Deborah."

Deborah started and then recovered, carefully replacing the cap on her pen. "Rosalie, lovely to see you."

Rosalie could've argued the point but instead found herself tongue-tied. What had she planned to say?

"I saw Alan land a bit ago," she said. "They had a rough night, it seems."

"Is he all right?"

"Yes, he is. The thing is, he wrote me recently that the squadron would be moving again—to Norfolk, this time. Swannington."

"Yes, I'd heard."

Rosalie swallowed. "Will you be moving to Swannington too?"

Deborah carefully laid her pen on the desk. "Rosalie, I hope you haven't mistaken what Alan and I are to each other."

"What is that, exactly?"

"A casual thing. Convenience. It's always been that way. I've understood it from the start."

"Do you want to marry him?" Rosalie asked.

She laughed. "Marry him? That isn't on the cards—I'm not his type. That is, not his family's type." Deborah looked at her closely. "You never thought he would marry *you*?"

That misty future of Rosalie's began to come into focus. "No," she said, "I never thought he would marry me."

★   ★   ★

Alan already waited for her in the library.

"There you are," he said, taking Rosalie in his arms. His hair was still damp and he smelled fresh. He kissed her. "I thought Mack was having me on when he told me you had been there, up on the control tower roof."

"You weren't hurt, were you?" she asked. "What about your navigator?"

"The smoke got to him, but he's fine now. I'm fine. You." It seemed to occur to him suddenly. "You're the one who's been injured. I can't believe you're back flying again. Come on, now let's sit down."

She did, but wished she could've continued to stand.

She took his hands. "I'm happy to be flying. There's so much to do. I feel comfortable back in an aeroplane."

"We had a night of doodlebugs last week," Alan said, glancing round the library as if looking for a safe subject. Perhaps he knew why she was here. "We try to tip them, you see—use our wings to nudge them off course so that they'll explode out over the water. We've managed to get a good few. We look for them at dusk or at dawn."

"Alan," she said, "I want to talk with you about . . . about the two of us." Best to get this over with. "As lovely as it's been, it's obvious, don't you think, that it won't work. We could never stay together."

He did not look surprised. Rosalie would always remember that. Instead, he looked as if he had at that moment noticed that he'd lost something. He kept hold of her hands, and tears sprang into his eyes.

"But I love you," he said.

Rosalie believed that he believed this, and didn't have the heart to argue the point. "I know you do. But it won't work, will it? You can admit that."

"It wasn't the time to make plans, but when the war is finished—"

"I don't believe the end of the war would make a difference. This was never meant to be forever."

"It isn't Deborah, is it?" he asked. "You have to understand, Rosalie. That doesn't mean anything."

It was as good as a slap in the face. Just what Rosalie needed to remind her of what was true.

"It is partly Deborah, yes," she said, pulling her hands away. "I thought it was the two of us. I certainly never imagined . . . but I'm not blaming her. It isn't her fault." Rosalie, weary, only wanted to finish. "I've got to be on my way now." She leaned over and kissed him on the cheek. "Good-bye, Alan. Good luck with your farm."

He didn't try to stop her, and it came to her that this last meeting of theirs was a mere formality, that actually things had ended between them . . . when, exactly? Even before her crash? Could they blame the war, or was it because they had never had any foundation to keep them stable? In her subconscious, she always must have known that it wasn't to last—why else keep up the pretense of "I'll tell my family when it's time"? Perhaps what she'd had with Alan, Rosalie thought, was not that much different from what Alan had with Deborah after all.

Rosalie hurried over to the WAAF quarters to collect her bag and parachute and then to the duty officer's hut, where she felt fortunate to find an Anson just arrived and about to take off again. She didn't even ask where it was going, and only after they were in the air did she learn that it was headed for Speke, near Liverpool. It would be a long journey back to Hamble.

CHAPTER 28

Autumn 1944

The first of September, the skies over Britain fell silent. That is, the assault from the doodlebugs ceased. No more listening to the approach of the ragged engine and then waiting, waiting for it to pass. Or worse, for its engine to cut out, letting it drop to the ground and explode. Had the Germans given up?

No, because a week later, a new and greater assault began from V-2 rockets—larger and more destructive. Rockets, air raid sirens, ack-ack guns. Once again, the world was not a quiet place.

And so the war went on and Rosalie flew—even Lancasters, which she did with another woman as copilot. Having completed the conversion course, she was, at last, First Officer Wright. She would brag about that to Snug next time she saw him. Whenever that was. He seemed to have vanished. He had gone to Lime Farm and saved her from spending the rest of her life hiding, and she had come to her senses about him. In her weakest moments, she hoped she hadn't imagined it. What about all his girls? Well, Rosalie wouldn't be one of a crowd—that was for certain. She'd had her fill of that.

She landed at Aston Down one afternoon in late September. Having been in and out of the place a dozen times since she'd been back flying, she had developed a routine. First, take a look in the Mess. If Snug wasn't there—and he hadn't been yet—she proceeded to the ferry pool's assignment room and found his name on the chalkboard. Today he'd been given three aeroplanes. The Aston Down's deputy CO nodded a hello at her. "He may not make it back until tomorrow," he told Rosalie. "Problems with that Wellington he's got."

A cup of tea on her own, then. Rosalie retraced her steps to the Mess, where Marjorie caught up with her.

"I'm gasping for a cuppa," she said, "and I think there are fresh cakes in the canteen. Care to join me?"

They settled at the end of a table and swapped stories of their jobs. Marjorie had some good ones about what it was like to work in ops as a plotter, where she saw not only the position of RAF aeroplanes in the sky but also where the enemy aircraft flew.

"And," Marjorie said, "my friend saw Mrs. Roosevelt herself when she visited White Waltham. That was ATA, Rosalie—you should've been there and told them all you've done."

"Oh, what have I done? Flown a few of the RAF's aeroplanes." Rosalie picked up her teacup and swirled the dregs around. She hesitated, wanting to ask Marjorie a question but not really wanting to hear the answer. Finally, she cleared her throat and took a chance.

"I haven't seen Snug in ages," she said. "It seems we're all so busy these days. What's he up to?"

"Barely seen him myself," Marjorie said. "I can tell you one thing, though. That Snug—he's become a monk."

Rosalie's cup clattered back into its saucer. "He what?"

Marjorie laughed. "Not actually a monk. It's just that . . . well, he's still friendly and all, buys a girl a drink, you know. But that's as far as it goes these days." She eyed Rosalie with a mischievous grin. "I think he's in love."

★ ★ ★

There was spotty flying in October—good days or even half days were sandwiched between periods of thick fog and poor visibility that kept the ferry pilots on the ground. Rosalie worked in the back garden at No. 6 a great deal, hoping Snug might drop in to see how the hens were and, well, to see her. But he didn't. He wasn't one for letter writing. Hadn't he said so himself? And she would rather see him than try to put her thoughts into words on paper.

When clear weather returned toward the end of the month, she felt grateful to be back at it. Her first day out, she flew the Anson taxi to Kidlington, leaving two pilots and collecting others to take to the Cosford ferry pool. Not a long day—she'd be back in time to clean out the henhouse.

Here it was nearly November, and they'd soon be celebrating Guy Fawkes Night. Or not celebrating, as fireworks had been banned throughout the war. Hadn't they had enough of the real thing? Perhaps, Rosalie thought, all the fireworks from every canceled celebration during the war were being saved up and, when it was all finished, everything would go up in one glorious Bonfire Night like no one had ever seen.

She delivered her two pilots to Kidlington and had time for a cup of tea in the Mess before reporting back to the duty officer.

"I've got two for Cosford, don't I?" she asked.

He ran his finger down the day's schedule. "You do. They're already aboard the Anson waiting for you, but now you've got one more." He looked up and pointed his pencil over Rosalie's shoulder. "That one."

She felt a presence behind her—a large one. She whirled round.

"There you are!" she said to Snug.

"There *you* are," he said, and looked down at the patch on her arm. "First Officer Wright."

"'Bout time, isn't it?" she asked raising her shoulder and admiring the patch herself. "You've been flying north a fair bit, haven't you?" she asked.

"And you've been back and forth across the south more times than you can count, probably."

"How would you know that?"

He leaned over and whispered, "I have a spy at your ferry pool."

Rosalie laughed, and the duty officer coughed.

"And *that* one," he said in a raised voice, "is for Aston Down."

"I'm going to Hamble," Snug said, glancing at Rosalie.

The duty officer tapped on his schedule. "It says here you fly to—"

"He's going to Hamble," Rosalie said. "So you'd best change your schedule."

She and Snug walked out to the Anson together, neither speaking but both looking out the corners of their eyes at the other.

Once in the air, Snug settled in the copilot's seat and let the other passengers crank the undercarriage up and then down again to land at Cosford. He had the task to himself for the flight to Hamble.

When they climbed out of the aeroplane and started across the field, the late-afternoon sun throwing long shadows in front of them, Rosalie stopped. "So, what are you doing here in Hamble? Have a date?" she asked, hoping to be proved wrong.

"I might," Snug replied, and Rosalie put on a brave face. "What are you doing this evening?"

She blushed and grinned and looked round them. "As it happens, I've no plans."

"Let's go out for a meal. I know a place this side of Southampton. Not too far."

"I'll go and change my clothes," Rosalie said. "It won't take me a minute." Snug looked at her long enough that her face grew quite warm. "Go on, now, sort out our transportation—no bicycles, please—and come and collect me."

She fair flew home to No. 6, making a terrible racket as she ran up the stairs, calling to anyone who was there to listen.

"I'm going out! I'm going out for a meal!" She left her bedroom door open and stripped off her uniform, pausing for a moment before the slim choice of clothes in the wardrobe. Then she grabbed her only nonuniform trousers, a blouse, and red sweater, while she continued to shout. "I'm going with Snug, and he's coming round any minute now, so someone answer the door for me, because I've got to change my clothes."

She was into the lavatory and out in two minutes, including running damp fingers through her curls. Rosalie landed, panting, on the ground floor to find Mrs. May, Pamela, and Zofia gathered in the entry, watching her.

"Did you hear what I said?"

"I'd say the entire terrace heard what you said," Mrs. May told her, but with a smile.

"And they would say the same thing we do," Zofia added. "It's about bloody time."

The landlady turned with a shocked expression at such language, but a knock on the door precluded any scolding. Instead, she gestured for the women to stand back and opened the door to Snug, still in uniform, but now in possession of an Austin Eton Coupe, looking its age and with its top down, parked just behind him at the curb.

"Have a lovely evening!" Pamela called.

Snug opened the car door for Rosalie, and such a simple gallant gesture made her suddenly shy. She covered by running her hand over the dashboard. "Where'd you get this?"

"Belongs to my mate Len in maintenance here at Hamble," Snug explained as they motored off. The wind whipped through Rosalie's hair—the journey reminded her a bit of flying her first Gipsy Moth, except they weren't going that fast. Fast enough, though. Rosalie braced herself as they beetled round a bend. It was no time before they pulled into a hamlet and up to a pub called the Cross Keys.

"They do food," Snug said as he opened the car door for her. "Not bad for the war too."

The pub had a separate room for those ordering meals. Rosalie couldn't remember the last time she'd been in a proper restaurant. She'd spent the war eating in the Mess at myriad aerodromes or at Mrs. May's table in the kitchen. Then she remembered eating in the dining room at the Feathers, the hotel where she and Alan would meet. How odd—that seemed like someone else's life now.

"Drink first?" Snug asked.

"Yes, let's."

They stood at the bar, Rosalie with a glass of the mild and Snug with a pint, and got to talking with a fellow on a stool at the end.

"My boy's RAF, and my sister's girl sews blankets from bits and bobs of old things for the children bombed out in London. Has done the entire war."

"And her efforts are much appreciated, I'm sure," Rosalie commented.

"What do you do for the war effort?" he asked.

"I fly aeroplanes," Rosalie said.

The man paused, his drink halfway to his mouth. "You?"

"Yes, me. Spitfires, Hurricanes . . . Lancasters."

"You never."

"She does," Snug said, leaning against the bar looking as if he quite enjoyed this. "Your son's RAF, so he has his Spit or whatever because Rosalie here delivered it."

The man scratched his head. "Seems you'd have trouble reaching all those levers and switches."

Rosalie and Snug left him to his disbelief and decamped to a small table on the far side of the dining room, sniggering along the way.

"Where's he been?" Snug asked. "Haven't you women been splashed all over the newspapers—the Glamour Girls?"

Rosalie shook her head. "There are others who fit that description, not me."

"That isn't true, and it's time you admit it."

She looked up and saw he meant it.

It wasn't long before the dining room had filled with people. The food was good and fresh and a welcome change from Woolton pie. "Not that there's anything wrong with it," Rosalie said. "In fact, I may miss it when the war's over." She took a bite of her ham loaf. "But not much."

They cleaned their plates, talking the entire meal about what they'd seen and done since last meeting in July at Lime Farm. In the occasional silences, they smiled at each other.

"Everything settled now with Will and Jean and the boy?" Snug asked.

"Moved back into the house and all is well. Little Robert and my mum are practically inseparable. Leslie has decided to keep working on the cottage so that he can move in himself. What of your mum and Mouse and Delfina?"

"They survived the Blitz and they survived the doodlebugs. Now they've got the damned V-2s coming at them. But they will not be moved."

"The war's got to end soon, don't you think? We have them on the run."

The waitress took their plates away, and Snug leaned his arms on the table.

"Yes, but what are we going to do, Wright, after it's over?" An uncharacteristic, defeated look settled on him like a cloud. "What'll they do with the likes of us?"

"The likes of us?" Rosalie asked.

"I've got one good eye," Snug said. "Do you think anyone will hire me as a pilot? And as for you, you'll be chivied off to do what they call 'women's work.'"

"I will not be chivied off anywhere I don't want to go, and I refuse to do what they all call 'women's work,'" Rosalie said with heat. She picked up her empty glass and set it down again. "I'll tell you what we'll do. We'll buy our own bloody aeroplane and fly a taxi service. Or we'll take over some small airfield—they'll be going for a song after the war—and we'll run it ourselves."

Snug cocked his head and squinted his eye. A smile threatened to break his glum look. "We will, will we? You and I?"

Rosalie reached across the table and took his hand. "If you'll have me. Because I love you." She laughed. "Took me long enough to figure that out, didn't it? But I do."

She held her breath, waiting for his reaction, and exhaled only when she saw his dark eyes sparkle.

"God, Wright. I've loved you since the day you stole my chair by the electric fire and then shouted at me." He squeezed her hand and stroked the back of it with his thumb, and a shiver of pleasure went through Rosalie. Snug glanced round at the other diners. "I tell you, if we weren't in public—"

"What, Snug Durrant—are you afraid of what people might think? Well, I'm not."

She couldn't wait any longer. She leaned over the table, grabbed his lapel, and kissed him. One kiss, she told herself, that's all. But it was too good. He hadn't shaved, and his face felt a bit scratchy, but the way his lips responded to hers, strong and yet soft, kept her going. She pulled away but kept near—quite near—looking in his eyes. He put his hand at the back of her neck, drew her close, and kissed her. And again. It came to her that she heard a smattering of applause from the other diners. They broke apart and Rosalie sat back, completely embarrassed and completely happy.

They settled up the bill and left, strolling out to the car hand in hand.

"I'll take you back to Mrs. May's. Len's letting me keep the car and drive it up to Aston Down. He'll collect it in a few days."

"Couldn't you put up with him tonight and then go back tomorrow?" It would mean they'd have the chance of a cup of tea in the Mess before they both got back to work.

"Can't. We're off early."

"Where?"

He grinned. "I'll be flying to France."

"No." She gasped.

"I will. Taking medical supplies and food. They say we'll be bringing back injured soldiers and children."

A few of the male transport pilots had started flying to the Continent. It was proof of the ATA's vital role and something to be proud of. She was happy for Snug, but she couldn't help remembering that the Germans were still putting up a fight with no regard for life—theirs or anyone else's. The battle now took place not over Britain but on the Continent. France. Near the end or not, Rosalie felt afraid of the war.

"You'll . . ." She did not want to give voice to her fears. "You'll mind how you go?"

"I will." He cupped her face in his hand. "And you. You'll be busy. We'll get through this. And if not before then, I'll see you when it's over—on the very day they announce it. We'll have something to celebrate, won't we?"

"Yes." What a relief to have that set. A day, whenever it might come, to look forward to. "Wherever we have to come from, we'll meet at Number Six. No! The Bugle. What do you think?"

"I think we'll find each other."

They drove back to Hamble without speaking. Rosalie's head was filled with thoughts of the present and of the future, the crystal-clear future. Now, to get there. At No. 6, Snug switched off the engine, and they sat for the longest time. But in the end, they had to part, and no amount of holding hands and kissing in the dark would make that fact go away.

Standing on the pavement at the front door, Snug leaned over, rested his forehead against Rosalie's, and whispered, "I love you."

CHAPTER 29

December 1944

Rosalie threw herself into flying with rarely a pause. Easy to do and preferable to the alternative, because if she wasn't flying, she was worrying. Just after the dinner she had with Snug in November, two ATA pilots in a Lancaster crashed in Cheshire, bringing home once again that the war still wielded its power.

★　★　★

On Christmas morning, Zofia, Pamela, and Rosalie marched down the stairs just as the post arrived, scattering greetings of the season across the floor. Zofia, first in line, scooped it up and carried it into the kitchen, where she distributed the cards and letters. Mrs. May wiped her hands on her pinny before taking hers.

They settled at the table, and for a few minutes the only sounds in the kitchen were the *plop* of the porridge, the tinkle of spoons stirring tea, and the tearing open of envelopes. Zofia remained standing, studying the letter in her hand before turning it over and opening it.

Rosalie looked up from a Christmas card signed by little Robert to watch Zofia read through the letter, bite her lip, and then read it again. Then she looked up.

"Dr. Andrews writes," she said, her voice thick and low. "He says my mother and my sister are found—safe, he believes. He hopes."

They leapt up from their chairs, all talking at once, and Zofia couldn't answer their questions quick enough. "It was the cousin of Dr. Andrews, working in government who gives the news . . . No, they are still in France . . . he says they have been living in the hills these past two years . . . British agents were there and found them. Perhaps they must stay to be safe, or perhaps they will be taken out, secretly." She paused and added, "The Germans are not finished with the French people yet."

Zofia swayed slightly. Rosalie dropped her post onto the table and took her arm, guiding her into a chair. Zofia trembled and her eyes were filled with tears, but she smiled.

"It is good news. Yes?" she asked, handing the letter to Rosalie.

After a quick read, Rosalie replied, "Yes, it is excellent news."

Her mother and sister had been located in the hills of Vichy, where the French Resistance had been strong but communication difficult. Now, joined by the Allies, people who had been thought to be lost were reappearing, including Zofia's mother and sister. Eventually they would be flown to Britain—a reminder to them all that the war didn't end in a day.

"A happy Christmas after all," Mrs. May said, kissing Zofia on the forehead before returning to the pot of porridge. Pamela took down bowls and spoons and pushed aside the post, but stopped.

"Wait now. Did you miss one, Rosalie?"

Rosalie hadn't noticed the postcard among the Christmas greetings, but she spotted it now. An illustration of the Eiffel Tower bedecked with a holly wreath slung over its pointed top. Rosalie's smile grew wide even before she turned the postcard over to see it was addressed to First Officer Wright and, in a heavy hand, signed *Happy Christmas XOXO Snug.*

★　★　★

March 1945

One midday when nothing much was going on, Rosalie's only chitty for the day was to deliver a Spitfire to Castle Camps in Essex. She hadn't been there in almost a year, but it felt more like a lifetime. She wouldn't be able to see Ellen and was sorry about that, but news from Leslie was promising. Ellen indeed had left the WAAFs and started her nurses training in Cambridge. She and Leslie were seeing each other again, and it looked as if things might be getting serious. *But Ellen has quite taken to nursing,* Leslie wrote, *and isn't sure she'd want to give it up if we marry. She mentioned you when she said this, saying you would continue flying no matter what and so why shouldn't she work. You're not easy to explain away, Rags, but I suppose that's all for the best.*

Skirting London, and noting that there were far fewer barrage balloons to avoid these days, Rosalie flew north through quiet skies as she mulled over Leslie's news. She wondered about Ellen's chances to continue nursing if she married and compared them with her own chances of continuing to fly after the war—married or not. Then, out the corner of her eye, starboard side, she noticed an aircraft. It headed west and would cross in front of her. No, not an aeroplane. A doodlebug. The bloody V–1s had returned, this time launched from the Netherlands.

As the rocket crossed straight in front ahead of her, three things happened in rapid succession. She saw flashes from the ground—ack-ack guns. They must've hit their target, for the doodlebug exploded. And Rosalie, unable to alter course quickly enough, flew right into the middle of a cloud of debris, smoke, and fire.

Bits of metal pinged off the hood and sides of her Spit. She couldn't see anything. She pulled the control stick to the left, but too forcefully, and suddenly she was out of the rocket's cloud and in the clear—but upside down.

The blood rushed to her scalp and she might have shouted something, but she took control easily, gently pushing the control stick further and completing the roll.

Once righted and with the remains of the rocket behind her, she gasped for air, not realizing she'd been holding her breath. She noticed a few small holes in the hood, but ahead of her the sky was a serene blue, and she saw the Castle Camps aerodrome. She felt something cold on her face and put her hand to her cheek. It came away bloody.

She laughed. *Good thing it missed my eye*, she thought. *Otherwise we'd only have one good pair between us.*

She put down without further incident, although she did take a moment to sit quietly in the cockpit and tell herself she was fine before climbing out and, along with the ground crew, assessing the damage.

"You took quick action," one of them said. "Can't ask more than that."

Buoyed, she told her story to the duty officer, who took notes.

"Sorry about the aeroplane," she said. "I'll write my report." Rosalie wondered if she could be blamed for damage to her aeroplane when she wasn't the one who had shot at the doodlebug to make it explode.

"Leave it with me," he said. "Those fellows on the ground get a bit trigger-happy, if you ask me. But who can blame them with these damned buzz bombs—thought we were finished with them. You go over to get that cheek fixed up."

It wasn't much. A cut about two inches long but not deep, and it required no stitches. A nurse washed it off, smeared something on it, and covered it with a bandage. Checking herself out in a small mirror by the door of the examining room, Rosalie decided she'd had worse growing up on the farm.

After a cup of tea, she asked about transport but could find nothing going anywhere useful, until one of the WAAF drivers said, "Aren't you a friend of Ellen's?"

They got to talking, and Rosalie discovered that one of the women had a car and a group of them would be going into London for the evening. They offered Rosalie a lift and invited her along dancing too. She declined the dance but accepted the lift, telling them she could find a way back to Hampshire. Couldn't she?

Rosalie had been in London three times in her life, but even if she had been a dozen times, she would've been hard-pressed to find her way. The car—four women in the back, three in the front—crept along streets lined with piles of rubble and empty lots of destruction next to completely intact buildings. They had to find detours around bomb craters. It was hardly to be believed. But then, at the next corner, she saw something she recognized. It was the sign for Liverpool Street Underground station.

"Here!" she shouted. "You can leave me here. This is just the place."

"Is it?" Ellen's friend asked.

"I know someone who lives nearby."

"Right, well, good luck to you." They waved and drove off. Rosalie, hugging her parachute in front of her and holding her bag, stood where she was and turned in a circle to take in her surroundings. People were coming and going out of the station, and so she stopped a man and asked if he knew the Bishop's Finger, but he shrugged and went on his way. So, she began her own search around the station. She quickly became lost, and it took her an hour to make it back to where she had started. After that, she made careful forays up one street at a time and then back. Still she had no luck, and she had begun to doubt her plan when she saw a Civil Defense warden. She stopped him and asked.

"Betty's pub? It's just up that yard there." He nodded to a pile of bricks that did a bang-up job of disguising the entry to a short street. She picked her way through the heaps of debris and paused to look ahead. There was a gap in the line of buildings, like a missing front tooth. Still attached to the remaining part of the terrace were signs that there had been life once—water-stained wallpaper with red roses, a light fixture dangling from a partial beam, and, incredibly, a half-broken cup hanging from its hook on a shelf. Rosalie had seen the damage from bombs in the villages and at the aerodromes, but she had never seen this—an entire city crumbling. Where had the people gone who lived there? Had they survived?

A passing woman with a shopping bag asked, "You all right, dear?"

"Yes, thanks." Because there, beyond the hole in the terrace, she could see a sign for the Bishop's Finger hanging over a door.

She walked on, but as she reached the door of the pub, her steps slowed. What would she do, introduce herself? Would Betty or Mouse or Delfina even know who she was? Had Snug ever mentioned her name? Perhaps she would test the waters by slipping in, acting as if she were just another punter, and get the lay of the land.

The pub, for all its hiding down a yard, was heaving. Several older women sat at tables along the wall, and the bar was lined with men. Between, small groups stood with drinks in hand, talking and laughing. But the crowd parted as Rosalie made her way up to the end of the bar. She set her bag on the floor but clutched her parachute to her chest.

A young man with one shoulder considerably lower than the other approached her.

"All right, there?" he asked. "What'll you have?"

"Oh, um, glass of the mild, please." As he pulled her half pint, Rosalie leaned over the bar and added in as quiet a voice as she could above the noise, "Is Betty about?"

He shouted over his shoulder, "Betty! There's a lady down here to see you!"

Anyone who was not already looking at Rosalie now did.

"Coming!" was the muffled shout. "I can't be in two places at once, you know."

From round the corner at the other end of the bar came a woman who, though not physically large, seemed so. As she made her way to Rosalie, she swept empty glasses off the surface of the bar, commented to her customers, and took orders.

"Inky," she said to the boy, "another round down that end, there's a good lad. Now"—she turned to Rosalie—"sorry, love, what can I do for you?"

When she saw Rosalie's face, Betty's eyes, small and dark, widened considerably.

"Hello," Rosalie said, now even more unsure of what to do.

Betty's gaze fell to the wing patch on Rosalie's jacket. "You're ATA," she said. Then she examined Rosalie more closely, starting with her hair. "Well," she said, amazement in her voice, "isn't this just . . ." She put a finger up. "Wait now, love. Right here." She turned and shouted, "Mouse! Mouse!"

"What d'ya want?" The voice came from a doorway behind the bar, and it carried well over the noise.

"Come out here this minute!"

A tall, thin woman popped out. She wore dungarees and a scarf tied about her hair with a knot at the top of her forehead.

"Look!" Betty said. "Look who's come to see us."

Mouse squinted her eyes at this new customer and then shifted her gaze to Betty and said, "Bloody hell."

"It is, isn't it?" Betty said, beaming. "It's Rosalie!"

★　★　★

Rosalie had a wonderful but exhausting time in the pub that evening. She talked with customers who knew Snug and who all wanted to buy her a drink. She tried to stop at two glasses of mild, but a third one appeared in front of her regardless. At last, Betty leaned over the bar and said, "You go on up now—you're looking a bit peaky. Mouse and Delfina will come down and close for me. I'll see you soon."

Mouse led Rosalie upstairs to Betty's flat and gave her a Spam sandwich. "I'm sorry we can't offer you cheese and olives and good country bread. They eat well in Spain, I can tell you. When this is all over, Delfina and I are going back."

Delfina—who was small, with a lovely, shy smile—appeared, and she and Mouse went down to the pub.

Betty put the kettle on the moment she walked into the flat. She and Rosalie had a good talk about both Snug's family and Lime Farm—Betty seemed to know a good bit about it. They talked about flying and the ATA, and they both wondered how Snug was doing.

"He's never been one for letter writing, more's the pity," Betty said.

"He sent a Christmas postcard," Rosalie said, pulling it out of the outside pocket on her bag and holding it out.

Betty smiled. "Ah, that's my boy. Now, love, let's put you to bed."

That night, Rosalie slept on the sofa in Betty's flat above the pub. It was one in a stream of odd places she'd put up for the night, but by far the most comforting.

★　★　★

Later that month, two ATA pilots died when an Anson crashed on approach to Aston Down. Rosalie didn't know them personally, but she knew who they were and was sorry for them and their families.

But worse for her was the combination of an Anson, the same aeroplane Snug was flying to France, and the mention of his own ferry pool. The event occupied a dark corner of her mind and wouldn't go away. She finished the month uneasy and, when she wasn't flying, distracted herself by ripping out her red sweater and reknitting it.

"You'll wear that yarn to nothing," Grace noted when she walked into the waiting room one day.

Rosalie had forgiven Grace for her treatment of Caro, and they'd formed a sort of friendship—she wasn't really sure what sort, but at least they could carry on a conversation. Rosalie was about to ask after the latest wedding plans when Grace said, "I've had a bit of news."

"Oh, what's that?" Rosalie asked, continuing with her needles.

"It's Alan Chersey. He's getting married."

Rosalie paused at that and looked up. "Is he? To Deborah Barlow?"

"Who?" Grace asked, but didn't wait for an answer. "No, to Veronica Hoare—you know, the London banking family. That settles what he'll be doing after the war."

"A banker?" Rosalie echoed. "Poor Alan."

"It's quite suitable for both families," Grace pointed out. "And actually, it was inevitable."

"Yes, I suppose it was." Rosalie remembered Alan's story of playing in the hothouse among the melon vines when he was a boy. So much for his hopes and dreams.

"And what about you?" Grace asked. "What will you do when it's all over?"

Rosalie stuck her chin out. "I will fly."

CHAPTER 30

May 8, 1945
Victory in Europe Day

On the seventh of May, word went out—Germany had signed an unconditional surrender. Although the event itself had been anticipated, the official announcement would be made the following day, already known as V-E Day and proclaimed a national holiday. The war, at least in Europe, would be officially at an end.

"We won't fly tomorrow," Commanding Officer Margot Gore told the women who had gathered in the assignment room late in the afternoon. Her announcement was met with such a din of cheers that she had to wait to continue. "I'm sure you'll all find other things to occupy your time. But the next day, please come in and have a talk with me. We have more aeroplanes to fly, but as I'm sure you have realized, the ATA won't last forever. But, regardless of where you go and what you do with your lives, I want every one of you women to remember that you made all the difference in the war. Well done."

More cheers, and then almost everyone set off for the Bugle to make an evening of it. Rosalie went along for a bit, nursing her glass of mild and watching the door every time it opened.

"Is Snug coming down?" Brenda asked.

"No," Rosalie said. "Not this evening. But he'll be here tomorrow. It's all arranged—we promised." It had been the last time they saw each other. The end of October felt like ages ago to her, and she'd heard nothing apart from his postcard at Christmas. Tomorrow was the day. Still, she couldn't help wishing he might surprise her and walk in any moment.

"What about Zofia?" Brenda asked.

"She left today," Rosalie said. Just as everyone had hoped, Zofia's mum and sister had made it to England and were staying with Dr. Andrews, and Zofia had gone to join them.

Rosalie left the revelers to it at the Bugle and walked back to No. 6 to find doors open, blackout curtains gone, and what seemed like every light in the village blazing. Music and chatter flowing like a tide over the road, and Mrs. May, standing at Mrs. Potts's open door with a cup of tea in hand, waved to Rosalie.

"Eggs for our evening meal," she called out. "As many as we want!"

★ ★ ★

The next morning, Britain sprang to life. Bunting appeared from nowhere to be strung up along railings and out first- and second-story windows, men were selling little versions of the Union Jack, and headlines screamed *Germany Quits!* Everyone's spirits were high to the point of mania, and Rosalie felt as if she were the only subdued person left on the planet. She took forever to put her clothes on. She'd spent eleven coupons for the dress three months ago in anticipation of this day. It was lovely—a dark mulberry with a nipped waist. She'd felt guilty handing over so many coupons for such a purchase, but at the same time it was a promise of things to come. She'd put it in the wardrobe, and there it had stayed until this day.

When she heard Mrs. May shout, "The porridge won't keep till Christmas!" Rosalie threw on her dress and ran downstairs to sit at the table and toy with her breakfast.

"We're having the celebration up and down our road," Mrs. May said. "I've already baked two cakes."

"Rosalie has another sort of celebration planned," Pamela said. "With Snug."

"Yes. That is, we said we would meet today, you know, the official end. But it's possible he's in France or Scotland or . . . he may not get back. In time, I mean. I must be practical."

"Practical?" Pamela asked. "I don't think that frock of yours says 'practical.'"

Rosalie smoothed the skirt of her dress. "I might go change my clothes." Because she would look the right fool if Snug didn't show.

"You'll do nothing of the kind," Mrs. May said. "What you need is to keep busy until he arrives. We've the tables to set up."

During the morning, people up and down Satchell Lane dragged out kitchen tables and every chair they could manage and lined them up so that they looked like a ribbon down the middle of the road through the village. Rosalie threw herself into the activity, although she couldn't help looking up and down the road every few minutes.

The Bugle was open—pubs had been given permission to open early and close late—and Rosalie nipped in once or twice during the morning to check on the growing crowd. The two old fellows were in their places, Bisby behind the bar.

"Looking for someone?" Bisby asked.

Rosalie shook her head, her stomach a bit queasy. "No. That is, I thought . . . no." She walked up and down Satchell Lane, exchanging a few words with villagers she'd never met, buying a Union Jack, and getting in Mrs. Potts's way as she brought out a tray of jellies.

"Come sit down and have a cup of tea," Mrs. May called from the doorway to No. 6, and Rosalie slipped between two tables and went for her cuppa in the kitchen. But she couldn't stay still and went back out to help with the plates and plates of cakes and sandwiches, after which she made another circuit of the village, putting her head once again into the Bugle. The place was chockablock with locals as well as every imaginable kind of uniform. But no Snug.

She sat at one of the tables with the children while they ate their tea, and she even had a few bites of cake, but passed on the fish paste sandwiches. She just might give up fish altogether now the war was over.

On her walk past open doors, Rosalie heard snatches of the prime minister's official announcement broadcast over the wireless, and sometime after that—on another circuit—Churchill speaking again. This time, he spoke to the crowds, who responded to his words with huge cheers and then began to sing "Land of Hope and Glory." It sounded as if the entire country were joining in. Rosalie, too, as she stood outside the Bugle next to a group of sailors.

When the wireless switched to a lively band number, one of the sailors said, "C'mon, darling," and took hold of Rosalie's hand. "Isn't this what we've been waiting for?"

He smelled as if he'd started on the ale the evening before and hadn't stopped. He danced like it too, but Rosalie obliged him until the song ended and his hands began to wander. She brushed them off, saying, "I'm waiting for someone," and slipped away.

"But you've got me!" he called after her, staggering as he held his arms open wide.

The children, finished with their tea, were running riot in the streets, darting among adults. Rosalie picked her way through the growing crowd. She began to allow herself to worry, just a bit.

At one point, someone called her name—did she hear that? Rosalie stood in the middle of the road and whipped round and round, but the rapid movement sent her vision spinning, and she caught hold of a chair to steady herself.

"All right now."

She looked up to see Mrs. May giving her a hard look. "I don't believe you've eaten a thing, have you? Sit down there now and wait."

Rosalie did as she was told, gazing up Satchell Lane at the serpentine arrangement of tables and chairs, now in disarray. Mrs. May returned with bread and butter—that is, the standard war loaf and margarine—and a cup of tea.

"He'll be here," she said. "Don't you worry."

Rosalie tucked in, realizing she'd had nothing since porridge that morning except for a bite or two of cake, and here it was gone six o'clock. She took the last swallow of tea and popped up.

"Are you sure you're steady enough?" Mrs. May asked.

Rosalie assured her she was and began another walk round the village.

Perhaps he had forgotten. No, that couldn't be—Rosalie was sure of that to her very core, as she was sure of his love for her. But if he hadn't forgotten, then something had prevented him from meeting her, and that led her thoughts down dark paths.

Perhaps he had forgotten.

She passed the Bugle and looked in. Pamela waved and shouted, "Come in!" but Rosalie shook her head as she backed out and into the same sailor from earlier, who stood in the street in raucous laughter with a few others. He caught Rosalie by the wrist and turned her round.

"Another dance, love?"

She shook him off, and he stumbled back. "No thanks," she said firmly.

Rosalie felt as if she were wearing a path through Hamble and so went further, walking down to the river's edge. She stayed there for the longest time, thinking but not thinking. The sky to the east began to darken. She would go back to No. 6. Let the others continue the party.

Up through the village she walked, squeezing between groups of revelers and the few children still on a tear and giving the Bugle and that sailor a wide berth. Not wide enough, for when she passed under a beech tree, she felt a hand on her waist.

She tried to shrug him off, saying, "Look, I've told you, you'll have to find someone else!"

"But I don't want anyone else."

She swung round on the spot, and there was Snug.

"About bloody time!" she shouted, releasing in one burst the fear that had been building inside her. She added weakly, "Where've you been?"

"Paris. We flew in last night, but they went straight up to Lincolnshire. You wouldn't believe the trouble I had finding my way here—the entire country has gone mad today."

"Oh." She sniffed, noticing his red eyes and haggard look. "At least you weren't in Scotland. That would've taken you three days."

"No," Snug said firmly, putting a hand up and caressing her cheek. "Even if they'd flown me to Scotland, I'd've been here. I wouldn't've missed this. Not for the world."

She was in his arms in an instant. They kissed. He kissed her. She kissed him. They looked for all the world like any one of the other entwined couples strewn about the village—probably across Britain. But they weren't. They were Rosalie and Snug.

The dusky sky above them burst into fountains of colored lights followed by an explosion that made them jump.

Snug laughed. "We'll have to get used to that, won't we? Well, Wright, what do you say?"

He held her close round her waist, and Rosalie leaned back to look up at him. She traced his lips with her finger and kissed him again. "I say let's go. We've got some celebrating to do."

HISTORICAL NOTES

It's common knowledge that in the past, young women—whether from the working class or from privilege—were not always allowed to choose a profession. Except, that is, under extreme circumstances, such as the Second World War. In Britain as in other countries, from the late 1930s, with men off to fight, women from all walks of life moved into the workforce. They became not only nurses but also factory workers, drivers, mechanics, and pilots. My research for *Glamour Girls* took me into the lives of many British women, and I found that for them, those years were filled with a heady mixture of power, heartbreak, and good times. At the end of the war, this power was taken away from them, and many went back to their former lives taking care of homes and families. But not all.

Glamour Girls was inspired by the life of Mary Wilkins Ellis and drawn from her autobiography, *A Spitfire Girl* (as told to Melody Foreman; Frontline Books). She was a farm girl from Oxfordshire who loved to fly. Just after the start of the war and once Pauline Gower had broken the barrier for women, Mary joined the Air Transport Auxiliary (ATA) and began ferrying planes to Royal Air Force bases around England, Scotland, and Wales.

The ATA comprised more than 12 percent women, and they were known as Attagirls (or Atagirls). Most of them were based at No. 15 Hamble and No. 12 Cosford, the two women-only ferry pools. I sent my character, Rosalie, to follow Mary Wilkins to Hamble.

By 1945, Mary had flown four hundred Spitfires and seventy-six different types of aircraft. Even better, after the war, she continued to ferry planes for the RAF and in 1950 became the manager of a private airfield on the Isle of Wight. She married fellow pilot Don Ellis in 1961 and died in July 2018 at age 101, one of the last surviving Attagirls.

The incidents woven into Rosalie's story in *Glamour Girls* are based on actual events and drawn from Mary's life as well as others'—shaken and stirred with a good bit of literary license when it comes to the characters' personal lives. Many other women pilots wrote about their time flying during the war, and many names, dates, and places are included in *The Hurricane Girls* by Jo Wheeler (Penguin).

In *First Light* (Penguin), RAF pilot Geoffrey Wellum draws from his journals of the time to tell an evocative story of his life flying Spitfires.

Online research provides an amazing array of material, from photos and written firsthand accounts of British life during the war to film and audio. I was particularly taken with the short film "Five Inch Bather." That and other informational newsreels of wartime, including "Tea Making Tips" and "Mrs. T and Her Cabbage Patch," are only a quick search away on your computer. Many stories told by those who lived the war can be found at the BBC WW2 People's War website.

The Imperial War Museum and RAF Museum websites boast broad collections that cover not only the military side of the war but also details about life in Britain. The RAF site has a useful timeline, too. The websites of the Air Transport Auxiliary Museum, housed at the Maidenhead Heritage Centre, and the British Air Transport Auxiliary both contain a wealth of information.

The Second World War is still within reach in stories from our parents or grandparents and remarkable archives, and fortunately there are still places we can visit to help us understand the larger events of those days, the battles won and lost, but also the soldiers and civilians who did their best in bad times.

All four of the Imperial War Museums are worth a visit, but I especially enjoyed the day at Duxford near Cambridge where I could look at many of the World War II planes up close.

I have stood on the roof of a wartime control tower in Britain. My father-in-law was stationed at the U.S. base in Lavenham, Suffolk, and he often told the story of how they would wait on the roof, counting the planes in. Many of the more than seven hundred air bases were carved out of farmland across Britain, and many went back to being farms after the war. But in some places, evidence still exists of their temporary use.

The exhibitions at the Air Transport Auxiliary museum include everything from uniforms to chits, those slips of paper with daily flying assignments. The museum also houses a Spitfire simulator, where I spent an exhausting session learning how to—or perhaps how not to—fly a Spitfire. Mary Wilkins—and in *Glamour Girls*, Rosalie Wright—did it so much better.

Air Transport Auxiliary Museum: https://atamuseum.org

BBC WW2 People's War: http://www.bbc.co.uk/history/ ww2peopleswar/

British Air Transport Auxiliary: http://www.airtranspor- taux.com/index.html

Imperial War Museum: https://www.iwm.org.uk

Maidenhead Heritage Center: https://maidenheadheritage. org.uk

RAF Museum: https://www.rafmuseum.org.uk

ACKNOWLEDGMENTS

I have loved every part of writing Rosalie's story and thank all who have had a hand in it in any way, shape or form. My agent, Christina Hogrebe at the Jane Rotrosen Agency, helped me sharpen my focus and was a great advocate for the book. It's been a delight to work with Alcove Press, especially Melissa Rechter, who shepherded *Glamour Girls* through every aspect of the editorial and production process. Thanks to my editor, Martin Biro, who saw my intentions even in the murky spots and off suggestions that made the story stronger, and to copy editor Rachel Keith for her attention to detail.

Glamour Girls came alive for me in discussions with my sister-in-law Katherine Wingate and during weekly sessions with my writing group: Kara Pomeroy, Louise Creighton, Sarah Niebuhr Rubin, Tracey Hatton, and Meghana Padakandla. These women keep me honest by asking the important questions—not only "What's the point of this scene?" but also "How can she walk down the stairs if she didn't walk up them first?"

I share love for this time and place in history with my husband, Leighton Wingate, and so he never minded my rabbiting on about the forage cap as part of the ATA female pilot's uniform or when the first and last bombs of the Second World War dropped on Southampton or what time the pubs opened and closed in 1945. He particularly likes discussing the pubs.